About BRIGHTWING

A Criminal Love Story

Edgar and Mallory Battle are on the run after a spectacularly violent escape. Now, with a trail of bodies behind them, they need a hostage against the inevitable standoff with the police. Their first doesn't last long, thanks to sociopathic Mallory. Edgar has been hiding his brother's crimes since they were kids. Now he's torn between loyalty and self-preservation.

They carjack Lucy Brightwing, a criminal fresh from her own heist, with a fortune of uncut gems hidden in her vehicle. She could escape — but she won't abandon her millions. She could kill the Battle brothers, but she has to be careful. For one thing, if the law investigates, they'll find her ill-gotten loot. For another, her own life is sacred. She's the last member of a Florida paleoindian tribe thought to be extinct — the Tequesta. With her share of the money she plans to buy, bribe and blackmail her way into her own ancestral tribal lands in the heart of the Everglades, a Tequesta nation.

Lucy leads them into her beloved swamp, determined to kill them. But when she falls for Edgar she must decide whether to risk her heritage and the future of her tribe to save the doomed brothers.

BRIGHTWING

SULLIVAN LEE

First Print Edition: July 2011

For my sister M
Who begged me to kill Mallory

Chapter 1

It was a shame about the hooker.

Lucy Brightwing left the high class call girl tied with her own thigh highs and convincingly roughed-up in the lobby of a diner that opened for breakfast. The early fry cook would find her, and probably not rape her, since she knew from a background check he had a clean criminal record.

Lucy always did her research.

Still, as she shed her own clothes at the back door of the jewelry store she felt a momentary qualm. She had a soft spot for hookers. She occasionally taught a women's self-defense class on the Res, and most of her students were professionals or enthusiastic amateurs who wanted to make sure their johns didn't get out of line. Lucy taught them easy chokes, painful joint locks, and when no one else was looking, the tender places where a blade, slipped in a slim half-inch, can turn a criminal into a corpse.

The curvy red-head bound in her own hosiery hadn't taken Lucy's class, and did little more than squeal when Lucy deftly and mercifully made her unconscious before adding a few decorative bruises.

Now, standing superbly naked, she said a silent prayer to her ancestors that the hooker wouldn't suffer anything more dire than the few marks Lucy had given her — for her own good. She had to look like what she was: a victim. When you're dealing with twelve million dollars in uncut gems, people tend to assume everyone who knows about them is a suspect. And once you get into the millions, suspects have a way of meeting unpleasant ends.

It was the hooker's fault, of course. She was unwise enough to blab to her madam about how the jeweler liked to take her in the strong-room and dress her up in priceless emeralds, diamonds and pigeon-blood rubies then make her perform acts he considered unspeakably, titillatingly foul, but she considered no more than an easy night's work. More recently, he'd taken to having his sweaty way with her on top of mounds of things she thought looked like pretty pebbles, which he swore were uncut jewels of untold worth. She didn't like that as much as the necklaces and tiaras. The rough rocks left bruises on her posterior, and her other clients were beginning to complain.

No, really it was the madam's fault. She was the one who ran up six figures of debt at the Seminole Casino. When closeted in the back room with two of Billie Bald Cypress' larger heavies she decided a finder's fee might get her out of her jam, and hinted broadly at what she knew. Billie stepped in before the minions could get ideas of their own. Minions are so tricky. The dumb ones are no use, the smart ones invariably betray their handlers.

Billie got all the information and ran with it. He paid half of the madam's debt, leaving her to pay the rest in trade, which, she decided as she got deeper in the robbery scheme, she should have done in the first place. But Billie had his hooks in her now, and once he knew about the jewels he didn't much care how she paid off her remaining debt. After all, he wasn't officially connected to the casino, though as the head of Seminole organized crime he had his finger in every tasty, lucrative pot. He was paid well for helping the casino collect what it was owed, but the payoff from shaking down the scared little madam would be the biggest of his life.

He immediately saw the way to get past the jeweler's impressive security. It wasn't a matter for thugs with guns — no smash-and-grab here. They'd get the job done, all right, but not without leaving blood and destruction behind, and the last thing Billie wanted was for the cops to know a thing about it. This needed a subtle touch, a woman's touch.

So he called Lucy Brightwing.

Now, naked in the back alley, she smoothed the long red tresses of her wig and slipped the wooden mask over her face. Then she broke into the jewelry shop the old-fashioned way — she rang the bell. If all had gone according to plan — and it better have, or there'd be hell to pay — the madam had called the jeweler up just a few minutes ago to let him know his favorite girl had concocted a special treat for him. A new dance she'd been working on, something exotic. Since exotic dancers were the jeweler's second favorite type of woman he was rampantly excited even before the bell chimed.

Nakedness is often the best disguise. He saw what he expected to see — lavish red hair, mounds and declivities in the accustomed places. He saw the mask, of course, carved from pale cypress heartwood into a demonic owl face, but didn't notice that the eyes glowing behind it were not blue, but deep black. He smiled, reached out to touch her...

Two minutes later, before he could *quite* discover the ambivalent joys of erotic asphyxiation, he was choked unconscious, then encouraged to remain that way somewhat longer by a precise blow to the head. She pried open his eyelid for the retinal scan, slapped his limp hand on a pad to read his prints, wedged his body in the doorway to keep it from locking, and discovered that there was one more barrier to a successful heist.

Pit bulls are the softest, gentlest dogs in the world... until they decide not to be. This one had been trained since puppyhood to defend shiny things. Unfortunately for the jeweler, he'd also been conditioned by very frequent exposure to ignore naked women in the strong-room. His master had given his customary grunt and was now apparently asleep, as usual, so all was well with the world. He licked at the layer of super-glue covering Lucy's hands while she gently pulled his pink ears, then settled down for a nap while she stole slightly more than twelve million dollars worth of gems. He was a pretty dog, so before she left she looped strands of sapphires around his neck and narrow waist. He thumped his tail twice and went back to sleep.

3

It was those two trusting thumps that made her start to feel guilty. The jeweler was a criminal; Billie Bald Cypress had assured her of that. The gems weren't covered by his insurance or listed among his stock. He'd gotten them illegally, or at least unscrupulously, and kept them off the books. What would happen now? No crook is an island. Surely he was cutting the stones for some high-powered fence to shift, or trading them for arms or drugs. Either way, someone besides the jeweler was going to be mightily peeved that the gems were gone. And since they'd never find her—Lucy was sure of that — they'd take it out on the jeweler.

Or the hooker. That's why she'd taken such pains to bruise her face without doing any real damage, and leave her to be discovered by a model citizen who'd no doubt call the police. Even if she didn't want to pursue it, there would be a record of her name, her injuries, an alibi in case anyone wanted to accuse her of being in on the plot. The madam might have a harder time of it, but then, it had been her idea in the first place, so she got what she got.

None of them were very high on the sliding scale of goodness and morality, but maybe they didn't deserve what might be coming to them.

Lucy looked up into the security camera with her bird mask and said aloud, "If it was just for me, I might walk away. But it's for my tribe. For the Tequesta."

Then she disabled the camera and erased the video and the backup, her fingers feeling strangely disembodied under the layer of superglue that covered her prints without the awkwardness of gloves.

She would drive back to the Everglades, to the Seminole and Miccosukee reservations, where two entire tribes would swear that she'd never been anywhere near the jeweler's shop. Then as soon as the gems could be turned to cash she'd use the money to finally fulfill her lifelong dream — establishing a homeland for her people.

Even if her people had been officially extinct for more than two hundred years. Even if, at the moment, her tribe consisted of just one person: her.

She checked on the jeweler to make sure he was still breathing, then rolled him into his strong-room with her high-arched bare foot.

She decided she didn't have much sympathy for him after all. "You called the hooker," she told his unconscious bulk as she left. "You should have expected to be fucked."

Chapter 2

"Ha! The first palm tree. I win!" Mallory's face illuminated in a flash of joy so guileless Edgar could almost ignore the flecks of blood on his brother's cheeks, and how they got there. A stubby Washingtonian palm poked from the underbrush of elderberry and palmetto scrub at the side of the road.

Edgar pushed hard against his broad forehead, temporarily smoothing engrained frown lines. "Seven states worth of cops gunning for us, and you play Mom's old road games." He shook his head. Edgar didn't tell him that palmettos are palms too, little runty good-for-nothing palms, but palms nonetheless, and he'd seen the first one forty miles back on the Georgia side. He'd known Mallory since he was two days old. That's when Mom pulled him out of the incubator, four weeks premature, swearing no doctor would mess with her little boy. None ever did, or they might have discovered something wrong with Mallory even then. Can a baby be insane? She died when Mallory was nine, and from then on Edgar was brother and mother both, doubly protective.

Anyway, Edgar had seen the first red dirt in Georgia, so he let Mallory have his victory.

They were on the road from New York to Florida, a tedious drive even when beaches and Disney are your goal, so much worse when the law is hounding your ass. Edgar had thought about going to Canada, but Mallory yearned for the sun. So Edgar slapped together a plan. He had a friend in Miami who owed him. He'd get them transport out of the country on a merchant or fishing boat. They'd slip across the gulf to some tropical paradise of sun-browned skin and cheap rum.

Lay low, Edgar cautioned, but the body count since the journey began hovered somewhere around six, possibly as high as ten — it wasn't always convenient to stick around and wait for someone's prognosis. They'd started out with $50,000 and a stolen car, so you might think there was no need to hit up gas stations and bars along the way. But things happened. Especially when he wasn't working alone.

Mallory had a tendency to overreact. That's how Edgar explained it to himself, when he didn't want to delve too deeply into his brother's mental plagues. Most of the time they lay dormant... then he'd turn his back and his seemingly rational brother would do something stupid. Again, that label, stupid, was a cover for the more unnerving truth. But thirty years of someone's company can make for a whole lot of ignoring, and as a rule Mallory was no more than touchy.

Anyone who didn't love Mallory would call him a sociopath.

Edgar was pushing forty, and thought he'd found his place in the world. He was a successful mid-level criminal, a jack of all trades, so long as those trades related to theft or burglary or beating someone until they decided to pay what they owed. He was the one even big guys would back down from, not just the bouncers and failed boxers, the heavies, but the suits, made men. Mallory was just Edgar's kid brother, and that was enough to earn him a measure of respect. Edgar's crimes were generally commissioned; Mallory's indiscretions were all personal, and much more obscure.

Edgar had done most of the driving, past frost-covered roadside jonquils as a hard, lingering northern winter breathed its death-rattle, down to the Florida-Georgia border where now, in the hour just before dawn, it was seventy degrees. His muscles felt dull, with that warm heaviness that comes from a daily five minutes of desperate adrenaline rush, followed by twelve hours of driving on desolate back roads.

It would be over soon, though. Just a few hours to Miami, and they were home free.

Just a few minutes earlier they'd been awakened by a trooper, certain anyone asleep in their car on a back road was drunk, an easy arrest stat. Edgar had put on his reasonable face. If the cop hadn't watched the news lately he might be able to talk his way out of it. But when the trooper refused to be swayed by Edgar's affable pose and reached for his shoulder mic to call backup, Edgar heard a whining noise of protest from Mallory in the passenger seat. There was a blur of motion, a hand clapped hard over his ear, then the barely muffled explosion of a .357 point blank.

"Damn it Mallory!" he'd said, his own voice sounding distant and metallic in his echoing ears. "Low profile!" The trooper was on the ground, still moving, only wounded. Mallory acted on impulse, but Edgar always had to clean up.

He won't live anyway, Edgar told himself as he glanced at the trooper's wound, and dragged him, moaning, toward the ditch to administer the coup de grace. But the shot he fired went straight into the dirt and, hating himself, he pressed the red emergency button on the trooper's radio. Maybe it wasn't too late. Taking the gun — a splendid Glock — spare clips, handcuffs and pepper spray, he trudged back through the waist-high grass.

"I saw the first palm tree," Mallory said again as they left blue pulsing lights far behind them.

"Look." Edgar paused, wondering if there was any point in trying. "We have money. We're four-hundred miles from a safe house. If we can avoid attracting attention for a while we can be in Argentina partying with all the retired war criminals. But we can't even make it to the next town if you shoot everyone we meet. Geez — have a little self-control."

Stocky piebald cows watched them from behind barbwire. "Florida cows are better than Texas cows," Mallory said suddenly, making Edgar jump. He'd been calculating how long it would take for someone to find the trooper, whether he'd run their tag before he pulled over behind them. "They're pretty and....cleaner, and....kinda unexpected. You know you're going to see cows in

Texas, but in Florida they surprise you. I read that Florida has the second-highest number of cows, after Texas. But every time I see one, I can't help thinking, hoo boy, a cow."

As if their rude awakening hadn't happened.

He wasn't stupid, and Edgar would have knocked the front teeth out of anyone who said he was crazy, but there was no getting around the fact that Mallory was a pretty funny bastard. And though Edgar had looked after him for thirty years, and learned almost boundless patience, he sometimes thought the kindest thing would be to put a bullet in his brother's head some night when he was sleeping. It would be the best thing for Edgar, certainly, and for the world. But he remembered his mother's pleading eyes as she said, clutching his hand, "Take care of him! Whatever else he is, he's your brother."

He fought back the fantasy of killing his brother and ruffled his golden hair instead. Maybe I should have set a better example, he thought.

It might have been a smooth ride all the way to his buddy in Miami, if not for Mallory. Now he had to ditch this car, and hell, maybe take a hostage against the increasingly likely probability of a standoff. At the very least, hole up for a while.

They stumbled on a Bronco at a rest stop, and found its owner, a woman alone, using the bathroom inside. When she emerged, they explained they'd be taking her truck, and would she be so good as to remain quietly tied in the back under several layers of blankets and tarps?

They went to ground that afternoon in a little cabin so old and shabby they figured no one even knew it existed any more. They were wrong, of course — it was one of the traditional stops for hikers and backpackers along the edge of the National Park trail, frequented by explorers, and it was only a matter of chance that no one came by to bivouac there that particular night. It had no electricity or running water, but was comfort enough for Edgar, whose only desire was that people not shoot at him for a week or two. They ate from the assortment of canned beans, condensed milk and dried fruit they found in the cabin, not knowing, or not caring, that by convention such provisions were reserved for emergencies, and that the next visitor, when he saw the supplies were gone, would immediately become suspicious, and look for any clues that might tell the story.

The Battle brothers left plenty that night. Or rather, one left the clues, the other, despairing, tried to cover them up.

The next morning they set out before dawn, with the Bronco but without the girl, and almost immediately upon departing found themselves lost. The terrain became flatter and less woodsy, but within ten miles, when they crossed the Marion county line, they hit their first lake. It was a negligible obstacle, as were the next three—Edgar simply retraced his route and found another road that led around it. But then they hit Lake Harris, not so big, as lakes go, but still stretching several miles across, blocking their southerly route. Edgar turned left, when right would have been the better choice, and wound up going straight north again when the lake curved.

By ten Edgar was growing frustrated. He wished he could stick to main roads, but with the threat of the law breathing down his neck, he quite sensibly stuck to little back byways, no more than twisty, turny paths that connected grovers' estates and fish farmers' spreads, without having anything to do with the rest of civilization. On every side was water — little ponds creeping almost up to the shoulder, sunken springs fringed by mossy carpets — water that would suddenly pounce on him, cutting off his escape. He felt like he was in a dream, one of those nightmares of impotence where you can't make your legs move, where your fist is suddenly limp and useless. He drove until they were almost out of gas, and dusk was approaching. He would find a way around a lake, only to be routed by an impenetrable wall of orange or lemon trees. He would start down a path, only to see it dissolve into dirt and woods a half-mile later.

Mallory, bored by the scenery but not terribly anxious, said, "Why don't we find a main road?" He had been consulting a tourist's map with big mouse ears in the center, a map that knew no vacationer would set foot in the real Florida backwoods. The place they were — where they guessed they were, in any case — was represented by a patchwork of green and blue, with nary a road depicted.

Edgar fixed his brother with a look so long he nearly ran off the road into a water-filled canal.

"Because they know," he said at length, returning his gaze to the road, "within a hundred-mile radius, where we are. Because they know that not only are we the dumb fucks who shot a trooper, and dumped a dead girl behind a cabin, but I'm willing to bet they know we're the dumb fucks who pulled the prison bus break in New York, without even having a fucking plan of escape." His voice managed to stay even through his tirade, but the muscles in his cheeks were tight, almost as though he were smiling. It made it easy for Mallory to overlook his brother's anger, and he turned to look out the window again.

"Can we stop and pick some oranges?" Mallory began, but Edgar pounded the wheel with his fist, the gesture accentuated by the sharp report of the horn.

"Don't you even *think* before you do anything?" he demanded. "We could have cruised all the way from New York to Miami without anyone noticing us. Why would they think we'd go to Florida, huh? Just two guys on the road. But no, you had to knife that man at the filling station in Penn, with his little boy watching. You think he's ever going to forget what we look like? Bet the cops had us ID'd within five minutes. Do you think it took them much longer to figure out the string of bodies you left all point in an arrow directly to us? Maybe, maybe if we'd had *just one day* where you didn't leave a blood puddle with our name in it they'd have been thrown a little. Maybe thought we were heading for the Mexican border. Maybe thought we'd gone to ground. But no — you practically send the Florida law an engraved invitation with fucking calligraphy and gold trim, telling them where we are, and where we're going."

"But they're too stupid to..." Mallory began. Edgar slammed on the brakes and swerved to the grassy shoulder.

"Do you want to get caught?" he growled when the car skidded to a halt. "Do you want to spend the rest of your life in prison, absolutely helpless, waiting to die? Do you want to see me gunned down by thirty rabid cops when they remember that we've killed a few of their own?" Mallory, stunned, wondering if he had whiplash, shook his head. "Then you're going to keep a low profile, got it? You're not going to make eye contact with any one.

You're not going to kill anyone…"

"Even if I have to?"

"If you have to, you have to," Edgar admitted, knowing in his heart that Mallory's idea of necessity differed considerably from his. "But we're still alive now because of a damn big pile of luck, and I have a feeling that's going to be gone before long."

His voice softened as he watched his kid brother rubbing the back of his neck. "You all right? I hurt you? Just try to be careful. All we have to do is lay low for a while, and then we can see about getting out of the country. Just please don't do anything to attract anyone's notice."

"Like driving in crazy circles around every freakin' lake in Florida?" Mallory asked.

"Yeah, kinda like that." Edgar flipped on the radio to clear the air, and until nightfall they listened to Latina contraltos sing sad-sounding songs they couldn't understand.

Chapter 3

The panic that had hovered along the edge of Edgar's mind, kept at bay only by the dreamlike quality of the day, the labyrinthine waterways and absolute solitude (for they had seen no more than a handful of cars all that day) asserted itself during the eight o'clock news update on NPR, the only station they could receive, other than the one in Spanish and another with someone screaming about hellfire. The cool, detached tones of Pilar Romero informed him there was a massive manhunt underway in central Florida for two men wanted for questioning in the brutal attempted murder of a state trooper, who the police had reason to believe were the same men involved in the recent New York prison bus break, and a host of other crimes. Edgar and Mallory Battle. The Battle brothers. Edgar sighed and rubbed his tired eyes as Pilar ran over a rough physical description of them.

"Attempted murder?" Mallory asked. "What, you miss from two inches away?"

Edgar didn't answer.

"Hey, they say we're both six-foot-two." Mallory persisted. "You know I'm an inch taller than you. I wish they'd get their facts straight."

"Maybe if you're caught, you can get off on that one. Golly officer, I can't be the man you want. I'm six-foot-three. That oughta work." Surprisingly, Edgar was in a better mood now that he heard the report. The news might be dire, but at least he knew where he stood. He rotated his head to stretch out his sore neck (ignoring the crackle of crepitus) and felt refreshed, like a general preparing for war. He could feel his cool returning, the real thing, not the act he kept up that was so good he could usually fool even himself.

"We need to get rid of this car, and we need another hostage. And this one has to last." He closed his eyes to the memory of the woman, hardly more than a girl, bloody and splay-legged in the woods when he woke up the next morning. Edgar was always a deep sleeper, and Mallory had enough practice to do his work quietly.

"They probably haven't found her yet — they didn't say anything about it on the radio — but when they do they'll know what car to look for. If we can just get a different car, we'll have the whole night to put some distance behind us. But Mallory, it can't be messy. Promise me."

"Of course, bro. Anything you say."

It was Mallory who spotted the red flashing hazard lights of a car pulled off to the side of the road, and he elbowed Edgar to attention.

Edgar slowed as they neared, and in the intermittent red glow caught sight of a form bending down by the driver's side. A woman, he could tell a second later, for her position spread her up-raised hips. Edgar smiled as a phrase floated through his mind — broad where a broad should be broad. Her car was an older black Volvo, a nice, reliable car, but nothing that would attract attention. Big interior. Big trunk.

"That's the one," Edgar said. "Get ready."

They pulled up behind her, and it was only when she heard the sound of their emergency brake that she stood and slowly turned to face them.

For a long moment Edgar looked at her, knowing she couldn't see beyond the headlights. "Wait," he said, and started to put the car in gear again, but Mallory was already out the door. "Not her," he whispered in the empty car.

She was tall — he liked that — and she looked evenly into the glare. Her bright brown hair, curling wildly around her shoulders, caught the light, but her eyes were the deep black of unlit coal. She wore tight black pants and a tank top the color of an overripe plum. He flipped off the headlights and got out of the car slowly, hanging over the door with a half-smile. Mallory, on the other hand, walked right toward her in his apparently affable way. The girl did not move.

Lucy Brightwing was annoyed when the car pulled up behind her, having the situation well in hand and not anxious for company after dark on a lonely country road. Particularly when she had millions of dollars in uncut gems hidden in the body of her car. But she'd never met a man she couldn't handle (though women still baffled her sometimes) so she braced herself to be charming and get rid of them quickly.

"Evening," the younger man said, approaching to within a few feet. She nodded in return, and her hand reached up to dally coquettishly with her neckline. She had a small serrated Spyderco folding knife clipped between her breasts. Her philosophy of social relations was simple — be friendly and polite to everyone, but always be ready to kill them if you have to. Most people caught the friendly part; few noticed what lay beneath.

The two men were dressed respectably enough, both in dark clothes evidently chosen with some care as to fit and style. The one nearest her, the friendly one, was big enough to be imposing, but had a certain sweetness about him, she thought, which she was consciously aware set her at ease. Her immediate counter-reaction was to be suspicious.

The other one, though, she couldn't quite figure. His craggy face was shadowed, but as near as she could tell he seemed almost handsome, though worn and tired. He was burdened by something, his friend was not. He carries both packs, her people would say. She knew a thing or two about the weight of responsibility.

"Do you need some help, ma'am?" Mallory asked.

"I have everything under control, I think, boys," she said smoothly. She held her ground when Mallory took a step, not a very big one, toward her. Something about him made her uneasy. It took a lot to make Lucy nervous. She'd taken bigger men to the

17

ground without a thought.

"We got a little lost on these back roads, figured we'd kill two birds, so to speak. Help you and get our bearings. Do you know what the next town is, up ahead?"

"I don't know the area well," she confessed briefly.

"Not from around here?" he asked, measuring her up. "Well, what's wrong with your car? I thought Volvos were supposed to be so reliable."

She laughed, and the sound was low, like water moving over rocks. "Not reliable, just safe. The brake lights aren't working."

"Doesn't sound too safe to me," Edgar said, not shifting from his pose beside the Bronco. Lucy met his eyes, and didn't even notice that Mallory edged a bit closer.

"That's why I stopped," she said. "I think it's just the fuse. I have a few spares. I'll be ready to go in a minute."

"Would you like us to stay here until you're done?" Mallory asked, his voice soft.

"And you'll keep me safe?" she asked, the corners of her lips curling upward. She thought of the past few hours, the subtle ploy that got her inside, the burst of violence when the jeweler proved reluctant, the feel of those rough baubles running through her hand... Not that she cared about rubies and emeralds, per se. She would turn them over to Billie Bald Cypress and Lazarus Night-eyes and take her share of the money. That, she cared about. She already had enough money to live on — the two tribes saw to that — but for what she had in mind she needed millions. For her own tribe.

"Something like that," Mallory said in a tone of insinuation she didn't quite like, but dismissed it when he lit up cheerfully, spying a copy of Vonnegut's *Hocus Pocus* on the passenger's seat. "Wow, I loved that book."

The ploy worked, as though two men with guns need a ploy, and she immediately relaxed by two or three notches, turning away from him to follow his gaze to the novel, smiling to find him a kindred literary spirit. When she turned back to him, her eye was level with the barrel of Mallory's .357.

She didn't act surprised, really, a fact which in itself startled Edgar. A little gasp, flared nostrils, and that was all. She looked down the barrel, then refocused on Mallory's face. For a moment Edgar thought the shock of it all was taking a while to register, and he waited for the trembling, the tears, the screams. But instead she stood loosely, and glanced over into her car briefly, longingly. Did she have a weapon? A phone? But she made no move.

She considered it, though. She was a skilled grappler, though more comfortable on the ground than standing. It would be easy to deflect the gun. Maybe not wrest it away, but if she could distract him, knock him off balance, she'd be in the woods like a deer. Twenty feet into that wilderness and only a lucky bullet would find her.

But she couldn't die, couldn't take the chance. She was too important. She was the last; if she died, her people would be gone.

And of course, she couldn't leave her jewels.

She weighed those things, her past and her future, against these two men. She examined Mallory again, then looked at last to Edgar, who still hadn't moved. I know I could take them, she thought. I *think* I could take them. "But of course," she said aloud, "you have a gun too."

To prove her right, Edgar languidly drew the trooper's Glock. "Don't make a sound..." Edgar began.

"Or do anything to piss us off..." Mallory interjected.

"And you'll probably get out of this alive."

She digested that for a moment, then, her voice creaky, said, "Who are you boys running from?"

"Oops," said Mallory. "You forgot the first rule already." He pushed the .357 closer to her head and cocked the hammer, so it would fall at the slightest trigger pressure. The bullet, Lucy could not help thinking, would not have far to go at all.

"Mallory!" The harsh command brought him tightly under control, for the moment at least. He was used to obeying that voice, for a while. "Don't screw up this time, ok? We might not find another one. We have to make this one last."

And despite the gun that still threatened her face, Lucy chuckled grimly, thinking that she was a valuable commodity. She wondered what happened to the other one, and again considered escape. But unless she managed to dispatch both of them, she'd have to go alone, and those jewels were too good company to lose.

"Shut up!" Edgar said to her, coming around the side of the car and taking over his brother's place. "Do exactly what we tell you, if you want to live." She cocked her head to the side, and Edgar wondered, could she really be as fearless as she seemed? She might be a bit edgy, but she looked at him evenly. He wasn't sure if even he himself would look so cool in her place. Then again, he wouldn't let himself get in such a state. If someone had been stupid enough to pull a gun on him within arm's reach, well, to hell with the gun, then. The man would have gone down, felled by one of his famous punches. But no girl would have the guts, not to say the strength, to pull off something like that, and he'd been right in thinking she wouldn't put up a fight. But the last thing he expected was for some random girl on the side of the road to stare coolly into the black maw of a barrel without flinching. He thought about leaving her here, but it was too late for that.

"What's your name?" he asked her, but she said nothing. He asked her again, looking more intimidating, but she only raised her eyebrows and glanced toward Mallory, to see if he would understand.

He did. "You told her not to talk, Edgar."

Edgar sighed. He was not in the mood for this. "Speak when I want you to speak."

The girl paused, and then said, with a little lilt, "Lucy."

"Well, Lu, you're going to get in the …"

But of all things, she interrupted him. "Not Lu. Lucy."

For a second he didn't react, then swiftly he raised his arm, shifting the grip on his gun so he could smash it across her face. He didn't — he didn't want to, it was too good a face — but he did want to see the sudden fear in her eyes as she cringed to evade the blow. It was satisfying to see her loose her cool like that, and though she regained much of it a moment later when she realized the gesture was only a threat, she looked vaguely subdued, defeated. Much better.

"Now *Lu*," he said, pausing on her name to see if there would be any further protests, "are you going to cooperate?" This time she only nodded, though by Battle brothers logic she was allowed to talk that time. "You're going to be with us for a few days, if you're lucky." An involuntary image of the last girl flitted through his mind again, and he shuddered. Had she still been alive when his brother went to work in earnest? "You might not always have a gun at your head, but don't let that fool you. We will always have the ability to kill you, and we will if you give us any trouble."

Though she remained obediently mute, Edgar could tell she was doing some pretty serious thinking. She was a smart cookie. She knew they wanted a hostage, not a victim, and she was worth more to them alive than dead. He could see her self-possession returning as this realization sank in. That was good. It would make for a quiet trip. Few things got on his nerves as much as whimpering.

Almost at once he stopped thinking about the girl, concentrating instead on his next move. He would drive south all night, hoping to get to Miami — if he could ever get out of this lake country. In Miami was someone who owed him a favor, a big one. He was sure Vargas would take him in and arrange transport out of the country. He didn't know the kind of price on his head. It was easily enough to outweigh any favor, to circumvent the tenuous loyalty of criminal brotherhood.

"All right," he said, at once decisive, "in the car. You in the back, Lu." After the briefest hesitation she got in. If she was going to make a break for it this might be her last chance. She always taught her students that anything is better than being trapped in a car. Fight, she told them, though it might be a death-struggle, because being dragged into a car spells doom. And yet she had a feeling about these boys, a feeling she could scarcely define, which amounted to little more than a premonition, that cheerfully obeying them would be her best bet. There would be time, once their guard was down, to get away with her life and her fortune both, if only she was alert for the right moment. And then again, they needed her, more than they knew.

Lucy had been occupied with her own affairs for the past few days, not in any position to hang on the news. She was wholly in the dark about these two men, otherwise she might have reacted differently. All the same, she thought she could tell their tale fairly well, and though she had no illusions about their character they didn't strike her as entirely irredeemable. She was used to criminals. They were her best friends, her drinking buddies. Her great-uncle Billie Bald Cypress, head of Seminole organized crime, thought he was her boss. And so she took these men at face value, desperate criminals, to be sure, but not so different from herself. Not that she'd let them know that, of course. She wanted them to believe she was simply a terrified hostage, a girl like any other.

So when she was ushered into the back seat of her own Volvo, she went without protest, scooting over so Mallory could take the seat beside her. Edgar transferred their belongings to the new car and sat up front, starting the car roughly. He was about to pull away when Lucy said softly, "Edgar?" Damn, she knew his name. He should have been more careful, particularly since he hoped to let her live. But Lucy was already making plans to change the nature of their relationship.

"Do you want to be gagged?" he asked, glaring at her through the rear-view mirror.

She wisely didn't answer that directly, but calmly went on, now that she had his attention. Mallory still held the gun loosely on her, sometimes so distracted she was sure she could have gotten it away, sometimes squinting down the sights at her like a sharpshooter.

"Are you going to leave your car there?" she asked. "On the roadside?"

He looked like he wanted to hit her. At last he unlatched his seat belt with a rattlesnake's click and hiss, and got out of the car, irritated for a number of reasons, not the least of which was that the girl was perfectly right. "Shoot her if she does anything stupid," Edgar said to his brother, fervently hoping that she wouldn't — they'd be out one hostage, and probably a car too, unless the blood and bullet-holes weren't too noticeable.

He hastily wiped the steering wheel, clutch and dash with a handkerchief in a half-hearted attempt to remove fingerprints, then threw the car in neutral, unlocked the emergency brake, and with some effort pushed the Bronco into the grass where it caught the downslope and rolled freely into the brush. It paused and shimmied before slowly sinking into the dark, still canal waters until only the rooftop showed.

He'd been in too much of a hurry to think of it — but he should have, damn it. The day was when Edgar Battle was a competent criminal, who didn't leave any evidence. This wild caper, since the moment of his escape while en route to the upstate prison where he'd just been sentenced to spend the next eighteen years, had been a farcical disaster in all ways but one — they hadn't gotten caught yet. Get on the ball, he hissed under his breath as he stalked back to the Volvo. He would get his brother and himself to some safe haven where they could live out their lives in dissipation and peace. In his mind there hovered an idea of some sort of criminal sanctuary, a *home* in life's game of tag, where they could be contented and safe. Despite all that he'd done, he still felt he deserved it. And he would not go there without his brother. He'd promised their mother, and that's a promise you don't break.

"Man," Mallory said when Edgar got back into the Volvo. "That was about the stupidest thing I've ever seen." But he was talking to Lucy, not Edgar. "You helping us hide our evidence now? You better keep your trap shut before we all get away free and clear."

Lucy said nothing, only caught Edgar's eye in the rear view mirror, giving him the faint smile and raised eyebrows of a co-conspirator. He glowered. Edgar thought he understood her reasons, and it unnerved him that she should be so self-possessed, and so crafty.

Lucy might have been frightened, but it was mingled with curiosity, and a sense of adventure. She'd been in several situations almost as dangerous in her twenty-five years, and this had enough novelty to be exciting. She was supremely confident, used to getting her own way, and had absolute faith that her ancestors were watching, commenting, and placing bets on the outcome even now. And then, having lived a great deal of her life in the Florida swamps, she was prepared for just about anything.

Edgar gunned the engine, skidded onto the pavement, and the trio was on the road.

Chapter 4

As it turned out, the Volvo was no good luck charm for navigating through the uncharted backwoods. Several times Edgar passed what he was sure was the same spot — though by now, in the moonless black of rural night, everything looked the same. The world past the compass of his headlights was full of shadowed arms of tree branches, the quicksilver flash of stars on the marshes. He clenched his fingers in white-knuckled frustration around the wheel. There was no logical reason why he couldn't escape this maze of lakes, and yet he had just passed the same lightning-cleft tree for the third — or was it fourth?—time. He was having that bad dream feeling again, but drove relentlessly, not speaking of his fears, knowing that eventually luck, if nothing else, would lead him out. Mallory, occupied with watching their hostage, which he did with feline intensity, didn't notice their absurdly circular path. Lucy, who knew the area moderately well, did notice, and as she avoided Mallory's eye, she smiled again at Edgar's reflection.

"What the fuck are you looking at?" he asked testily, catching her. She lowered her eyes demurely and glanced at the charred tree, making sure that Edgar saw where she was looking.

"Where are we going?" she asked.

The gun was now pointed at her stomach, its range bouncing between her breastbone and her thighs as the car jostled along the potholes and puddles. It was the natural question of any worried hostage, but coming at that moment, and with that archness, Edgar was sure she was mocking him.

I should have gagged her, he thought. Do the thing right from the beginning, rough her up a bit so she knows what she's in for if she crosses us. But he hoped to show Mallory that brutality isn't always the answer. It's generally *one* of the answers, and when you can't quite come up with the absolutely right solution, it usually suffices. But it's not mandatory. At least, not the way Mallory did it. That wasn't business; it was something else entirely.

So he ignored her, but she wasn't content to stay silent and whispered, "If you take a hidden path that'll be coming up in a mile or so, on the left, you'll get to a town called Dodge."

"I thought you didn't know this area," Mallory said.

"You never tell strangers the truth," Lucy said, pulling her eyes away from Edgar. Mallory, for some reason, thought this was pretty funny stuff, and Edgar saw Lucy's eyes dance in response. *Don't attract him more than you can help*, he silently begged her. The last one tried to get on his good side.

"So … what's in Dodge?" Edgar asked, the name giving him a premonition he didn't like.

"In Dodge? Oh, a town hall, a barbershop, couple of traffic lights…" She shut up when Mallory pressed the cold muzzle to her temple. Edgar held his breath, remembering how loud a gunshot sounds in a car. Lucy gave a little shrug and returned to staring out the window.

Edgar found the turn-off, though he spotted it at the last minute and had to pull a jerky three-point-turn to get to it. "Find Dodge on the map," he said to Mallory. "And tie her hands."

"With what?"

"Find something." Edgar said, exasperated, forgetting about the stolen cuffs. But there would be a town up ahead, a reference point. From there he could chart a sure course down south, without the help of any aggravating hostage-girl.

Lucy's Volvo contained a collection of seemingly random objects that might have clued another man in to the fact that she was outside of the normal scope of girls. It was a combination of a survivalist's storehouse and a teenager's room — chlorine tablets, sparkled hair-clips, a helmet with an odd contraption attached to it (it was a carbide caving lantern, but Mallory didn't immediately recognize it) a dive mask, silver nail polish, books ranging from *The Story Of O* to wildflower identification guides. Amidst all this Mallory found a scarf in midnight blue silk shot with fine silver threads. He coiled the ends around his hands and jerked to feel the strength of the goods. "It's pretty," he said, as the fine material snaked around his big fingers.

"If you don't tie me up, it's yours," she said, and winked at him, bringing a laugh.

"Less conversation back there," Edgar ordered, uneasy, and Mallory tied her wrists together.

"Is that too tight?" he asked her, soft and solicitous.

She studied him, knowing there was something wrong with him but unable to place her finger exactly on it. He was looking at her kindly now, and when she squirmed her wrists and said that yes, it was too tight, he loosened it. He made her nervous, as she might be nervous of a water moccasin on a cold morning. It was torpid now, and she was safe, but she could never know the exact moment when it would absorb enough heat from the sun to be actively dangerous. For now, she felt she could pet him with impunity, and granted him a smile of thanks. But she knew, or rather felt, that it would not take much temptation to entice him to strike.

She tested her bonds, and found them even looser than Mallory thought to make them. Like the willful horse that holds its breath when the saddle is girded on, only to exhale later and easily throw the rider, she had subtly held her hands in such a way that she now had an additional half-centimeter of slack to work with. Not enough to escape, yet, but enough at least to provide an extra measure of comfort. With a sigh, she closed her eyes and rested her head against the window, watching the dark flash of passing scenery, waiting. She was a bit like a moccasin herself, waiting for the signal that would rouse her to action. She felt Mallory's eyes settle on her once more.

Some time later Lucy spoke yet again. Too much trouble to

shut her up now, Edgar thought with a sigh.

"I never did finish fixing the brake lights."

She let the statement hang there, and at first Edgar thought it was a non sequitur, a means of keeping up her end of a very sporadic conversation. But eventually Edgar half-turned and said, "What the *hell* are you talking about?"

"It's nothing, I guess, but I just remembered what else is in Dodge."

"And what might that be?" Edgar asked, knowing that it would be something — something else — he wouldn't much like.

"Crooked cops."

"Are there any other kind?" Mallory asked.

Some of her best friends were cops. Sure, half of them were on the take, but things are a little different on the reservation.

"Not in Dodge," she said. "It's a speed trap. General orders say stop everyone you can. The force is made up almost entirely of the Fritillary family. Old guy who's been the sheriff for seventy years, his son, and a few more generations. No out-of-town plate will get through without a ticket. They'll stop you for anything."

"Can't we just go around Dodge?" Mallory asked.

"You guys want to go south? Someone after you up north? Well, unless you want to backtrack about a hundred miles you'll have to go through Dodge. There aren't all that many roads around here, you know. Not that go anywhere you want to go."

Mallory turned on the dome light and studied the map. As Edgar slowed, delaying what seemed like their inevitable entry into Dodge, Mallory confirmed Lucy's advice. "Looks like it's Dodge, Bro. We got any more .357 ammo?"

"Don't think so. Plenty of .38 Special. And three clips from the trooper's... for the Glock."

"Why are you preparing for war when if you just fix the light we might get through?"

"I thought you said they stopped everyone," Edgar reminded her.

She rolled her eyes dramatically. "They can't stop *everyone*. And they probably wouldn't stop me. But *you* driving? With no brake lights?"

"Can you fix the lights?" Edgar asked.

"Sure. I told you it was just the fuse."

Edgar slowed more, and at last, choosing a particularly dark spot under the deep shade of an oak, stopped the car entirely. "Get her out," he said to Mallory.

"Now Lu," Edgar said when she was standing at the Volvo's side "Two things. You can guess the first one. Try anything — anything at all — scream, run, anything, and I will shoot you in the face. Understand?"

"Perfectly." After all, it was nothing new. "And number two?"

He got up close to her, cupping his body over hers so she was backed against the car door. They did not touch, but they were very close. "Why are you trying to help us?" She was supposed to be curled up in a frightened little ball, whimpering, praying, while he planned all of their moves. He was tempted to get rid of her, whether in the easy messy way, or simply leave her at the roadside, one more piece of incontrovertible evidence pointing out their route. But particularly now, so close to her flesh, he wasn't inclined to part with her. The law could pounce at any moment, he told himself, dismissing that other reason. It would be comforting to have that warm body to hold before them like a shield, to make the cops think twice about shooting.

Lucy seemed to echo his thoughts. "If you get caught, I'm probably going to die. That's what you have me for."

"You won't be killed if you cooperate."

"Don't bullshit me, Edgar." Her voice was still amused, but somehow harder. He wondered if she was the sort of person who smiled more and more, the angrier she got. He'd never liked that in men — but he'd never encountered it in a woman. "You'd kill me in a heartbeat, if it was in your best interests. But that's not what I'm worried about. If I'm your hostage, I have to be alive, more or less, to do you any good. The part that scares me is when the law comes. I don't know how deep you guys are, but I have the feeling you have someone pretty serious sniffing after you. When they come, they're going to come hard. They'll sort out the bodies later, apologize to my family, and that will be it for me. I don't like that idea. So it's my job to keep you from getting caught."

"Do you know who we are, Lu?"

"No," she said, with a frown. "My name's Lucy." And this time he didn't threaten to hit her. Lucy considered it an important step in their relationship.

With her hands still bound by the scarf, she knelt gracefully and replaced the brake light fuse as Edgar watched her, and Mallory watched the road.

"Have any other suggestions?" Edgar asked her wryly as Mallory slid into the back seat, gesturing for her to follow. She paused, leaning against the car.

"I do," she said, "but you're not going to like it." She sighed. "I should be the one driving."

"Hell no, you crazy woman!"

"Hey Edgar, did we get a new partner without you telling me?" Mallory asked from the car. "Cause last I heard, it was you, me, and one fucking hostage. Do you want me to put her in the trunk?"

The girl was taking over. She was absolutely right. If their only choice was to drive through a booby-trapped town, they damn well better take every precaution they could. Women just don't get pulled over as often as men. Edgar was as sexist as they come. He'd never met a woman who gave him a reason not to be. When you take a hostage, it's always a woman — there's never any question about that. Children are too annoying, men fight back, even if they're craven weaklings, out of some vestige of masculine pride. But women, even tough women, are a piece of cake. At least, such had been his opinion until a bare half-hour ago.

With some reluctance, he said, "All right, get in the front. But my brother will have a bullet waiting for your spine."

"Don't you think he should be lying down? They're looking for two of you, right? Don't make it easy for them."

"Get a load of her," Mallory said with a snort. But he didn't suggest getting rid of her now. He remembered the way she smiled at him when he tied her wrists, and it made him think of the things that usually followed tying someone up.

Edgar, of course, felt tempted to disregard her recommendations simply to maintain his position of control. But it was good advice. He gave the girl a nod that was more a jut of his chin, and she started the car, putting on the turn signal to re-enter the road, though no cars passed them since she'd been picked up. He almost laughed at her, then realized it was just such attention to detail that would keep them off the radar. The kind of thing he usually thought about himself, but for some reason, never seemed to remember in this current caper. He shook his head to clear it, but it only aggravated the traces of headache that had been playing around his temples for the past day.

It irritated him even more when he found a hint of sympathy on the girl's face as she saw him rub his forehead. "Get down, Mallory," he said, glad to have an order to give. "Cover yourself up with some of that shit back there. But stay on the ball. I might need you."

Dodge had fared better than many of the other inland Florida towns. Florida gives the impression of affluence, but the high life is all around the coasts. There's plenty of outback where rednecks and hicks abound. Travel through the center of the Sunshine State and you'll encounter much the same sort of backwoods mentality you might find in deep Appalachia. But Dodge was something of an oddity, an economically strong haven in the midst of white trash wilderness.

The mayor, who was also the sheriff, Boo Fritillary, had devised a plan to keep both his family and the town financially secure. He sank every drop of revenue into roads, even donating to state coffers, designing them so that for fifty miles around, all roads led to Dodge. The state thought that Dodge was doing something noble and generous; the Fritillarys, of course, had their own best interests at heart, for they supported the town on citation money.

Lucy wasn't keen on driving through Dodge, but there was little choice. She led the Battle brothers in, and hoped, for her own sake, it would not prove a death trap.

Chapter 5

It took Lucy a moment to recognize what lay a few hundred yards ahead of them. But Edgar had been anticipating just such a scene for so long now that he jumped to his own conclusion.

He stared for a heartbeat at the flashing red and blue lights, as Lucy drove slowly on. Then his brow knit, he inhaled one quick hyperventilated breath, and it was on.

"Oh fuck oh fuck oh fuck!" he said, reaching for the gun he'd settled beneath his leg. "It's a road block. Mallory, up! Shit! They're too close." And he reached across for the wheel, trying to spin it as Lucy fought him, first instinctively, then with good reason as she came to her own conclusions about the situation.

"Edgar... damn it Edgar, listen to me!" She elbowed him away, catching him in the chin with a resounding crack, and held the wheel firm. Edgar shouted at her to turn around, and both brothers, in their adrenaline rush, pointed their guns at her, which by now she barely noticed.

"Let go of me! It's not a road block. Look! It's off to the side, and there are ambulances." He loosened his grip on her arm and took a closer look, his breath still coming fast. "Stop jerking the wheel or we *will* get pulled over. Mallory, stay down!" And to her surprise, he hunkered obediently back into the pile of clothes.

"Edgar, this is perfect. I don't care what kind of hard-asses the local deputies are, they're not going to stop us when they're dealing with an accident."

As they approached the scene they could see a crumpled sports car and an overturned semi. Oranges lay spilled in saffron piles, squelching under their tires as they approached.

On she drove, keeping well below the speed limit (or rather, the hypothesized speed limit, for to better increase their ticket stats, no speed signs are posted within ten miles of Dodge) and watching the milling assortment of people carefully, alert to any undue notice.

"Two cruisers," she said, "and an unmarked, might be a cop, might be with the FD. And one engine."

"Turn your head away," she said to Edgar as they passed. "Pretend you're asleep." The rescuers were too involved in pulling a body from the wreckage of the sports car to pay much attention as the Volvo maneuvered around ruined fruit and shards of metal and glass. A fireman in a fluorescent vest waved them on and turned abruptly away. Lucy only noticed that she was holding her breath when the long exhale made her chest ache. The wreck was in her rear view mirror — they were free!

Her relief was cut short by the sickening sound of puncture, quickly followed by tilting and a heavy bump. Lucy hit the brakes. "Shit!" said Edgar, then "What are you doing! Keep driving!" and in the same breath "Mallory, stay down!"

"We have to stop."

"No! Drive!" And again, the gun. It was getting annoying now.

"If we don't stop they're going to think it's pretty odd, Edgar. Do normal people keep driving on a flat like this? Didn't you hear? The tire was ripped apart — it's not a little leak. We have to stop."

"But there are cops…" He gestured, half frantic, behind them.

"I have to change the tire. Please, listen to me!" And he had to, because he suddenly didn't know what else to do. "You two pretend to be asleep. If anyone comes I'll give them a story. We can't get away on this flat."

"I say we take off," said Mallory. "If they follow us we shoot. They don't have a chance. There's only, what, three of them. Not bad odds."

"Shut up!" Edgar shouted to his brother. "Let me think!" But he wasn't really thinking. His mind, his overtaxed nerves, had nearly shut down. "Ok, Lu, get out of the car. But if I see anything I don't like, you're dead."

"So tell me something I don't know," she said wryly. "Now you boys be chill. Pretend you're asleep, or drunk. Just keep your faces covered. I'll be right by the car the whole time."

"Can you change a tire?" Edgar asked, but she only replied with a look, and killed the engine.

Working fast, but keeping her movements steady so she wouldn't alarm her captors, she opened the trunk and got out the spare. I can run now, easy, she thought as she tied her hair into a knot. And with cops this close and the tire flat they'll run them down in half a mile. But what happens next? A shootout, dead cops. So what if they're on the take? She was on the take herself. Didn't mean they should die, and someone certainly *would* die, all that desperation and firepower hunkered in her Volvo right now. And then the car impounded for evidence. What if they found the jewels? She was looking at twenty years, at least, if everything came out and the jeweler was ballsy enough to testify.

No, not yet, she told herself. Wait until there's no one around. You'll get your chance. These boys are nothing compared to you. She flexed her muscles as she hauled out the tire, a real one not some dinky spare, and mentally rehearsed her favorite moves. She'd dispatch Mallory quickly, if she could. Edgar, now… it might be nice to take a little longer.

Lucy got the car jacked up, taking pains to avoid soiling her clothes, before she saw a shape break away from the at the accident scene and begin to approach her. No, she pleaded silently, don't complicate this for me.

"Any trouble there?" he asked, still from afar, and Lucy recognized the youngest Fritillary brother. He'd stopped her once for speeding a bare three miles over the unknown limit, but contrary to tradition, didn't ticket her. He'd been decent about the whole thing, only casually suggesting she should sleep with him, and while she was glad he was someone who wouldn't give her too hard a time, she was sorry to put him in any risk.

SULLIVAN LEE

"No trouble at all," she drawled. Edgar noticed her voice had
changed. Before, it had been cultured, with no discernable accent.
Now she fell into that peculiar Florida voice reminiscent of the
traditional southern accent, with harsher edges—Cracker. Her
pronunciation clearly indicated to the cop that she was like him, a
Florida girl. She slipped into his confidence, onto his side, almost
as easily as she had the Battle brothers.

"That's a mighty bad hole you put in your tire," he said in
friendly tones.

"I got off lucky, compared to that little car. Anyone hurt too
bad?" Her voice was soft, charming, and though she was just out
of Edgar's range of vision, he could imagine how she looked, eyes
a little widened, head to one side, gazing up sweetly at the deputy.
Damn, he thought, a clever woman can get away with anything.

"Nah," said the deputy. "Guy in the convertible was passed
out drunk and went right under the truck. If he'd been awake and
sitting up, he'd have had his head lopped clean off. As it was, bed
of the truck just sheared his windows, then he went into a tree.
Couple of scrapes, but he's fine. You travelin' alone?"

She didn't pause before she answered. "No, my two brothers
are in the car. Pretty much passed out too, or asleep would be a
nicer way of putting it." She elaborated on the story neatly, deciding it would be better to provide too much information all at
once, and make him loose interest, than to seem reticent and
prompt further questions. "They were at a bachelor's party up in
Eustis. Started around noon on the beer and barbecue, and you
know how things go from there. Luckily they had the good sense
to call me around six and ask for a ride, 'stead of tryin' to drive,
drunk as skunks. We're visiting our grandma in St. Cloud, but
we're from Miami." She remembered her Dade County plates at
the last minute, and altered her story to fit.

"You like it down there?" the deputy asked, moving closer, but
not in the least suspicious.

"Yeah, there's a lot of crime, but it's nice. I go to the Keys almost every weekend." Lucy broke off as she saw movement in the
back seat. "I'm fine, really. My brothers taught me plenty about
cars. I can have this tire on in three minutes. My younger brother
races." All the while, as she was babbling, she tried to subtly steer

36

the deputy away. But he was too nice, too friendly, to leave quickly when a woman was in trouble.

From the corner of her eye she saw Mallory sit up, and almost desperately said, "You should go back to the accident. They need you there more than I do."

Leave, she pleaded with him silently. Leave now before… But the back door opened, and as Edgar shouted huskily, Mallory swung out of the car, firing as he stood His gun glinted blue in the emergency lights, and the muzzle flash blinded her for a second. The deputy just managed to draw, but held his gun before his chest like an offering as he slumped to his knees. "Gee, thanks," Mallory said politely, and he plucked the weapon from the deputy's grasp as he toppled backward.

Edgar got out of the car slowly, suddenly so weary that for a moment he sincerely doubted he could stand. But he already had his weapon drawn and instinctively sought a target. He met Lucy's eyes briefly and wasn't quite sure what he found there. Pity for the fallen deputy, wide-eyed surprise, disgust, but nothing quite approaching shock.

"Why didn't you control him?" she asked, with more sadness than accusation, so quietly that only Edgar could hear her.

"Mallory, get back here!" Already, his irrepressible younger brother was setting off on foot toward the accident scene, where the emergency personnel were still milling. The gunshot hadn't registered at first. With the lights, grumbling engines, and the clanging of metal as they pried wreckage apart, one more piece of fireworks was scarcely noticeable. "Damn it!" Edgar swore under his breath, and started to go after him, then remembered Lucy. If he left her, she'd run for sure. "Get in the car, Lu, and get down." Why he added this last piece of advice, he couldn't say.

"Edgar, don't go," she said as she obeyed. "Leave him. You don't want to do this."

He leaned into car, and she thought, crazily, that he was going to kiss her goodbye. "You're right," he said, and pulled the keys out of the ignition before stalking away.

Edgar gritted his teeth and watched as his brother took up a strategic position behind a cluster of pines. A moment later Mallory opened fire, and still the law didn't respond until one of the cluster fell. Then they scattered and sprinted for cover, the deputies drawing their weapons, the civilians just running.

Almost weeping, swearing all the while, Edgar joined the action, sliding down into a dry ditch at the roadside. He shot blindly and high, providing cover fire for Mallory as he dodged closer but making no effort to aim.

There was no point in shooting that deputy in the first place, he growled as he lay down fire. We should have just driven off, and if it came to a pitched fight later, so be it. But this slaughter...

He saw one uniformed figure with a rifle in his hands fall, and he desperately hoped it wasn't his fault.

It's *all* my fault, he thought. I should have stayed in prison. Even with my brother and freedom calling me out, I should have stayed.

But he kept firing.

They were scattering now, though whether in panic, or to fan out into a better defensive position, he didn't know. If they'd been smart, if they knew what they were up against, they would have turned tail instead of facing the combined firepower of the Battle brothers.

Lucy followed orders and kept low, but it was only so she could try to rip out the ignition and get her car started without a key. She raised her head tentatively when the firing stopped.

"Edgar," she whispered out the door, "are you still alive?" She wasn't sure what she hoped for. He rose silently from the dust, grim and hard-eyed. "How many people are dead?" she asked as she stepped out of the car. Her flat tone was worse than condemnation.

"I don't know," he said quietly. "If there are any, it's too many." He rubbed his hand across his eyes.

"And your brother?"

"Mallory," he called softly, then "Mallory!" in a sharp yell. There was no answer, and with elation he felt a great weight lifting from him. It was worth it, all this death, if it freed him from his responsibility from his brother.

Lucy's eyes were sharper than Edgar's, but more importantly, she knew how to use her night vision, and looked at things peripherally, not directly. There's no deeper darkness than that of the Everglades, and she could prowl the swamps as well as any panther.

"He's over there," she said, peering through the blackness.

What she saw shocked her, and she was not easily shocked.

Lucy took a deep breath, then another, and even then, when she thought she was composed enough to speak, she found she needed one more, held longer than the others, to steady herself. She looked at Edgar, who could only just pick out Mallory's outline, and that of another person. But he could tell by the sounds, and from past experience, what must be happening, and he felt a dizzying sway of nausea, and looked away.

"Edgar," Lucy said, very low, "what's wrong with your brother?"

"Nothing," he lied bitterly. "Don't dare ask me that again." And jamming his gun in his back waistband, he strode across the street to get Mallory.

Chapter 6

Lucy and the Battle brothers were on the road again within two minutes, Lucy still driving, Edgar beside her and Mallory sprawled in the back. No one had spoken since they regrouped, and Lucy continued through Dodge then picked a westerly route without instructions, heading for I-75. She was trying — trying very hard — not to think about what she saw.

Thought I saw, she corrected. *I could have been wrong, and it was dark.*

She repeated this to herself as mile after mile of black-tarred highway passed under her tires. Crime, she could understand. She was tough, and could certainly hurt people, but she was never cruel. This went beyond even cruelty. She knew, almost the first time she looked at him, that Edgar could kill, without much compunction and very little regret. But Mallory made her feel like fire ants were crawling over her bare skin. She glanced at the rear-view mirror, but he was asleep. Asleep after that?

I have to get them out of the car, she decided. There's no way I'm giving up my people's future, and all my plans depend on the money. I'll never see this much again. This is my only chance. Lagrima. It has to be Lagrima. When they feel safe I can get rid of them. You always stroke a chicken into calmness before you twist its head off.

Two guns rested on Edgar's lap. Several times she tried to catch his eye, but he stared into his own reflection in the window. He was sure it was over, and to tell the truth (not that there was anyone he could tell it to) he was glad. He wouldn't turn himself in, of course. He just wouldn't try any more. Planning never did any good anyway, with Mallory around.

"The cop knew who we were," he'd explained to Edgar after the firefight. "I saw him reach for his gun. He would have gotten us if I hadn't been on the ball. Lucy was good, though. Cool little chick."

Edgar had other things on his mind just then, like what he'd interrupted his brother doing to the female deputy who'd been gutshot, still alive. Off in the tall grass, barely conscious, still struggling. If she'd been dead, or hadn't moved, Mallory might have left her alone... maybe. But she'd dragged herself to a firing position, and when all of her comrades had either fallen or fled, she continued the fruitless struggle for life and victory. And Mallory found her.

Mallory had scowled at Edgar when he pulled him off, but then cheerfully said, "I think we got 'em all. See, I was right."

Already he began to forget about the woman lying in the dirt — not forget, exactly, because before he went to sleep that night he'd recall those gray eyes full of hate and fear, the sound she made when he first touched her. But he lost interest, and quickly turned his attention to explaining how right he'd been to forget the whole plan and undo all the trouble both Edgar and Lucy had gone through to put as much distance as possible between them and any recognizable blood trail. He was actually proud of himself, and in quite a good mood.

Edgar had looked long into his brother's puckish eyes, trying to think of a way to admonish him, a way of explaining things that would finally sink in. At ten, Mallory had done things to cats. But he couldn't get a cat to plead, so he moved on. For years, Edgar had vacillated from ignoring to raging to lecturing, all to no avail, until he thought he had built up enough calluses to close his eyes and mind to the things his brother did, the way his brother was. Loyalty, and a sense of utter helplessness, kept him from doing anything about it. You don't turn your brother in, no matter what. You protect him all you can, because he's family. Even if that makes you worse than him.

Mallory slept soundly now, his breathing slow and heavy, with the occasional hint of a snore, his long legs curled up on the seat.

"Where are we headed?" Edgar asked, and the suddenness of his voice, after nearly an hour of silence, startled her.

"I thought we could go to a place I know, a little coastal city. No one will think to look for you there."

"Why?" he asked, and thought, and why are you helping us without being threatened? Why, after you saw what Mallory did, do you still look at me like you *want* to help me?

"It's a resort and vacation town, upscale. They'll look for you in shitholes and dives, not an expensive beachside cottage. We can stay there a day or two, then you can head south, to wherever you want to go."

"You mean *we* can head south."

"Don't you think I've paid my dues? You're on your own from now on." And she said it with such certainty, such authority, that for a moment he paused. Then he laughed.

"Not a chance, sister. You're our only ace right now. You know the state, and you're smart. I like that combination. No — you stay with us until we leave the country."

"Hey, it was worth a shot," she said, her eyes creasing at the corners. "But you'd really do better with me on your side. Here, give me that phone. I'll call ahead for reservations. The owner knows me—I stay there a lot. Do I get the warning this time about not doing anything stupid, or do you think it's sunk in by now?"

"Babe, I don't think you could do anything stupid if you tried," he said, shaking his head.

"You got that right."

Slowing the car a bit, she scrolled through the menu of numbers until she found one for the Plover's Nest. *"Hola Ruth, lo siento que llamarte tan tarde."* She quickly switched to English, for fear of rousing Edgar's suspicions. "It's Lucy Brightwing. Do you have any rooms available? I'm on the road now, and I should be in town sometime tonight. The Bijou? With the gulf view? Perfect.

Will you leave the key under the whelk again for me? I really don't know how late I'll be, and I don't want to wake you. You still have my credit card number? Oh, that's sweet of you. You'll be out of business if you treat all your customers like that. Let's say two nights, tonight and tomorrow night. But I'm not sure yet. Oh, and I'm bringing my new beau, so you can pretty much assume I'll have the do not disturb sign out. Don't be surprised if you don't see me this time!"

When she hung up she tossed the phone into Edgar's lap. "I hope," she said pointedly, "when the time comes you think about killing me, you'll remember how much you owe me."

Edgar tried to reestablish their mutual positions in his mind — *hostage, criminal, hostage, criminal* — but she kept disarming him with her easy smile, her seemingly friendly banter, the overall impression that she was in charge, and they were just along for the ride.

He couldn't figure her, couldn't ask her, so he changed the subject.

"Brightwing, huh? Where did you get that name? You indigenous?" He got that from a big brown mean pecker of an Iroquois construction worker he knew in New York.

"Yeah," she said.

"You don't look it."

She shrugged. "It's that way with any race, other than Caucasian. If you have a little in you, you get credit for the whole thing. My mom was, er, indigenous."

"What tribe are you from? Seminole?" He knew that from the college team, and from the casinos they'd passed.

Lucy was about to speak, stopped herself, then sighed. What did it matter?

"No, not Seminole," she said, watching his reaction. "Tequesta." But to him it was just another funky name, not a long-extinct tribe, and he thought nothing of it. When she said that to some people, they looked at her like she was a cross between Elvis, Obama in his Messiah days, and the pope. She sighed, which didn't go unnoticed by Edgar, who found his chief occupation of late was watching this peculiar girl for some clue. With Mallory asleep, and no sign of pursuit, he was beginning to relax, and almost enjoyed leaning his temple against the headrest, looking at her.

"So where's the name from? Is that a family name, like a last name?"

"No, the name was given to me. My mother's given name was Two Moons. But people know me by different names."

"Mysterious. How'd they pick yours?"

"Mmm. You're not the only one to wonder. On the day of his manhood ceremony, a young brave can approach the elders and ask them any questions he has about what it means to be an Indian. A boy in my village who came of age last year said, 'I have just one question, honored elder. How are we given our names?'"

It took him a moment to realize from her tone that she'd slipped into a joke.

"'Well, my son,' said the elder, 'when a child is born to us, the mother stays indoors until she is strong enough to go outside. Then, when she beholds the world after her confinement, the first thing she sees will be the infant's name. When my uncle was born, his mother saw a bear, so he was called Standing Bear. When my sister was born, her mother saw the creek flowing by, so she was named Rippling Waters. But tell me, why are you so curious about this, Two Dogs Fucking?'"

She didn't crack a smile, just stared at the road ahead, her own straight-man. But Edgar laughed, not for the joke itself, but because for days there had been nothing, absolutely nothing, to laugh about. How strangely things had turned out, he thought, when by rights she should be tied hand and foot, tossed in the trunk. How peculiar that he should be lounging, half-asleep, in the front seat of a car listening to his hostage tell him bad jokes. In his experience, things are simple. You like someone or you don't. You trust them or you don't — and mostly you don't. You rob them, blackmail them, extort them, kill them, or you leave them alone. There was none of this ambiguity shit. He had no idea what to do with Lucy Brightwing, other than watch the lovely curve of her mouth as she spoke, and wait for those raven eyes to meet his again.

As he was pondering these things, he somehow fell asleep.

He awoke, some time later, to a comfortable tickle on the side of his neck. He opened his eyes with a start to see the flash of Lucy's slim white wrist as her hand retreated from the caress.

"We're almost there," she said, and shushed him as he began to question her. "Your brother's still asleep. Let him rest until we get there."

He nodded and rubbed the sleep out of his eyes with his knuckles. He shouldn't have fallen asleep, he chastised himself. Lucy could have escaped. But she probably didn't even know I was asleep. We got lucky. I won't be so careless next time.

Then he noticed his guns weren't in his lap anymore.

Lucy, watching him narrowly with a wry smile, soothed him just as he was starting to look angry. "I put them on the floor, Edgar. You had your hand over them, and they were pointing at me. I didn't want to be shot accidentally — bad enough if you decide to do it deliberately. But I'm not about to die in some stupid way."

He felt his breath coming fast, more baffled than when he'd been driving in the dark through lake country. Who the hell was this girl?

"Why didn't you run?" he asked helplessly. "Why didn't you shoot us?"

In response, Lucy shrugged noncommittally, the smile of a secret touching her lips. "It was never quite the right time," she said. "C'mon, Edgar, stop giving me ideas."

"As soon as we stop you go back into official hostage mode."

"Bondage and all?" she asked coyly.

"Bondage and all," he confirmed. "And no more talking, or I'll have to gag you."

She snorted. She didn't take the threats seriously any more. He might kill her, but he wouldn't gag her. He was already relying on her too much.

Certainly, once she had the guns, it would have been a relatively easy matter to shoot the brothers. But she didn't really want to kill Edgar. And then, by the time they were both asleep she was driving through populated places. She couldn't conveniently dump the bodies, and even if she could, there would still be a long ride to the Everglades, the only place she'd be truly safe, in a bloody car. Odds are she wouldn't be stopped, but if she was, it was over. And so she waited.

Edgar was making plans for the night. The girl (he tried to call her that) would be tied securely, so they could finally get a solid night's sleep. Long days of driving, and only brief, nervous rests were taking their toll. One good night without worry, he told himself, and his head would be clear. The old Edgar would be back, ready to plan, scythe-sharp and on the ball. No more relying on the hostage.

And then he noticed something.

Was it possible? Just before he dozed off, he'd seen the gas gauge at just below the quarter-tank mark. He'd thought, dimly, that there could be a problem getting more fuel, but fell asleep before he decided anything. Now the gauge read a hair below the F.

He didn't ask. It was just too unsettling, like having an alligator rub against your leg like a kitten. It was contrary to nature, and unfathomable.

"What's the name of the town we're going to?" Edgar asked instead.

"Lagrima."

"Is that Spanish? What does that mean?"

"It means tear. Some say it was named for the salty ocean, but there's another story. When the Spanish came it was a prosperous fishing village. It wasn't a barrier island then, but part of the mainland, and the people there were known far and wide as shark hunters."

Lucy's voice slipped into a distant, dreamy richness, as though she were reciting an epic by heart. "They were great warriors, too, and their weapons were made from the teeth of the sharks they hunted — big bull sharks and makos made the deltas of their spears, and they would fix the long narrow tapers of sand tiger teeth to their clubs, to make a spiked mace. They even wore shark-skin armor, cured like rawhide, the scales standing upright like mail.

"One day, Spanish galleons came, and the women and children went inland. An hour after sunrise, the village was empty, save for one woman, who refused to leave."

She raised her chin proudly, and Edgar saw that woman in her.

"I do not know her name, but I know she was very young, and

beautiful, just given as a bride the winter before, and already she carried her mate's first child. She would not leave lest the gods think she didn't have absolute faith in her husband. Her doubt would kill him. So she stayed in the village, alone, making her morning porridge as usual, eating fish broth, surrounded by a silence the likes of which she had never known. Then she sat down in the center of her deserted village and waited for her love to return.

"The Spanish came at last near nightfall, and leading them with a weary step, bound in cruel metal chains, was her lover. He'd fought like a panther and was wounded many times, but in the end he was the only man of his tribe left standing, and in disgrace he was made to lead them back to the village.

"He was sure the village must be deserted. Perhaps, he thought, if I give them what they want, they will go away. But conquerors never go away. And when he saw his lady there the defeated warrior turned into a wild cat again, and sprang at the nearest Spaniard, choking the soldier with the very chains that bound him, turning to attack another one when the first had fallen. In all, the young warrior managed to kill four of the Spanish before one of the officers had the presence of mind to shoot him, right before his wife's eyes."

Lucy stared at the road, but Edgar saw her knuckles whiten on the steering wheel.

"The manner of her husband's death was so alien to her she could hardly comprehend it. A bang from afar, and her mate, the strongest man in the village, would fall? But at length she saw the blood, and when he did not rise she uncrossed her legs and walked to the water. The sea beckoned her. She would walk in, and keep walking, until the waves swallowed her, then she would take that first breath that would usher her into the next life, for her tribe knew that each creature returns to the sea, and must breathe in the salt to be reborn.

"But the Spaniards wouldn't let her die. They still craved gold, and thought she could tell them where it was. So they put upon her the selfsame chains her husband had worn, still flecked with his undried blood, and bound her to a palm tree that stood between the village and the Spanish camp.

"She pulled against her chains until her flesh bruised, straining to find death in the waves. She called out to the Spaniards to free her, she called to the gods, but though the gods always hear, they rarely answer. At last, as the dusk deepened and night sank into full darkness, she began to weep.

"The Spanish in their camp heard her crying, crossed themselves against unseen forces, and slept. All through the night she cried, her salty tears flowing down her cheeks, coursing across the sand in rivulets, more tears than any mortal had cried before, tears that turned from a trickle into a stream, from a stream to a river, until she was sitting in a pool of briny tears that reached her waist. And still she wept, silently, her grief absolute, as the sea of tears rose to engulf her. Near daybreak, she lifted her shining face to the heavens, where it glowed like a moon against the ocean she had made, and took one last breath of sweet air. A moment later she slipped beneath the gentle waves of her tears, and took her first breath of the afterlife."

Two tears rolled down Lucy's cheek, gone before Edgar could think to catch them.

"When the Spaniards woke, they found a deep channel had been cut between their camp and the abandoned Indian village. On that day the Intracoastal waterway was created by the tears of a woman crying for her love, and the Spanish named the new island Lagrima."

"Do people really love like that?" Edgar asked.

All she said was, "We're here."

Lagrima was a quiet quaint beach community, with pink stucco cottages and teak stilt houses. Building heights were severely restricted, and from almost anywhere on the tiny strip of land you could see two coastlines.

Edgar got out and breathed the salty air, wondering if he was tasting tears. The streetlights were dim, for the sake of turtle hatchlings, and he could see silhouettes of happy couples strolling slowly to nowhere, pursued by nothing. A night heron called, sharp and strident, but the cry created no more discord than a wave crashing on a silent shore. It's only because I'm so tired, Edgar thought, but he couldn't shake the feeling Lucy had led him into another world, the sanctuary he was seeking.

Chapter 7

"Mallory," he said as he patted his brother's arm. "Up and at 'em, boy. We're here."

Mallory screwed up his face like a sleepy child and looked past the low buildings to the dunes alive with wafting sea oats.

"We're in Lagrima, kiddo. We're going to stay here for a couple of days, rest up. It's safe." Because Lucy said so.

"You stay between us," he told Lucy. The key is under a shell?"

"Under the big lightning whelk."

She walked in flanked by the two men, pressed tightly against them with a pair of gun muzzles chilling her ribs.

"Did you remember to lock the car door?" Lucy asked, thinking of her own millions.

Damn it, she saved us again, Edgar thought, remembering his fifty-thousand in a duffle tossed in the trunk.

Inside everything was cool and tasteful, more like a house than a hotel. The Battle brothers sighed in unison. Seeing them relax, Lucy came on her game. This is where I'll have to act, she thought. Dispatch them, get to the car.

"Dibs on the bathroom!" Mallory said, and peeled off most of his clothes on the way.

Now it will be easy. She slid up beside Edgar, so close her bright curls brushed his shoulder, and he caught his breath. It's not real, he though. She's not real. She leaned closer still.

"Time to tie me up?" she breathed, and snaked her arms around his neck to choke him, whether to death or unconsciousness she would have to decide soon.

There was a crash in the bathroom, and Edgar jumped up, shouting, "Mallory!"

She read it all in his eyes then, the panic, the hope, and her golden arms dropped. It was the same way she'd looked at her own brother, before he was a pile of bones in a cairn on the land that was once her homeland and would be again. You love him, she thought. You love him like your own flesh. But you wish beyond anything he were gone.

No, don't soften. They're vermin, she told herself. Disease. I should wipe them out. Both of them. All of what I want in life is in that car, and these two monsters are standing in my way. If he was just a thief, like me, or a smuggler, or hell, even a hit man, maybe I could help him. But I can't save this one.

"It's okay, bro," Mallory called, opening the door a crack. "Tried to do a chin-up on the shower rod." He locked himself in again and started singing Irish folk songs as the shower ran.

Edgar stood before her, desolate and desperate.

"I'll do it for you," she said softly.

"Do what?" he asked, though he knew.

"You can't, I understand that. But I can. Then I leave. Then you're free."

He looked like a drowning man staring at the hand held just out of reach.

"You walk out the door," Lucy said. "I say Mallory broke in, attacked me. I never saw you. Maybe he told me you died on the road. They'll stop looking for you soon."

Edgar closed his eyes. It would be so easy, hardly even his own decision. Just leave. Lucy, astounding Lucy, would take care of everything.

"He's my brother," he said tightly. "I promised I'd take care of him. You say anything like that again I'll put a bullet in you." He meant it. He couldn't fight that kind of temptation.

Lucy nodded. "I understand. I'd do anything for my family too."

"Mallory's all I've got. You have a big family?"

"You're looking at it. So far."

"But..."

"So why are we here," Lucy asked. "What did you two do?"

It should have been an easy question — he knew his rap sheet by heart, from youthful auto theft to the most recent RICO charges that led to his arrest. But the story, he realized, wasn't his. He was supposed to be the big brother, the leader, but lately was no more than a spectator, carried away by Mallory's actions.

"Why don't you see for yourself," he said at last, grabbing the remote. He thought he might flip through for a while and eventually find their story. He wasn't prepared to be a media darling. Even past midnight, Bay News 5 was running constant updates on the deranged criminals marauding their way through the country, who had finally reached Florida.

Edgar turned the volume up and settled down to watch, awestruck, with a twinge of pride and a detached sort of disgust.

Music swelled in a crescendo of low drums and horns, with a final plaintive note from an oboe. The news channel had given the brothers their own theme song, as it did only for the most dire tragedies, 9-11, tsunamis. The screen faded to a smoldering wreck, a pile of charred metal Edgar recognized as the prison transport van Mallory had gleefully demolished during the break. They made it look like fucking Afghanistan, he thought. The scene, which would later be used as a backdrop for the text summaries, faded out and a somber Bret Stone greeted the audience with a sincere "Good evening," though it was fast approaching morning.

"Our report on the escalating manhunt for the Battle brothers, both wanted on multiple charges of murder and sexual battery, continues as the search reaches day seven." Stone paused, giving the audience time to absorb the topic, or run for Doritos. "For those of you just joining the story, it all began with Edgar Battle, arrested in New York City on charges of extortion and racketeering."

They cut to an image of the courthouse — there was no footage of his arrest or conviction, for then he hadn't been interesting

53

or important. "After a short trial, involving several reliable witnesses, he was sentenced to eighteen years in prison. The world rested easy, knowing another criminal was behind bars." They showed a photo, what looked like a mug shot, of Edgar, with two days of beard growth and a cut above his eye. Lucy glanced at him, as though to make a comparison, and turned back to the television. The clever production people at the news office had slapped a graphic of bars across Edgar's photo.

"But the citizens' relief was short-lived, and the law enforcement world was rocked when one Mallory Battle, Edgar Battle's younger brother, stormed prison van convoy the next morning. Armed with automatic weapons and a hand-held anti-tank missile-launcher, he destroyed the lead cruiser in a fiery mushroom cloud of devastation. Stunned by the explosions, the guards were caught off guard," (a fraction of a pause, as Bret Stone appreciated his own cleverness) "and the driver and two guards, as well as one prisoner who was appealing a life sentence, were killed in the exchange of gunfire that followed. Edgar Battle and his brother escaped in a red Mustang and managed to evade capture.

"The Battle brothers left a distinct trail behind them as they headed south. They were first definitively spotted at a Pennsylvania gas station, where they stabbed the attendant, a single father, to death."

No, not *they*, Edgar thought—Mallory. The screen showed a bloodstained floor, a lumpen mass covered in a sheet, then cut to a little boy looking bewildered and tired.

"The next clear evidence was in Maryland, where two sisters were raped and killed. The Battle brothers escaped in the girls' Volkswagen, which they abandoned a few hours later, and carjacked a Lexus. The owner is still in serious but stable condition with multiple skull fractures."

The disembodied voice of Bret Stone continued, listing atrocity after atrocity, a red line tracing their route along a map, interspersed with shots of body bags and distraught family members. The update traced their exploits all the way to Florida, through the bloody Dodge encounter. Then the statistics appeared on the screen, as Edgar and Lucy watched, mute.

Total dead: prison transport staff—3; prisoners—1; law enforcement—4;

paramedics—1; civilians—7. Number wounded, some seriously—5.

"This concludes out update on the hunt for the Battle brothers. Stay tuned for complete coverage at the seven o'clock news hour."

For a moment Lucy was silent.

"Man alive," she said at last, blowing a stream of air out through pursed lips. "Man ah-Lve..." And then, remarkably, "How much of that is true?"

"All of it, more or less, but..."

"Him, not you. Right?"

"I was there."

"Did you rape the girls?"

"No."

"Or kill them?"

"No. Maybe one of the cops... I don't know. I didn't try to." He scrubbed his forehead and told her about the wounded trooper he couldn't dispatch.

"That's you. That's who you are. You're not him. What's going to happen to me?"

"I don't know."

"You're supposed to say 'nothing.'"

He looked toward the bathroom door.

"Yeah..." Lucy said.

"You stopped and got gas, didn't you? Why didn't you run?"

Because my cut of the heist is four million, she thought, and I'm not leaving that behind. "I don't know," she said.

This is crazy, she told herself. So he loves his brother, so what. Mallory's a sociopath and Edgar's a fool to protect him.

But Lucy had longed for a family, a tribe, all of her life, was now risking everything to secure it, and she couldn't help feeling sympathy for a man burdened with love and responsibility for someone so unworthy.

I'd be the same way, she thought, if I had people of my own. And when I do, someday, I'll protect them with my last drop of blood. When I have my land, my children, when I can adopt people into my tribe, I'll fight any white man or Indian who tries to interfere. I wouldn't care if my people were sick killers. Well, I would, but I'd take the responsibility of dispatching them myself, and kill anyone else who tried to do it.

She turned toward the bathroom where Mallory had switched to Cole Porter tunes. She was contemplating doing the stupidest, most reckless thing she'd ever done, and it excited her. Once she fought a biker on meth who was harassing a waitress — that was nothing, because the bar was full of Miccosukee who were obliged by oath, and the threat of a death-curse, to help her if she needed it. Once she dove to almost two-hundred feet on straight air, searching a sinkhole for her ancestors' spearheads, and that had been nearly suicidal, but she'd risen, pleasantly in the grip of nitrogen narcosis, with a fistful of beauties. And just that morning she'd stolen twelve million dollars worth of rocks, to split three ways with the people who set up the deal but lacked the will and charm and physical prowess to make it happen.

This was crazier, by a long shot.

I'm going to help them, she thought. Ancestors help me, but I'm going to help them.

"You know," she said offhand, "I was going to kill you just now. I decided not to, but we have to understand each other. I'll help you if you want. For a while anyway."

He chuckled, not thinking she meant it, so she threw him down on the bed, mounted him, and put him in a triangle choke before he knew what happened. He reached for the gun with his free hand, and she clamped the hold tighter until he went limp.

She took the Glock and rolled off him, watching from across the room until he fluttered to consciousness a few seconds later.

"I'm not so good against two at once, though," she said as he gasped, his head throbbing. "Now, before Mallory gets out we need to settle a few things. I have a place you can go, where no one will ever find you. I'll take you there, but I need to know you're going to keep your brother in check. He's family, I get that, but I won't help if you let him off the leash. Man up and take responsibility for him."

He just eyed her, or rather, his gun in her hands.

"Who the hell *are* you?"

She grinned on one side of her mouth. "Lucy Brightwing, last of the Tequesta. Sacred object of the Seminole and Miccosukee tribes. And if you guys don't kill me, founder of a new nation.

Now give me the phone."

He picked up the cordless phone but cradled it in his lap, watching her warily.

"Aw, geez, can't we just agree that we can all kill each other whenever we want to and get on with life?" Lucy said.

"I just... I mean I... you could have killed us any time?"

"One of you, for sure."

"And you didn't? I give up. I just give up."

"Good. Then you get the gun." She slid onto the bed beside him and placed it in his hands, leaving hers cupped on top. "I like you, Edgar. Not enough to die for you, but enough to help you. Not him, though. You know I'll kill him if he tries anything with me."

"And then I'll..."

"You'll what?"

"Christ, who knows? I hope I don't shoot you. Lu, this is crazy. We'll leave. Tell the police if you want. We'll take your car and just..."

"No!" She forced herself to lighten it with a laugh, but she started to sweat. You do that, you won't give me a choice about killing you. "No, just trust me."

He'd been running, fighting so long, with no one to rely on but himself. Trust her? How could he? But it was like falling asleep — he couldn't fight it forever.

"I have to call someone who's worried about me. If I don't, trust me, he'll find me, wherever I am, and that means he'll find you." She dialed her great-uncle, Billie Bald Cypress.

"Unc," she said when he answered on the eighth ring, groggy and growling. "Sorry, I should have waited until morning, but I didn't want you to worry. No, it all went fine, I've just been delayed."

Edgar clearly heard a voice on the other end roar that she better not fuck with him.

She smiled sweetly, and her voice became saccharine. "No, nothing like that, Unc."

More yelling on the other end. "I'm sorry, it can't be helped," she said through gritted teeth. Then he said something that made her eyes widen, their coal depths glowing. She drew herself up regally.

"I'll thank you to remember who I am, Billie Bald Cypress! When I arrive, you might get an explanation, but I rather think not." She was interrupted briefly, then snapped, "He can wait! He's waited this long. A few more days won't matter." He evidently said some conciliatory words, for she answered more softly. "Of course I do. Good night Unc." She set the phone gently into its cradle.

"Ah, family," she said lightly. "We were planning a reunion, and I think I just spoiled it."

"I thought you didn't have any family."

"I have his blood, but he doesn't have mine. There's a difference. I'm the only one left with my blood." It echoed in her mind, an endless ache. The only one. Two Moons took my brother and left me alone. But she knew I could handle it. Cub could never stand to be by himself. Even his bones would weep to be alone. But someday there will be children to play around their ossuary, his nephews and nieces, my mother's grandchildren. I promise, Mommy. I promise, Cub.

Mallory walked out, quite naked. He finished drying himself, then, seeing no other purpose for the towel, let it puddle to the floor.

"My turn with her," Mallory said, and it made Lucy's skin horripilate. "I even saved you some hot water."

Edgar told his brother, without providing any real explanation, that Lucy was going to help them. He still didn't really know why himself, and that uncertainty made him want to chuck the whole thing.

"Cool," Mallory said. "Go on, take a shower, the tiny little shampoo smells like mint."

Edgar glanced at Lucy. "Nah, I'm too tired to move. Maybe later."

"You're worried I'm going to hurt her, aren't you?" he asked, genuinely distressed. "I like this one, and besides, she's useful, and she hasn't pitched a fit yet like the others. She can hang around for a while."

"She'll hang around as long as I say," Edgar said sharply. "Mallory, promise me you won't... you won't do anything..." He had never directly confronted his brother about his proclivities.

"Do what, bro?" he asked, all innocence, and Edgar couldn't bear to push it.

Chapter 8

There is a place where few men go, on the swampy shifting border between the Big Cypress Seminole Indian Reservation and the Florida State Miccosukee Indian Reservation. One of the longest and most dangerous highways in Florida bisects the two trust lands, but few roads lead more than a mile or two into the swamp. Even the Indians don't want to delve too deeply into much of their homeland, and besides, the land isn't land all year long. There's a government road, largely shunned by the residents simply because of its name, running along a north-south route, and a few recognized airboat trails which lead to the two or three named settlements. There are acres that haven't felt the sour breath of a human for generations.

The Everglades is a good place for secrets. On the Seminole side the marshes are part of a great woodland where cypress knees are so dense that passage is often limited to slogging on foot thorough thigh-high water and mud and lurking alligators, or to particularly agile pole boats. But the Miccosukee swamp is like a vast wet prairie, where the grass grows above a man's eyes. Entering the grasslands is like stepping into a particularly dangerous cornfield, one where the waters underfoot can swallow a man up, where the loss of a compass might mean death, where, when the temperature is right, and the wind not too strong, mosquitoes can cover the body in a dense black cloud, repelled only by netting or the sort of chemicals that almost killed off the eagles and kites that circle overhead. It is a treacherous and beautiful place that consumes travelers.

It was into the Miccosukee swamp that Billie Bald Cypress sallied just before dawn, the morning after his terse chat with Lucy Brightwing. He took an escort, for though he knew the swamps well, and had as a youth survived months in their heart, he was now in his eighty-second year and it was only common sense to bring someone young and strong and not particularly astute on this important rendezvous. Generals and kings of old had deafmutes. Billie Bald Cypress had Jimi Golden, also known as Jimi Three Toes.

Jimi Three Toes was a byword for failure. His share of casino revenues prevented him from losing his ramshackle house outright, and kept him in beer and cigarettes most of the month, but by the twentieth or so he was always looking for a way to score some quick cash. He was a dreamer, though, and knew he was destined for greatness. Throughout his thirty-odd years he'd tried any number of self-improvement schemes, but every business folded, every plan crumbled, and the one time he ventured away from the reservation he came home three months later with a limp and a new nickname. He never told anyone how he had lost the two smallest toes of his left foot, but rumor eventually reached the Big Cypress reservation that he tried out for the part of Kachunga the Alligator Wrestler at Sunken Gardens in St. Petersburg, and lost the job at his first performance.

When Billie Bald Cypress took him into his organization, the reservation considered it an act of charity.

All Seminoles, all Miccosukee, and many outside the reservations knew the name of Billie Bald Cypress, but his exact position was hard to define. He wasn't the tribal elder or head of the council, but he was probably the most respected, and the most influential Indian in Florida ... short of Lucy Brightwing. It was always a sore point with him that when they spoke, the gathering would listen just as respectfully to the Brightwing girl as they would to him. But then, he told himself, they were bound to by oath. She hadn't really earned her status. She wasn't a member of either tribe — her only power was as a symbol.

Still, he always tried to cultivate her friendship, to maintain an influence over her, to seem in league with her even when they were violently opposed. He was her great-uncle, and since her mother and that unfortunate brother of hers had died when she was sixteen, and no one knew her father, he was now her closest living relative. It was according to the nature of things that she should be under his control. But then, Lucy Brightwing was an anomaly. The last surviving member of her kind, she lived entirely by her own rules.

It would be difficult to say that Billie Bald Cypress was involved in organized crime, just as it would be difficult to say that he was in fact the head of such an organization. Difficult to say, and if he covered his tracks as well as he hoped, impossible to prove. A reservation is a sovereign territory, and though U.S. federal statutes generally apply, reservations also write their own laws, so Billie's criminal status largely depended on which side of the border he stood.

Most of his activities centered on gambling, but he didn't turn up his nose at loan sharking or extortion, and the necessary roughness that these activities require if they are to be enforced. The kind of thing that could have a Mafia boss dragged to court was only a slight infringement when perpetrated by a Seminole. Gambling, sanctioned by the U.S. government as a sop for having all of North America taken away, was regulated within the tribes, and thus any funny-business was their own business, and the tribal police, with a little pay-off, looked the other way.

Billie Bald Cypress was honored in the community for two reasons — he never let his activities become so obvious that the council of elders was forced to do something about it, and, like Robin Hood, he gave away a lot of his money. His name was on countless meeting halls and recreation centers; Seminole youths attended universities on Billie Bald Cypress scholarships; the Museum of Seminole Culture and Heritage had a statue of him in full regalia adorning its entranceway. As leaders of organized crime go, he wasn't a bad sort. He rarely had anyone killed when broken fingers would suffice.

Billie had slept fitfully after Lucy's call, visions of failure slipping into his dreams to jolt him to consciousness. This was the biggest thing he'd ever attempted, and he and the Brightwing girl had planned each contingency down to the smallest permutation. It wasn't particularly dangerous or taxing for a girl of Brightwing's abilities, and she seemed willing to risk the twelve-thousand years of cultural heritage that converged in her.

The Brightwing girl had been involved on and off with his organization for many years, mostly on a small scale. She would act as a courier, occasionally as a negotiator, at which she excelled, but she had her own interests, and felt no need to work for him unless the money was particularly tempting, or for the excitement. Despite her reliable history, he feared betrayal, and at dawn he reluctantly decided to arrange a palaver with his partner in this exploit, his counterpart in the Miccosukee tribe, Lazarus Nighteyes.

Lazarus was in his fifties, robust of constitution, with a keen intelligence that was contemplative rather than quick. He'd been educated at Georgia Tech, then got an engineering degree from Cornell, but upon graduation promptly decided the past twenty-six years of effort were more than enough for him and settled into an easy life on the reservation, living off modest proceeds from a device he'd invented in grad school that had something to do with regulating the flow of electrical currents. (When asked about it, he claimed to have forgotten exactly how it worked — he'd invented it, and that was enough for him.)

Lazarus fell into the criminal game quite by accident, but took to it in his natural, easygoing way. Within the first year of returning to the reservation, he made a few loans to casual acquaintances. Most people paid him back, but one fellow proved recalcitrant, even after the normally laid-back Lazarus gave him a few subtle hints at the local bar. The debtor brushed him off, insulted his mother, and that was the last anyone ever saw of him.

Of course, the logical explanation — and the truth — was that he'd gotten drunk and wandered into the swamp. He either drowned, got sucked into the mud, choked on his own vomit, was eaten by an alligator, or met some other inglorious end. But because his death followed the public reminder of his debt, and because the body was never recovered — and because Lazarus never denied it — rumors naturally spread that it was not a good idea to renege on his loans. Eventually Lazarus hit on the bright idea of charging interest, and since he was the only Miccosukee loan shark at the time, he set his rates unusually high.

Thus in a few years he amassed a fortune, in addition to his royalties. He gradually expanded his enterprise until he was a slightly less successful, less ambitious, altogether happier version of Billie Bald Cypress. Their proximity and close racial bond made it natural that they occasionally work together.

The two men met in their accustomed place, deep within the swamp that bordered their lands in neutral territory. Billie and Jimi Three Toes drove on roads known to only a few people until the dry dirt stopped, then took an airboat for a stretch. When they reached such land where custom and practicality prohibited the mechanical and the modern, Billie stepped into the bow of a pole boat and had Jimi Three Toes push him through the still, shallow, secret waters between the reeds until they reached a hill of land that heaved itself out of the swamp.

The site was ancient, belonging to a people far older than either the Seminoles or the Miccosukee, but hallowed ground remains forever sacred. Though there was only one person alive with a blood right to lay claim to it, the new natives had adopted it as their own. It was a midden of shell and bone, of mud and earth and grasses that collected for thousands of years. It was very low; in flood the crest barely peeked above the waters. In the misty past it had been no more than a trash heap, but it grew until it formed the only reliable land for leagues around. It was not holy until the day a great shaman came and there performed five great spells, which might be called miracles, before he was ritually sacrificed and buried, standing up and facing east, in the midden.

At the summit, up a gradual, hard-packed rise, stood a domed hut with a wooden framework and paneled walls of bark. The half-circle doorway was low to the ground, so one must crawl to enter. Billie saw another shallow-draft boat, with a man in Miccosukee garb kneeling in the stern, carving a snail out of a gnarled root. He looked up and nodded briefly, then returned to his task. He was good with a knife, all of its uses, but had the mind of a child.

The two crime lords exchanged formal greetings, then Lazarus sat silent with a serenity that irked the Seminole boss. It's his money too, damn it. Four million of it, anyway. Why isn't he worried? Is it a double cross? Is he in on it?

"I got a call from Lucy Brightwing late last night," he began, and Lazarus met this interesting tidbit with a mild curiosity expressed only by the slight, slow raising and lowering of his dexter eyebrow. "She said everything went fine, but she won't be here for a few days. Won't tell me why."

"Indeed," Lazarus drawled, regarding Billie as though he were slightly less interesting than a rock or a tree, somewhat more interesting than the bare bark walls of the hut. "And what is the problem?"

Bald Cypress hesitated, suddenly sorry he'd called the meeting. What, after all, was the problem? She'd called to let him know that there would be a delay. Probably she got spooked, thought someone might be on to her, and decided to lay low. Perfectly understandable. There was no reason to panic.

Was it possible she was on the run with their money? He picked her specifically because she was discreet, and wealthy enough that greed wouldn't set in. She got tithes from the two tribes, enough to maintain her quite comfortably. Even if one of his men was reliable enough to bring the jewels home, he couldn't trust anyone to behave responsibly after being paid his share. Even the best of his men would be like a sailor in a whorehouse, lavishly horny to spend and spend until the extravagance could not remain unnoticed even by feds who were well paid-off.

He'd trusted her; now he wasn't so sure. He has a lurking suspicion that if she ever wanted to really screw him, she could, with very little effort. But to both his relief and his disappointment, she never showed more than a passing interest in the establishment he'd created. Relief, because it left him no one to fear. Disappointment, because she was really the only member of his dwindling family who could take his place when he was gone. Unless some arrangements were made soon, the empire he constructed might crumble after his death. In a way, though, he didn't care. He couldn't imagine a world without him in it.

He intended to be factual, but as he told his tale he recalled the arrogance of Brightwing's tone. Reminded of his annoyance, and spurred by the fear of losing millions, the story that emerged painted Brightwing in a none-too-favorable light.

"If you doubt her competence, why did you send her on such an important assignment?"

"I've been thinking about sending someone after her," Bald Cypress said.

Lazarus sighed, and gave a gentle chuckle. "Just what do you think you'll do, Billie-boy, if she decides to run with it?"

"She couldn't. How would she sell them? But if she did, we could track her down fast enough."

"And then what would you do with her... to her? How would you catch her? How would you punish her?" Bald Cypress fell silent, and looked uncertain.

Lazarus laughed more richly. "You know who Lucy Brightwing is. She cannot be touched, she cannot be harmed. She is sacrosanct. Do you forget the penalty for the man who harms her?"

He didn't, though the code that protected her had been forged generations ago, passed unwritten through the ages.

"You have sent, upon this mission that is so important to you, the one person over whom you have no control. You can't threaten her, you can't intimidate her. We are both sworn to protect her, the last Tequesta." A final laugh, which left Billie almost trembling with anger. "We rely upon her good will to reap our unearned rewards, my old friend. Have patience, Billie Bald Cypress. I think she will come yet."

With a nod of his head, the Miccosukee crawled out of the hut, and a moment later Billie heard the plash of his boat shoving off.

Damn, he thought. Damn him to the devil, whichever kind he believes in. "I'll get that money," he vowed out loud, scarcely realizing that he was speaking. "I'll get that money and be damned to Lazarus Nighteyes, and double-damned to that Brightwing bitch. She'll make the delivery, or, Tequesta or not, she'll know the penalty!"

He left the hut, knees crackling, and curtly signaled Jimi Three Toes to help him into the boat.

It never occurred to him that Jimi was listening. He considered him on par with Lazarus' idiot, though lacking even artistic skill.

He measured intelligence by success, and so thought Jimi must be the stupidest man on the reservation.

Jimi had been working as a jack-of-all-trades for the Bald Cypress organization, hoping to make his mark and eventually rise in the ranks. He thought that if he could shine, make Bald Cypress notice him, he might be destined for great things. He didn't mind doing drudge work for the time being. Everyone has to start at the bottom. He thought Bald Cypress liked him, saw his potential, because he often called on him to drive him around the reservation, or pole him about the waterways to this meeting or that. He didn't think for a moment that Bald Cypress equated him with that half-wit who served the Miccosukee man, as someone too dense to be dangerous.

But Jimi had ambition, albeit of a rather lackadaisical sort. He hoped to do something spectacular that would launch him instantly into a position of respect and power. He had fantasies about saving Bald Cypress' life, of thwarting some grand scheme against him, of discovering a lucrative deal he could bring to his master's attention. If he could see his way to such a fate, he would be catapulted into the spotlight.

He was lost in just such a reverie while he squatted in the back of the shallow boat waiting for Bald Cypress to emerge. What if, he thought, Lazarus tried to kill Billie now? The probability of that was so remote it was almost nonexistent. But if it happened, he, Jimi Golden, would be there to save his life. And in his gratitude, Billie would...

Then he heard him curse Lucy Brightwing, and he knew at once how to prove himself. He had no knowledge of Henry II, else perhaps he would have dismissed the plan. But in his mind, Jimi had heard, *who will rid me of this turbulent priest?* And he decided that it would be in his interest to seek out Thomas a Becket.

If she'd gone to ground, there was only one place she'd be truly safe, a place so secret no one knew its location. No one but Jimi, because he'd built it for her.

Chapter 9

Every animal has a sense of when it's being hunted. Lucy, who often tracked animals for fun or food, was well aware of that uncanny ability creatures have to feel when a hunter has fixed them with a death-gaze. As long as her eyes were unfocused, looking at the animal peripherally as a part of the environment, she could easily approach skittish deer and wary weasels. But the instant she fixed her eyes on the animal, it would spring away. Years of following creatures through the woods and wetlands gave Lucy certain atavistic abilities of her own. She did not wake to discover Mallory's intent gaze — it was his look that dragged her from sleep.

His smooth, pale appearance, his floppy fair hair, his gentle voice created an impression of innocence that Lucy had a hard time overcoming, despite abundant evidence to the contrary. She was afraid of him, yet she found herself for seconds at a time *not* being afraid of him, and that scared her more than anything.

She had a friend, Junior, who trained bears for movies. There was a grizzly he'd raised from a cub, and he could roll and wrestle with the animal as if it were a puppy. But he told Lucy he never quite lost his gut terror of those monster claws and teeth, never forgot that it could turn from a baby sucking on his hand to a throat-ripping nightmare in an instant. Mallory is like that bear, Lucy thought, generally harmless but uniquely unpredictable. And when he turned on someone, the results were horrifying.

"I'm going swimming," he whispered conspiratorially.

"You can't."

He leaned down from the bed he and his brother shared to where Lucy slept on the floor, and touched one of her curls. She wanted to attack. He's not just a bear, she thought, he's a bear with rabies. Do I dominate? Do I placate? She didn't know what would work with him. She managed not to pull away.

"Want to come?" he asked.

She shook her head, using the motion to place herself slightly out of his reach.

He shrugged and slipped outside in his rolled-up trousers before she could think to wake Edgar.

Edgar lay curled on his side, his dark, lined face softened in the morning light. He was relaxed for the first time since they met, and she was so struck by the difference she slid into the bed next to him. She traced a line along the side of his neck, from the softness behind his ear to the tender depression at the base of his throat, the line she would open to bleed out a deer or kill a man.

My tribe has always taken in outsiders, she thought. I could test him…

His eyes fluttered open. He still felt the phantom tickle of fingers below his ear.

"Where's Mallory?"

"Swimming. Wait!" She pulled him back into bed. "What are you going to do, go out there? Call his name? No one's on the beach yet. He'll get cold and come in on his own. Edgar… Edgar, look at me."

She pulled him back down onto the bed as gently and inexorably as a mother panther pinning her cub with a velveted paw to bathe it. He stared out the window at his brother kicking up sand as he walked.

"I took him with us, me and my girlfriend, to Coney Island," Edgar said, gazing at his brother, and into the past. "He was six, I think. We stuffed him full of cotton candy, left him by the carousel and found ourselves a place under the boardwalk. I thought he'd stay put, and I forgot about him. Then at some point she said no — she was a good Catholic girl — and I went looking for him. He was under a dock, with this gray and white pigeon in his hands. I thought, how sweet. He was a kid, you know, I didn't want him to be a tough like me. I wanted something better for him. But the bird was pecking at him, and making this sound I never heard a pigeon make before, and then I saw."

She snaked her foot around his calf.

"He was pulling the feathers out, one by one, slowly, and he was so focused. His fingers were smeared with blood. He had that same floppy hair, and when he pushed it out of his eyes he got blood all over his face. The pigeon was almost bare. Mallory looked up and smiled at me, then went back to work."

He rolled onto his back. "I should have beat the tar out of that little shit, showed him how it felt. Maybe it would have changed everything. But I couldn't believe what he was doing. I didn't understand. I remember I laughed, kind of nervous, like he just did something to embarrass me, and told him it was time to go. He dropped the pigeon and forgot all about it, far as I could tell. And I tried to forget too. At six he was screwed up. Six!"

"Was that the only time?" She laid a hand on his chest.

"I found the cats when he was ten. I didn't even ask him about it. Mom was dead by then, and I was all he had. I wasn't going to let them put my brother in the nut house. People came later, once he was big enough to handle them, mostly girls. I don't know how he didn't get caught. He wasn't careful. I think the only thing in his favor was that it was totally random, completely on a whim. He had no connection to them, he didn't stalk them. He just felt like hurting something and he did, then he walked away. He doesn't even have a record."

"Why does he do it?" she asked gently. "I mean, did something happen to him when he was little?"

"He was premature, but he was fine, the doctors said, just small. Mom was great to us both. She loved us. We went on picnics and to museums and all that... you know, normal. Never knew my dad, but Mom made enough to take care of us. She died when Mallory was nine, in a fire. Mallory was there too, but he got out."

"Did he start it or did she?"

"What? It was an accident."

"Ok," she said.

"No, what do you mean?"

"It's not important. I just thought maybe your brother either had a ... a whim, or..." She broke off, then, with an effort, said, "Or your mom did what my mom did."

"What was that?"

"My brother. He... Okay, you know I'm the last one, the last Tequesta. Well, so Mom was the next to last, and she had a cousin who was half Tequesta. My dad was Irish, I think. Never knew him, but mom said he had curly red hair. Mom decided she shouldn't dilute the line, so she tried with her cousin. It was too close. You know what can happen. My brother was... wrong. But he was my best friend, just a year younger. Then one day he tied me to the bed and gave me this."

She pulled up her shirt and showed him a thin scar running from her sternum to her waistband, and farther.

"He wanted to be an uncle, and thought he'd save time by taking all the babies out of me at once. See what comes of an incomplete education?" She gave a rueful laugh. "It wasn't deep, though. Mom taught us how to skin an animal when we were toddlers, so he was used to making a shallow cut first. The next one would have slit me open. Mom found us like that, just in time, and took him into the swamp. I think she knew what he was before that, but who can believe it of their own child? She decided she couldn't let him live after what he did to me. But he was her baby, and she couldn't let him go to the spirit world alone. There was one bullet in each of them."

"That's why you're helping us, isn't it?"

"I'm helping you. Don't worry about why. Oh no... look."

A mother and two little girls were running to the surf, squealing in delight. Mallory waved to them, and the oldest girl, about nine, veered over with a giggle and splashed water on his legs. Suddenly shy, she ran back to her mother, but Mallory coaxed her over with a pretty shell.

"Will he do anything to her?" Lucy asked. She crossed to the sliding glass door and stood, poised on the balls of her feet, looking out with shining predator eyes.

"He's never hurt a little kid before… that I know about. I have to go after him."

"I'll go."

"I don't want you to be alone with him," Edgar whispered. "What if he…"

"I can take care of myself," she said automatically.

"He has a razor. He always has a razor."

"Okay, long as I know that. If you go, and anyone sees the two of you together, you're done. Maybe we'll be lucky and she doesn't watch television on vacation."

"Did you see the news? I don't think there's anyone in the country who doesn't know the Battle brothers by now."

"Do you want to leave him here? We can get in the car right now."

He sighed. "You go. I'm through."

She dashed out the door.

No doctor ever attempted to diagnose Mallory's psychosis, but if one had tried, he probably wouldn't have gotten very far. Mallory would have either ignored him or killed him.

He simply did not comprehend the existence of other people. Oh, he was aware of them, of course — he was neither moronic nor autistic. He just lacked the capacity for truly believing in anyone other than himself, and thus it never occurred to him that someone could be laughing at him, or hate him, or think anything of him whatsoever. He was immune to the world, and this gave him full license. The only real person was Edgar. His universe was peopled with himself, and his brother, who was a sort of godlike figure to the boy, and the dim phantom that was his mother. The rest were props, automatons, which had no feelings, needs, terrors, because they did not really exist. And yet, he found that they could be probed and prodded almost to life, like a child's toy violently shaken in a simulacrum of sentience, and it sometimes interested him to see how real he could make them by acting upon them.

This little girl, for instance. She was a blur, a happy sound, like a bird, here and gone and back again. If he held her under the water, would she become real for a time, before she stopped moving?

"Mallory," a low voice called from close by, and he turned to behold an angel.

The rising sun was directly behind her head. The blinding orb itself was blocked, but the light seemed to radiate from her body in a bright golden nimbus. Her curling hair was afire, her skin molten honey. Her face, what he could see past the light, was serenely smiling. He stared, open-mouthed and wide-eyed, unsure for a moment what he was seeing. She looked like the hostage, who wasn't real, but she also seemed like his brother, who was. He felt a moment of panic, confused for the first time in his life.

The celestial creature walked toward him, stretching out her arms, and he rose in the water, half lifting his own arms to meet her. She pushed through the breaking waves, and he had had never seen anything so beautiful as Lucy was at that moment, bathed in the sun.

The sand dropped off, and as she stepped deeper the illusion shattered in a blinding flash—Mallory found himself staring not into the face of a goddess but into the sun itself. With a cry he shielded his face with his arm, as a man will when he witnesses the divine.

"Come," she said. "Come back inside."

Now she was just a woman, but the angelic effect lingered in Mallory's mind. It was as if the gods had given him a gift, and fashioned in mortal flesh the nearest duplicate they could craft to the radiant apparition he'd seen. The woman was accessible; the woman was real, as no other person had been, and he realized with rush of blood that he only had to reach across the small space that separated them to take her, there on the shore, however he liked. Sunblind, he stretched out his hand, meaning to pull her to him, but somehow he found himself drawn to her instead, as if he had no will of his own, and he wondered, am *I* real?

They're my responsibility now, Lucy thought as she led Mallory back to the hotel. My people did it for the Seminoles, the Miccosukee, so long ago. We took in the fugitives, made them as our own children, gave them life in the swamps that would have killed them. Once you help someone, they belong to you. You'd think they'd owe you, but it never works that way. You just owe them more and more.

It's just for a little while, she told herself. I'll let them stay with me until the media loses interest, till people forget their faces, then Edgar's on his own. After all, it's not like he can stay in the swamp forever.

Into the carefully conceived path of her life had stepped two men, the dark, hard, crumbling Edgar and his gentle-visaged madman of a brother. Blood will tell, Two Moons always said to her, and even with that Irishman's blood in her veins she was still Tequesta enough to feel that ancestral urge to aid the desperate.

And look what it got my people, she thought. Unfathomable honor, and a vanished tribe.

Chapter 10

Jimi Three Toes lived at the end of a dirt road on the outskirts of the main reservation town, in a region known as Dungle. It hadn't rained with any enthusiasm since November, and the roads were sere and dusty, the parched pigweed and trailing mints maintaining a scruffy existence along the shoulders. When the rains finally came the road would become a sucking morass of mud, the ruts of truck tracks breeding grounds for mosquitoes and tadpoles for months on end, until winter frost and drought turned the land once again to tinder.

Dungle — an abbreviated version of the area's original name, Dunghill, was built on a garbage dump. When the reservation was being formed, the Seminole carried their waste as far from civilization as they could. It was distant enough that the stench of rotting food and human excrement didn't drift into town, but close enough so that whatever child had the onerous duty of disposal wouldn't get home late for dinner. As the years went by and some degree of plumbing reached the reservation, it became a landfill, and it was only in the last thirty years or so that fires and rains and decomposition leveled much of the land and people built houses on top of the refuse.

Living in Dungle carried a certain disgrace, but Jimi Three

Toes had never much minded. He'd been born there, and now owned the rickety little house of dust-colored cypress and brick that stood at the end of the lane. Dungle, he reasoned, was really no more than a comparatively modern midden, and if a thousand-year-old midden is sacred, what was his home other than a young piece of holy ground?

Jimi Three Toes' life had been gradually picking up speed over the last few months. His haphazard existence finally developed some purpose, first in his moderately steady work for Billie Bald Cypress, and now with his decision to ferret out Lucy Brightwing. Despite his enthusiasm, he did not set off at once to discover Lucy — firstly because he had to sweep the dry-season dust out of Billie Bald Cypress' main office, and edge the browning grass that bordered its meager lawn, but also because he knew an enterprise such as this required careful planning. When he got home that afternoon he poured himself a beer, set a bottle of tequila beside it, and sat down to consider.

After the first shot, he remembered the stories he'd heard about Lucy's exploits — the fights, the shadowy activities under Billie's auspices. He chugged the flattening beer and thought about the oath all Seminoles and Miccosukee made to her, of the torments that awaited anyone who broke their vow. He wasn't sure who would dole out the punishment, the Council, the spirits, or Lucy herself. He was bound to protect her, to offer her aid whenever she should call for it. How, then, was he to drag her from her swamp (presuming she was there in the first place) against her will. Even without the curse, she wasn't someone he wanted to cross. One man he knew had, and ended up with an even worse nickname than Jimi's—Harold No-Teeth.

By the time the bottle was considerably diminished, his confidence had returned, and he was ready to start at once. She was just one girl. If she didn't listen to reason he'd cold-cock her and drag her back to Billie. He threw some necessities into a garbage bag and loaded them in his car, an old butterscotch Plymouth Valiant.

He heard a growling shout from the house next door, a place somewhat more decrepit than his own, for, with all his faults, Jimi was a good carpenter, and though he only plied his trade for pay near the end of the month when cigarette money ran low, he kept his own home in decent repair.

Fagan Blue was at it again. Jim shook his head. He had no re-spect for the stereotypical mean-drunk Indian. Jimi himself drank as steadily as he could afford to, as an Englishman drinks tea, part of his daily ritual, but it never changed him, for his core personali-ty was that of a slightly intoxicated man anyway — friendly, lan-guorous, self-aggrandizing without feeling pressed to prove it.

There was a high-pitched wildcat scream. That would be Fa-gan's wife Sue Blue, seventeen, eighteen tops. The scream was cut short, and Jimi sighed. He hated getting involved in other people's personal lives. It occurred to him that rich people probably slugged their wives just as often as poor people, but their walls were so thick, their houses so far apart, that no one ever knew.

He knocked on the door and told Fagan it might not be a good idea to beat up the lady who might someday bear him children and be the prop and support of his old age.

"Mind you own fucking business," Fagan said, producing a steel pipe.

Which was Jimi's idea exactly, particularly now that he saw the pipe, but he suddenly realized there was no way he could drive that night, and no way he could sleep it off with the Blues going at it a layer or two of clapboard away, so he invited Fagan in for a drink. There was still one more bottle of tequila, and it was as good a way as any to keep his neighbor from beating up his wife.

Completely without his knowledge or volition, two days passed. He woke up on his own sofa to find Sue Blue and another woman, a mournfully beautiful decayed charmer, trussing up the unconscious Fagan.

"The hell?" He had no idea what was going on, but by the looks of things, whatever happened in his blackout had been pret-ty interesting.

"Oh, I've had enough of him," Sue said. "Will you help me drag him home?"

"No."

"You'd rather have him wake up here?"

She made a good point. When Fagan was safely in his own bed, tied hand and foot, Jimi went home, only to find Sue shoul-dering her way in past him. The other woman had never left.

"I heard you're looking for Lucy Brightwing."

"How'd you hear that?"

"Outside your window last night. You drinkers always babble. I also heard she's starting a new tribe in the middle of nowhere."

That was news to Jimi.

"I'm going to join," Sue said.

"You're Seminole. What makes you think she'll take you?"

"I have an idea for her, a good one."

"What is it?"

"It's for her, not you, Three-Toes. For my new chief."

"Just go on home, would you? Fagan will kill me if he finds you here."

"I'm not going home," she said, crossing her arms.

"Why?"

"You know. You've heard us. I'm sick of it. This is my aunt, Dolores Otter. We're joining the Tequesta." She looked down at her chipped nailpolish and picked off a flake.

He tried, and failed, to convince her to go home. He got in his car and she followed before he could lock the door. He tried to extract her from his car, and she bit him.

If I can't handle Sue Blue, what in the world am I going to do with Lucy?

Chapter 11

Lucy was torn between wanting to get to the safety of her beloved swamp as quickly as possible and the prudence of waiting until nightfall to transport her dangerous cargo through the more populous parts of the state. She was convinced to start right away when she saw how restless Mallory was — pacing, staring out the window at the gathering vacationers, rubbing his fingertips together like a fly. If he escaped control again...

"Give me your bags," she said. "I'll put them in the trunk and pull the car up to the door for you."

When she tossed them in she saw the duffel, and made a note to check it later, when the Battle brothers' eyes weren't on her.

"Mallory, I want you in the back, all the way down and under the blanket. Don't sit up for anything. You can wear this, Edgar." She tossed him a dirty canvas Foreign Legion hat with a long sun flap in the back.

When she had them loaded she told Edgar, "Keep your face toward me," and pulled into the slowly cruising beach traffic.

He was happy to oblige. She was frighteningly lovely. Hell, just frightening. The way she'd choked him out almost before he knew what was happening. Who was she? Oh, he knew what she'd said, the last whatever it was, Tequesta? But that didn't explain her skill, nor the perplexing fact that she had taken them both under her wing. She'd had a psycho brother too, but that's no reason to put her own life on the line.

He was firmly resolved not to kill her, but if this sojourn had taught him anything it was that most of life was beyond his control.

He watched her; she watched he road with predatory intensity, her black eyes sliding from Gulf Boulevard to the side roads, looking for trouble, for ambushes. A little guilty, he let her do all the work, have all the worry. It's just like road trips with mom, he thought. I'm just a passenger, and it hardly matters where we're going. Just the fact that we're being taken somewhere is wonderful in itself.

She drove them south on 275, opting, with some reluctance, for the shorter toll route across the Skyway Bridge. She had a Sunpass, so she didn't even have to exchange smiles with the elderly tollkeepers, but still, it was a bottleneck, and therefore risky, just the kind of place a trooper or deputy might be stationed to check, even casually, all passing cars. Just a glimpse of either famous face, and they'd be done. Maybe farther south she had a chance in a pursuit, where her knowledge of back roads might give her an edge, but on the open interstate they'd pit her inside of a mile, and then the shooting would start.

"Cover up," she warned them. Edgar pulled the hat down over his face and closed his eyes.

They got through the toll plaza without incident, and then, engine straining up the bridge's incline, they soared aloft with ospreys above the emerald bay. She got in the right lane and slowed.

"Take a look."

Edgar opened his eyes to the golden beams of steel cables that capped the span like two great gleaming sails, then turned to see the water far below. Mangrove islands dotted the bay, and the color of the water changed depending on the substrate — blue-green where the shipping channels were carved deep, white where sandbars and new islands were forming in the tidal current, black where shoals of rooted mussels and oysters clung to rocks in the shallows.

A huge tanker eased below them, and pleasure boats with tails of foaming wake dotted the expanse. For a moment a white-capped pelican, like a pterodactyl with its tucked-back neck and jutting beak, glided beside their car just off the rails, watching them with its crafty prehistoric eye, then winged sharply away to dive after some choice morsel.

"You should see this bridge at night," Lucy said. "From over there, a place called Fort DeSoto." She pointed to the mainland that curved to the west. "Floodlights illuminate the cables, but you can't see the rest of the bridge, so it looks like two glowing triangles are just floating on the bay."

"I'd like to see it," he said softly, looking out the window, and Lucy felt a fresh flush of profound pity for the poor doomed man. I could keep him, she thought. No, that would be crazy. This is just temporary. When it cools down, he's on his own.

"I'll send you a postcard, when you get where you're going," she said casually, but the words cast a temporary pall over both of them. You'll never get where you're going, she thought. You'll never live long enough. I'm just giving you a respite, a stay of execution. Get rid of them as soon as you can, she told herself, and finish what you started before they stumbled into your life.

But when she looked over at Edgar again, there was something in the longing way he gazed at the water that made her think more fondly of him. For just a moment, she tried to picture him really living in Florida, knowing the state as intimately as she did.

No, he's a New York boy. He'd be miserable here.

It can't all end, Edgar thought, looking at the vastness of sea and sky. I can't see something this beautiful one minute and be gunned down the next. It's simply not possible.

He stared, spellbound, and then gasped.

"What?" Lucy asked.

"I just saw... I thought I... nothing." Was he losing his mind? He hadn't been sleeping much, but...

"This is a bridge of ghosts," she said casually. "The Blackthorn went down here, twenty-three hands lost. The original bridge collapsed when a tanker hit it, thirty-five died. And about ten people commit suicide from the summit every year. What did you see?"

"I told you, nothing." How could he tell her he'd seen a flock of shimmering people flying like seagulls just over the wavelets, only to dive and disappear in a flash of luminescence. Maybe it really was seagulls. Maybe it was flying fish. Maybe it was nothing. He kneaded his forehead and faced Lucy again, taking comfort in her profile, the strong line of her jaw, the invitation of her lips.

If he can see the Skyway spirits, that's good, Lucy thought. The Tequesta have always been close to the spirit world, and if he...

She brought herself up short. I don't even have tribal lands yet, and I'm thinking of taking Edgar into my tribe? He might be handsome — she snuck a glance at his broad, grave forehead, his creased gray eyes — but if you took in every man you wanted to sleep with your reservation would get crowded fast. Her lip curled on the side away from Edgar. Perhaps that wouldn't be such a bad idea after all.

But then there was his brother, and no force in the world — this one or the next — could induce her to welcome that madman into her tribe.

They descended the far slope of the Skyway and came almost level with the bay. Terns dove, and orange-billed skimmers sifted the wave tops for a meal.

"Look, near that boat," Lucy said, pointing, and Edgar was quick enough to catch a sudden rush of motion beneath the waves as the water broke into a thousand shimmering fingers of fish that twisted their bodies in a frenzied dash. Behind them he could just make out dark torpedo shadows closing in on them.

"Kingfish," Lucy explained. "They come inshore about this time of year." The shapes moved in, and the water churned again in a silver sheet of baitfish that rose as a single desperate organism into the dubious safety of the sunshine. When they fell again into their tight school, their numbers were not diminished to Edgar's eyes, but the kings must have been satisfied, for their dark forms sank into the obscuring depths.

As they continued along the long curves of I-75, Edgar found there was yet another aspect of Florida that didn't meet his expectations. He had a vision of Florida as a lush paradise of flowers and beaches and above all, perpetual greenery. But though the roadside was lined with slash pines and elderberry shrubs, grasses and oaks, he soon saw that brown rather than green dominated

BRIGHTWING

the palette.

All of the vegetation was quick, but in the dark, sere green of hardy plants at the end of a seasonal drought. They were alive, true, but had stayed alive at a sacrifice. In the dry season they retreated into vegetative meditation and took most of their verdure with them. It is no different than northern winter, when plants shut down to survive. The only difference is that Florida seasons depend not on temperature but rainfall. Edgar had expected lush perpetual summer, and he was disappointed in the brown tones that shadowed the greens.

Florida was shabbier than he'd imagined, too. The open spaces on the roadside were dotted with smatterings of old rusted sheds and dilapidated trailers that might have housed migrant workers. Everything was so flat, so open, like a raw wound, the shacks and tires and corroding barbed wire of cattle fences like oozings of putrescence from the native scrub woods. The beach town had been charming, but the other cities they passed were gray and largely unattractive, the sky crossed by power and telephone lines, the vista bisected by jutting erections of microwave towers.

"They're haphazard towns," Lucy said in explanation. "The victims of extreme planning of tiny sections, but no overarching vision. They were fine when they were just little cities, scattered, but together they have no cohesion. Roads have four different names as they pass from town to town, power lines are strung up as needed, all above ground, when any fool knows they'll come down in the next big storm. But undergrounding them is too expensive.

"Parts are lovely," she added, coming to her state's defense. "But Florida doesn't have many old towns, and character is mighty hard to come by in just a couple of generations. Most of Florida, the urban part, anyway, is just one sprawling suburb."

"Suburb of what?" he asked, trying to remember which was the biggest local metropolis.

"Of New York, of course," she said with a laugh. "Where the New Yorkers come to die." She chuckled again, briefly, then cut her laughter short with a guilty gasp. "I'm sorry, I didn't mean..." she whispered.

He pretended it didn't matter, but the sense of doom that had been briefly dispelled by the beauty around him returned, hard. I shouldn't be thinking like that, he told himself. But he'd been expecting death to lay its chill hand upon him since the moment he got into the car with Mallory on the roadside after the break. Though he'd been planning and scheming, grimly trying to stay alive all these days, he had a premonition that all his effort would be wasted.

Now that Lucy was in charge, he could push his premonitions aside for minutes at a time. One look at her, and the certainty of death subsided, but there were still occasions when thanatos overwhelmed him. Maybe he should tell her to drive back to the Skyway. If the end was coming, better to hurl himself into that sublimity than be gunned down in the street.

Edgar's mood rose and fell. He found that Florida improved on familiarity. Soon he became accustomed to the muted greenery and the little shacks that peeked like sneaky beasts from behind palms and castor-oil plants along the roadside. Shabby trailers, looked at in the right light, became quaint migrant chateaus, rusted cattle sheds grew picturesque in their nestled obscurity.

He began to pick out uniform patterns in the roadside foliage, and realized some of the palms and magnolias and oaks were not the random dispersal of nature but the calculated rows of arboretums. Many of the patches he'd mistaken for young roadside forest were actually farms — tree farms, which he'd never encountered before. Baby palms with just three leaves above the ground grew in ordered columns, and fields with older sabal palms and low squatting coonties wafted in the wind kicked up by the interstate. The plantation trees fit in so well with the landscape that it took Edgar a good fifty miles to see them for what they actually were. The only clue, other than the unnatural order of the fields, was the occasional human habitation, the odd trailer or run-down cottage where the tree-tenders took their lunch. When he realized this, the decrepitude seemed more picturesque, the old outhouses like the antique farms he knew up north. It's not so foreign after all, he thought, just that my expectations are different.

Along the way, in a quiet sort of voice they could ignore if they chose, Lucy pointed out scenes they might otherwise have missed. Looking through her eyes, he saw glimpses of Florida that few ever notice, for even from the highway at seventy miles per hour, Florida holds wonders. She pointed out a tall stately bird bending its neck in exaggerated elegance, with a fuzzy, russet baby running between her stilt legs, almost tripping over its own feet.

"A sandhill crane," she explained, telling him it was one of the rarest birds in the state.

Later she called his attention to a bold mockingbird family mobbing a hefty lone crow, a sight which even Mallory appreciated.

"Mockingbirds hate crows," she said, "and with good cause. Crows are smart, and there's nothing they like better than eating mockingbird nestlings."

The gray-and-white family attacked the dark marauder with aerobatic assaults that would have put the Red Baron to shame, seeming to stop mid-air, banking and diving to harass the crow with beak and claw and raucous scream. Finally the crow yielded with a throaty caw and winged ponderously off.

"But he was probably just a distraction. Crows work together like wolves or lions, so I wouldn't be surprised if the rest of the crows are feasting on baby mockingbirds while the parents are busy with this one."

As they went south the vegetation grew thicker, and even his untrained eye could distinguish new plants among the old familiar oaks and slash pines. Most notable were the extravagantly spiked epiphytes, which clung to trees and took their nutrients and water from the air. Spotting the first one in full efflorescence perched high in a tree, Edgar said, "Look! A porcupine," proud of his own contribution.

Lucy told him as gently as she could that it was only a plant. "But a very nice specimen," she added, to appease him.

Poor Edgar, Lucy thought as she pulled onto Alligator Alley. So out of his element. Would he learn? Could he adapt? Perhaps, but she thought he could never really love Florida as she did. It was in her blood. His blood, cold and northern, was the very antithesis.

Maybe I should bring them to the Big Cypress res instead, she mused. Uncle could find them a safe house. No, Lazarus Night-eyes would be a safer bet. Family or not, Billie Bald Cypress would sell the Battle Brothers out in a heartbeat. He might keep her out of it, because of the oath, but he'd claim the reward money nonetheless.

It would have to be her own home. Well, not quite her own, not yet. Technically, the land belonged to Lazarus, his personal holding, not the Miccosukee reservation land. It was a useless tract for any investment purposes, and he was happy to let her use it as her own, and deed it to her after she paid him from this heist. She hoped her delay wouldn't sour the deal. She'd worked too long, jumped through too many hoops securing her own Tequesta reservation, to let anything get in her way now. Still, a few days shouldn't make any difference. Fondly, with the side of her forearm, she brushed against the car's paneling, almost able to feel through the thick layer of plastic and metal reinforcements the warm glow of the fortune hidden inside.

Dusk was approaching when she turned onto an exit that, among other things, promised a Burger King, Checkers, Cracker Barrel, and a family eatery known as Ye Olde Pube, which the DOT had, either through good humor or ignorance, allowed to remain. They arched across an overpass and then Edgar found himself briefly cruising along a country main street like those in upstate New York — a little town hall of brick, cobblestone side streets, a pedestrian shopping square and a patina-green statue of the town's founder. He half expected, when they rounded the corner on the outskirts, to see frost on the ground, and the bare, stripped boughs of aspen and birch.

The next moment they were on a street that was paved only in the loosest definition of the word. The bare earth shoulders made deep inroads onto the lane, and each of the potholes had developed its own ecosystem, with dirt and dandelions blooming freely in the infrequent traffic. A leafy canopy overshadowed the road, flecking it with flashing variable shade. The foliage was dark and dappled on the underside, with mosses hanging down, and Edgar had the impression that he'd crossed over into something primeval. For half an hour they traveled down this road, slowly and swervingly to avoid deep yawning crevices, and as they drove the way grew darker. Edgar told himself this was only because the sun was setting, but the gloaming that settled around the travelers seemed like the darkness of crossing between worlds.

Chapter 12

Everything familiar to Edgar was behind him now. He might have seen Florida as an alien place, but there were still things he essentially recognized. Roads and buildings and people, even the ever-haunting menace of the police, were familiar to him, comfortable in their familiarity. But here there was only the deep wilderness. Even the smell of this place was different, coming stealthily through the car's open air vents. It was denser and more dangerous, with murk and generations of dead damp leaves, yet purer too, to his city-bred nostrils and tongue, than any air he had ever tasted. Yes, that was it — you could taste the air here. It settled on the tongue, like cool spring water, given a foreign flavor by the rocks and earth it passed through on its way to the surface.

As they drove deeper Edgar felt a twinge of fear. This was not the way it was supposed to be happening. He should be heading to Miami now, to familiar city haunts, familiar regardless of the city. Not journeying deeper into something he didn't understand, at the mercy of a girl who led them like a will-of-the-wisp. He was tempted to order her to turn around and take them down to Miami, maybe even take the guns out again. So what if they were stopped by police at a roadblock. At least he'd know what was happening to him, where he was, not trapped in this *terra incognita* of Lucy's.

But again he felt his resolution drain away. After the pressure of making all the decisions ever since the break, and the frustration of seeing his good judgment constantly thwarted by Mallory, there was a peace, a surrender, to letting Lucy stay in charge. He didn't pretend to comprehend the full reason she was helping them, and yet he did not think she would betray them.

They were on a true dirt road now, without the slightest pretense to pavement. She turned right, then left, then right again, and Edgar tried to make a mental note of the directions so he could backtrack on his own if need be. But the way was so convoluted that he was utterly disoriented. For a while the paths were moderately well-used jeep trails (though the only sign of civilization was a fellow in a canoe in a roadside canal, who did not look up at their passing) but eventually she turned onto paths he could scarcely recognize as such. Weeds overgrew what might have been the faint spoor of tires, or may have merely been rabbit runs. But Lucy drove as if she was sure of the way, and handled the Volvo like an off-road vehicle.

At last, when the sun was well below the tree line and very little light remained, she made a tight turn through some trees, zigged and zagged around some others, and finally came to a stop behind a dense tangle of briars and vines that choked the bushes they climbed upon.

"End of the road, boys," Lucy said, and swung her shapely legs out of the car.

"Where's your house?" Mallory asked, peering through the trees and sprawling shrubbery.

"Over there," she said with a vague nod. The Battle brothers looked, but could see nothing.

"Beyond those trees?" Edgar asked dubiously.

"More or less," she replied. "A bit farther."

"How much farther?" Mallory asked, setting out.

"About three miles, as the crow flies. A little longer the way we have to go."

"Shit," Mallory drawled in a reasonable imitation of Cracker. "I don't have the right shoes for this. Can't we drive there?"

"Car's gone as far as it can. You guys can't do three miles? I thought you were big-bads." "We can do it," Edgar said, glowering. "But there's an awful lot of dirt."

"That what you get when there's no pavement. You're lucky this is the dry season." She didn't tell them the dirt would change to mud in half a mile, and water beyond that.

"Don't take more than you have to," Lucy said, collecting her own essentials, except for the gems. "Stuff gets awfully heavy after the first mile, and I don't want my woods junked up with your trash. I'll be back in a minute."

"Where are you going?" Edgar asked, suddenly certain she was going to abandon them.

"Just to cover our tracks a little."

"I'll come," Edgar said, and Lucy shrugged and set off, backtracking a few hundred feet through churned dirt and bent grass.

"So," Edgar began as she moved branches and kicked clods of dirt level, "you really live out here? Out in the boondocks?"

"Part of the year. When I feel like being alone."

"This is your own land?"

"It will be soon."

"What was that you said before, about your own nation?"

She laughed, startling a foraging armadillo, which crashed through the underbrush. "You remember that? Well, I might be the only one, but I'm still part of a distinct tribe, and we don't have a homeland. If everything goes right, this is going to be my reservation — the Tequesta reservation."

"Reservation? I thought those are kind of like prisons. Where the government makes you live so you won't scalp them all."

"Oh, the Tequesta never scalped," she said lightly. "Tortured, yes. Sometimes ate. But never scalped."

He didn't know whether to laugh.

"That's how reservations started, but now they're something different. This will be a sanctuary against the world, a place that can never be taken away."

"This is where your people lived?" he asked, looking around the inhospitable density of the woods.

"Not at first. We lived on the coast, mostly, around Miami — but can you imagine the government giving up even an acre of that land? The Tequesta moved here later, when..." She broke off abruptly. "Anyway, no one wants this land, except me."

"So the government will give it to you?"

She couldn't tell him she was buying it in an under-the-table two-million deal from the Miccosukee crime boss. "Someone is donating it to me. Then I give it to the U.S. Government, and they hold it in trust."

"Trust? You trust them?"

"These days they don't break treaties as often as they used to. They hold it, it means no matter what, my descendants can't lose it. I can't gamble it away or do something stupid. It's mine, ours, forever."

"And you'll be the chief?"

"I suppose. I'll be the only one for a while, but eventually I'll adopt a few people into my tribe."

"Who?"

"Oh, friends, orphans. Not too many."

"I'd like to see it."

"Yeah. You'll be, where? Argentina? Mexico?"

"Something like that." He didn't want to talk about it, and they started back to the car.

"Maybe you'll like it out here, for a while," she said. He enjoyed listening to her voice, so quiet and clear, barely rising above the wood-sounds of droning cicadas and trees that murmured to each other high in their hammocks. She walked near him, beside him, her stride matching his, as though they were lovers on a stroll. From where they walked they could not see Mallory, and this added to Edgar's illusion of isolation.

"Unless you hate it already. Some people can't see past the drawbacks. Sure, there are mosquitoes, and you might have to walk through mud once in a while, but there are worse things in New York, aren't there? You don't have to breathe smog here, and you won't get mugged." Or can't mug anyone.

"I don't hate it yet," he said. "Maybe after the hike." He gazed about him, and though his countenance showed guarded apprehension, there was also evidence of wonder in his eyes as he looked on the trailing mosses, dripping quicksilver from the darkening canopy. A nightjar called from afar, and another answered from so near that Edgar jumped, bumping into Lucy, who took his elbow briefly to steady him. She stopped walking and leaned into him, tilting her head up.

"Where the hell are you guys?" Mallory called, and they drifted apart. "I'm getting eaten alive out here." He swatted at the air.

"They're not too bad right now," Lucy said. "It's still a little chilly at night for mosquitos, and the breeze will keep them down. They're too light to fly in much of a wind."

While Edgar sorted through his things — the duffel of cash was his first priority—Lucy set about camouflaging her car with branches and vines. She rubbed handfuls of dirt into the chrome. Not that anyone would be near it, but she didn't want to take any chances. She couldn't take her gems out now, with them watching, so the loot would have to sit unprotected for an hour or two. She might like Edgar, but he was a criminal, and she couldn't trust him with her treasure. If it was just money, maybe, but those gems represented her future for generations to come.

Lucy traveled light. Her house was equipped for survival, though not luxury. She found it comfortable, but she wondered how the Battle brothers would adapt to what was surely by their standards a remarkably primitive life.

She planned to lead them a mile or so into the swamps toward her shelter and then, without warning, abandon them. She'd hide the gems in the swamp — she had a good place in mind — just in case someone did happen on the car. Rangers wouldn't be on private land, but you never knew when an ambitious botanist or poacher would be out in search of orchids or black bear gall bladders. In an hour she'd rejoin the brothers, and if they wanted an explanation, too bad.

She took the lead, first selecting a stout branch a bit taller than herself. "There's not much quicksand, per se, in the Everglades," she told them, "but plain old mud can suck you down to the hips. Not to mention the pools covered in slime and debris that look like regular ground. You'll be under water in an alligator wallow before you know it."

"With the alligator?" Mallory asked.

"Probably," she said, "so stay close, or get your own stick." The staff could also shoo snakes — more than once in her life, Lucy's staff had received a strike that otherwise would have reached her leg, from some sleepy moccasin or rattler — and provided balance on the notoriously uncertain terrain.

The way was easy at first, and as she walked she offered them advice. Though Edgar had a flashlight, she forbade him to turn it on. She needed her night vision for her temporary escape. She only implied that it would attract too many mosquitoes, which wasn't exactly the case. Moths come to light, but mosquitoes are lured by carbon dioxide. She temporized by saying, "You'll see a lot more mosquitoes if you put that flashlight on." Which, strictly speaking, was true.

To Lucy's eyes, it wasn't at all dark. Full night had not yet come. Remnants of the sun would persist for an hour or more, and already the moon was rising. But the Battle brothers were not having an easy time of it. As Mallory said, their shoes were all wrong, and their nice clothes were a psychological hindrance, for they minced along as though there was a chance they might not get dirty. Though the swamps were unusually dry after a record drought, they were still swamps, and Lucy heard Edgar curse creatively and at great length the first time he went up to his ankles in viscous ooze.

She didn't make the walk particularly easy for them, and they, being men, could not ask, or command, her to slow her pace for their benefit. All the same, it took them the better part of an hour to make the first mile. Edgar, who considered himself a fair physical specimen, began to feel his thighs burn in the first ten minutes. There were no hills, but the dense brush and undergrowth, the trailing roots and the variation between earth and log and water, forced him to lift each leg unnaturally high, or risk tripping in the dark — which he did often enough despite his best care. He watched Lucy walking just a few steps ahead of him (always threatening to outdistance him, making him scamper to catch her, and almost invariably stumble) and tried to emulate her walk, a sort of smooth heron's gait with loose ankles and knees that were never quite straight. Her feet rolled, while his shuffled, and though she walked quickly she also walked silently, shifting her weight so that few branches snapped beneath her, the water failed to splash at her step. He and Mallory sounded like wounded bears charging through the wood. Soon he began to pant and his brow felt that clammy chill of sweat quickly dried by a nippy wind. Lucy fell silent. Edgar longed for her voice to make the night seem friendlier, but he decided to save his own breath for the arduous hike and said nothing to encourage her.

They were surrounded by a stand of old cypress whose crowns blocked out much of the sky. It was as dark now as it would ever be as long as the moon was up. When they were mired in a particularly muddy patch of dense cypress knees, she whispered in Edgar's ear, "Stay here, I'll be right back," and was off like a deer into the darkness.

"Little bitch," Mallory said when he saw her sprint away, and drew his gun from the waistband of his trousers. Before he could fire Edgar was in his way, running after her.

"You're in my line of fire! Damn!" But both his brother and the girl were gone into the night. He could hear them clearly — at least, he could hear Edgar barreling through the undergrowth — but he could see nothing but the dark ghosts of trees beyond twenty feet. "Damn!" he said again, and finding the cleanest, driest log in the immediate vicinity, he made himself comfortable to await the outcome.

She honestly hadn't expected pursuit. They were helpless, hopeless in the woods. How could Edgar (she could tell it was him, from his curses) possibly think he could catch her in her motherland? And yet, against all odds, he followed, at a reasonably fast clip, calling down wrath on the cypress knees, vines, and yes, even Lucy Brightwing as he ran.

It was exciting, being chased, even better than when, as a little girl, she'd teased a mother black bear with two cubs, and the normally docile she-bear charged her. She'd expected teeth or claws in her back, but it had been a thrill, too, staking her life on her own skill. Lucy had escaped the bear easily. It was faster than she, but eager to get back to her cubs. Edgar was proving more persistent.

The fool, she thought. He'll get too far separated from Mallory and I'll have to spend hours tracking him down. He'll probably manage to kill himself before then. Why couldn't he be like anyone else and give up after a hundred feet? If he chased her much farther, she'd have to let him catch her and take him back, and she had a feeling they'd object to her going off on her own again.

When Edgar saw that she'd escaped, he thought of nothing except that he must catch her. Not just because he was dependent on her guidance in the swamp, nor yet because he believed she had certainly undergone a change of heart and was running to turn them in. The instant he spotted her fleeing form it occurred to him how unbearable all of this would be without her. Unmindful of the thorns that raked his wrists and throat, forgetful, even, of his brother, he could only think, in a feral, animal way, that he must pursue her, must catch her. His legs beyond sore, his chest aching, he pounded after her.

There are forces in this world that protect small children and fools. Perhaps that is why, though he ran through hurdles and obstacles of cypress knees and trip-wire roots, he did not stumble once in his headlong pursuit of Lucy. Dumb bad luck was the only force acting on Lucy. The girl who from birth, from her very bloodline, had been trained to run through dark swamps, who'd accomplished sprints like this one a hundred times before in a nocturnal hunt or sheer animal good spirits, hit a gnarled root and crashed to the ground, striking her head against a low cypress knee. She lay stunned, sprawled on her face with her head ringing and her eyes closed.

Edgar heard her fall, and the exultation of victory swelled in him as he closed the distance. Her golden outflung limbs rose from the formless blackness when he was only a few feet from her, and when he pounced on her he was almost growling, his face bestial. Kneeling atop her with his legs on either side he flung her over to her back. He was panting with more than the run, the passion of pursuit hot in his blood.

What he would have done if she'd resisted him right away he didn't like to think. Already, as he rolled her over, his hard fist was clenched to smash into her face. She'd turned on him! He trusted her and she betrayed him! She would be punished, taught to fear him as she ought. Covering her helpless body with his own he felt the at once shameful and exciting thrill of dominance, and some animal part of him realized what an easy matter it would be to spread her legs and take her as thoughtlessly as Mallory would have.

But she didn't resist. Her eyes fluttered loosely and her head fell to the side, shrouded in a tangled cloud of bright brown hair that caught the moonlight. The sight of her helpless leeched all the violence out of him, and his grip softened at once from clench to caress as the stunned girl fought through her daze and at last opened her eyes. She blinked heavily, her chin tilted up toward him, and he knew that he wanted to use his strength not to punish but to cherish her.

She lay pinned beneath him on the loamy earth, her eyes large not with fear, but with a sort of waiting expectancy. Those lips allured him, and his hands slid up from her shoulders to encircle her throat in a caress before resting on cheeks begrimed from her tumble. His eyes softened, his head lowered toward hers and he felt her chest rise briefly to touch his in a quick little gasp as her eyes widened. And then, as he was about to find comfort in the yielding pillow of her lips, his balls — ready for something quite different — were filled with explosive pain.

For a second his world was coming to an end, a little Armageddon in his groin. A breath later it was slightly better — it was never as bad as he thought it would be — and he noticed Lucy was making no further effort to escape.

He fell on her, clumsily but effectively pinning her flat, his legs covering hers, grasping her wrists spread-eagle in his hands. She relaxed under him with a palpable shudder as he bowed his head to her shoulder, fighting back the last spasms of jaw-clenching pain.

Lucy's chest and throat were warm with his weight, and she smelled the sharp, sweet odor of new sweat over old. She let him lie silently, controlling his pain, before she turned her face to his downturned head and summoned his attention with a brief nuzzling caress against his temple.

"I'm sorry," she breathed into his ear, like the murmuring of water.

"Sorry?" he croaked.

"My head hurts. I wasn't... It was instinct. I wasn't sure who you were for a second."

Mallory would have had a razor to her throat. Possibly in her throat.

"You abandoned me," he said, making no effort to roll off her.

"You left me in the swamp. Were you going to call the police or just forget about me?"

"I was just going back to the car. Would you have let me go if I'd asked you?"

"Alone? No." Though what he could have done to stop her, short of shooting her, he had no idea.

"Well then."

"Why were you going to the car?"

"I needed to get something."

"What?"

She hesitated. "Something I'm not going to tell you about." She didn't want to talk about that. She wanted to abandon herself to the dizzying sensation of Edgar above her, and the whole earth below, crushed between two primal forces. She pressed herself against him but, to her dismay, he rolled off her and stood.

"Just go," he said, turning away from her. "Come back, don't come back, I don't care."

She rose like a snake slithering up his legs and dug her fingers in his hair, pushing his head back and kissing him so fiercely his balls thought things might be looking up again.

"I'll be back in an hour. I move faster than you. And Edgar, next time you get me pinned on my back, you better not let me get away."

She vanished silently into the blackness.

"Didn't catch her, huh?" Mallory asked, still perched on his log, when Edgar stumbled back.

"I caught her."

"You should have let her live. She was useful." He peered into the darkness, wondering if there was anything left for him.

"She's going to her car. She'll be back."

"Are you high?" Mallory asked, suddenly the rational one. "You let her live? You let her go? They'll have a helicopter out here in an hour."

"No, no, you don't understand her."

"Come on, we can still catch her."

"No, bro. Just wait. She'll be here."

She was back before the hour expired, her gems safe in a hollow gnarl under a squirrel's cache of mast.

"Let's go," she said as soon as she joined them. "The breeze drops after midnight, and the mosquitoes will be out in full force. I want to be home by then."

"What the hell did you..." Mallory began.

"Leave it," Edgar said sharply, and fell into step behind her.

Chapter 13

They tramped for another hour, moving through walls of branches that seemed impenetrable before Lucy revealed a path, and mud pits that swallowed them to their knees.

"We're close," she said at last.

As the night deepened, Edgar wondered if he should be suspicious. Had she really returned to her car on some innocent errand? Then why not tell him what it was? And why on earth hadn't he pressed her, with persuasion or violence?

Maybe she was leading them to nothing, though for what purpose, he couldn't say. His unpracticed eye could hardly pick out the contours of the ground five feet in front of him. How could she navigate through these miles of indistinguishable trees with no sun, no compass, only a few stars peeking through the canopy? Could she really have a house so far into the wilderness, through trackless swamp and thickets so dense no construction equipment could get through it? It had to be a trick or trap of some kind, but what? Why?

At last she raised her hand without looking back, and they stopped before a patch of scrub and clinging bullbriar that looked, to him, the same as any other.

"We're there?" Edgar asked.

Lucy stood silent; he did not know she was forming a prayer of sorts, to gods her ancestors had known, to her ancestors themselves who watched her, but more than anything to the swamp and trees and mosses of her homeland. Please let me be doing the right thing.

Then, lifting her bowed head, she parted the branches with both hands and the moon shone silver on a still sheet of water that crept in unseen currents. She ducked her head and slipped through, leaving Edgar behind a solid wall of greenery again. He followed, found himself on loose wet sand at the bank of... he didn't know what to call it. It wasn't a lake, certainly not a river. In the world he came from, bodies of water had defining features, boundaries that allowed you to positively identify them. Here, it seemed, the water simply started up out of the ground wherever it chose.

To Lucy, it was all simply the Everglades. Water would be here one season, gone another, only to reappear elsewhere. In her mind, the mutability was natural. She didn't expect a waterway to be the same from one year to the next, while Edgar would have been quite disturbed had the Hudson River suddenly changed course. He lived in a world that was essentially stagnant, while Lucy's, though it seemed to move at a much slower pace, was always ready to fool anyone who presumed to know it too well.

"Home is across this," she said.

Mallory, coming up behind them, tossed a branch into the water, then, seeing it didn't sink, cursed and found a pebble to throw. It was still a futile effort. He couldn't see past the gently shimmering surface, but it was easy enough to guess there was some depth to it.

"I'm not wading through that," Mallory said. "I bet there are alligators out there. Are there?"

"Of course there are," she said with an edge of scorn. "There have been alligators all around us for this whole trip. Haven't you seen them?" She shrugged, as if to say it wasn't her fault he was night-blind. "But we don't have to wade. If you'll come this way."

She poked around a few yards downstream, and from among what looked to Edgar like a pile of driftwood produced a dugout canoe of simple, ancient design. She'd made it herself from a log that had been water-seasoned for eighty years then smoked and hollowed out with fire and a gouge in the ancient method. The inside was polished to silken smoothness and tinged a subtle green-gray with dye from grass and moss. The outside was decorated in a wood-burned motif of marsh reeds bending in a current. Only when he saw it later, in full daylight, did Edgar notice another figure in the design — carved on each side of the dugout was a lurking bittern hiding in the stalks, its beak pointed to the sky like another brown grass blade, its thrush-streaked chest crossed by sawgrass and cattails.

The canoe was barely big enough for three, but the Battle brothers hunkered in with their gear between them, nearly upsetting it and sinking the dugout's already low lip even closer to the water's surface.

She stood in the stern, perfectly balanced, and slid the long pole up through her palms, pushing off in a sure stroke that sent them gliding with otter smoothness across a black expanse that parted in moon-touched silver before their prow. It seemed, as they quit the shore, that they left the noises of the forest behind, but it was only that the cicadas happened to fall silent, as they do every few minutes, leaving a heavy solemn emptiness in the wake of their droning song.

As the night noises faded they were replaced by the subtle plashing of water against the canoe, and occasional stirrings of beasts that twisted at the surface, or slid from the banks. Edgar could not see their destination, and after only a few pole strokes their launch site too had melted into blackness. He would have thought he was taking his final journey across the wide river Styx, had he not been leaning his back against the ferryman's legs, smooth and cool and solid like marble.

Mallory, in the bow, trailed his hand over the edge. Lucy slowed her poling and said, "I'd keep my hand in if I were you."

"Yeah?" he said, flicking his fingers under the water. "Why's that?"

"You said it yourself just now. There are alligators out here."

"Don't believe her," he said to Edgar. "She's trying to scare us. There's nothing that bad out here."

"The biggest alligator I've ever seen here was fifteen feet. But they can get bigger than that, if they have plenty of food. There's one in a hole nearby that could bite you in half, eat the top bits for breakfast and save your legs for lunch. Even a little guy could take your hand off pretty cleanly. But if you won't miss it..."

Mallory, stubborn, not only left his fingers trailing in the water but flung a leg over the side. "I don't think I have to worry about any gators," he said, but she could tell he was trying to look across the shimmering water, just to be sure.

"Oh, they're here all right — you just can't see them yet. Wait, I'll call them."

She made a noise in the back of her throat, something like a kitten's husky mew of protest, something like the call of a rutting frog. Suddenly the water around them came alive with a roiling tumult of unseen inhabitants. There were splashes like big logs rolling off the bank, and nearer — much nearer — the softer and more ominous sounds of quick snorted breath and gently yielding water. Mallory scrambled back into the boat so abruptly he nearly capsized it, and Lucy had to half-crouch against Edgar's back to steady herself. Edgar didn't shift in his seat, but his eyes darted frantically, knowing that he looked terrified and hoping the darkness hid it. Lucy, with one hand on Edgar's shoulder, laughed, high and clear like the call of a night bird.

"Where are they?" Mallory cried, his voice unusually shrill. "Oh, shit, what'd you do? Where are they?" He had drawn his gun, and was looking for a target, his eyes wide.

"Put that away," she said. "You won't be shooting any of *my* alligators."

"Yours?" Edgar asked weakly.

"I called them, didn't I? They protect my home. I told you this is a safe hideout. Put that gun away. Now, Mallory, or I'll flip the boat. That's better."

She could hear that the alligators were already losing interest in her call, and she still had a show to put on. She pulled out the flashlight she'd refused to light before. "Look over there." She turned it on and sent the powerful beam skimming across the surface. A dozen pairs of eyes illuminated, watching them. One was very near, within six feet of the dugout, and they could see its body stretched behind glowing eyes. Edgar would later swear it was twelve feet, but Lucy guessed closer to eight. Still, at close range, to the uninitiated, an impressive beast, and she felt Edgar catch his breath, and saw Mallory reach once more for his gun.

"Put that away!" she commanded again, and this time she rocked the boat with her legs, pitching them toward the gator, which seemed profoundly indifferent. She turned the flashlight on a slow circuit of the waterway, showing them how many reptile eyes stared in their direction, then she raised her long pole and with the very tip touched the nearest alligator gently on the snout. He sank down obediently, leaving Edgar to ponder whether it was worse to see them, or to know that they were there, lurking invisibly beneath him.

Lucy abruptly shut off the light and resumed poling. They made the rest of the trip in utter silence, and it was terrible and wonderful knowing such creatures were out there in the blackness, waiting for her orders.

Lucy was pleased at their reaction to her little game — for that's all it was, really, a clever parlor trick. She'd imitated a baby alligator distress call, a sound most adult alligators will investigate. A mother alligator guards her clutch viciously. She carries her hatchlings in her mouth to a pool, staying nearby for weeks to protect them. Though most alligators won't go so far as to protect unrelated young (and, as is the case with many animals, might even eat them) all alligators will instinctively take a look around when they hear a baby alligator's distress call. Their reaction would have been better in full summer, with new crops of infants combing the waterways for frogs and bugs to eat, but even in their partial night torpor in the chilly water, Lucy's call brought the alligators to attention with a nerve reaction they could not ignore. She did not tell the Battle brothers this, nor did she tell them that even without her call there would have been a dozen reflective eyes resting at the surface. Let them think she could summon alligators to her aid. It was one of many tricks her people had used to maintain power over those they invited onto their lands.

Solid ground was upon them before either of the brothers realized it. They were still recovering their composure when the craft struck shore, beaching the first foot of its prow on the bank. She held the boat still with the pole while Mallory clambered out, and accepted Edgar's hand when he offered it, though she was the one who steadied him. She secured the canoe loosely to a bush, tying it off with a supple vine she found growing nearby. There was no current to speak of to steal her boat away. She would hide it the next day; there was no danger of discovery that night.

From there it was another short trek through a thicket of brambles. Edgar noticed a slight incline to the ground. He'd taken it for granted that Florida was all flat.

At last, after a journey that seemed to have taken the whole night (though it was only a bit past eleven) Lucy again stepped through bushes and held them aside for the brothers.

"There," she said simply.

The woods ended abruptly in a small clearing, and with the canopy absent the moon, now risen to its zenith, was strong enough to cast shadows. Edgar let out a low whistle, which was answered by something — an owl?—from a nearby tree. She'd called it her house, but he expected something like a cabin, a little homemade shack set so deeply in the wilderness. What he saw instead, even in the moonlight, was startling.

It was not a particularly large house, having one grand open room and two or three small side-rooms, mainly for storage. But it was crafted with an intricacy that astounded him. It was not possible for such a dwelling to be built so far from civilization. She must have been lying, he thought. There must be a road that leads to this place. The lumber alone would have taken years to haul to such a remote location, the way they'd come.

When he first entered the clearing, Edgar almost missed the house itself. The first thing he saw was what looked like a grove in the middle of a meadow. Tall, stout columns resembling tree trunks sprouted from the earth, and it was only a moment later that he followed them upward and realized the house was built on stilts more than ten feet high. The house was perfectly round, and a porch circled it like Saturn's rings. There were two sets of stairs, each starting on opposite sides of the house and spiraling halfway around in a perfect segment of double helix.

The trees around it had been felled, but just a little beyond the woods was so thick it was impossible to see the house until you were in the clearing. And though the house was high, it did not reach above the canopy. Not even the roof could be seen from afar. Had it been daylight, he would have seen that the roof was shingled with an overlay of bark and mosses, and that the cypress nearby all seemed to lean toward the house, so that from above — say, from an inquisitive plane or helicopter — it would be very difficult to tell there was a clearing at all, and almost impossible to distinguish a house within it. Over the last five years she had pruned and tied the upper branches of the nearby trees to encourage such growth, and had herself seen the effect from the air. The house was nearly invisible to the outside world.

She didn't give them long to contemplate the façade. There would be time enough for that in the morning, and she wanted to keep them just a bit disoriented for now.

She mounted the curving stairs and led the Battle brothers into safety.

Chapter 14

You're an old man, Edgar told himself. A three hour hike and a short sprint should be nothing, but as he mounted the stairs his calves ached and his thighs were starting to spasm. Those stairs were almost the last straw. If he'd been alone he would have sunk down on the third step and spent the night there. But with Lucy bounding with her inexhaustible energy ahead of him he forced himself onward and upward. "Excelsior!" he mumbled through gritted teeth, though no one heard him.

He was drained by far more than physical exertion. The uncertainty, the emotion, and above all that terrible longing for a moment's security, were all taking their toll. Ever since the escape, every time he started to relax all hell had broken loose. Now his nerves were ready for another such betrayal, and no matter how safe he started to feel, he constantly fought the temptation to relax. The lure of security stalked him, and once again he felt it flex its claws to pounce. All he'd wanted since the moment of the break was one honest-to-goodness hour without worry.

"We won't have any electricity until I get the generator going in the morning," Lucy said as she opened the door.

"No locks?" Mallory commented.

"It's kind of a tradition with my people, some other Indians too, especially in out-of-the-way places. Anyone who needs help or shelter out here needs it badly. So they're welcome to it."

"Has anyone ever used it?" Edgar asked.

"Never."

She lit a stubby candle and began to circulate around the main room, lighting tapers as she went. Mallory stayed at the limen, waiting to get his bearings, but Edgar followed her on her tour as gradually, in halting, flickering orbs of illumination, the room came into view.

To Edgar, it felt like a church, even a cathedral, except for its size. It was spacious and, even in the semidarkness, very open, perfectly round with high ceilings and a great many windows. The candlelight danced upon these, and on the pale polished wood that seemed to make up whatever was not glass in the house. The windows, he would see in the morning, were heavily tinted to keep out prying eyes and the brutal sun. There were no curtains. Her home was open to the swamps. Like a church, the house was refreshingly cool even in the height of the summer, and on that night the crispness was pleasant, a touch of chill without the breeze that continued outside.

Even candlelight was enough to show the extraordinary craftsmanship the woodwork. It was not particularly ornate; quite the contrary, it seemed that all of the artisans' skills had gone into making the house appear simple and understated. In that way it had an aura of Japanese construction, though the woodwork was closer to what one might find in the oldest Appalachian homes.

Edgar picked up a candle and looked more closely at the walls. He'd seen such intricacy on inlaid boxes. This was similar, though on a much grander scale. It was all made from the same kind of wood, cypress, joined with unseen connections and polished smooth until the surface seemed shimmeringly alive. The grains varied to form a pattern, and yet no pattern, for though he could find nothing repeating in the design it possessed a certain continuity of idea. Some of the pieces were in long traditional planks, albeit slightly concave. while others were in segments of only a few inches. Most were rectangular, but occasional trapezoidal segments added depth to the whole.

The wood floors were less ornate, but just as expertly crafted, and the wood used for them seemed to have more character, with dark whorls and knots that looked like animal faces rubbed smooth, as though the three-dimensional personality of the tree had been captured and flattened. There were no nails, no glue, no splinters to be seen. He ran a hand along one wall, closing his eyes. He would have sworn it was made from a single slab of wood, smoothed to perfection.

From what he could see of the furniture — a table for eating and a rougher one for working, two simple chairs and one that rocked, and a bookcase filled with titles he couldn't make out — they must have been crafted by the same hand, and their components seemed made to be joined, rather than forced together with hammer and nail.

He should have known it was too good to be true.

"Close the door," he said to Mallory, his voice low and harsh. "And lock it." For though there was no lock on the outside, there was one inside.

Lucy didn't notice the new edge in his voice. She was debating whether to light a fire and make something warm to eat, or wait until morning. At the slide of the bolt she turned around and saw the Battle brothers ready for a fight. Mallory was the only one certain they'd win it.

Lucy had no idea why the room was suddenly charged, but her posture shifted subtly. Her legs bent slightly, shifting her full hips to lower her center of gravity. Her nostrils flared, and the muscles of her forearms danced as her hands prepared to grapple. What the hell's going on, she wondered. I thought we had everything ironed out.

"Did you think you could get away with lying to us?" Edgar asked, his voice even. "That we were stupid?"

"What are you talking about?" she asked impatiently, thinking if she had to kill them both now, at least no one would ever find the bodies. Still, it would be tough, two on one, and those two so big, with guns and a razor.

"Far from civilization? A safe haven? No one around for miles? What are you cooking up, Lu? Trying to get us caught, or just plain turning us in? Do you really think I'd believe that all this was built miles from nowhere? It would have taken a dozen men years to get the supplies here the way we came, and there's no way you got those stilts up without heavy equipment. You expect me to believe you got a crane through that mess?"

Lucy looked at him, confused, as he ranted on. "There's got to be a highway nearby, probably a road leading right to the house. We just can't see it in the dark, right?" He took his Glock from the duffel and stalked toward her with the weapon held at arm's length. Mallory just watched.

On the other hand, Lucy thought, there's something to be said for close quarters.

Quick as a heron striking she attacked the gun directly, one hand underneath, gripping, the other on top, pushing the slide out of battery so it couldn't fire. They stood that way for an instant, Edgar armed with his useless weapon, knowing, suddenly, Lucy had all the power. The next moment she twisted and pulled his arm and had him on the ground, the gun in her own hand. She tapped and racked it, clearing the chamber in case a round got jammed in the manhandling, and pointed it at Mallory while she knelt on his brother.

Yes, the majority voted — her common sense, her self-preservation. Shoot Mallory now. No, her heart and her deepest instincts said, because Edgar will never forgive me. I don't want that.

She locked eyes with Mallory.

"This is my home, my territory. I can live out here naked, kill what I want to eat, destroy whatever threatens me. I have fangs and claws you can't imagine." She bared her gleaming teeth.

Mallory couldn't look away. He ran his thumb along the dull edge of his razor and stared into eyes like the rippling black of midnight water, animal eyes. He was painfully, blatantly hard.

Lucy saw, and for the first time her courage almost failed her. A madman, she could handle. Not a madman focused on her. The scar on her belly, that relic from her brother, itched like a centipede crawling down between her legs. She meant to intimidate him. Instead she'd enflamed him. Kill him! her mind screamed, but she mastered it at last and loosed Edgar's arm, letting him sit up. He didn't notice his brother's turgidity. He could only see Lucy standing dominantly over him. He could reach the gun as easily as she had a moment before, but it never occurred to him to try.

"The nearest house is a little cabin about twenty miles back the way we came, off the dirt road, and they don't know I live here. On the other side, there's nothing but water and sawgrass for thirty miles."

"There's no way you could get a house built all the way out here."

"Start walking," she said. "See how far you get before the swamp swallows you up. I built the house myself. Me and one other person."

"How'd you get the wood here?"

She laughed. "What did you spend the last few hours hiking through, Edgar? We used cypress. We cut it ourselves, sawed the planks. Jimi did most of the technical woodwork. Took about two years."

"I thought you said no one knows about this house."

"Jimi doesn't know where it is, not really. I made sure he was good and drunk whenever I walked him back and forth. He lived out here for weeks at a time, working. He knows it's here, but I doubt he could find it again."

She handed him the Glock. "I don't need it to take you on," she whispered.

"Put that away," Edgar said to Mallory. "I made a mistake."

Edgar deliberately sorted through his bag so he didn't have to look at either of them. This will be good for both of us, he thought. He'd relax, finally, and be able to plot their next move, for he still planned to flee the country, for good, as soon as he could. Mallory might calm down too. There were no threats to put him on edge, nothing to force to the surface those terrible, unfathomable sociopathic tendencies Edgar still couldn't fully believe inhabited his little brother. There were no temptations, unless he wanted to exercise his proclivities on bunnies. He'd shown no sign of wanting to hurt Lucy, and Edgar was sure Mallory had put her in a unique classification — like himself, inviolate.

While Edgar's back was turned, Mallory rubbed his cock and looked longingly at Lucy's upraised backside as she bent to brush a dead millipede off the bed.

Lucy slept on the floor that night. Edgar tried to protest, but she told them it was the host's privilege to make the sleeping arrangements. They should share the only bed. "I'm used to sleeping on the floor," she said.

If I have to fight Mallory, it'll probably end up on the floor one way or another, she thought. Might as well start there.

Chapter 15

Lucy dreamed unmolested that night. Sleep sometimes has a stronger call than sickness, and Mallory thought he had plenty of time.

She woke early, as one almost always does when sleeping on the ground. She wasn't particularly uncomfortable with only the negligible down of her sleeping bag between her back and the wooden floor, but it wasn't a position for indolence, and at the first hint of dawn she silently rose and pulled on her boots. Already the sounds seeping into the house had changed their timbre, night hunters replaced by day stalkers, and she could hear trilling cries of the earliest birds catching their drowsy worms.

She slipped outside and gripped the porch railing in her hands, letting her head hang back so her face caught the first golden haze of morning sun filtered through boughs of greenery. Ah! She was home! She might leave often, but she would always return to this place. She took a deep breath of the heavy air. In the swamps her lungs seemed to expand, and the air was sweeter to her than anywhere else, each inhalation a minor ecstasy. Out in the world she shut half of herself down, drowning out the drone of modern life, but here it was impossible to be detached from her surroundings. The swamp filled her in a sensual explosion — the hum of a hundred kinds of insects, the undertone of barely moving water, the dark secret smells writhing up from centuries of decomposition, the caressing warmth of the newborn sun, all welcomed her home, and she closed her eyes to relish it.

Fear, what little there had been, was gone, slain like an enemy at her feet. She could only feel a nameless ecstatic joy. Suddenly, stillness became impossible, and in a rush she dashed a step or two and vaulted, holding onto the railing until her feet swung down to the cypress stilts, then she slid to the ground. In the quick vigor of morning, stairs were just too staid. As soon as her feet hit the earth she was off at a dash.

She wove in and out of trunks, dodging as if evading some shadow pursuer, and ducked under vines almost sturdy enough to swing from. When she came to a log or puddle she hurdled it like a deer in a soaring leap. She slowed as the ground turned damp and yielding, her breath coming hard more from excitement than exertion, and when she reached the bank of the waterway she'd ferried them across the night before she found a familiar tree and climbed it with squirrel-like grace. She settled herself in a crook fifteen feet up, wrapping her thighs loosely about the chafing bark, and leaned her back against the broad silvery trunk.

Below her the water was cloudy red from the tannins of decaying matter, darker at the banks where eddies churned up the mud. She could see the reflection of her swinging feet, and little fish shied from the mirrored movement, while bigger ones cruised over to investigate. For a quarter hour she scanned the surface, observing through shade and ripples the life that lurked below. When she knew where the fish were congregating she climbed halfway down the tree and jumped the rest of the way, landing almost on all fours, and tripped silently away from the water until she found a crumbling bit of log overgrown with moss and swarming with baby pillbugs. She turned it over, rolling the log towards her body so any snake slumbering beneath couldn't strike her, and appraised her bait store.

The earth was dark, though with less aeration than northern dirt, which kept some species from thriving. But the bacteria that foster decomposition — the foundation of any healthy ecosystem — were having a field day in the wet rotting swamps, and in some spots the ground was like peat, a slightly younger version of that ancient fuel. In drier areas, when forest fires rage through the land, that peat can burn a foot below the ground, keeping subterranean fires smoldering for weeks. The area around Lucy's house was damp, and the house itself built on a limestone rise with only a thin accumulation of dirt, so any fires that crossed her path snaked through quickly, searing dry foliage but never taking firm hold on the land. She welcomed even the fire, for much of the Everglades could not survive without it. It cleared out crowded old growth, allowed seeds to set, drove off invaders.

Lucy pounced on two fat white grubs, but rejected a writhing red centipede, four inches long with a painful bite, and a salamander, whose flaming orange neck and belly were a sure sign of its toxicity. She found a handful of grubs under other logs and took her bait to the water to set her lines. Fish were plentiful, and could be caught without much effort. Usually she kept a fish trap or two nearby, spiral arrangements of reeds that fish could easily get into, but couldn't escape. It kept them alive for weeks, and she could harvest them by hand or with a net whenever she was hungry. But she was never sure how long she'd be gone, and she dismantled them whenever she left the swamp.

That day she set out a half-dozen lines, which she'd check every few hours. Sometimes fish would steal the bait, sometimes an alligator would poach the fish after it was hooked, but generally two or three fish would prove cooperative and volunteer for her pot.

Most of the time, Lucy used hooks, either metal or carved bone, but on this day she used a more traditional method. She whittled slivers of wood to a point and nicked a notch in the middle. With a silent prayer for their spirits she pierced a grub on each spike, tossed them out on monofilament lines and tied the lot to a bush on shore. The fish would swallow the whole thing and the wood would twist and lodge in their gullet, holding them fast. It was survival fishing, not recreational. With a tiny spear in their gut, there was no catch and release for those fish.

While she waited for fish to sacrifice themselves, she checked the area immediately around her home. She liked to assure herself there was nothing new, aside from a crop of spring ground flowers, and the far more subtle sprays of orchids adorning the treetops. They looked more like insects than blooms, and their mission in life was deception, luring lustful flies and bees to mate with their provocatively shaped petals and spread their pollen.

But flowers were scarce that year. Everything was waiting for the rain.

It was unusual for the rains to be so late. The alligator wallows and low sloughs ensured that the place maintained some growth year-round, but it wouldn't come into full flower until the first deluge. It was lovely, but to Lucy's practiced eye there were still several more stages of green quickness to progress through before the land achieved perfect beauty. Soon enough the leaves would burst forth in that palest green that is almost yellow — they're so anxious not to miss a day they sprout before they have enough chlorophyll. The eager vine tips would grow so fast that if she napped away an afternoon on the ground she could be a prisoner by dusk, entwined in eager greenery. Then she would know the blood of the swamps flowed again.

Lucy found the woods surrounding her cabin much as she'd left it several months ago. A cypress had fallen, but it had been dead some three decades, and its toppling was only a surprise to the family of woodpeckers who nested in its hollow. She found deer tracks, smaller than their northern relatives, if not so diminutive as Key deer. Though they didn't love the swamplands, the foraging there was better in the winter. She also found the telltale scratchings of black bear claws high on a trunk, and a tuft of hair he'd left lodged in an outcropping of bark while luxuriously scratching himself. Black bears, small compared to their brown cousins, aren't generally a threat, though they are opportunistic hunters who in lean times will risk stalking a human. But we are large prey for them. They don't know how yielding our flesh can be, and Lucy, who knew how to intimidate them, didn't fear her bears.

There are so many ways to die in the swamps — four kinds of poisonous snakes, assorted meat-eaters, and a host of toxic plants, not to mention quicksand and intestinal parasites — that no single threat loomed very large. It was safe as long as you knew what you were about, and Lucy did. Tell a Bushman to cross the street in rush-hour traffic and he will have something to fear. A native city-dweller will do it without a thought. Few dangers remain dangerous once they are properly understood.

Lucy was satisfied in the most important thing — she found no prints or other spoor that might indicate human presence. No one had found her sanctuary in her absence.

It was nearly eight when she strolled back to the cabin, swinging a bunch of mushrooms in a satchel quickly knotted from a vine. She saw Edgar pacing above her on the deck. He hadn't spotted her yet, but he scanned the border of the wood anxiously, and his hands, clenched in fists, distractedly pounded the railing at intervals. Lucy whistled, and when he spied her his body seem to shimmer with relief.

When he woke earlier and found her sleeping bag empty and cold he was sure she'd fled. And why not? She trusted him enough to bring both brothers to safety, and he'd repaid that trust by sticking a gun in her face.

He decided he'd make no effort to find her. They'd have to move out that day, of course, and how he would get them back to civilization (and what he'd do once there) he had no inkling. Vague ideas about the sun rising in the east were about as far as his navigational skills went, but they would have to make the attempt. He was willing to bet she wouldn't even turn them in. The swamps were prison enough, a death sentence. There was no need to send them to trial and incarceration when the alligators and mosquitoes would do the job just as well, and much more quickly.

Then came the whistle, which at first he could hardly pick out of the baseline cacophony of bird and insect noises. It was sharp and close, and he turned around to find Lucy almost directly below him, waving, and smiling in mischief. He ran down the helix two steps at a time, skipping the last four entirely in a leap that brought him almost on top of her.

"I thought you'd gone," he said, taking her arms first to steady himself and then not letting go.

Lucy laughed and laid her hands carelessly on his waist. "I'm not leaving you," she said steadily.

He clutched her arms more tightly. "Why won't you run away, Lucy?" His voice was an urgent whisper, and his deep eyes were darkly shadowed. They looked bright and open compared to hers, black with the secrets of centuries.

"You sound like you want me to leave," she said, forcing her voice to stay light but only wanting to close what minimal gap remained between them.

"I want you to stay for me. I want you to go for you. You shouldn't be here."

"It's my home. I'm staying. And you can't leave."

For so many reasons, he thought.

"Come to the water with me," she said. "Let's see if there are fish for breakfast." She gently disentangled herself and led him into the bracken. Edgar followed, meek as a lamb.

The woods were easier to negotiate by daylight, and Edgar had no problem keeping up with her easy pace as they headed to the banks. Two of the lines were taut, and she pulled out a pair of fat fish Edgar couldn't identify. She slit their throats and gutted them on the dry grass, tossing the entrails far into the water where almost immediately something dark and leathery rose in a churning froth and took them.

"A bull," she said. "He'll be testy because he's anxious to mate." I know how he feels, Lucy thought, eyeing Edgar sidelong and wondering if she should pounce now. But then, he might be a disappointment, and afterward the rest of his time here would be so awkward. Of course, I could always teach him.

"That's it for my trotline. I'm surprised he didn't get the first two. He'll steal the rest. Don't worry, there's a clear spring where we can swim. Do you like alligator meat?"

"That thing has to be ten feet."

"Yeah, but there's less meat than you'd think. The good stuff's in the tail and tongue. My mom swore by the eyes, but they give me the creeps."

"You're going to shoot it?"

"No, we use spears. I don't like to kill things too near the house, but then, I never had guests to feed before. Edgar, come here," she added softly, but he was following his own thoughts and didn't hear her.

"People like you aren't supposed to exist." He was almost talking to himself. "A girl who can kill me, and call alligators, who treats the swamp like a resort, who helps murderers. Yes, murderers, me too, even if I didn't..." If she'd been looking at his face, she would have seen tears shining in them. But she was staring intently at a spot near his feet. "Lucy, what are you? What am I not seeing?"

She took a step toward him and pulled him firmly into her arms. "Lucy," he breathed, and bowed his head to kiss her, but she abruptly pulled him another two steps.

"Soon," she said. "Look there." She pointed where he'd been standing. "That's what you're not seeing."

He stared at the spot for a full minute, seeing nothing but fallen brown leaves. Only when it shifted one of its coils in contemplation of retreat did Edgar see the wedge-shaped head and dead-leaf pattern of an irritated rattlesnake.

"Shit!" he said, stepping behind her then feeling like a coward. To recover he scooped up a stone from the river bank and drew back his arm. Before he could throw, Lucy grabbed his hand and pulled it down easily.

"We don't kill snakes," she said firmly.

"But that thing could have killed *me*," he said, annoyed she seemed to be taking the snake's side.

"Probably not, unless you stepped on her, which you almost did. She's still pretty torpid from the night. Towards noon, you might have a problem."

"How do you know it's a she?" he asked, calming enough to admire the snake's striking patterns and the glittering crescent of its eye. Now that she'd pointed it out he could see it clearly, but he'd never have spotted it on his own.

"I don't, but the first rattlesnake was a she, so I think of them all that way. Very long ago, so long that the oceans were bound up in glaciers and the seas had retreated, snakes had no teeth."

"What did they eat?" he asked, slipping an arm around her waist as he watched the hypnotic flicker of the snake's tongue.

"I never thought to ask, but knowing our legends, probably dreams, or fear or something. They were gentle and kind, though, and never harmed a living soul. One day there came a man, a very bad man, who — and again I don't know the reason, probably just for fun — found a mother snake with thirteen babies, and he killed them all with his knife. The mother escaped into a gopher tortoise burrow, but as she slithered down the man cut off the tip of her tail."

The snake eyed Edgar unblinkingly. The bad man came, Edgar thought. For no reason. For fun. He shuddered. There is a bad man even in the most secret woods — and I brought him here. Two bad men, he corrected.

"Later, when the tortoise told her the man was gone, the mother snake went weeping to the shaman. In those days, shaman were more than they are today. The greatest among them were almost gods. This one was so moved by the mother snake's story he promised to make her a set of impressive teeth, as fierce as a panther's, from a piece of ivory. But after he carved only two teeth, the ivory splintered into a thousand tiny pieces, and so the snake had to make do with only two large fangs, and the rest of the teeth very small. The shaman knew a thing as big as a man would laugh at just two teeth, so he took the poison away from the cattail and the coontie — that's why they're edible now — and gave them to the snake.

"She was very grateful, and bowed to the great shaman, but as she left he noticed the tip of her tail had been cut off. She hadn't thought it worth mentioning, next to her grief for her babies. Now, I have said that this shaman was very powerful, and his greatest power was to call the winds and storms. He had a magic rattle, made of a gourd filled with enchanted beans, and when he shook it the wind would come from the four corners of the earth, rustling through the bushes, to do his bidding. But such compassion had he for the mother snake, and such shame did he feel that a fellow human would kill her children, that he promptly tied his rattle where her tail had been, and so gave up his greatest power. Now it is the snakes who can call storms.

"And that," she said, "is why we should not repeat the evil of our ancestor and harm a snake, and why the rattlesnake, who stayed gentle despite her two great fangs, will always rather run and hide instead of biting you. And that is also why snakes and gopher tortoises still live together, and why no snake will ever bite a tortoise, no matter how clumsily it steps on her. Tortoises are known for their hospitality, and hold salons of snakes, spiders, scorpions and burrowing owls, where everyone gets along. I wish you'd scared her a little more. Then maybe she would have rattled. We need the rain."

"This place isn't wet enough?" he asked, looking over the expanse of water and cypress, remembering the mud and sloughs on their trek.

She slipped out of his encircling arm and crouched about six feet from the snake.

"Be careful," Edgar said, then felt foolish. She must know what she's doing. And indeed, he was hardly surprised when she held out her hands, palms outward, and began to sing to the snake. The snake shifted, and she moved her hands in a circle. Then, as if on command, the snake abruptly turned and vanished into the grass with a shivering undulation.

"You speak to animals?" he asked, amazed.

"Of course," she said simply.

"Er, what did you say?"

"I told her you were friendly, but she made you nervous, and asked if she would mind staying away while you were here."

"I don't believe you," he said, in a tone that clearly meant he almost did. "She went away because you asked her to?"

Lucy shrugged noncommittally.

Lucy *could* talk to snakes. So can you, for all the good it would do. It was just another trick her ancestors had used centuries before to keep their guests in check. She had the magician's gift of making the mundane seem impressive. She understood snakes, that was all. This one had lost the edge of its aggression and probably wouldn't strike, but was still nervous, and wanted to find a lonelier place to bask. By moving closer she'd just given it incentive to do what it already intended to do: leave. Then again, in a way, she *was* communicating with the snake. It told her plainly with its posture what it meant to do, and she gave it instructions by moving dominantly forward. The song, a Tequesta lullaby, meant nothing, was in fact unheard by the snake, and was solely for Edgar's benefit. Edgar had every right to be impressed with Lucy, though it wasn't for quite the right reason.

They strolled back at a slow, meandering pace, side by side. Edgar took her hand, swinging it easily.

"Do the Tequesta have an explanation for everything?" he asked.

"Yes," she said. "But mostly we just make it up, for white people."

When Edgar and Lucy returned to her cabin, Mallory was just waking up. He opened his eyes carefully, then wrinkled his nose and hid his head under the pillow. "Ugh! What's that I smell?" he asked, muffled.

"That's fresh air, bro," Edgar said cheerfully, grabbing the covers and pulling them down to Mallory's feet. "Clean, pure, smogless air. Get used to it. You're going to be breathing it for a long time."

"Not too long," Mallory and Lucy both said at once.

You can't keep him, she told herself. He's not a puppy. Fulfill your stupid Tequesta duty to strangers in need, have your fun with Edgar and get rid of them. Soon the bill will go through, and it will be official. You'll have your very own nation. By then the Battle brothers will be in South America, and good luck to them.

"Well boys, I have a few things to do if we're going to live comfortably while we're here. Do you two want to take a walk, look around?"

"I don't know..." Edgar began, thinking of the rattlesnake.

"Go on, pussy," Mallory said. "I'm going back to sleep." He pulled the covers over his head and turned his back to them. "Fish for breakfast... geez," he grumbled from his cave. "What did I get myself into? I should have left you in prison."

"You'll be fine if you don't go too far away," Lucy told Edgar. "If you go back to the water where we were and head right along the bank it should be fairly clear and dry. It's mostly either cypress swamp or hardwood hammocks near here. You won't have any real trouble unless you get to the sawgrass, and that's the other direction. Just don't go in the water, or too near it."

He'd rather stay with Lucy, but she was bustling in a way he recognized from childhood, the determined, efficient busyness he remembered in his mother when she cleaned house and really wanted her boys out of the way. Even when he offered to help she'd shooed him off with the broom, knowing despite his best efforts he'd only be a hindrance.

"Take this," she said, handing him a whistle on a chain. "I'll come save your ass if you run into anyone you can't handle."

"I thought there was no one else out here."

"I mean the snakes, and the bears, and the panthers."

Edgar had some misgivings about leaving the two of them together, but so far his brother hadn't shown the slightest inclination to harm Lucy. Well, he'd been perfectly willing to kill her for treachery, but not to... do what he had to the others. Anyway, what could happen in a half-hour, with Mallory asleep and Lu busy with other things?

"You'll be okay?" he asked softly.

"Sure," she said, glancing at Mallory and wondering if he was shamming sleep. Despite all she had seen, she still underestimated his danger. She equated Mallory with a particularly vicious dog. He might be dangerous, but he still acted fundamentally like a dog, and could be read and controlled in more or less the same manner. She didn't fully understand that Mallory was a rabid dog, completely unnatural, utterly unpredictable.

But Edgar left, Mallory slept, and Lucy went outside to start the generator. It harvested a combination of wind and solar, both scarce in her neck of the woods, but it could store a fair amount of the power that trickled slowly in. She'd been talking to Lazarus Nighteyes about rigging up hydroelectricity on a small scale, either in one of gushing springs or just in the steady, inexorable flow of water that constantly traveled from the Okeechobee to Florida Bay. It was a little too ambitious for her at the moment, and parts of her didn't want her home to become too civilized. When she had her reservation she could build something less primitive near airboat access, or closer to the path they drove in on, but she planned to keep this section, her home, the home of her family's bones, as pristine as possible.

She rarely made use of what electricity was available. There were lights for emergency or when she was engrossed in a good book and it was too hot to build the fire to a blazing light. She had a radio and small television, static-y connections to the outside world, but they were seldom turned on. There was no refrigerator. She had a good store of canned and dried food, but she preferred to live off the land as much as possible. There was no air conditioner.

The primary purpose of her meager electrical supply was to pump water to her house from the nearby spring, and filter it of any impurities before delivering it through the modern-looking and efficient plumbing system. The spring welled up pure from the limestone, with enough force to keep a sizable basin filled with clear water. From there it overspilled to other semi-connected waterways, making the transition from vodka clarity to shades of blue-green, tannic red, brown and at last the near-black of the creeping swamps. She could, and often did, drink it directly from the source, but like every swamp dweller Lucy lived in mortal fear of stray amoebas that could, at best, give her a few unpleasant days, at worst strip away all her body's moisture and desiccate her to death. Her filters cleared out giardia and other nasties, and strained the assorted leaf litter and insects that fell into the spring. When the water reached her house it was pure, better than the best city water, uncontaminated by chlorine. Extra water was stored in an underground reservoir that, once the system got going, held enough for several days.

The generator hummed, but it would be a few hours before she could pump fresh water. Now at last she heeded the call of her ancestors. Her mother's voice was most plaintive of all. After all, she was closest, in a charnel house in the middle of a small dense hammock just a few hundred yards from Lucy's home.

Lucy began to sing, a continuo of sound from deep in her chest that rose a few measures later to form words no other living person could speak. Lazarus Nighteyes knew a few phrases, and all Seminoles and Miccosukee learned a single word in their late childhood, roughly translating to "I swear with my blood," spoken when they reaffirmed the oath of protection every member of the two tribes had made since the Tequesta first welcomed them in their time of trouble.

Lucy Brightwing sang of her people, of their lives before Europeans came, of their dwindling numbers, of their own retreat to the deepest swamps where no white man could go. She sang loudly, for her mother and brother to hear, and for the more distant shades of all those others who came before her, whose bones lay scattered. She sang so loudly she did not hear Mallory's footsteps behind her.

She climbed the hill, a rise of no more than a few feet, but a mountain in the swamps, high and dry even at the full flood of the rainy season. Most such hills were only a few inches above the baseline. Her family's bones deserved this monument.

The land around the hill was dry now, but in a week or two even that would be underwater, and it would be an island. Tropical mahogany trees mixed with temperate live oaks made a wall around the ossuary. At the center stood the hollowed-out stump of a massive oak, with a peculiar sculpture around it. Nearer, it could be seen that the structure was actually an intricately assembled tangle of cypress knees, cut from the swamp and fit together to make a sort of cage with protruding rounded spikes. Fire might sweep through the undergrowth, but it would catch hold in neither the hardwoods nor the cypress knees. Her family's bones would never burn. A bold mouse might steal a fingerbone to gnaw on, but the important relics, the skulls, the long thighbones, the platter-like pelvises, were safe from marauders. There wasn't a scrap of flesh left to tempt larger scavengers like raccoons or bears. She had watched over the decomposition process herself, hurrying it along by luring scout ants to the feast. Some cultures sit up with the dead until burial. The Tequesta stay with the body until it is no more than bones.

She lay her hands on the tangle, still singing even as she formed her questions in her mind. Through gaps in the matrix of cypress knees she glimpsed the stark white of bone, the telltale curve and fissure of a skull. She didn't know if it belonged to Two Moons or to Cub. But it didn't matter. For what she had to ask, the opinion of a madman might do just as well.

"Mother," she asked formally, "he followed me home. May I keep him?"

She heard a whisper from the bones, a melding of two voices. "You can have whatever you want, if you pay the price. There will be a trial..."

The heavy rosewood butt of a .357 struck her bowed head, and she crumpled on top of her family's bones. Her last conscious sensation was of hands at her waistband, fumbling and pulling.

Chapter 16

The day began to warm as Edgar picked his way through the woods, and it felt as good on his exposed hands and throat as it did on the snake's scales. Until that day, Edgar had labored under the impression that all trees are green, all bark brown. But now as he meandered almost spellbound through a thousand-thousand myriad leaves and tendrils and jutting knees he found that, whereas the green had all been suffused with gold a half-hour ago when he walked with Lucy into the sunrise, the foliage now glinted like silver chain mail where the sun struck it from five degrees higher. Each leaf shone like polished steel, and when the wind stirred them the trees seemed an army of armored warriors joining in battle. In the shaded understory the ground was dappled with bright shifting spots of light that danced on deepest shadows. Here and there were nooks that never saw light at all, in the lifted skirts between tight-pressed cypress knees, in hollows excavated at the base of trees. In these microsystems pale bloodless things bridged the gap between plant and fungus, furling their corpselike flower-heads into their twilight world.

Above him birds with thrush-streaked breasts came into sight just long enough to tempt his eye, then blended seamlessly into the wood. Ants foraged unseen at his feet — not fire ants, which prefer drier terrain, but a less pernicious sort of red ant whose bite is significant only in quantity. On higher ground lived a species of black ant, passive creatures that did not bite at all. Each had mapped out its territory generations before, and only rarely did expanding populations call for border raids or outright war. Edgar only saw the large, the gross, and that was impressive enough, but had he examined any square inch in detail he would have found it teeming with life such as he'd never imagined.

He was not converted all at once. He still thought the only worthwhile place for a man is the city. But if pressed, he couldn't have said what seductions kept him there, other than habit. Lucy herself would never wholly abandon civilization, the truly civilized kind, that is, because of the many pleasures it could bring. Lucy liked the opera; she liked museums; she liked to explore stores for exactly the right cheese and lotion and clothing. But these were occasional pastimes, treats or periodic temptations. She was nourished by the daily life she loved, her life in the swamps, but would succumb at times to the lure of such desserts as Miami or New York had to offer.

Edgar as a rule did not patronize museums or the Met, and though he indulged as freely as any other metropolite in the rampant consumerism inspired by commercials and well-dressed store fronts, he found no particular joy in purchase. That he had been born in a city, that men throughout the world, to the extent of his knowledge, were built to live in cities, were the only justifications in his mind. It was the same excuse used by so many people for so many things — that's the way it is done, the way it has *always* been done. Life in a city was the only way of life that, until this moment, had ever occurred to him, and New York was the only city of any significance, to his mind. New York was the hub, and as you declined, you might find yourself in Newark, or D.C., or Chicago. Everything else was for people who didn't matter, small-town life for small-time people.

Part of him saw winding up in the Everglades as a sign of his utter failure. Life had been good in New York. He had his career and the respect of those he worked with. He had money. Then everything had gone wrong. He'd progressed steadily from the center of the world to the upstate prison, to the backwoods of

Appalachia as they drove south after the escape, and now, to this, the most primeval wilderness in the country, populated only by three people and a whole lot of trees and water and biting things. Looking at the big picture, he thought, it was like a descent to hell.

But that morning, with the sun changing the world's colors from hour to hour, it was not possible for him to see anything like a big picture. Everything around him captured his immediate attention. Before, he thought of the world on a grand but essentially impersonal scale. Images of maps — the eastern American states they had traveled — filled that matte board behind his eyes; lines of police cars; gyro-stabilized shots from helicopters, of smoke rising from the overturned transport van, of a body being pulled from a ditch. All of it concerned him, yet he was oddly disconnected from it. It was like a parable, or at best a floundering student's clumsy outline of a complicated plot that bogged him down with its gravity without giving his situation any clarity. Now, as he had only on rare occasions since the break, he forgot to recite that constant background litany of the last two weeks, and let the world simply caress his senses.

The trunks around him made a sort of prison, keeping his mind from wandering over both regrets and future plans. He found himself smiling at things. Not people or ideas, but things — a lizard defying gravity on the underside of a glossy leaf, a knot in a cypress knee that resembled his uncle, a bird that bravely swooped almost beneath his feet to snatch a grasshopper.

He didn't mean to wander so far, but when he reached water he turned and realized that all the features that had seemed such unique landmarks on the journey out now blended into formless greenery. He was lost, and he realized only now that he'd left his gun back at the cabin. He tried to remember the route from the night before, but that trek had been almost surreal. It couldn't have been far from the waterfront to Lu's cabin, but as he glanced behind him he saw nothing that looked familiar.

He had the security of his whistle, but what man would deign to sound the shrill herald of defeat and disorientation? Men do not ask for directions on the highway or in the wilds. If minutes of confusion turned to hours he might give in and purse his lips in disgrace to blow, but as long as there was a chance of finding his way, he'd rather wander unassisted.

The dark black still waterway wasn't too far from the cabin, he knew that much. There was the grassy sward where she knelt to gut the fish, and there, the shallows where an alligator lurked. All I have to do is walk away from the water and I should find my way back, he assured himself. Instinct told him the moment he feared himself lost was the proper time to try and retrace his steps, but manliness urged him to make light of it, and stay and explore the banks, which latter temptation he of course yielded to. He did remember her one piece of advice. He turned right along the bank.

In all his time in the Everglades, he never met a body of water he could quite put a name to. He knew of lakes, oceans and rivers. The Glades has sloughs and wallows and floodplains, all of which change with the season. The body they'd crossed last night was broad and seemed to run more or less in a line, with thick cypress on either side blending into mixed hardwood forest, but it did not flow like a river, nor yet did it have the quiet configuration of a pond or lake. It was connected, by partly underground conduits, to several springs, keeping the water active enough to prevent sawgrass, which prefers even stiller water. Yet it was also part of that steady southward flow that begins in several central Florida rivers, feeds into Lake Okeechobee and filters through a dozen kinds of ecosystems until it reaches salt water. If he had stood in the waterway he could not have felt the movement of the current, yet it moved much faster than most of the rest of the Glades, which like a great inland sea keeps an almost tidal rhythm that stretches the expanse of the state.

Fish and frogs gathered in the reliable water supply, and flocks of birds followed: herons and egrets stalking with long-legged elegance among the scattered rushes and floating water-plants, coots and gallinules with wide-spread toes, poking their short beaks fretfully through the mud near the banks. In other seasons there would be roseate spoonbills and ibis, both the white and the scarlet, and occasionally a non-native escapee flamingo. On some mornings the water was strewn with a cloud of pink or white feathers, and on those days the replete alligator would bask in the sun, his hunting over for a time.

A female coot greeted him with its queer cry before scuttling to the far bank, where, with a rather haughty manner, it ignored him. Edgar stood on the bank with his arms folded, surveying the scene. He found no snakes (there was a hognose snake quite near, but being good-natured it didn't make its presence known with its puff-headed threat display) but he did spot the bull alligator floating with eyes and nostrils visible near the far bank, and Edgar was very proud that all he did was take a few scuttling steps backward.

All in all, he thought he was handling the wilderness in a serene and manly way, tramping through the woods without squeamishness. (He still felt inclined to avoid mud. It takes weeks to reach that stage where one walks through ankle-deep ooze without pause.) To put off making a decision he took up a stick and poked around the water's edge, stirring up creatures that spiraled with indignation at the disturbance. He was lost, or almost lost. He knew where he was, but not how to get back, and soon he'd have to prove it by trying. But not yet.

He headed right, like Lucy had told him, and before long came to a patch of churned ground he could have sworn was the work of a small dozer. The earth was broken up against a rise near the bank, rooted and furrowed, and dotted with sharp little cloven indentations. The broken line, some dozen feet long, was like a great rent in the skin of the earth, exposing, within the torn loamy flesh, arteries of mangled roots, clots of pebbles and the less-edible bits of grubs. Edgar got down on his haunches for a closer look and smelled something deep and rank, like old heavy sweat, along with a less definable odor that made his nose tingle and itch.

Just then he heard a sound, one that startled him to full attention. It was close, the sound of something large moving through bushes. He stood, cautiously with a wavering balance, and peered over the rise into the brush. The sound came again, like something quite heavy ponderously rubbing itself against bark, but as yet Edgar could see nothing. He retreated, realizing too late this brought him to the water and cut off escape.

His first thought was that it must be a person, and after his initial wariness almost charged forward to confront them directly. For weeks, other people had been the danger, the enemy.

The sound grew louder and nearer, and he heard a low rumbling grunt. He saw movement in the brush, but could make out no form. Then, shadow made flesh, out stepped a giant shaggy body, a long snuffling snout and a clever little eye, and just below both, a curl of ivory tusk. It took him a breath to realize it was a pig. Pigs are supposed to be pink and indolent, knowing their lot in life as hams or breeders of more ham. This was a wild boar, a feral descendent of pigs that escaped from the first Spanish settlers, which through the generations added bulk from genetic donations of more recent escapees. They are by far the fiercest things in the swamps, their tusks razor sharp, placed just right to rip out the belly of a panther or open the groin of a man.

Nearsighted and impetuous, it gave a sneezing snort and charged as soon as it saw Edgar. He hurled himself backward into the water and the razorback gouged viciously at the mud and froth. Thinking she'd done the job, she left him there and fled on her dainty trotters.

He lay stunned, almost more terrified in the aftermath than he'd been in the attack. He'd been helpless. He was still helpless. If that thing came back determined to kill him, it could. Or the alligator. Or a bear, or a snake, or any one of a hundred things in this treacherous land.

"I have to get out of here," he said aloud, pulling himself out of the muck. "I don't belong in this place." But then there was Lucy.

Would she come with him? He didn't even know where he was going, other than out of the country, to Central or South America, most likely, wherever his buddy could manage. It didn't matter, as long as it wasn't this deceitful place. It had lulled him with its beauty, its temporary serenity, then exploded in a rage of slathering boar tushes. Facing down an opponent with a gun only steeled his nerves; having that hulking, drooping-dugged she-beast on top of him, slashing with her primitive daggers, weakened him to the very core. He could handle his own kind of danger, but not this... not this!

Chapter 17

His way suddenly clear, he ran. In ten minutes he was at the stairs and climbed heavily up, only to find the house deserted. He went out again and circled the deck, looking into the noon-lit woods. He thought he saw movement, and went toward it, down the stairs again and through the woods.

He heard singing, at least, he thought it was singing, though it sounded like a melodic conversational chant, the words unclear. Lucy's voice, undoubtedly. He hesitated. There was something holy about the song, something that told him it shouldn't be interrupted.

It was Lucy Brightwing's death-song.

She sang of the ice crossing, fifteen thousand years ago, that lingered in her people's history like fragments of a dream. She sang of the great beasts that ranged Florida in the last Ice Age, the bellow of the mammoth, shaking the earth, the bone-breaking hug of the giant ground sloth. Her voice crescendoed and fell as she sang of the rise and fall of the Tequesta, from days skimming bright waters of the Keys harpooning Caribbean monk seals to nights in the depth of the swamps, covered with mud to ward off mosquitoes. In her mind a chorus sang with her, first thousands of voices, then hundreds, until only her mother and brother sang with her. Then it was just her own voice, the last, a voice which at any moment might be silenced by a little more pressure from the razor that already cut into her throat.

It was a song of acceptance, but not of defeat. Blood was streaming down her breast. The cut was shallow so far, the blade so sharp it would close again quickly, but only a centimeter, a flick of the wrist, stood between her and the end.

"I will kill you if I can, swiftly like a beast," she chanted to Mallory in her own tongue. "And if I cannot, I call upon the gods to witness this oath: my home will swallow you. If you kill me, your bones will be scattered in this land, and in the next world my spirit will torment you with sky-fire and burning peat, with poison and loneliness."

Her voice gained strength even as the cold razor pressed closer, and something else, hot and hard, pressed against her elsewhere.

Edgar almost went away before he could see her, then he heard his brother's voice above the singing, a laugh, a sound of satisfaction. He eased his way through the trees.

His first instinct was to leave, as quietly as he had come. She was standing, almost, leaning forward against a peculiar pile of wood, with Mallory tight against her. The first thing he thought, with a flush on his cheeks, was the phrase *beast with two backs*. He'd never been able to illustrate that expression, but now it was clear. Mallory, trousers bunched below his knees, moved against her in a slow rhythm, first upward with delicious friction along the deep crevice of her buttocks, then shifting slightly to slick himself between her legs. One hand was sunk in her hair, the other apparently caressing her neck.

And Lucy was singing, with a half-smile on her face. She was willing.

Edgar felt nausea, and shame, and confusion, and could not look away. It's not possible, he thought. It made his stomach flutter with rising bile, but if it was true, if she really wanted Mallory... what could he do other than be a man, and a gentleman, and a brother, accept his own defeat and leave them to enjoy themselves?

This, all in the first second or two. Then Mallory pulled Lucy's head back to lick her throat, and Edgar saw the cascade of scarlet down Lucy's chest, an empurpled spread of fresh, swelling bruise stretching from her temple across her eye and cheek. The next moment Edgar launched himself across the clearing and barreled his brother to the ground.

Edgar had been in fights, had been angry, murderously angry, but never before had all reason left him, in its place a red rage. He tumbled Mallory halfway across the small clearing, scattering interlaced cypress knees in their wake. They rolled, and when Edgar was again on top he smashed his fist into his brother's face, remembering when he felt his own knucklebones chip and grind why he never threw punches. He switched to elbows, and landed two more hard strikes against the side of Mallory's head before hauling his brother to his feet. Mallory was taller, but his feet dangled as Edgar held him up against a tree, his entire body now flaccid.

Mallory, dizzy and confused, hardly recognized his brother, and didn't know why he was acting in this unforeseen, painful way.

"Easy, bro," he stammered, plucking at the hands that clenched in his shirt like talons. "I was just…"

Edgar didn't want explanations. To ease his guilt, he wanted to inflict pain. Tightening his grip, he slammed his knee into Mallory's unprotected groin, then let him crumple in a whimpering heap.

Mallory still clutched the unfolded razor in his hand.

Only then did Edgar spare a glance for Lucy, who had raised her head and closed her legs, but still rested against the ossuary. Edgar didn't know if the violation had been complete, didn't know if that even mattered.

He left his brother long enough to run his hand over Lucy's throat. Cleaned, the cut was shallow, though it stretched halfway across her neck, and now barely oozed blood. Assured she would live to blame him, he left her and snatched up one of the fallen cypress knees. Before Mallory could curl his body into a protective fetal position Edgar was astride him.

"She was helping us, damn it!" he shouted, hoarse and broken. "She risked her life for us, and this is how you repay her? By rap-ing her?" He shook Mallory to emphasize the words, rattling his head against mahogany roots, and brandished the club-like knee in his face.

"You like to be threatened, huh? How does it feel to have someone on top of you?" Mallory tried to say something, but as he opened his mouth Edgar thrust the knee in, chipping his front tooth and hitting the back of his throat. "Shut up!" Mallory tried to squirm away; he was crying now, half naked and exposed and in terrible pain, but even more than that, utterly confused and frightened by the big brother who had for all his life been nothing but kind and forgiving and protective.

Edgar held him firmly, and pulled the knee away slightly, only to push it back sharply against Mallory's throat. "How does it feel, Mallory?" he growled. "How does it feel to have something sticking where you don't want it? How does it feel? How does it feel?" He pushed the wood again and again down his brother's throat, repeating that question incessantly, Mallory answering only with cringing and weak mewling cries.

Mallory was sure he was going to die. With the world gone topsy-turvy and his brother like a demon, he could feel himself about to lose consciousness, and after that, he was sure, would come death. He didn't clearly understand exactly what he'd done wrong, but he knew that everything he'd counted on for a lifetime had been shattered into a thousand pieces, coalescing into this furious man who was hurting him. His whole body throbbed with pain, each pulse sending radiating shocks through him. His vision grew fuzzy, and for the first time in his life he tried to tell his brother he was sorry, but the wooden gag choked off his words. The sky was pulsating, first in swimming darkness then in blinding light. He could hardly breathe, between the gag and the blood welling up from his broken nose.

Then, along the edge of his dimming vision, came a figure he'd seen before, an angel from some long-forgotten dream, with eyes dark as thunderclouds and an aureole of bright hair. The angel placed a hand on the raging demon's shoulder, and a voice like cool water said, "That's enough, Edgar. It's not his fault. He can't help it."

With that gentle hand she made Edgar rise, and the shaking,

the yelling, the choking wood in his throat were all mercifully gone, and he rolled to his side trying to remember how to breathe.

Edgar stood panting in the clearing, diamonds of sweat on his face, hands clenched in tight knots at his side. Gradually, the rage dissipated, flowing in eddying currents from the hard muscles of his arms, his tensed stomach, his strained nerves, replaced by a shocked emptiness. He would have killed his brother, the very thing Lucy had urged him to do, the thing he knew he should do... and then she stopped him.

She'd pulled her pants up and was methodically rearranging the charnel house's interlocking puzzle pieces. He watched her pick up a skull that had rolled free — nothing in this place amazed him anymore — kiss its ivory dome and put it back inside. She took the bloodied cypress knee he still clutched in his hand and slipped it into place.

Edgar fell to his knees at her feet, and looked up at her with worshipful, grieved eyes. Hesitantly he touched her face, first the uninjured side, then tenderly, gingerly, the dark swollen bruise from the butt of Mallory's gun. He held her face cradled in his hands, but he was the one who needed care and pity.

After a long silence, Edgar managed to ask, "Did he..." He could manage no more.

"No," she said, and gave him a wry little smile. "Not quite. You came just in time." He laid his head against her thighs and wept, for that hour, and for all the days since his escape. Lucy stroked his hair, and ran her hands over shoulders that heaved like quaking mountains.

"Forgive me," he said from the warmth of her legs.

"You didn't do anything," she said soothingly, but she had to fill her eyes with him, to blot out the image of his brother.

"You shouldn't be here. *We* shouldn't be here." He stood quickly. "We're going to leave, right now. We'll find our way out. Or you leave. Leave us here, and come back in a month and see what's left of us." More bones for the ossuary.

She shook her head.

"Damn it, I should have killed him! Whenever anything starts to go right, whenever I find... damn!"

"It doesn't matter. It's over now."

He looked at her, incredulous. "He was about to… to rape you. He might have killed you."

"He *would* have killed me, eventually, if you hadn't come. He did all the others, right?" Edgar nodded grimly. "He caught me off guard, but I was lucky. A scratch, a bruise, and you as my protector." She swayed on her feet. "I need to sit down."

They sat by her family's bones while Mallory moaned at the edge of the clearing.

"Why did you stop me?" he asked softly. "I would have killed him."

"And then?"

"Then?"

"It would have been my fault."

"What?"

"You'd have done it for me, in rage, not because you'd accepted it was the best thing to do, and you would have hated me afterward. Me, and yourself."

"I know what he is now. I've always known, but I never thought he would do that to you."

"How is it that you're both so innocent?" she asked him gently, taking his bloody hand.

"Innocent?"

"Mallory can't help what he does, the way he is. It's not a matter of will. He doesn't think, *what can I do to make someone's life unpleasant.* He's like a baby pulling wings off butterflies, not to be malicious, but because they're pretty, and he wants to at the moment, and he lacks the capacity to understand what it means to the butterfly to have its wings plucked off. There's something wrong with his brain. It's not his fault, it's not society's fault. It's just genetic bad luck."

"So you forgive him for what he tried to do to you, for what he's done to so many others?"

"It's not a matter of forgiveness. You know the story of the scorpion crossing the river, don't you? It's his nature, and you can't find fault with him for doing what he was born to do. You can abandon him, or kill him, or drop him off at the police station, but you can't be surprised, if you keep him around, that he'll do something like this. But I couldn't let you kill him. Later, when you're calm again, but not now. Oh Edgar," she said suddenly, her eyes growing heavy. "You're such a good man, and I bet you don't even know it." She sighed. "I don't think I'll have a problem with Mallory anymore."

"What makes you think that?"

"My mother told me."

Edgar looked incredulously toward the bones.

"I asked her for something, and she said if I want it, I can have it, only I'd be tested. I guess that was the test. Spirits don't usually work so fast, but when they have an instrument like Mallory handy..."

He didn't quite understand. "What is it you asked for?"

"Let's wait a while and see if I still want it," she said.

Mallory rolled himself partially upright and spit out a back tooth. A few yards away, Edgar had his head buried in Lucy's hips.

"Oh," Mallory said aloud, beginning, dimly, to understand. He felt, not that he had done wrong — he was not capable of that — but rather that he had been incorrect in something. Slowly, a new set of definitions settled into his mind. Before, there had been himself, and secondarily, his brother Edgar, the only real and true things in the world. The rest of the people had been like trees in the wood, distinguishable but impersonal, their felling of no moment beyond a thrilling violent crash.

It occurs to us all, at times, that we might be the only actual creatures in a world of fictions, that the rest of the people, perhaps the rest of the universe, exists only as a trope to keep our minds stimulated. It is a philosophical excursion we take, in our misanthropic or bitter (or extremely egoistic) moments, but most of us dismiss this thought, which amounts to absolute selfishness. With the single exception of his brother, though, Mallory had never given up that notion, had never even considered the possibility of it being otherwise. Other people didn't matter. If it amused him to hurt them, if it was convenient to kill them, he could do so with no qualms. Most cruel people know that they are cruel, take pleasure in it, or else they excuse it as being for a greater good. With Mallory, violence was a whim, without consequence.

The shocking beating he received at his brother's hands did little to change this mindset, except for one thing: it now occurred to him that perhaps Lucy was a real person too, and his world of two might be expanded to three. In that moment of his most extreme terror and pain, when he knew death was close by, she'd stretched out a hand and saved him. He frowned painfully. It was evident, now, that he had made a mistake somewhere along the line. Where, he could not be sure; things were still settling uneasily in his brain. But it turned out that Lucy was right. Her ordeal had been like a rite of passage, and she entered what amounted to a new state of immunity. She, like Edgar, was now real to Mallory, and he would no more attack her than he would shoot his brother or mutilate himself.

She came to him a while later.

"Are you too badly hurt to walk?" she asked.

He shook his head, which of course made everything hurt far worse. She looked at his face, the chipped tooth and the bloody hollow of the missing one, and felt along the outside of his throat for swelling. He gazed at her as he had that brief moment on the beach, and when she'd calmed Edgar's rage — as though she were a thing somewhat more than a woman.

"Can you stand? Come back to the house then. This thing is over. Right?"

He nodded, and like a child who was sent away as punishment, but brought back, in the end, because he is only a child, Mallory followed her back to the house.

Chapter 18

They ate—Lucy cut Mallory's food fine — and calmed in the homely ritual. Edgar still glowered, and couldn't see how Lucy could bear to be in the same room with either of them. He still planned to leave, if a guilty half-thought without action counts as a plan.

Mallory crawled into bed and Edgar passed the afternoon on the deck, staring, trying to think. Lucy absented herself to spend a few hours with her family.

As dusk softly approached the swamps, lengthening shadows by degrees, Lucy returned and spoke a word in Edgar's ear, and he followed her into the wood.

"I want you to see something," she said, leading him onward without turning. "My mother said I should. No one alive has seen it. I think you should. I want you to know about me." He trailed behind her tantalizing lure.

Lucy noticed with pleasure that his step was quieter, his gait freer than it had been the night before. His feet still balked at the uncertainly of rough natural earth, and he was loud enough to warn all creatures within a quarter-mile of his approach, but the improvements were apparent. Already, instincts buried deep in the twists of his DNA were beginning to surface, offering tentative clues about how his ancestors, not so many generations removed, walked on yielding carpets of earth through vaulted chambers of forests roofed in greenery.

She brought him to the bank where the dugout was tied. He almost knew the route now, recognizing certain trees, and a little ditch lined with pebbles. She pushed the boat out of the reeds and held it steady while he clambered in. He took pains not to get wet, still not realizing how futile that ambition is in the swamps. Lucy had no such squeamishness and stepped in the shallows to mid-calf, maneuvering the boat to a depth where it could float with their combined weight before pulling herself in. She knelt in the stern for a moment, finding the balance of the boat, then stood with admirable ease, her feet braced to shove off.

"Is it far?" he asked, but still didn't press her to name their destination. He knew she wanted it to be mysterious, and he liked the weighty sense of anticipation that was building, though it occurred to him, briefly, that it could turn out to be something unpleasant. He was still far from at ease in his surroundings, and had a nagging sense of impending... something. Doom, perhaps, though he confessed to himself that sounded too dramatic. Here in the woods, despite even the events of the morning, he still felt perpetually tempted to let his guard down, to relax and stop anticipating the future. But he knew with grim certainty that any moment something would happen, as it always did, to crush that incipient peace timidly trying to settle itself into his bones. However happy, however safe he might become deep in the woods, it was all bound to end, and in that case, why let it even begin? But he couldn't help himself, and despite the lingering dread haunting him, he found himself again and again abandoning himself to pleasures of the moment.

Lucy was chief among those pleasures. He sat facing the front of the boat, looking away from her, but he was as acutely aware of her presence behind him, of her movements and postures, as if he was watching her. From time to time he would turn, when he asked her a question about some animal or plant they passed, but it was almost better to simply know she was there, a reassuring certainty that didn't have to be constantly reconfirmed with sight.

He was also avoiding seeing the bruise his brother had inflicted, and that more disturbing crusty line of blood at her throat, trying, as she did, to dismiss the matter, at least superficially. The blow to her head wasn't nearly as bad as he'd feared. After her self-treatment with some unknown poultice the swelling had gone quickly down, and she assured him she had no concussion.

He still didn't know whether to leave. Going back to civilization right now, with his image so fresh in everyone's mind, would be suicide. As for the swamp itself, he was still torn, at times hating it, fearing it, other times getting lost in its apparently serene beauty. It would certainly be better for Lucy if they left, but she expressly told them to stay. Could she be right? Was Mallory no longer a threat to her? At one point, teetering on the edge of sanity, he wondered what Miss Manners would recommend. What is the proper thing to do when your brother has just tried to rape your host?

They had gone their separate ways all afternoon, and as dusk approached they'd reached an accord of forgiveness and acceptance. Edgar was beginning to see (though not understand) that the things that mattered in the real world were of little significance here in the wilderness. He felt bound in a spell, in a suspended state just outside of reality. It was torment to know he'd eventually have to rejoin that outside world of cars and cities and police and guns, but at least there he knew what was real, what he should feel.

Now Lucy pushed him along the waterway as darkness closed snugly around them. Edgar's eyes adjusted more quickly to the change, and it didn't seem so frightening this time, exchanging the security of walls for a boundless darkness where unseen things crept with hushed skitterings. He no longer started at every sudden owl cry, and he could bear unflinchingly the bombardment of insects which, though they didn't bite, seemed to positively enjoy bumping into him. A large pale moth beat her dusty wings against his face for a moment, and he closed his eyes, smiling, suffering her fleeting caress.

"Look up," Lucy said.

Overhead, in the narrow break of trees through which peeked milky glimpses of starry sky, Edgar saw a living arc bridge the space between boughs. It took him a while to realize that the undulating line, several yards thick, was not one draconic creature but countless thousands of small beasts that fly as fish swim, in a responsive school of twisting defense, each member looping and maneuvering to secure a safe inside place, only to be ousted by the next jostling body. The bats kept coming in a stream for as long as he could see them, until the canoe passed a bend in the waterway. He couldn't imagine such numbers, masses like a biblical plague swarming over the forest.

"What do they eat?" he asked.

"Moths, mosquitoes. There's plenty to go around. In a little while they'll spread out to hunt, but when they first emerge in the half-light they're the prey. Owls take them, and the hawks stay up late just for a mouthful. The late hawk gets the bat, as the old Tequesta saying goes. There's one!" she said, and Edgar saw a dark wedge dive through the swarm, carving a hole that reformed itself seamlessly an instant later.

"There's never too many of anything out here," she told him. "Everything eats, everything gets eaten. If there were too many bats they couldn't find enough to eat, and some would starve. Or their cave would get too crowded, and a disease would spread through their ranks. Everything works out well in the end, if you leave it alone."

Before he even knew they were close to land he felt the boat ground with a little bump. Lucy thrust the bow high onto the flat muddy bank. He scrambled out and she tied off the boat before taking his hand in a way that was gratifyingly natural. It implied not so much affection as responsibility, for away from the water's break in the canopy the night grew suddenly closer and Edgar felt that instinctive urge to be near another of his kind, a little protective swarm of two. He ran his thumb over her knuckles, rising and sinking with their warm topography. She led him silently away from the water, deeper into blackness.

In the night, in the loud quietude of droning insects, the way seemed endless, though it was only a few minutes later that Lucy slowed and said in hushed undertones, "We're almost there." Until that moment he hadn't given much thought to what she would show him. Now his imagination inexplicably got the better of him, and though he could not seem to settle on any single possibility his mind reeled in a nightmarish swirl of things lurking just out of sight. He squeezed her hand. She wouldn't be leading him into danger, would she? She knew these swamps, these woods, and though there might be plenty to fear out here he thought he was safe as long as she was at his side. But what if — suspicion countered reason — she sought revenge for this morning. What if she was leading him into some terrible place, a pit of snakes, or quicksand, or... He shook his head to scatter the thoughts, trying to laugh at his fears, but it was not until he looked down on the sleek part of her bright hair, and a second later at her upturned face that seemed to glow with its own light, that his last suspicions fled.

"Right there," she said, her breath warm against his shoulder. "You can just see it through the trees."

He looked, and at first saw nothing more than the shadows that danced in varying patterns of dark and darker. Then, at the corner of his perception he thought he saw a flash, gone too soon for him to focus. He dismissed it as a trick of the eye until another came in front of him, a few feet away. This time, sure he'd seen something tangible and real, he squinted and took a few steps forward, striking off on his own as Lucy hung back, letting him discover for himself.

It was brighter ahead. He thought it must be a clearing that let the moon's glow through the canopy. A few steps more and he stopped. The light, low and dispersed, flickered. It must be a fire, he thought now, and felt another twinge of uncertainty. Were there people here? Was it a trap? But he squared his shoulders and went on, trusting her, trusting himself to handle whatever awaited.

With Lucy now far behind he parted the last cluster of branches that separated him from the glow, and with a sharp intake of breath that expired in a sigh he witnessed the mystical sight that no one alive, save Lucy, had ever witnessed.

In a clearing ringed by an inward-folding circle of trees rose a great earthen mound bathed in a pale yellow-green glow. Around the mound in a flickering aura floated moving spots of light that winked on and off, a glittering of fairy-dust sprinkled over a domed fairy castle. He stood, dumfounded, by what was probably the most beautiful, outlandish sight he'd ever seen in his life, and it was not until one of the specks of light landed on his forearm that he realized they were fireflies.

They gathered in a profusion that rivaled the swarm of bats, to meet and copulate on this hill. On the ground, females flashed a pattern known only to their species, and above them males responded in kind, and somehow chose the perfect mate (or a dozen of them) from among the incandescent nubiles.

Edgar knelt, whether to keep from disturbing the phenomenon or in innate reverence for beauty and mystery, he didn't know.

"This is the only place in Florida, probably the only place in the world, where fireflies gather in such density in such a small space." Lucy crept up behind him on silent cat paws. "The species will only mate on this mound. I don't know how far away they come from, but for two or three weeks in late spring they gather here, the females on the ground, the males flying."

"Why only here?" he asked, not pulling his eyes away from the glowing hill. It looked like a space craft about to take flight under the power of a million tiny wings.

"I don't know, at least, not for sure. I asked a few entomologists, without giving them all the details, and they suggested it might just be because in the swamps they seek out the highest ground. But my house is at least as high as this, and there are mounds on other hammocks. I didn't tell them this is a Tequesta burial mound."

"Someone's buried in there?"

"Yes, someone, more or less. More *more* than *less.*" She chuckled. "But not a person."

"What then?"

Another long hesitation, wondering how it would sound to say it, what can of worms it would open. People who knew her, any Indians, really, accepted gods and spirits and talking to dead ancestors, but she was a little leery of telling Edgar, a thorough outsider. At last she said, "A god."

He didn't smile, and that encouraged her to continue. "That's what they say, at least."

"Who're they?"

"Well, my mother mostly. She's the one who preserved the knowledge. But the Seminole and Miccosukee elders know some of it. What they're allowed to know. Edgar, I need to tell you

about myself. About my people. I think… maybe you'll understand why I'm helping you, after you hear it."

"I'd like that."

"Are you comfortable? It's a long story. Fifteen thousand years
long."

Chapter 19

Lucy took a breath and uttered a silent prayer to everything around her. It was a sacred story, one she rarely told it in English. She'd grown accustomed to her role, and most of the people in her life already knew her history. She accepted their respect, the measure of awe with which they regarded her, but she'd never been comfortable telling the tale from the beginning. She sometimes spoke to historians and ethnologists eager for her story, but it always made her feel awkward. When she told outsiders, she felt that she was either bragging — a princess of a lost empire — or lying. Then too there were details she could never tell an outsider, and other things, deeper things, that only a child of her own blood could ever hear from her lips. If she ever had a child of her own blood.

She moved nearer the golden glowing mound and settled herself down on the earth, will-of-the-wisps so bright they robbed her of her night vision, cutting off the world outside the circle with a solid wall of light. She beckoned to Edgar, who had a vague feeling he shouldn't approach the spectacle too closely, and he sat beside her, facing the mound in its splendor but listening to Lucy.

"I'm going to tell you a story," she said, her voice taking on the otherworldly atonality he'd heard before. "A story that begins many thousands of years ago. We will say fifteen thousand, though properly speaking, the story goes back to the beginning of time. But that would take too long to tell, wouldn't it?" She broke out of her chant to look at Edgar with a little giggle, but when she stared again at the mass of fireflies she soon fell back into her trance-like state.

She told how the glaciers ate up land and water, how her ancestors crossed into Siberia and Beringia to follow herds of bison and mammoth.

Dazed by the light, Edgar fell into her story, seeing her ancestors, one with Lucy's own face, trailing behind a herd of shaggy behemoths.

"Some reached Florida and could go no further, though indeed my people traveled in sea kayaks as far as Cuba. You would not recognize that Florida. There were extravagant beasts: mammoths and mastodon, horses, camels, great bison with horns six feet across, ground sloths standing twenty feet tall, giant tortoises, armadillos the size of a Volkswagen. And preying on them, sabre-toothed cats, dire wolves, the bone-crushing hyena, the American lion, bigger than any lion alive today. And eating, and being eaten by, all of these were humans.

"The stories that come before this time are shadows, dreams, my mother calls them, real and not real." He noticed Lucy spoke of her mother in present tense. Death had hovered so close to Edgar for so long the line didn't seem as sharply drawn as it once had, and her way seemed almost natural to him now.

She spoke of her ancestor, Kaya-Ka-Hichi, who bargained with beasts to learn the arts of agriculture, and when even that wasn't enough to feed her people, tricked a deer-god into showing her the way to the vast fertile sea, eating bits of him along the way until he was a tiny Key deer. There, her people lived in a bountiful paradise for many generations.

"The women in your stories are braver than the men," Edgar said.

"Maybe those are just the stories I remember best. She nuzzled his shoulder with her cheek and shooed a firefly that landed on her nose.

"This happiness lasted a long time, but it could not last forever." There was a change in her voice, a harsh note of lamentation and suppressed bitterness. "The Tequesta built a great civilization, creating a world that rivaled the Maya, the Egyptians, in complexity. They understood astronomy, the solar and lunar years, and could predict eclipses and celestial alignments. They had a religion that sought to explain other mysteries, and they came far closer to the truth, even thousands of years ago, than the Spanish had when they arrived in the new world.

"It would be wrong to think too badly of the Spanish, for they were no more fools than most men. They wanted gold, and later wanted land, and set about getting what they lacked, just as a Tequesta would seek to get a fish if he was hungry. Men don't always know what they should hunger for. They killed many of the Tequesta, there's no denying that, but then again the Tequesta killed many Spaniards, for though the invaders had guns, a musket at that time was a clumsy thing indeed, and a Tequesta arrow or at-latl-hurled spear could pierce armor as easily as an English longbow. If it had only been a matter of outright war, the Tequesta might still rule this land. The indigenous people might still hold dominion over all of the Americas.

"The Spanish brought with them little viral diamonds of DNA so eager to reproduce themselves at any cost: smallpox, influenza and a host of other lesser ailments that nevertheless were enough to kill those who had no immunity. The only thing we in the Americas could give them was syphilis. We died… "

Edgar shuddered at the pronoun.

"We died by the thousands, by the hundreds of thousands, even Tequesta who never laid eyes on a Spaniard. Villages were laid to waste by the sicknesses. At times, the disease would come so quickly an entire village would perish in the course of a day, and by night the hearth fires would all still be burning, untended, in a city of ghosts.

"Illness and death spread far faster than Spanish swords or muskets ever could. The terrible part, the part that is the Europeans' only salvation, is that even if they'd come with the noblest intentions, in true peace and brotherly love, they would have killed the Indians just as surely. Florida was hit particularly hard, and within a decade few were left to make war, or to be converted into good pious Christians, or sent for slaves to the Indies."

Lucy Brightwing lowered her eyes. It still pained her, though she felt a little foolish for being bothered by something that happened centuries ago, a thing that's part of the natural, if harsh, course of evolution and migration. She felt no malice toward anyone for the events of the past, and harbored no resentment of whites today. Of course, she was half-white herself, and lived a life of privilege, bridging the barriers of both status and blood. But though she was well-adjusted in this modern world, she could not suppress the poignant sadness that crept over her, tightening her throat and bowing her head, whenever she dwelt too long on the history and demise of her people.

Light from the fireflies settled restlessly on the curve of her lowered cheek, and Edgar asked her softly, "You said the Indians of Florida are gone, but you are Tequesta, and you're still here. And the Seminoles."

"The Seminoles and the Miccosukee are newcomers," she said. "Guests on this land. Yes, I am Tequesta, and I'm still here. When the sickness began to spread, the wisest shaman knew something must be done. He gathered up such Tequesta as had not fallen ill and led them deep into the swamps. The Tequesta knew the Everglades, though they preferred the seashore where life is easy, the mosquitoes scarce. But they were sure the Spanish, or the English who followed them, wouldn't venture into the interior when there was such choice land near the coasts. And so a band of some hundred Tequesta, women, men, and babes at the breast, retreated, and... disappeared.

"Perhaps they would have been safe even without magic, but the shaman wanted to be certain. This great magician gathered up all his considerable power and cast a spell over the swamplands, so that no one should see the Tequesta again until they willed it. With his lifeforce he spread the magical protection across the land, from the Okeechobee south almost to the ocean's edge, and when his work was done and he was drained to a husk he settled himself upon the ground and died, content that his people were well protected.

"And so while all the other Indians in Florida perished, this little pocket of one hundred souls survived, unseen, for some three hundred years. Survived, but not thrived. There was less to eat in the swamps, and more disease, not the Spaniards' disease, but simply those fevers and grippes common where there is standing water and mosquitoes. Then too, they were naturally disheartened, knowing that all of their brothers, and mothers, and friends were gone forever. For centuries they lived as if in a dream of their past life. Their population grew a bit at first, but soon declined. Fewer babies were born, and it was harder to obey the strict incest taboos that generally kept even distant cousins from mating." She bit her lip. "My mother violated that, and made my brother."

"But they maintained the old traditions, keeping relics of past glories: carved figures of gods, metal plated headdresses and moldering capes of cormorant feathers, which they replaced, when they had to, with anhinga plumes. They still sculpted, still made fine weapons for hunting, and most of all, they kept their old stories and songs alive. They knew their culture was dying, and did what they could to preserve it, like a man with a wasting illness who must nonetheless complete his memoirs. Every night each surviving member sang the songs of his lineage, taking their bloodline back as far as they could remember. The song of my family goes back seventeen generations before the landing of the Spaniards. It takes three hours to sing it properly.

"After they had lived so many years in hiding, not knowing the Spanish had abandoned the state and English now ruled the land, which had become its own sovereign country, the Tequesta were surprised to find a troop of men, foreign, but not as unlike themselves as the Spanish had been, approaching their village.

"'Help us,' the men begged. 'We are Creek, and we have traveled hundreds of miles to escape death. We thought to hide in the swamps, but we cannot find food here. It is nothing like the home we knew, and we will die here as surely as we would in war. Help us, and we will be your loyal friends and serve you always.' Though they were proud, they were desperate. The new Americans were trying to relocate them to a reservation far to the north and west, to a rocky barren land they did not care to see, and they fled with their wives and children, who still lingered a day's march behind.

"The Tequesta held a council, and decided the spell had broken itself. They'd been found, so it must be their duty to help these fugitives. They bound the Creek with strange and terrible oaths, oaths so sacred that to even think them would make you tremble, and the Tequesta opened their homes. They taught them to find fish in the swamps, which are far more elusive than fish of the oceans and clear rippling streams. They taught them what plants to eat, what to use as medicine, how to keep the mosquitoes away with smudge fires, how to walk, even in mud, without leaving a trail. They lived beside them... and yet they rarely intermarried. The Tequesta remained a people apart, almost as gods. And indeed they were, for it was only through their generosity and good will that those Creek, and many bands who followed them, and black slaves too, found a congenial home in the deep swamps of the Everglades.

"They came to be called the Seminoles, a corruption of the word *cimarron*, or renegade. When all of the other tribes were sent to reservations, or fled across the snowy border to the Canadian woodlands, only a few Seminole tribes managed to avoid that fate, both by fighting, and by staying hidden in the Everglades. They are the only Indians who never surrendered to the white man. All thanks to the Tequesta.

"The Seminoles, and the Miccosukee, who came later and were bound by the same oaths, never forgot their debt to my people. They protect us, revere us. For many years no one outside of the tribes knew about the existence of the handful of Tequesta. Wary of white men, mindful of the past, they felt it safer to remain in honored seclusion until well into the twentieth century. In 1900, there were just eighteen Tequesta left. At the half-century mark, only my grandmother and two others. The rest had died, or run off, yielding to the temptations of modern life. Now they and their descendants probably live in some southwestern slum, and don't even know what ancient blood runs in their veins.

"But my grandmother was a descendent of the singers of songs, and she, more than any, had preserved the knowledge of the Tequesta. In her youth there were only two men left to choose from, two full Tequesta. One was too close kin, and the other she despised. And so against the wishes of the council she chose a young man who had been fathered by an old Tequesta, now dead, on a Seminole girl. Her children would not be all Tequesta, but it was the best she could do. She knew there was no way to save her people. With only three left, and one woman, the line was as good as severed. The only hope was to keep the words alive, the ancient language, the songs, the knowledge.

"She only had one child, my mother, Two Moons, but she taught her well, both of the ancient world and the modern. She knew that in this day no one can exist in isolation, and she took my mother travelling, let her be educated, but also taught her the song of our family, and all of the stories she knew. The Seminole and Miccosukee elders shook their heads in despair, thinking all their work at helping to repay their debt to the Tequesta was coming to nothing. The man my grandmother didn't like died in a brawl with a young Seminole (who was exiled for the crime) and the other, who was too close kin, left a half-Miccosukee child behind. My grandmother and mother were not heard of for many years, and the Elders had given up on the Tequesta.

"Then one day there came to the reservation a woman in a smart Chanel suit, carrying a child in her arms. It was my mother, the child none other than me."

Edgar tried to picture that child, bright brown pigtails, those impossible black eyes innocent.

"They welcomed her coldly, like a traitor. They thought she'd abandoned the old Tequesta teachings. But then, as she nursed me, she sat on the earth and began to sing the story of our family, stretching back so many generations. Oh, I can still hear my mother's sweet voice!" Lucy's breath caught. "I hardly remember her speaking when I was a child. She always sang, chanting old tales, lulling me to sleep with stories of my past. They saw that she had in her all of her mother's knowledge, all that was left of the Tequesta, and she intended to pass it on to me. They held a great festival of welcome, and set her up almost as a queen. She passed her lore to me, and parts of it, not the deepest secrets, to a select few Indians and even outsiders. I was the only one who ever learned the full language of the Tequesta. My mother began to write our history, too, in the old Tequesta tongue, and I will finish her work.

"And so, I was raised in the Everglades, but by a thoroughly modern mother, one who happened to hold in her mind and in her heart all that was Tequesta. She wanted to strengthen the Tequesta blood, and found the son of her mother's kin, the half-Miccosukee. She had Cub, two years younger than me. We learned to hunt and stalk, to knap a spear or arrow point from stone we harvested with our own hands. We went to the sea, and recreated the ways of my more distant ancestors, fashioning traps with reeds, spearing fish and squid from our canoes by moonlight. She showed us where all of our mounds are, the shell middens and the great earthworks where chiefs and magicians are buried. We learned to live unclothed in the wood. And I also went to college, and lived in cities and watched television, and did so much of what every child, every young woman, does. But I also held within me everything that remains of my people.

"When I was sixteen…" She swallowed hard. "Well, you know that much. Cub took me off guard, like Mallory did, and started to carve me up with the best intentions. Then it was just me."

Distance and time blurred for Edgar. Thousands of years, told by Lucy, seemed to encompass but a moment, and yet these few seconds since she had fallen silent seemed an eternity. Likewise space, the hair's breadth separating them seemed an expanse as great as a canyon, and he longed to press her, hold her, get as close to merging with her as he could, the only way he knew how.

"It must be a burden," he said at last, when the silence grew too much for him to bear.

She looked up at him, surprised. Most people didn't understand. They only thought of the honor, the prestige, the superiority of knowing what no other person on earth could know. They didn't think of the responsibility involved, the overwhelming weight of so many pairs of eyes looking at you in a regretful sort of wonder.

"It is," she said. "I'd rather be almost anything than a symbol. That's what it means to be the last Tequesta. I'm everything that is lost, the iniquities of the conquerors. Like that last sad Carolina parakeet that once hopped around in a zoo, waiting to die, I'm the belated realization that through carelessness or ignorance, good things come to an end. Do you know, I need only ask a thing of any Seminole or Miccosukee, and it will be done. No matter what it is. They've honored their obligation well."

The night pressed closer around them. "The fireflies are almost finished," she said. "They don't stay in love for long."

"I never did finish my story, did I?" she said a moment later. "I was trying to tell you about the firefly mound, and I wound up giving you the history of the world. My world.

"This land is officially part of the Miccosukee reservation, but no one would dare set foot on it. It was sacred land even when the Tequesta still lived on the coast, before the coming of the Spaniards. Here, the shamans and magicians conducted their most secret rituals.

"There was a god who came to earth in the shape of a man. He lived among the Tequesta, taught them many things about the worlds beyond what mortals can see, and in that time he fell in love with a Tequesta maid. Their love is one of the great stories of my people. We have so many songs about them that it would take a whole night of singing, from dusk 'til dawn, to give voice to them all. Whenever they looked upon each other, their faces shone like stars. Their radiant love lasted many years, and together they had children who bore the blood of gods in their veins.

"One day a blight came upon the land. The sun shrank behind clouds, and the new seedlings withered in the earth. Neither prayers nor the magic of mortals were of any avail, and at last, when the people were starving, the earth dying, the god who walked among them knew the time had come to sacrifice himself so the land might live.

"The Christians think it such an exceptional thing that a god should lay down his life for the good of humans, but among the Tequesta it is always the gods who make the greatest sacrifices. Many gods have shed their divine blood for the land; Florida is full of gods' tombs.

"He told the shaman, he told the elders, and last, because it pained him, he told his wife. She did not weep, only looked at him with an unimaginable sadness welling up inside her, which she somehow contained, though it was like a great pressure against her breast as it struggled to escape. She followed him to the mound he'd prepared with his magic, to attend him in his final moments, and still she did not weep.

"His wife handed him a stone knife and he cut out his heart with great solemnity. Still she did not weep. One would think, to see her dry cheeks, that she did not even know him, that she hated him, for who could see anyone in such great pain without weeping? (For though he was a god, and though he killed himself without flinching, even a god feels pain.) Holding his heart, still beating, in his hands, he descended into the bowels of the mound, and when he had interred himself, crushed his heart between his palms, and died.

"His wife stared unblinking at the mound where her love lay dead, holding in her tears, trying to tell herself she could not mourn that he performed his duty so bravely, that he saved the land, saved her people. The grief built inside her, searching for an outlet, and she would allow it none. Such sadness, such tears and such love cannot be contained for long, and the pressure against her breast grew until at nightfall her body exploded into a thousand shimmering, radiant pieces, each one so full of emotion that it would glow forever. From her body the fireflies were born, and when they feel the tug of love they flock to this site, searching out the god, gathering in a fruitless effort to rejoin their many parts into one."

"Do any Tequesta love stories end happily?" Edgar asked.

"Of course," she replied. "But those ones aren't worth telling. Happiness doesn't make for good stories."

"Well," she asked a while later. "Do you believe my story?"

"I like your explanation better than any a scientist could come up with," Edgar said.

"But do you believe it?" she challenged.

He shrugged. "What does it matter if it's true? It's prettier than any story about magnetism, or geothermal activity under the mound. Why can't a firefly be a bundle of love and sadness? But Lu, tell me... why did you show me this? Why let me in on your secret?" He looked at her almost playfully, clearly fishing for words of fondness. Because I like you, he thought she'd say, at least, and he hoped she'd look just a little bit shy when she said it.

But she only looked away with a frown between her brows. She sighed, and the cool air seemed suddenly weighty around him. All at once he knew why she felt so free to show him what no one else had been permitted to see, why she could speak so freely about her people's past, tell him stories of long-forgotten secrets. He knew it. He'd felt his doom all along, but always managed to forget it. He didn't know Lucy knew too. Once she knew, it was real.

"It doesn't hurt to tell your secrets to a dead man," he said, with a bitterness that surprised him. "It's like a deathbed confession, isn't it? But the other way around. You feel safe telling me anything because you know I won't be alive long enough to pass it on. That's it, right?"

He stood, though he legs were numb from sitting cross-legged, and stalked stiffly away. He was angry she'd allowed the outside world to crash into his treasured preserve of peace, and more than that, frightened that her own thoughts confirmed what he'd hoped were only his own paranoid fears. He looked back at her, desperate for her to deny it, to tell him he was being foolish, that he wasn't going to die, but in the moonlight that gradually replaced the fireflies' glow he could read a countenance clouded with compassion. He clenched his teeth, thinking that he would scorn her pity... but when she went to him he waited, and when she reached her hand up to him he bent his cheek to meet it.

"I didn't show you these things because you're going to die," she said gently. But she didn't say he wasn't going to die, he noticed, and he took a deep breath to help stifle whatever unmanly emotions threatened to surface.

Tell me what to do, she pleaded with her ancestors. You told me I can have him, but I asked the wrong question, I know that now. Should I help him? Really help him, all the way. There's a world of difference between hiding him out here for two weeks, dallying and dabbling for my own fun, then turning him loose, and committing myself to him, my life to his life.

She thought about animals she'd rescued, always against her mother's sage advice. When she tended them unseen, setting their bones in darkness, feeding them through a hole, she could release them without consequence. They still hated and feared her, they stayed wild. They belonged to themselves. But those few times she'd nursed them with love it was always bliss ending in disaster. There was the storm-blown baby squirrel who never left her side for five years, chewing up all her clothes and soiling her bed in its passionate loyalty to her. The bobcat cub she tended after his mother was hit by a car was himself run over when he stalked his beloved Lucy through a parking lot. The half-dozen rescued deer, released but unafraid, fattened on her corn, were picked off by hunters amazed at their luck.

I can do my duty, keep him until he has a chance, and turn him loose. We will go our own ways, and never think of each other again.

Or I can own him, and he will own me. He'll be my responsibility then, and it will end badly. It will end badly either way, but if he's mine, I'll know about it. At best, I get him out of the country and never see him again.

Then there's Mallory.

She didn't want to be responsible for him, but knew it was a package deal.

Give me a sign, she asked, holding Egdar's face in her hands. He was warm and alive, though she could see the death-specter hanging over his head.

A firefly lit on Edgar's shoulder. He started to shoo it away but she caught his hand. It was a female, late to the game, flashing her tail for whatever dregs of males were left. One tried to settle on her, but she flicked her shell-covered wings and sent him toppling. Another landed next to her, and this one she accepted, though he had to clamber over her awkwardly before they were joined.

"Two Moons always said signs don't tell you what to do, they just shove in your face what you already planned to do anyway."

He looked at her quizzically.

"Just thinking about something. Listen, I'm too tired tonight, but tomorrow let's talk about your plans. I might be able to help." She was doing rapid mental calculations. Two million for Lazarus Nighteyes, for the gift of her swamp acres. Nearly another million to assorted bureaucrats as high as a senator to sneak her reservation grant on the coattails of a bipartisan environmental bill that would pass quickly and easily. She'd planned on using that last million for infrastructure. She didn't want anything to spoil the pristine woods and waters, but it would be handy to at least have a gravel road, maybe power lines.

Whatever Edgar had planned for his own escape, it couldn't be enough. Lucy knew it takes money to circumvent the law, probably half a million at least to set the brothers up with airtight documents, new identities, and a trip to a third-world country. Cash in their pockets wouldn't hurt either.

Oh well, the electricity could wait. She could always pull another job for Billie.

"You've helped so much already," Edgar said.

He pulled her closer, the length of his body warm against her, and she wanted to push him down on that grave of joy and slake her compassion with some good old honest fornication. But she really was tired, and there was plenty of time.

It was past midnight when at last they mounted the stairs and found Mallory lying on his stomach in bed, fiddling with Lucy's world band radio. "Good news, bro," he said, grinning at the pair. "I've been listening an hour and I haven't heard a word about us."

"Yeah?" Edgar said without much interest. "That's great." And he went into the bathroom to shower.

"Of course, I didn't tell him the only stations I could get were in Spanish," he added with a wink to Lucy.

"So what did you two get up to all that time?" Mallory asked, rolling to his side.

"Oh," she said lightly, "We went to see some fireflies."

"Is that what you kids are calling it these days? Hey Edgar!" he shouted over the running water. "What was that crazy song mom used to sing about fireflies? I can only remember a little bit of it. Something about an aeronautical boll weevil in the woods primeval."

He serenaded Lucy, humming the parts he couldn't remember.

Edgar came out, scrubbed clean, in a pair of dark blue clinging sweats.

"You think of the damndest things," he said, sitting next to his brother. "Does that hurt?" he asked softly, touching Mallory's nose, now slightly askew.

"Hell yeah it does," Mallory said without animosity.

Even if he was staying, I could never touch that brotherly love, Lucy thought, and settled herself into her hard bed.

Chapter 20

Jimi Three Toes had been good and buzzed every time Lucy took him to her swamp, so he knew he'd have to poke around a while before something tickled his memory. It was adjacent to Big Cypress, he knew, and there was a turnoff somewhere… East or west on Alligator Alley?

"You don't have a clue where you're going," Sue said contemptuously from the back seat. She'd stayed there even after he offered her shotgun, perhaps thinking she'd be more comfortable, perhaps less difficult to extricate. Dolores sat up front.

He swung the car east, just to look decisive.

Jimi's lank hair hung to his shoulders, kept out of his eyes by a scruffy red beaded headband his mother made the year before her death from untreated diabetes. He rarely took the band off, and never deliberately washed it, though it sometimes got sluiced in a swim. He was under six feet, not by much, but that little lack had always been a sore point, and despite his best efforts at gluttony he was slightly built, an unkind person might even say skinny. The best he could manage was a little beer belly that pouted out from his abdomen, which made him feel, when he caught sight of his profile in the mirror, much older than he was. Funny, he spent his teen years desperately trying to be mistaken for someone older, and now that he was past thirty he did everything he could to seem younger. What ever became, he wondered, of those priceless years in his early twenties when he was exactly the age he wanted to be? He couldn't even remember anything he'd done back then. What a waste!

That doesn't matter, he told himself. Right now I'm etching my name into tribal history.

Jimi cruised on broad, nearly bald graying whitewalls. He never bothered with a macho speed kick. His Valiant, generally reliable, would complain past sixty. Traffic was light. Occasional citrus haulers passed him, leaving a sweet rotting smell in their wake, but he had plenty of leisure to slow at each turnoff and see if anything looked familiar.

"I knew it," Sue said.

"Go home if you don't like it."

"Bite me."

He looked at the tooth imprints on his arm where she'd bitten him a while ago, and decided he didn't like the odds.

They passed signs of traditional life mixed with modernity. The Everglades was popular with tourists; the tamer outskirts, that is, the civilized airboat and jeep tours, the air-conditioned hotels and questionable native guides who escort visitors along carefully manicured tracks of swamp, where mosquitoes are controlled with regular spraying and the alligators wake up from their naps on cue to yawn and show their blunted teeth.

Even in the heart of the glades, motorists were encouraged by signs scores of miles from their object presaging shops with 'authentic' arrowheads or a savory taste of gator flesh. Not many people stopped. Perhaps there was something a bit too ominously enclosing about the swamps. Or maybe the unconquered Seminoles pretending to be a tourist attraction seemed too much like a trap.

"Fagan's going to come after me, you know," Sue said after Jimi almost turned down a dirt road, then changed his mind. "I only came with you because I thought you knew the swamps. You built her house, didn't you?"

Lucy's home was supposed to be a secret, its location impossibly obscure, but since she was the most well-known Indian, though not a member of either tribe, everyone knew her business. Out of courtesy they pretended they didn't, and left her alone out there in the swamp to do whatever sacred things she did with the shades of her ancestors. Also, Lucy herself had spread the rumor that one unfortunate interloper got an arrow in his throat and a very temporary grave in an alligator wallow. (It's not quite a grave anymore once you've been digested.)

"Built half of it. She did the rest."

"How come you don't have more money if you can build houses? Didn't she pay you?"

In a way — she'd settled a debt he owed to someone who was threatening his knees. Jimi didn't answer.

"Look, you better get into the woods fast. Those ropes won't hold him long. Soon as he wakes up he'll be after me, and it'll be pretty easy for him to get you on the Alley."

"Aw, that old man of yours is too wasted to drive, and what makes you think he'll come after you anyway? Way I hear the pair of you going on next door you'd think he'd be happy to let you go. All you do is fight."

She leaned her bony arms on the back of Jimi's seat, one of her side-braids swinging onto his shoulder.

"Yeah, but when we make up, I'm a blast." For a moment she was a seductive nymphet, then she was a petulant child. "But I'm getting kind of sick of the black eyes, so me and Dolores, we're striking out on our own."

"You've been married for two years. Why screw up my life by leaving him now? You could have left a long time ago."

"And done what? It's different now. Protection and opportunity. Lucy Brightwing's going to have her new tribe, and I'm going to start a business there."

"What kind of business?" Jimi asked, thinking she would sell beadwork or dance for tourists.

"Something I'm well-trained in. The family business, you might say." She winked at her aunt. "I'm going to open a whorehouse."

"I need a drink," Jimi said.

"Ok, but hurry. He'll get loose soon, and he knows your car. He's not gonna let me go easy."

"Why will he think you're with me?"

"'Cause I left him a note, telling him."

"What!"

"Told him you were taking me to Lucy Brightwing's. He won't go after me there. He knows what she'd do to him, if I told her what he did to me."

"That's it, I'm taking you home."

She smiled, her black eyes narrowing. "No story you tell will keep him from knocking your teeth out. We better keep going."

Jimi was fond of his teeth.

Chapter 21

Lucy rolled out of her sleeping bag early again, stiff in her long muscles from the hard floor, but with twitchy restlessness in the shorter ones that comes of not getting enough sleep, and yet not being sleepy.

I might as well live like I always do, she thought. Even alone in the wilderness for weeks at a time, she could always occupy herself. Survival took considerable effort, and after she fed herself she had several projects in various stages of completion. Deer hide, cured thin and supple, lay rolled in a closet waiting to be made into a garment decorated with shells and porcupine quills — a present for Lazarus Nighteyes. A grass mat, half-woven, was propped up behind the door, and on a shelf a bowl worked from a rough gnarled chunk of cypress seemed trapped in the birthing process, the smooth curves of art just starting to emerge from the harsher lines of nature.

And when work, both necessary and voluntary, was done, she was content simply to be. To walk, sit, and swim in the swamps and woods she adored.

But now there was an added element to survival. Three had to eat. She got her bow and quiver ready for a hunt.

"You're a real injun," Mallory said, watching her.

"Real as they come. Want to give it a try?"

Mallory pulled out his pistol and twirled it around his finger so clumsily Lucy flinched. "I'll stick to technology," he said, looking fondly at the steely sheen.

"Yeah," Edgar said, "but what happens when you run out of bullets?"

Mallory made a huge fist. "Hasn't been a problem yet."

Lucy sighed, and glanced at Edgar. How had he survived so far with a handicap like Mallory? It was like trying to hunt with a drummer perpetually following you, beating warning.

She fletched a few arrows with new turkey feathers, twisting them in her fingers to test their spin, while Edgar turned the radio dial until he found a fuzzy station in English.

"You're quite an embarrassment," she said after they listened a while. "They're not coming right out and saying you disappeared off the face of the earth, but you can tell how frustrated they are." She chewed pensively at the end of an iridescent brown and black feather. "They say they have roadblocks set up along some of the major roads, but they know they can't cover everything, not for long, anyway. The airports and sea ports are covered, though. It'll be a while before you can get out of the country. I wouldn't even try it for a few months."

"Where would you go?" he asked.

"Someplace with a non-extradition treaty. But not necessarily. The law might stand in theory, but in practice the U.S. can get almost anyone they want. If they caught you, say, in Mexico, it would cause a delay, and cost this country a pretty penny. On one hand, you'd be awaiting extradition in some little dung-heap of a foreign jail. On the other, you wouldn't be on death row.

"You should pick a country that isn't overtly hostile to the states, but doesn't maintain particularly close ties. One that has a degree of domestic upheaval, someplace where they have enough to worry about without checking out every white boy throwing dollars around. Most of the smaller southeast Asian countries would do, but the islands would be even better. Indonesia is pretty, most people speak English, and they're constantly hovering on the brink of a low-grade civil war. Papua New Guinea. Irian Jaya." He wasn't sure where that last one was. "Do you have any money?" she asked casually.

"Fifty thousand, a little less."

"That will get you started." Yeah, that might bribe a bondsman or get you out of a DUI, but it wouldn't get a pair of notorious murderers across the border. Oh well, its just money. I can make more.

"The trick is getting there," Edgar said.

"Which you won't be able to do for a while, so don't even worry about it yet. Listen, they're talking about you."

The reporter introduced a Mrs. Harlin.

"Oh god, Mrs. Libby Harlin, PS 139! She was my fifth-grade teacher, English and history. Where did they dig her up, I wonder. She must be ancient... she was pretty old when I had her, as I remember."

The reporter said, "This feisty seventy year old former teacher knew the elder Battle brother as a juvenile delinquent when he..." He was cut off by a firm, grave voice.

"I never called him that, young man. Don't twist my words."

Edgar was focusing on one thing. Seventy? So she must have been about forty when she taught him. At the time it was impossible old. Shit, he thought, I'm forty! How the hell did that happen, and where had he been all that time? Mrs. Harlin had been a kind, somewhat arch woman on the slender side of matronly, with harlequin specs and honey-colored hair in a loose upswept bun. It seemed not so very long ago. He could still remember her telling him (the entire class, but it seemed especially him) about the exploits of the Roman emperors, hinting at her admiration for Napoleon, toying dangerously with the good sides of Communism, heady stuff for a ten year old boy. He didn't know which affected him most, to hear that Mrs. Harlin was seventy, or to realize he himself was forty. Neither was quite believable.

"I think they're sorry they're talking to her," Lucy said, bringing him back.

"I always gave her a hard time," he said, and in his smile she could see faint traces of the fifth grade boy. "Nothing mean, but I argued with her, asked her a lot of questions. What's she saying about me?" With the static it was hard to make out.

She said Edgar was one of the cleverest, nicest boys she ever met. She never said she was surprised, or she didn't know where Edgar had gone wrong. She didn't try to analyze him, just talked about what she remembered. She said he drew leaves in the margins of his assignments, where other boys usually drew heroes or cars or monsters, and each leaf had character, she could always tell what kind of tree it came from, even though when she asked Edgar, he didn't know himself. She still has one of his old essays somewhere, she said, but she only laughed when the reporter suggested she give it up as evidence.

The reporter tried to lead her into some early warning sign he'd go wrong, but she said, "You know, I always hoped Edgar Battle would go into politics. He had just the right combination of charisma, intelligence and unscrupulousness I admire in a leader. I always checked the papers for his name."

"And one day," the reporter said, "there it was. What are your views of the Battle brothers' murder spree?"

You could almost hear the shrug in her voice. "I don't know all the details. Things happen, I suppose. If you'll excuse me, I have a pie to bake."

"She always was a sport," Edgar said. "Libby. We liked to call teachers by their first names, behind their backs, of course. It made us feel awfully adult. Once, in front of the class, I slipped and called her Libby out loud. The class gasped, and I felt my stomach drop. Goodbye cockiness. But she just raised her eyebrows and answered my question. She was cool that way."

They pulled everyone out of the woodwork, old girlfriends, bagboys at the local A&P, a plumber who'd fixed a leak in Mallory's apartment once. They all had stories to tell, those hindsight Cassandras who spotted something odd about Edgar or Mallory and should have known it would all come to this. One of Edgar's neighbors said he rarely spoke to anyone, and that taciturnity was a sure sign of mental instability. One of Mallory's neighbors said he approached people too freely, and that lack of reticence was a sure sign of mental instability. They dug out some far distant cousin, who swore that their mother was crazy as a bedbug. Someone from New Jersey said Mallory kicked her poodle once. One of Edgar's former girlfriends made an unpleasantly catty comment about his lovemaking skills, which made Lucy blush.

The only people who weren't talking, as far as she could see, were Edgar's former employers.

"Who were they?" she asked, after pointing out this deficit.

"Can't say."

"Nonsense."

"I took a blood oath." She had to look at him to make sure he was joking. "Seriously, Lu, it's not a good thing to talk about."

"How about I guess, and if I'm right, you just nod. Good? Well… the logical guess would be the Italians. People keep talking about other organizations gaining a foothold, and Mafia movies have made them almost a joke, but when it comes to real influence, real control, you can't top the Italians." Except in south Florida, she thought. "Only problem is, you're not Italian, so you couldn't be part of the inner circle, so I'm gonna say you're a freelance worker, but one that only contracts with one employer. About right?"

"About." He was impressed she'd gotten so close. "It's all pretty much business now. With a criminal twist, of course, extracting money under pressure. But still business, making legitimate people, legitimate organizations, pay. The garment industry, garbage collection of course, plenty of commercial ports. But that's steady skimming, and securing contracts, and protection payoffs. Very well organized. Mostly they just sit back and collect, with occasional enforcing. And of course there are different branches, different families, different cities, always battling it out. But I stayed away from that. Oh, sometimes I'd make a collection … "

"A collection?" she asked innocently, though she'd made one or two herself.

"Someone borrows money, forgets to pay it back. Sometimes they need to be reminded."

"Did you ever kill any of them?"

"That's not good business. Usually they didn't even get hurt. You just go to their house, preferably when the wife and kids are at home, sit down in their favorite chair, real friendly, and remind them that they owe money. It helps if the kids like you, sit on your lap. Remind them about the money while their baby girl is on your knee. Flirt with the wife a little. They usually pay right up then, even if it means shifting the debt to a shark." He spoke matter-offactly, no bragging, no shame.

"I bet you were good at that. Better than any of the heavies I've known. Even when they try to be suave, they come off cheap, and cheap is even worse in a guy. I can see you doing it, though. Like a gentleman."

"Do you hang around with Mafia heavies?" he asked, amused.

"Oh, I have a wide circle of acquaintance." It was easy enough to let him think she was joking. "But that's not what you did, as a rule," she said, leading him back to the conversation.

"No. It wasn't really what I enjoyed. The Mafia, as much as anyone, likes a good chunk of ill-gotten gains. But being businessmen, they think robbery is a little beneath them. All the same, when they hear about something juicy, they're not going to pass on it, just because theft is blue-collar. So when they know that someone will be holding a bag of money in their house overnight, or a chorus-girl who just got a diamond necklace from a senator, they give me the information. I do the dirty deed, they get most of the money, but I get a good cut and a guarantee of protection. It's not too risky, if you know what you're doing. Most of the people I hit were already in Mafia clutches, one way or another. The chorus-girl complains, they show the senator compromising pictures and he convinces her to shut her trap. Guy with the suitcase full of bills gets upset, he's told sure, the money will be returned — to the IRS. So he cuts his losses and holds his tongue. It was the perfect job, work a few nights a year and make enough to live well. When I got caught, it wasn't for that."

"RICO, as I remember."

"So they say. They want to hit the Mafia, but they're too chicken shit, or too smart, to try anything. So they crack down on guys like me. Mafia satellites, they call us. We had protection, but not as much as someone in a family. I hardly even understood the charges they made against me. Nothing too big, but a lot of it. Apparently eighteen years worth. You know, I wouldn't have minded so much if they got me for what I really do. Catch me stealing a painting or lifting some cash, it's a legitimate thing, you know? I was doing something dangerous, and I always expected to be caught for it eventually. But this shit... they had me on tape saying a few vaguely incriminating things, and some guy I beat up when he didn't pay fingered me. Not for that, for things I didn't do. Geez, if they caught me for the things I did, I would've been looking at a few hundred years. But it's pretty damn demeaning to be put away for shit you're not responsible for. During the trial I felt like making a full confession, just to shock them. Tell them everything I stole in the past twenty years, just so I'd go for the right things. But I held my peace, and got off with eighteen years. I made a few of my employers pretty happy when I didn't talk. Not that it helped me any. I don't know, maybe they would have done something for me in the end, gotten the sentence reduced. But they didn't have time."

Or maybe, she thought but didn't say, they were the ones who gave you up in the first place. To placate the law, they gave away a few of their expendables. Maybe you were good, Edgar, but maybe there were others, just as good, to replace you.

But all she said was, "That's a shame." And it was. A guy like him, he didn't ever really hurt anyone, and it was always people who had it coming, one way or another. You can't expect to get mixed up with organized crime without being screwed eventually. As Edgar had discovered.

"I like thieves. You can be good guys."

"You know any thieves before me?" he asked, amused, but with the faintest undertone of jealousy.

She only said, "It takes skill to be a thief. That's probably why you take to the woods so well. You have a knack for being quiet. And when you do talk, your voice doesn't seem to interrupt things. So how'd you come by the fifty thou?" A decent take, but paltry next to her millions.

"That wasn't an assignment. That was luck. I was doing a little recon work, checking out a fellow trying to skip out of his debt. Tracked him to Atlantic City. Good place to be inconspicuous, get yourself lost. But this idiot—I got word he hired a guard, one of those body builders who work out all day but never learned to punch. When people win big, but want to stay in town, they hire guys like that, to walk with them and make them look important. Any little schmuck who has a lucky roll can look like a big shot with a bodyguard escorting him everywhere. It's a regular business. This guy had a hulk about four inches taller than me, and maybe twice as wide, walking next to him with a briefcase chained to his wrist. The guard looked impressive enough, but it took all of one punch to take him out. He was too worried his pretty face would get broken, and once he was down, he stayed down. I took the case—I had to dislocate a couple of bones in the guard's hand — and didn't bother reminding the man about his debt. I told my employer I couldn't find him, which was believable enough, and stashed the case. Around a hundred, starting out, but Mallory had it when I got picked up and used a lot of it for the escape. It's dwindled a little since then."

"It was a lucky break," she said. "Odds are always better with money." She was thinking of a forger she knew, who could get them squeaky-clean IDs as Honduran nationals, for about two hundred thousand each. Should they have plastic surgery? She'd hate to lose Edgar's craggy worried face, even if she never saw it again.

"And what chance do I have *with* it?" He wanted to avoid the gloom of dwelling on his future, but somehow he couldn't stay away from the subject.

"You don't want to talk about this," she said.

"But I have to," he said. "I don't get to do what I want to do." What he wanted to do was be with Lucy somewhere safe. Would she come with him?

"You want to talk about what's going to happen when you get caught?"

"Are you so sure that I *will* get caught?" But she wouldn't answer him. "Come on, your honest prognostication. Will I get caught?"

She sighed, then said, "Unless a miracle happens, yes." She wasn't sure he'd accept her help, not when he knew what it entailed, and she wanted to paint a bleak picture so he'd be more willing to take her money.

Edgar wanted to get angry, but could only manage sulky. It was what he already knew. Was it worse, that she should know it too?

"So, they catch me, and I get the chair. Is that it?"

"It won't be quite that easy."

"What do you mean?"

"Basic scenario? Ten years or more of hell before they strap you in. First thing, you'll have to face the police, troopers, agents, whoever, who catch you. That won't be pretty. You killed some cops, and they don't forgive that, especially in Florida. The only thing that will stop them from beating you to death, once they have you, is the thought that you'll suffer more going through the courts, and waiting to die in Starke."

"Starke's the state pen?"

"Yeah, up in north Florida. Not a bad little town. The law is real nice to you when you're driving through. But I've talked to people who have been there, and I was inside once."

"Inside? You weren't ever in prison."

"Not that kind of inside. I was visiting someone."

"You have an unusual circle of friends."

"You might say that." She'd been retrieving information from one of Bald Cypress' heavies, who had been convicted on felony murder charges — that is, someone died while he was committing a felony, though he wasn't the one who killed him. In an odd twist of Florida statute, he'd been charged with murder because his partner, an alcoholic sixty-year-old Seminole, had keeled over from a heart attack in the middle of a robbery, which the coroner directly attributed to the stresses of the crime. The incident had pissed off Billie Bald Cypress to no end, for the man was scheduled to do a big job for the Seminole boss, and was naturally prevented by his unrelated incarceration. Lucy had to pay him a visit, speaking to him through the perforated plexiglass in ways ambiguous enough not to arouse the guards' suspicions. Lucy was so vague, the man so dense, that it proved impossible to get the information she needed. But the experience gave her a first-hand glimpse of the penal facilities.

"Prison isn't a nice place, you know that, but Starke's worse. The guards are bad. Well, they have a lot of bad people to deal with, don't they? They had a lot of trouble a few years back, stomping someone to death in X-wing, so for all the press knows they've reformed, but there's always someplace off-camera. We know what goes on." He did. How did she?

"You don't have to worry about the other prisoners at Starke. The guards will kill you quicker. Of course, that's not what winds up on the report.

"The state will *decide* to kill you soon enough, but even if you're ready to die, even if you beg for it, they'll stick you with appeals for a decade at least. It's a way of easing their consciences."

"They won't take me. I'd rather die fighting."

"Sure, if you have a choice. Suicide by cop's the easy way out. You might not end up in Starke, though. New York has dibs on you, right? They'll try you in the order of the crimes committed. New York doesn't have the death penalty, but some of the other states you passed through do. Lethal injection, which is better than the chair, at least. Have you heard about our Old Sparky? They have a new one now, much more efficient. Oh, and bigger. They had a 400 pound guy on death row, and couldn't kill him until they had a chair he'd fit in. You should have heard the way the press talked about it, like they were *Architectural Digest*, or *Better Homes and Gardens*, going on about the clean Shaker lines of the chair.

"If you're lucky, another state will get you. With the right lawyer, you might not even go to trial in more than one state. But I think Florida will fight to keep you, even over New York, which should take precedence. Florida has a grudge against you two. It will take a whole lot to get you out of this state. Hell, you could be in court the next thirty years."

"Hey, come look at this," Mallory interrupted, peeking in from the deck. "There's something out here, and it's frickin' huge."

Chapter 22

"A bear?" Lucy asked.

"Looked more like a giant pig, with a bunch of little ones running around."

Lucy's eyes widened slightly, then narrowed. She placed a finger to her lips as she silently took her bow from its hooks on the wall. In one smooth motion she hooked her thigh around the spine and bent the bow, slipping the looped string over the notched end, and took up three arrows with large knapped killing tips.

"You're going to kill it?" Mallory asked in a whisper.

"It's a feral pig. They're aliens, they don't belong here. They tear up the native vegetation, and plenty of the plants around here are endangered. There's a kind of ground orchid that only grows within ten miles of this place. If there are hogs here, they'll destroy the land."

Every true Floridian loathes two things: feral pigs and Brazilian peppers. They're like northern tourists: destructive, invasive, and almost impossible to get rid of. But Lucy had to try. She gestured the men to be quiet and stay back, and crept up to the door, swinging it open on well-greased hinges.

There, below her, rooted a big charcoal-colored animal. It was the biggest feral pig she'd ever seen. Most are lean and weigh perhaps a little more than she did, but this one must have topped four hundred pounds. Her hide was thick, and long outward-thrusting tushes curled from her mobile snout. Around the sow trotted half a dozen brown and white streaked piglets, a few weeks old and already proficient at nosing up miniature trenches of earth in their search for grubs and nuts.

This, thought Lucy, is a far more serious matter. One pig, though bad, was tolerable, especially since she'd probably migrate north where feeding was better — though this sow was obviously finding plenty of food. But a mother pig would stay put, and in a few weeks there would be not one but seven full-sized ferals terrorizing the landscape.

She wanted to get rid of the pig, but more than that, she wanted meat. It was harder than she thought to feed two big hungry men, and this sow and her farrow would supply them for weeks. She would dry some of the meat, make that smokehouse she'd intended to build for the past year, but never had time. She eyed the sow's meaty haunch. That would make quite a ham.

Here was the perfect opportunity to dispatch it, without any risk to herself. Wild pigs are dangerous, even with several hunters and a pack of game, well-trained dogs. A sow in farrow was even more vicious. Killing it unseen, from the safety of her home, was a gift from her ancestors. She crept up to the railing and waited for her chance.

But the sow proved stubborn. Lucy was downwind of the beast, and could smell its sweaty musk, but it probably couldn't smell her yet. And pigs are used to predators coming from the ground, not the sky, so she never raised her head above eye level. But she kept her back to Lucy, her plump rump in the air presenting an easy target, but not a lethal one. Lucy couldn't shoot until it turned broadside, and she could get an arrow in the heart or throat. With the patience of generations of hunters bred into her she held her position with the arrow drawn. It was a tortuous pose, and soon her arms began to shake with the strain. She thought about making a noise. A whistle might make the sow turn, or it might spook her headlong into the woods. Lucy decided to wait, trusting to luck and patience, both of which seldom failed her.

Before she could find a perfect shot she heard the door latch click behind her. She didn't turn; nor did the sow, though she raised her snout briefly at the sound, eventually deciding it wasn't worth her concern. From the corner of her eye Lucy saw a shape creep up behind her: Mallory. Annoyed, she ignored him, hoping he had the sense to stay still and not ruin her shot. The sow, a little nervous now, seemed on the verge of turning.

A second later a gunshot rang out, so close and so loud that Lucy flinched and almost loosed her arrow. She glanced quickly at Mallory as the pig squealed, and turned back to her quarry just in time to see that the bullet had only grazed the sow's shoulder. With a growl of protest Lucy tried to find a target for her arrow, but the pig's haunches bunched and in an instant she had disappeared, crashing through the undergrowth on her swift narrow legs, her piglets trailing behind her with excited squeals. Frustrated, Lucy shot one arrow blindly at the retreating ruckus, hoping to at least wound the pig and slow it down, but she only heard the dull thump of her arrow hitting dirt.

She turned to Mallory with her teeth bared like a thwarted panther.

"Hey," he said with a grin, "at least I hit it. You missed completely. I told you guns are better." Too angry to say anything, she shoved him roughly aside and stalked back in the house.

"Your bastard of a brother ruined my shot!" she snarled, slamming her bow down on the table. "Now the sow's wounded, but not enough to bleed her out, just enough to make her harder to catch, and mad and mean as hell. I'm getting that pig today!"

"I never guessed you were so vicious and vindictive. You'd kill all of those cute little baby piglets?"

"If I let those stay, there would be twenty more by next year. This kind of environment isn't meant to support large numbers of pigs. So whenever any wander in — and they very rarely do—I have a pig hunt." She sighed. "I'll have to track her. Shouldn't be too hard to find her, but it might be a hell of a fight once I do. Will you be cool here by yourself all day?"

"If you're going on a pig hunt, I'll go with you. It's my brother's fault it got away. I have to make up for that. It's the least I can do."

Lucy chuckled, but told him quite seriously that she wouldn't let him come.

"But I shoot pretty well."

"No guns."

"What? You can't go after that thing with those little arrows."

"This is my land," or will be soon, "and I'm not going to let anyone hunt with guns. Not you, not me."

"All the more reason for me to go with you. That thing is too dangerous for you to go after alone."

"You didn't even see it. It won't be so bad."

"I saw one the other day, when I went out on my own by the river or whatever it is. She charged me." His voice dropped. "I've never been so scared, except a few minutes later when I saw Mallory... Look, after all you've done for us, after all you've been through, I won't let you put yourself in any more danger. I'm coming, and that's that."

She laughed. "I get ten feet into the swamps you'll never find me. Sure, wander around for a few hours, I'll track you and bring you home when I'm done with the pig, but you're not coming with me. Really, it's not that dangerous at all, if you know what you're doing, and you don't. You'll get yourself killed. I won't, I promise. The best way to hunt pigs is with dogs. They get the pigs at bay, surround them, and you move in. With good dogs, you can take down a whole herd of pigs in no time. But sometimes the dogs get gored. And a pig that breaks loose will charge like a bull at the first thing it sees. A friend of mine was killed by a feral pig, and another had his entire calf muscle ripped out. But don't worry about me. One pig shouldn't be a problem." Not even a four-hundred pound protective mother.

Edgar, however, was adamant. Whether from a desire for adventure, a need to tease her, or genuine concern for her safety, he insisted that she wouldn't go alone. "I can take care of myself on a hunt," he said, "and I won't get in your way. If you try to go without me, I'll stop you. He grabbed her bow and raised it over his knee, prepared to snap it in two. She looked at him, aghast, but didn't really believe he'd do it. "I'd hate to do it," he owned. "It's such a pretty bow. But once I make my mind up, I'm determined to have my way."

"And so am I. I'm not hiding you out here so you can be killed by an angry sow. If I have to, I'll hunt that pig with my bare hands."

Edgar almost believed she would — and could — do it. But he held the bow up threateningly. "Please, Edgar, don't snap it," she said, suddenly beseeching. "I'm awfully fond of that bow." She edged closer and took the bow in both her hands, not trying to take it from him, but asserting her possession. "If you insist, you can come with me today. But if you spoil the hunt, you won't go again tomorrow. And if you get killed, well, I told you so. Oh, and I won't come back to tell Mallory you're dead. I don't think he'd take it well."

Satisfied, he released the bow. "When do we leave?"

"Soon as I get my arrows ready, and get you a lance."

He watched her gather her arrows, and picked one up before she slid it into the quiver. "Where did you get this?" he asked, stroking the blade lightly with his thumb.

"Careful, it's sharper than it looks." And it looked pretty sharp.

The arrow was longer than her outstretched arm, so that even when the bow was fully drawn the lethal tip protruded some inches. It was wood, but though it gave the impression of being hand-hewn it was smooth and uniform. The end was fletched in trimmed turkey feathers, two brown and one speckled, only a little frayed from previous flights. But it was the point that intrigued Edgar the most. It was stone, marbled yellow and cream, and scarcely more than an inch long. It curved inward at the base in a narrow neck, where it was hafted to the bolt and bound in what Edgar thought might be wire, but that was in fact sinew which, when wrapped wet, shrank and tightened as it dried.

"I made it," she said, taking it away from him and wiping away the line of blood he'd left on the arrow edge. He couldn't even felt the sting from the razor-sharp blade.

"You made the point too? Or you just put it together?"

"It's chert, harvested from an outcropping near the coast. It's Florida's version of flint, and fractures the same way."

"What kind of tools did you use?" He returned that arrow, and took another from her loose buckskin quiver. This one had a longer, heavier point, and the last six inches of the shaft were not wood but bone, or perhaps antler. The arrowhead was larger and thicker, but edge was just as fine.

"Other stone, harder stone. And bone, for some of the finer work."

"That's remarkable," he said. "You're like a cave girl."

She laughed, not at all inclined to take offense. "My mother taught me, along with the rest of it. This, more or less, is what the Tequesta were using when the Europeans came."

Edgar felt the edge again. "With these, I'm surprised you didn't give them more of a fight."

"Oh, we killed plenty, but you can't kill microbes. At least, you couldn't then."

They set out within ten minutes. Mallory, inspired by his first hunting experience, wanted to join them, but this Lucy flatly refused. "It will be bad enough having one extra person around to make noise," she said. "That pig would hear us a mile off if you were there too." Edgar, though still far from silent in the woods, at least made an effort to be no louder than necessary. Mallory didn't even try.

Lucy carried her bow strung, with a quiver of a dozen broad-tipped arrows at her side. Her only other weapon was a long knife, a pig sticker, she called it, and Edgar thought she was joking. Despite much protest she didn't let Edgar carry a gun, telling him he was merely a spectator, not an official part of the hunt. But she let him carry a long heavy spear, almost a lance, of the sort once used to hunt European wild boar. Two feet from the tip it had a heavy crossbar.

"The best thing to do if the sow charges you is get up a tree, but if that's not possible within a few steps, don't turn your back on her. Hold your ground and run her through with this. When she's pierced, drop down and brace the butt in the ground. Whatever you do, don't let go of that spear until she's dead, or I get there. I'll be close. The bar will keep her from running herself all the way through just to get to you. Believe me, she'd do it, if she was mad enough."

Her ultimate advice was to stay out of the way, hers and the sow's.

"Wild pigs can be unpredictable. She'll probably just try to run away, but you never know. When we see her, stay behind me. And keep your eyes open. Anything can happen. And Edgar..." She leaned close so her breath warmed his throat. "I don't want anything to happen to you."

It would be good to have someone to hunt with again, she thought. In many ways it was easier to hunt alone, easier for one than two to stay silent and sharp, but it was sometimes worth it to have friendly companionship, a person to share observations, to join in the thrill of the chase, the triumph of the catch. And of course, when going after bigger game, it was handy to have a masculine body to help carry the kill home. That was one thing that kept her from hunting deer with any frequency. She had to range far afield to find them, and though she was strong, she couldn't carry a full-grown deer corpse very far by herself. Unless she made a lucky kill close to the house, or at least to the water, she was generally reduced to butchering the deer where it fell, taking only the hide and the best cuts, leaving the rest for nature to dispose of. It was wasteful, though there was always someone to eat what she left. She loved venison but she rarely allowed herself the treat when she hunted on her own land. With Edgar here, though, with a companion well-suited to the woods, a man whose company she enjoyed...

Chapter 23

In the past three days the season had begun its change. Lucy knew it intimately, the sun rising at a new time, in a new position, every morning; each noon almost imperceptibly warmer than the last. Edgar noticed too, though not so concretely. The air was unusually heavy about them, muffling the swamp sounds to a near hush. Now and again, a frog trilled hoarsely.

"What is it today, Lu?" he asked, thinking he was allowed to talk this early in the hunt. "I feel like something is about to happen. No, that's not it, exactly. I feel like everyone else thinks something is about to happen."

"It's the end of the dry season," she said. "Everything is waiting for the rains to come."

"But it's a swamp. Isn't there water enough?"

"The frogs don't think so. Do you hear them? They're making sounds like trickling water, trying to lure the rain. The same as using a duck call. If the storms think their friends are here already, they'll come sooner. Then the frogs can lay their eggs."

"Every time I go outside I step in water; it's everywhere. They could lay their eggs all winter."

"Try telling them that. Even in the dry season, even in heavy drought, this region always has some water. But when the rains come — oh, Edgar, you should see it! Places that are dry now will be flooded up to your knees. Why do you think I have a house on stilts? Well, that and the fires. Later in the summer, if we have a wet year, I can tie my canoe up to the house. The frogs always wait until the rains come. Now, all of the water has things living in it: fish and turtles and alligators, all living on top of each other. They'd eat the eggs and baby frogs. But when all the dry holes fill up, there will be places the frogs can have all to themselves. That way, if they all mate at once, at the start of the rains, more froglets will survive.

"Smart of them."

"Not smart, exactly, but it works. Can you feel the air? The way it seems to cling to you? And it's gotten much warmer. Everything is stiller now, even the wind doesn't blow as much. Everything is waiting, waiting. It won't rain tonight, I don't think, but soon. Very soon. It makes all the animals edgy, waiting for it. You have to be extra careful of snakes in the last week of the dry season, and sometimes the bears get mean too.

"But when the rain starts at last, it's like the entire swamp sighs a breath it's been holding for months. As soon as the first drops fall, the frogs start their mating chorus. *Brek-ke-ke-kex, koax, koax!* Oh, that's something you shouldn't miss. They sing every night through the summer, but the first night is the best. All different kinds, deep-throated bullfrogs and leopard frogs, chirping spadefoots and trilling treefrogs, all singing together. It's so beautiful, even the cicadas stop to listen to them."

"I wish I could be here to see it," he said softly.

"Would you like to be," she asked, almost afraid to hear the answer. "You know, you could…"

She held up her fist suddenly, signaling Edgar to stop as she sniffed the air.

Once again the wind was in her favor, and she caught the strong gamey odor of pig. She crept silently forward, and before long heard the contented squeals of nursing piglets. Through the ferns she could just see the hulking shape of the sow stretched on her side. Her babies were shoving and grunting at her full teats, and she alternated between nuzzling the nearest and trying without success to lick the trickle of blood that snaked down her shoulder.

She wanted Edgar to stay behind now. It was starting to get tricky, requiring careful, silent stalking and positioning, and it wouldn't do to have a companion who might tread on a dry branch at an inopportune moment, or misunderstand a silent signal. But the way the hunt was laying itself out made that impractical. To get to the pig she'd have to circle around it. There was no way to shoot through the bracken. If Edgar stayed in his current position, he'd be hidden behind the bushes, true, but directly in her line of fire, not to mention the line of a fleeing pig (if it decided not to charge her) who could easily tear through the undergrowth. When she might only have one, or at most two chances to shoot the sow, she didn't want to have to worry about Edgar's exact position.

The hunters backtracked away from the pigs, and Lucy led him in a wide circle to the far side. She brought Edgar just close enough so he could see the pig family, then silently ordered him to stop. At this range, she must go on alone, for only she could move stealthily enough not to be detected until she was near enough for a clean shot. Though her bow had a good reach, it lost power at distance, and she didn't look forward to chasing — or running from — a wounded pig.

Unless Edgar watched her constantly, it would be hard to see that she moved. Using trees, vines, even shadows as cover she crept as close as she dared to the resting pigs. Each step was agonizingly slow, her foot touching the earth first at the outside ball of the toe, testing each fraction of ground as it rolled back to the heel, ready at any moment to snatch it up again if it encountered an unexpected twig or dry leaf. Only when she was sure of each step did she commit her weight, and then she paused, looking just beyond the pigs, to make sure they hadn't noticed. It took her fifteen minutes to get near enough, for sometimes she had to stop altogether when a piglet looked directly at her. But she seemed no more threatening than a tree moving slowly in the breeze, and the piglets failed to notice that one particular tree came ever closer. The sow's eyes were closed. At last Lucy took a position at the edge of a trunk, where creepers descended in a shifting veil that helped obscure her movements.

As pig hunts go, she thought, this one is proving easy. She had an unobstructed shot, the pig didn't seem nervous, and Lucy was poised for the kill. Smoothly, she raised her bow, and drew her arrow so that the turkey feathers tickled the edge of her jaw. She knew just where the big vein ran along the sow's throat. The arrow, sharp and broad, would pierce even that thickened fatty flesh with ease. It was a better target than the heart, with no ribs to get in the way, though she was fairly sure her chert arrowhead would crack cleanly through the ribcage. She took a deep, silent breath, slowing her pulse and steadying her aim, and let the arrow fly.

She knew later she'd jinxed herself by thinking, prematurely, that all was well. When she was just about to release the arrow she heard a noise she couldn't immediately identify, and the sow heard it too. As the arrow bridged the short gap between hunter and prey, the pig threw back her head in alarm, turning toward the sound. The arrow lodged not in her throat, but in the muscular top of her shoulders. She squealed in pain and fury, a piercing, uncanny sound echoed by six confused piglets. In an instant the sow fixed on the source of her torment and, wounded but hardly slowed, charged Lucy, trailing piglets from her teats.

Lucy calmly held her ground and fitted another arrow. But as she drew it, she realized what the sound that startled the sow had been: the first strand of her bowstring snapping. As she drew her second arrow back the string gave way entirely, whipping against her arm and sending the bolt clattering uselessly to the ground halfway between her and the pig. All the same, it was probably that fallen, useless arrow that saved her, for it made the sow hesitate in her headlong charge, veering slightly toward the new moving target before fixing her little eyes back on the human. Lucy had just time enough to dive behind the tree and circle around her pursuer.

Pigs can be clever, but they're not good at thinking on their feet. Give a pig a chance, and they can solve most puzzles, but put a pig in the heat of action and they hardly use their brains at all. The pig wasn't fooled by Lucy's maneuver. It knew full well where she was, but so hot was its anger that instinct alone drove it. It wanted to gore something, anything. For a moment it couldn't see Lucy, so it turned its attention to the other large shape running toward it.

Edgar, unaccustomed to hunting scenes, was a bit slow to react. He didn't realize instantly that the first arrow failed to find its target, and it didn't occur to him to disobey his orders to stay put until the sow actually charged. When he saw that Lucy was in danger he dashed forward, not entirely sure what he should do, but certain he should do something. Despite the tusks, and the size of the beast, he still had a vague idea that it could be shooed away, and he came at it yelling and waving his heavy spear.

Lucy, panting, saw him coming and shouted at him to get up a tree. He didn't hear or refused to obey, and she cursed him as she wheeled and ran after the sow, tripping over scattering piglets. With the sow's head start she knew she could never reach them in time. Fighting visions of Edgar gored, Edgar bleeding, Edgar dying, she lengthened her stride. She stopped shouting, saving her breath for running.

Then she saw Edgar stop and plant himself firmly as he lowered the great lance. Her heart surged as she ran. Foolish Edgar! But oh, brave Edgar! It took more courage than most men possess to hold their ground in the face of a charging feral pig. Lower! That's it! Keep it steady!

His face was grim and frightened, a sheen of sweat on his brow, but he stood steadily, staring down the pig as it ran at him. It will be a good first kill, she thought proudly, still running. A good first non-human kill, she amended, then gasped. The sow had tripped, which anyone else would have thought was a good thing. But Lucy saw it all, almost before it happened.

As the raging pig fell the lance tip only grazed a long shallow gash on her flank, and she quickly regained her feet, now coming at Edgar inside the reach of his spear. At the last possible second he threw himself to the side, sprawling in the mud as he managed to shove her away with the shaft of the spear. But she was not to be deterred, and, snarling and snorting, lowered her head and twisted to gash him.

Edgar flailed on his back, trying to keep the pig at bay and escape at the same time. He could feel its breath hot against his leg, and flinched away as the sow flung up her head, seeking flesh to rip. Her curved tusk fouled on the spear, distracting her, but as she tossed her head this way and that to free herself she managed to jerk it out of Edgar's grasp. His only defense gone, he tried desperately to get to his feet before the first slash came. The sow, only a single bound away from him, paused, and Edgar fancied that the look in its little black eyes was one of triumph.

In that moment when the sow mocked him in his helplessness, Lucy finally reached him. With no apparent weapon she grabbed the pig by its hind legs and, throwing all her weight and strength into it, tripped the beast onto its back. While it thrashed and squealed, unable to right itself, Edgar heard the beautiful hiss of steel unsheathed, and saw the quick flash and fall of Lucy's long knife as it plunged between the sow's ribs. She held the pig down as it thrashed and struggled, then pulled the knife out with a spray of blood that dappled her body in red. She knelt for a time over the corpse, her breath still coming hard, her hand resting on the pig's haunches almost in a caress.

Unsteadily, Edgar got to his feet, the feel of death still upon him, and he leaned forward with his hands on his knees. But when he looked up again he was laughing, and suddenly Lucy laughed too, at the victory of the hunt, at death averted, laughing because they were both strong and alive and together.

Edgar caught her in an embrace that lifted her off the ground and crushed her to his chest. "You're magnificent!" he said, shouting wildly into her ear. "You're beautiful! I love you!" And before she could gauge the sincerity of this last, he was kissing her.

"I've gotten blood all over you," she said at last, weakly, a very long time later when he released her. But he only kissed her on the forehead, indulging casually in his new-found assurance of possession, and wiped his bloodied hands across his cheeks, leaving stripes like war paint. Lucy looked up at him breathlessly, not even bothering to tell herself that her heart beat fast only from the thrill of the hunt. But she made herself step back, still temptingly within reach of his arms, her eyes still crinkled and glinting in excitement.

"We have things to do... first," she said, and he swelled at the promise implied, of what might come second. "If we want to use any of the pig meat I have to dress the carcass right away, or the whole thing will be ruined. And there are the little ones to take care of."

Her lust quite spoiling her aim, Lucy managed to pick off four of the six piglets with her restrung bow. The last two, swifter or smarter than their brethren, scuttled off into the woods, to survive, or be consumed, it was up to nature to determine.

Lucy, now thoroughly covered in blood after her butchering efforts, let the bow slip from her hands and snaked her arms up around Edgar's neck. But she did not kiss him at once, only looked at him, from a blurry inch or two away, with fondness and pity and a last moment of hesitation. Is it kind to love a doomed man? Is it worth whatever pain she might feel at their eventual, unavoidable separation? But she let all logic slide away under the crush of affection, and coiled her arms more tightly about him, drawing him to her.

"There's another spring nearby," she breathed as she kissed his throat. "Would you like to get all this blood off?" He nodded, but didn't let her go. He slid an arm under her knees and scooped her up, making her giggle. She wasn't used to being treated so much like a girl.

"Which way?" he asked.

She tried to direct him, but it proved impossible to negotiate their way through the foliage without her legs tangling on every branch and thorn, and a moment later he was forced to drop his prize, but still kept her pressed close against his body. With many pauses to remind each other how they felt with gropes and squeezes, they slowly, and quite enjoyably, made their way the few hundred yards to the spring.

Lucy kicked off her shoes, flexing her toes luxuriously in the deep shaggy grey-green moss on the bank, and decided the rest of her clothes should quickly follow. With deft hands she exposed a body perfectly designed to satisfy the eye in its lean roundness, soft curves of hip and breast against the firm muscles of her limbs. Basking in his admiration, grinning at the happy turn of the day, keeping her eyes fixed on his like a snake charmer, she began to unbutton his shirt.

He had just reached the ideal point of nakedness (men, as a rule, look their best almost, but not quite, naked) when he felt Lucy stiffen, and saw her nostrils flare slightly. Wondering what personal flaw she had discovered he looked at her questioningly, but her attention was elsewhere.

"Hush," she whispered, barely a sound, looked around. "You haven't been smoking, have you?" she asked him after a moment. He shook his head. "Someone nearby has."

At last her eyes fixed on a place, and he followed her gaze until he found a face, almost hidden, watching them from across the clear little spring. It was a brown, weasely face, with long black hair held back by a tattered red headband, and it seemed so surprised at being spotted that it didn't move.

"Shit," Edgar said quietly, not entirely sure what to make of the new twist, but thinking more of the interruption at so delicate a moment than of any possible discovery and apprehension. When he turned to Lucy he found her face a predatory mask of anger and determination. She hadn't looked that intense, that enraged, when she wrestled the sow to its death.

"Wait here," she said, not taking her eyes off the man in the distance. "Wait for me, no matter how long I'm gone." And then before he could answer she dashed to the disheveled pile of discarded bloody clothes and snatched up her long knife. Only then, when she began to run, almost snarling, did the intruder break from his hide and disappear through the woods at his best speed. Lucy, a naked, bloody demon, pursued him.

"Lu!" Edgar called after her, but within seconds she was lost to sight, and a moment later he could hear nothing but the placid whistles of birds as the swamps around him recovered their calm after what was to them only a minor interlude of excitement. After all, bloody, savage things ran through their home every day.

With a heavy sigh and a flagging erection, Edgar put his pants back on and sat at the water's edge to wait.

Chapter 24

With her bloody pig-sticking knife in her hand, Lucy pounded after the interloper, barefoot, heedless of the rough ground. Running nude is not the most pleasant thing for a woman even moderately endowed, but Lucy ignored undignified jiggling and almost painful bouncing in this new and much more serious hunt. The man before her was swift, but though he too was an Indian he did not have her advantage of knowing this particular swamp's quirks. She found the easiest footing, seeming to know which patches of mud were only ankle-deep, and which would swallow her to the knee. Her prey had no such knowledge or instinct, and was hampered by the very earth itself. Still, he had a good lead on her, and he'd seen her weapon. He knew he might be running for his life, and that lends speed to any man's feet. Lucy was agile, swift as a cat over a sprint, though like a cat she had little endurance over the long haul.

She had one more advantage: she knew who she was chasing. And further, she knew that he recognized her, too.

When she felt herself beginning to tire she stopped abruptly and called out, "Jimi Golden! I'll run you to the next life!" And then she said something else, in a language only she could fully understand. They were the only Tequesta words most other Indians knew, the phrase reminding them of their oath to defend and obey the Tequesta tribe for all of their days.

Jimi stopped. He had no choice. He believed her threat. She had a deadly if obscure reputation, and beyond that, he knew the oath every Seminole and Miccosukee made, and the penalty for those forsworn. He turned, terrified, and saw a vision from a nightmare walking resolutely toward him.

Every Indian knows the most dangerous demons are also the most beautiful. The marsh maidens with hair like corn silk who caress men out of their wits and lead them to quicksand. The bear-girls, their voluptuous forms clad in fur, who offer their warmth to a lone hunter on a winter night, only to rip out his throat with hidden claws. Every man goes to hell of his own volition — he won't be seduced to his doom by something foul.

The creature that approached Jimi looked like one of the old war demons who fly over battlefields to feast on the fallen. She had no clothes — what does a spirit need with clothes?—and her skin was stained red with blood. Her face was stern and beautiful like the great timeless ones who used to walk on the earth, and her long knife, bloodied too, was like the daggers used in ritual sacrifice since the beginning of time. Jimi was a logical man, almost thoroughly modern, though steeped in the stories of his people, but even he was certain for a moment that a mythic creature had come in the shape of Lucy Brightwing to kill him.

When she grew nearer, he changed his mind somewhat. It was not a demon in the guise of Lucy, only Lucy herself. But she was still going to kill him.

She walked steadily up to him, heedless of her unclothed state, and Jimi did not move even when she placed the tip of her knife under his chin. Speaking not in English but in the formal version of his native tongue, she said, "Why do you trespass on land that is forbidden, Jimi Golden?"

Gathering himself up as best he could, he replied, "I've come to find you."

"You were sent?" she demanded, pushing the blade harder against his skin.

"No... no. Not sent. I heard Bald Cypress talking about you, that you were missing. I went to find you. He doesn't know I've come." He was glad he left Sue and Dolores in the car.

"You heard him talking, eh? It's not good to eavesdrop." She shifted her knife to the side of his head. "Those who do sometimes get their ears lopped off. So, what else did you overhear?"

"N... nothing!"

"Of course you did, Jimi. You heard what I was away doing, didn't you?"

"You were getting something, picking something up. Bald Cypress and Lazarus Nighteyes were talking about it. Bald Cypress was angry that you hadn't brought it back yet."

"And what did Nighteyes say?" she asked, and Jimi, to his intense relief, found a hint of amusement in her eyes. Perhaps he might not die after all.

"He said they had no control over you, there was nothing they could do but wait. He seemed to think the whole thing was kinda funny."

Good old Nighteyes! That boded well for her eventual return, for she still depended on him to sell her the land and spread baksheesh among the bureaucrats and politicians. But she made her features stern again and, tracing the lines of his neck with her point, said, "I could kill you out here, and no one would ever know. Your body would be eaten in two days, your bones scattered. No one would ever see poor Jimi again." She shook her head sadly at the possibility.

"You're not gonna kill me just 'cause I was worried about you, are you?" he asked, miserably.

"Worried about me? You thought you'd get a cut if you brought me in." But she took the knife away and stepped back. He tried, but couldn't quite manage not to sweep her lush body in one comprehensive, appreciative gaze as she turned her back on him.

"What did you see just now?" she asked him.

"Nothing. Not a thing," he assured her, pulling his eyes away from her buttocks.

"No, I don't mean what are you going to tell anyone you saw. That, of course, is nothing, or I will hunt you down and slit your belly open. What did you really see?"

"I... I saw you... with a man..."

"And who was that man?" She cocked her head to one side and looked at him sharply as a bluejay.

Now, Jimi, contrary to popular opinion, was no fool. Every news program for the past ten days had been dominated by two faces, and he'd just seen one of them in Lucy Brightwing's enthusiastic naked embrace. But if she wanted to live in the woods with the most wanted man in America, that was her business. Especially when she was the one holding the knife.

"I couldn't get a good look. He seemed tall and dark, but that was all I could tell."

She looked at him narrowly. He might be lying, she decided. She didn't realize how ingrained the Battle brothers' image had become in the minds of the populace. By now, every child, every bed-bound elder in the country could probably recognize the Battle brothers across a crowded room. The law was so eager to catch them, the media so willing to play upon the embarrassment of the pair remaining at large, that looking for the Edgar and Mallory had become something of a national pastime. They'd been spotted in twenty states in the past week, not to mention in Paris and Beijing, and Florida, where they were still thought to be, was attracting bounty hunters from around the world. People were already planning vacations tracing the Battle brothers' crime spree route from New York, delaying plans only until they'd been caught to determine the final destination of their tour. The brothers, though they hadn't been spotted in many days, were proving to be just another Florida tourist attraction.

But to Lucy, who only knew they were desperately wanted, not that posters of their mug shots were starting to appear on dorm walls, it seemed quite plausible that Jimi wouldn't recognize Edgar.

"After I... collected what I needed," Lucy said, "I thought it would be safer to lay low for a while. I called Bald Cypress to let him know. He shouldn't have been worried. I'll be leaving here tonight, though, and Bald Cypress and Nighteyes will see me soon. But until I choose to see them, I don't want them knowing anything about me. Is that clear?"

He nodded.

"If I didn't think I could trust you, I'd tie you up out here for a few days to make sure you didn't talk." That, Jimi thought, was a step up from death. Barely. "But I think I *can* trust you. I've always thought you were someone who could hold his tongue. Now you get the chance to prove it. I want you to go back to the reservation, and tell no one where you've been. If, when I return, everyone looks sufficiently surprised to see me, there might be a little something in it for you. But if anyone has even the slightest idea where I've been, it will be a contest between me and the curse of the Tequesta to see who disembowels you first. Now, down on your belly and take the oath!"

It was all a bit dramatic, and since Jimi had his face pressed to the earth Lucy allowed herself to smile, just a little. Her ancestors had created the oath to impress upon the Seminole and Miccosukee tribes just how important it was to protect the Tequesta, and it was full of promises of the horrible things that would befall the man who neglected his bond. Worms would gnaw his bowels, thorns pierce his eyes, dirt fill his lungs, his tongue would rot, his penis fall off. If Jimi doubted that the old gods of the Tequesta would visit such a fate upon him, he was quite certain Lucy would not hesitate to do their work for them. He'd always been in awe of her, even when they sweated side by side, working on her house. Now, she stood before him in her full glory as the last member of a dead race, and seemed to contain all the power, magic and ferocity of the Tequesta, distilled into a single body. Even if he didn't fear the oath, even if he did not fear her, there was no way he could refuse her.

"Get up, Jimi," she said gently, actually helping him to his feet. "I'll find you in a few days. And don't forget, you never saw me."

"Man," he said, brushing the dirt from his face, "I've never even *been* out here."

"Perfect," Lucy said, rewarding him with a smile that still looked strangely fierce, framed as it was by the blood, and the knife, and the nakedness.

She was gone, all told, two hours, for when Jimi left she followed him, unobserved, to ensure he was really heading out of the swamp. Only when he was well on his way back to civilization did she think it safe to turn her steps back toward Edgar.

She approached him from the far side of the spring, and he

didn't see her until she was very near, actually wading through the shallows. His impatience and anger and frustration and worry all evaporated in one long sigh, and he met her halfway across the spring, the water creeping up his trousers in a dark stain.

"Is everything all right?" he asked anxiously, taking her face in his hands. She nodded, and rested her cheek against his shoulder. She was exhausted, from the hunt, and her run, and more, from anxiety. Her feet were sore and her breasts hurt, and she had been bitten in several places by deer-flies attracted to the dry, caked blood. All she wanted to do was cling to him, to feel a strong masculine body give her reassurance.

He did his job well, stroking her hair calmingly, asking no questions until at last she looked up and said, "All that time, and you still haven't washed the blood off? I thought you were going to be nice and clean by the time I got back." She pouted at him, then crouched down in the water, sluicing her stiffening hair until the clear water clouded.

"I didn't know when you'd be back... or if you'd be alone. Did you... have to kill him?"

She considered lying. He would feel easier if he thought his sanctuary was still inviolate. But something about their new understanding prevented her. She would not, of course, be wholly honest. But she wouldn't lie more than absolutely necessary.

"No, I let him go. But he's not someone you have to worry about."

"You know him?"

"Yeah, he's a Seminole. He's the one who helped me build my house. He's one of the few people who know, more or less, where I live. But he was always half-drunk when I brought him out here, so he couldn't quite find the house. He was looking for it, and just stumbled on us."

"He was looking for you then?"

"My great-uncle was worried. Jimi came to see if I was here. I told him not to mention that he's seen me."

"But he's seen *me*! Now someone knows I'm out here."

"He didn't know who you were. And in any case, he's promised not to tell anyone."

"But how can you be sure?" Edgar began to pace through the

water. "We have to leave. There's nothing else to do."

"Nonsense. He's bound by oath to protect me. Just like all the Seminoles. I told him no one can know where I am, and he's not going to tell anyone. It's as simple as that."

Edgar had faith in her, but not in Jimi Golden.

"If it was any other situation," she agreed, "I'd be right with you. But this is different. If I ask a favor of him, there's no way he can refuse. And anyway, I told him I was leaving tonight, going somewhere else. We'll be good here a few more days. Come on, Edgar," she said, pulling him down into the water with her. "You're safe. You don't have to worry. You trust me, don't you?"

"I have so far."

"And I haven't failed you yet. Relax. Right now, we need to wash." She pushed him back in the water and straddled him. "Sweet Edgar," she said, kissing him lightly. But neither felt like making love now, and when they had bathed, they collected the piglets and the best cuts of sow, along with the curved tusks as a trophy, and walked home in the gloaming, their only intimacy a casual brush of arms.

Chapter 25

Edgar hovered nervously over her as the suckling pig, wrapped in layers of palmetto leaves, roasted in the coals. Are you sure we shouldn't leave tonight, he asked her time and again, whenever Mallory wasn't too nearby. He was sensible enough to realize no good could come of bringing Mallory into the conversation. Lucy assured him they had nothing to fear. They would stay in the swamps at least a week longer, then, when she had enough food harvested and preserved for them, she'd go out into the world and see if the hunt was still going strong. At least, that's what she told them. Actually she'd visit her friend the forger, and see if any freighter captains owed the Seminole or Miccosukee tribes any favors.

The fat little pig, its skin crisp and cracking over a layer of delicious fat, was ready just as the cool nighttime breezes began to blow. It was, she realized with a poignant sense of regret, probably the last night a roasted piglet would be appropriate. The days were already too warm for such fare. Only at night did the temperature still drop enough to make hot pork palatable. Soon the days would climb to the nineties, the weight of humidity making it feel a hundred degrees. A shame about the electricity. Air conditioning was one of the things she really loved about civilization. Soon the summer storm cycle would begin, as warm air rose from the baking interior of the state to meet cool sea breezes blowing in from either side. When they collided, great thunderheads would build, and travel across the peninsula until they died at dusk over the gulf.

For now, the land was trapped in a tormenting time of expectation, when every day was a degree warmer, and still the skies did not open to pour out their balm. The Tequesta, and the people who followed them and learned the ways of this land, consider it a dangerous time. People are on edge, nerves frayed by waiting. The quiet heaviness of the days becomes oppressive, and people find themselves disinclined to talk to their friends, to eat, to labor. It is a time of nervous activity, pointless abortive motion that begins, then stops in the futility of the dry heat, only to start again when restlessness takes over. The rains signal a return to true, archetypal Florida, and though people may grumble, they get tired of avoiding the truth of their state. Winter in Florida is a kind of denial. When the rains come, and with them all the delightful miseries of Florida, residents can at last relax, and stop kidding themselves.

Lucy gave Edgar the honor of carving the little pig, and the room filled with savory steam as the body cavity opened to reveal a stuffing of herbs, mushrooms and last fall's acorns, leached to sweetness in the spring. "Stuff an animal with the things it liked best to eat when it was alive," her mother had taught her. As they ate, Edgar regaled his brother with the story of the hunt, making Lucy sound so heroic she blushed.

"She saved my life," he said. "That sow would have ripped me open."

Lucy tried to play it down, but Edgar gave the dimensions of the pig, rather overstating her size, and then showed Mallory the curved white tusks Lucy had salvaged as a trophy. "Look at these," he said. "Your big brother wouldn't be here right now if it wasn't for Lu."

Mallory slapped her on the back. "See," he said affably. "I told you we shouldn't kill her." And he was permitted this little piece of revisionist history.

After midnight, while Mallory was drowsily occupied listening to the radio, Lucy and Edgar strolled out into the clearing at the bottom of the house.

"I'm tired as anything," Edgar said, reaching back to rub his own shoulders until Lucy took over the task. "But I don't think I'll be able to fall asleep. My eyes keep dashing around, like I've been living on coffee. But my body feels so heavy I can hardly move."

"It's from the hunt. Your muscles are tired, but your nerves keep replaying the exciting parts. That's why there are big feasts and ceremonies after a spectacular hunt, to burn off the extra adrenaline. You should spend the rest of the night dancing around a fire, chugging the black drink, then sleep all of tomorrow." Her fingers dug expertly into the bunched muscles of his back, a process that bordered on painful but forced him to relax.

"I was thinking of working these tusks tonight," she said. "Would you like a necklace? The straighter one would be perfect for that. I could drill a hole tonight, in about half an hour. You can help."

"Half an hour?" he asked. He was no handyman, but had an idea that holes are generally drilled in a matter of seconds.

"More or less, if you want to be authentic. I use a bow drill, which is a lot faster than a hand drill. Here, let me get a fire going and I'll show you." She took him to her outdoor workspace, a circle cleared of anything flammable, with a small shallow pit dug in the middle. The pit was lined with stones, with a circle of larger river rocks ensuring that the fire stayed put. She made a small, bright, quick-burning fire, one, she said, that would extinguish itself in an hour or two. "Even in the swamps, you have to be careful," she said as she added kindling and built a loose pyramid of narrow branches.

She knelt within the circle of firelight and took out something that looked like a miniature version of her hunting bow, complete with a scaled-down arrow. "This is the bit," she said, holding up the arrow-like piece, which was tipped with a very narrow stone point like an awl. "And this is the power." She looped the string around the shaft and strung the bow, with the shaft on the perpendicular. She held the bow in one hand, and with the other clapped a stone with a shallow depression over the top of the modified arrow. "You just saw, like this, and the shaft swivels. It takes a while to get the balance and the pressure right, but it's efficient. You can use the same principal to create friction to start a fire."

"But I saw that you used matches this time," he teased.

She shrugged. "Matches are easy to carry into the wilderness. Power drills aren't."

She drilled for a minute or two, then lifted the contraption and bent to blow away a cloud of ivory dust. He looked at the tusk, and found a tiny depression starting to form.

"That will take forever!" he protested.

"Not quite as long as that," she chided. "You said you couldn't sleep. This will help hypnotize you. And like I said, it's faster than a hand drill."

"Which is?"

"Same thing, but without the bow." She took it apart to show him. "Before someone made the leap of invention, a few thousand years ago, you had to do this." She grasped the drill stick at the top and rubbed it briskly back and forth between her hands, keeping a steady downward pressure so that in a few strokes her hands had slipped to the base. "Then, you have to start over again. For a very, very long time."

"And you can start fires that way too?"

"Yup. Friction makes heat. You do this on a piece of wood, long enough, fast enough, you get a little ember. But it takes a lot of practice to get a fire started this way. Every time you stop to reposition your hands, the wood cools. It's better with two pairs of hands. Want to see?"

She pulled a piece of wood from the fire and set up the drill along its edge. She directed Edgar's palms to the top of the drill, and each time she finished a cycle, he took over. It became a game, almost a race, to see who could drive the drill faster, and they worked so well together that their hands almost caught each other. "Look! There!" she cried at last, and bowed her head to blow on a little orange-glowing ember. It flared for an instant, then went out.

Edgar sat back on his heels. "All that work, for *that?*"

"Well, if you were depending on fire for survival or security, that would be a big step. Of course, you'd have good dry tinder ready, some shredded bark or dried moss, and you'd keep blowing and feeding the ember. Still, it would probably take you four or five tries before you got a fire going. It seems like a long time to a man who can flick a Bic and have a fire whenever he wants, but out here time moves differently. A few hours to start a fire, a few to catch a fish, and your day is filled. But you wouldn't have to start a fire more than a few times a year. Once you have a fire going, you try never to let it go out. You bank it the right way, so it lasts overnight, or you keep a coal alive."

"You know every way to survive, don't you."

"No one knows that," she replied.

He took her in his arms and pulled her down next to the fire. "I was so lucky to find you," he said. "I'd be dead by now, if it wasn't for you. I don't just mean from the sow. I would have been running all around Florida, thinking I was so clever, and not knowing jack. They would have gotten me in a couple of days, I know it. Funny, isn't it, how one little decision, one little turn in the road, can change your life. Do you know what I thought, when I first saw you next to your car? I thought, oh good, it's a girl. A pretty one. The pretty girls never give you any trouble when they're hostages. Huh! Shows what I know!"

She lay on his shoulder, and he rubbed his cheek against her hair. "I won't mind dying so much now," he said sleepily. "That's an odd thing to say, I know. Being with you should make me want to live more — and it does, really. But it probably won't happen that way, and somehow, these last few days with you will make whatever happens next bearable. I felt it when the sow was nearly on me today. I was terrified, but some little part of my brain was saying, it's all right, really. It was good at the end, and that's all that matters." His speech was soft, almost slurred, and Lucy realized that despite his professions of restlessness, he was drifting off to sleep.

"Lucy? If I do make it... someday... will you meet me? If I don't get caught can I find you here, in a year or two, and we'll see what happens?"

"Mmmm..." she said, affectionately but without commitment, and twined her body around his as they both fell asleep.

She woke near dawn to the smell of smoke, jerking to life so abruptly at the subliminal threat that Edgar opened his eyes too, scowling until he remembered who he was with.

"It's nothing," she said, laying her head back down. "I thought something was on fire. It's just the embers from last night." She stretched and yawned. "Do you want to go back in the house? The dew is starting to settle on us."

When they went inside they were accosted by a grinning Mallory who said, "Way to go, you stud!" and in a stage whisper, "Well, how was she?"

Lucy hid her smile and slipped into her sleeping bag, now almost too warm, to doze another hour or two. Edgar, blushing in the knowledge that he'd done nothing to speak of yet, endured a few playful fraternal punches and tried to go back to sleep too.

But the tides in his body were already surging toward morning, tides he had never known while he lived in the city where the sunrise is obscured by skyscrapers, the moon by smog. Now, though he didn't quite feel like getting up, he couldn't fall asleep again either. Smoke from the campfire seemed to cling to him, biting each breath with an acrid sharpness. He closed his eyes and lay still, but was roused by a periodic thumping noise. It sounded like someone was throwing pebbles or acorns against the window and, curious, he rose to investigate.

It took a great deal of staring before his eyes managed to tell that the little missiles striking the panes were in fact beetles. They flew headlong into the glass, the smaller ones tumbling to the ground, many of the largest recovering with an angry buzz of wings to continue their frantic journey, often as not right back into the window. It was unusual enough to interest him, and he wanted to ask Lucy about it, but she'd drifted back to sleep, and he wouldn't wake her for something so trivial.

He went outside to lounge on the deck, watching the pearly grayness of dawn stealthily lighten over the course of an hour to the golden glow of true daylight. He felt like he belonged here, like the land belonged to him, and there was a proprietary satisfaction in the very breaths he drew. The dewy air was soft, despite the strangely lingering smell of smoke. He would have to change his clothes, he decided, to escape the odor. But later. He was too content to think of moving now. He waited for the sounds he was beginning to associate with morning: the rail's cry, the rustle of sleepy squirrels, the good-night hoot of a great horned owl that roosted in a nearby cypress. But though he thought he had the pattern of matins down pat, none came this morning. Still, he didn't think much of it, only faulting himself for what must have been his own errors of observation.

I feel, he thought, like a patriarch Or at least a country squire. All around him were beautiful lands he was beginning to think of as his own, and inside the little round house, the only people he cared about. Nothing, he decided, closing his eyes, could be calculated to make him more content. Safety, relative solitude, good company when he wanted it, greenery, leftover pork and very few cares. I'll ask Lu about staying here longer, he decided. Unless he mistook her, she'd no doubt say yes.

He lay for another hour in a meditative daze, thinking how, only a day or two ago, he would have given anything to be out of this swamp and back in the frantic bustle of a city. In his other life — he thought of it that way now — he would have to be eating, or watching television, or walking the streets in search of stimulation. He would have scoffed at the idea of such rustic pleasures as watching the morning unfold, listening for beast and bird sounds that, oddly, still had not come. Now, the need to *do* something was not present. He was content simply to exist.

Lucy, closed in the house, was sleeping unusually late. But then, he thought, she had cause to be tired. Still, he wanted her company, and he began to consider whether it would be too selfish to enter the house and create a little accidental noise to prod her into wakefulness. No, not yet, he decided. It was full daylight, and past nine, but he would let her sleep herself out.

It was then that Edgar saw the first bird. It was not, in fact, the first, but the first he noticed, and he'd just reached a level of natural observation to be conscious that there was something wrong in its behavior. And in the one that followed it. Over the next half hour he became aware of a steady migration of birds heading east. They weren't stopping to feed or call, as birds generally do in their daily travels, but seemed to move with steady purpose, keeping low to the ground, skirting the house and moving on. Still, it made no deep impression on him, and he couldn't see any connection yet. He'd ask Lu, he thought. Probably some mating season thing.

He only began to worry when the snakes came.

They didn't come in horror-movie swarms. In fact, he saw no more than four or five snakes over the next hour. But as far as he knew, as far as Lucy told him, snakes were subtle and secretive, rarely leaving the underbrush unless on some specific mission. You won't see snakes unless you're looking for them, she said. You have to find them, they won't come find you. To stumble on a snake is something of a rarity. To see a handful of them, all different kinds, make their way resolutely across a clearing in the space of an hour, meant something strange was afoot.

Near eleven, Lucy came out, rubbing the sleep from her eyes.

"Lucy," he asked, "what does it mean when snakes all start coming out of the bushes?" He'd seen a dozen more while waiting for her to wake.

"Mmmm..." she said, stretching and yawning. "It means the end is near. Why?"

He pointed to the edge of the clearing, but no snakes emerged while she watched. "Of course, now that you're here, it stopped," he said. "Figures."

But as she sleepily looked down from her deck she saw a rabbit dash by, with nothing in pursuit. Then a bobwhite, leading a long string of fuzzy chicks. Her sharper eye picked out other things, lizards, normally arboreal, running on the ground, and she heard a sound in the distance like deer moving through the wood. The birds, even the insects, were silent. Then the wind shifted, telling her the cause of such unnatural events, and she spoke the word that strikes terror in the hearts of woodland-dwelling Floridians.

"Fire!"

Chapter 26

She breathed the word, almost to herself, as she looked wide-eyed, now completely awake, out into the swamps, smelling, sensing, thinking. For the first time in his memory, Edgar saw fear in her eyes.

"It's a forest fire, a big one. How long have the animals been coming?"

"I've been seeing snakes for the past couple of hours. And birds. And just before dawn, beetles kept hitting the window." He made the connections in a rush, reacting to her fear.

She forced herself to be calm. "They're running from the fire. It must be close," she said, almost to herself. "But I can't hear it, and I can't see any smoke yet." Even a quick fire would make the pine sap crackle, which could be heard far away. "I should have noticed it earlier," she chided herself. "I should have known that it wasn't from the campfire. We should have left by now, and there's still so much to do!"

She turned to Edgar. "We have to leave ahead of schedule," she said. "I'm sorry. I'll think of someplace to take you. But it's too dangerous to stay out here."

"It might be a small fire," he said, grasping. "What if it doesn't even come here? There's so much water around. How can it travel very far?"

"There's water, but the foliage is all dry. It should sweep through quickly. I don't think the trees will catch, the hardwoods, I mean. It'll just clear out the undergrowth, sear the bark, and extinguish itself."

"Then we can stay!" Please, he begged the fates. Don't make me leave now.

Lucy shook her head. "Even if the fire doesn't touch the house, we can't survive the smoke. It might not even reach my rise, but if it gets too close, we're done." She took a deep breath, forcing herself to think. "We have to leave, as soon as possible. But first I have to scout to see where the fire is, how fast it's moving. If we're lucky, it hasn't cut off our route to the car."

"Can't we all leave together?"

"No, you have to get your things ready. It'll waste time if we all set out, and have to turn back. If the fire's too big to the west we'll have to follow the animals and take the water route out."

"But then we'll have to leave the car."

She nodded. It was the very last option. At least gemstones can't burn.

"I'll come with you, then," he insisted, but she only patted his cheek.

"You'll only slow me down. I have to be fast today. I won't be gone more than an hour. In the meantime, if you want to help, there's something you can do."

While he told Mallory about their new predicament, Lucy dug through her storage until she pulled out three cylinders that roughly resembled fire extinguishers. "It's a fire retardant gel," she explained to Edgar as she assembled the spray nozzle. "Fires around here tend to stay low. Flames might lick the bottom of the house, but it should be safe. If the stilts burn through, though, the house collapses. Most fires won't be in one place more than a few minutes, and these posts are sturdy, but I'm not taking any chances."

She showed him how to spray the viscous gel. "It will last a few days. Cover the stilts and the underside of the house, then use this," she gave him an elongated attachment, "to spray the roof as much as you can. Cypress isn't particularly flammable, but a spark and a good breeze could do the trick in the right circumstances."

"Do you think you might lose your house?" Edgar asked. The thought disturbed him as much as if the house was his own.

"Possibly. It held through a fire when we were still building it. But even if the house succumbs, the land will recover in a month or two, after the rains fall. Fire is good for this place, at least, for the parts that really belong here."

She left him to his labors and scampered out into the swamps to seek the fire. She returned somewhat more than an hour later, panting, her face grimed by char.

"It's big," she gasped when she caught her breath. "The leading edge is a mile away, and it's moving, fast." That was good for the land, bad for them. Her eyes were haunted, and Edgar tried to imagine what it would be to face a wildfire alone. He put an arm around her. "Did you finish spraying? Then we have to leave, now."

Edgar's bag was packed, waiting on the deck. When Mallory went in to get his, she said, in a very low voice, "The fire is heading into the path we need to take to get to the car. Depending on how much wind there is, we might not make it."

"Do we still try?"

"If we don't, if we take a canoe through the sawgrass, we come out in a populated area. Without transportation. It won't be easy to get you out of that."

"If you think we can make it," he said, "we should go back to the car. We'll be faster than we were coming in. I promise."

She smiled. "A slug would be faster than you two were, coming in. But you've improved."

Could they make it, she wondered? Even traveling by herself, she wasn't sure. Fire is by its nature unpredictable. A shift in wind, a slope, a change of vegetation, and its speed could dramatically alter. A fire you thought was a safe distance away could circle around you, blocking your escape. She had seen this fire, and it worried her. Fires have personality, and this one seemed particularly treacherous.

But she said, resolutely, "We go to the car." It was her best bet to save Edgar.

As Lucy led them away, Edgar turned to look back on the stilt-ed little house. He had never felt attached to a place before, never regretted leaving anything as much as he did now. For a few days Lucy and her house in the swamps had offered an oasis in a parched world of strife. Now he must quit it, and return to that world, that life which now seemed so much less real than this brief one in the wilderness.

He felt a hand on his arm. "It will still be here," she said softly. "So will I. And someday, you can come back to us."

With a sigh almost lost in the strengthening wind, he turned away from the cabin, and headed back to civilization.

The first mile was easy, despite glum spirits and Lucy's contagious anxiety. Once they crossed the water (she tied her dugout to a mid-water cypress knee and waded ashore, hoping to save it from fire) they found the land much drier than it had been on their outward journey. Even Mallory, no woodsman, had an easy time of it. But before the hike was half over Lucy had spotted the first tiny flames licking the leaf litter.

"It's just smolder from an airborne spark," she assured them, stamping it out. "The main fire is still to the southwest. We probably won't even see it." But the next hundred yards proved her wrong.

The exited a thick copse to find themselves assaulted by a gritty wind that carried a cloud of ash. Behind it, flames licked the dry cypress and scrubby, skinny pines. Lucy froze, seemingly mesmerized, until Edgar gave her a little shake.

"Come on, Lucy. It doesn't look too bad." Few of the flames reached above knee-high, and though the pines were starting to crackle, the hardwoods weren't even charred. "If this is all there is, we can make it to the car, no problem."

But Lucy scarcely heard him. She was listening with all her might, feeling the shift of the wind, smelling the acrid air. This fire was not all it seemed. The wood was dense enough that in the best circumstances they could see no more than a few hundred yards, and that only in glimpses. This was not the inferno she had seen on her scouting foray. Somewhere, there was a vicious wall of flame that sent fingers of fire high above the treetops. This would be no more than an arm of the main fire. But where was that?

Frightened, she was losing her sense of direction — not that she didn't know where she was, but she felt herself losing her hold on the permutations of events that were influencing the fire's location. When she started out, she was confident she would know where the fire was at all times, and keep well away from it. Now she feared it had outdistanced her, or perhaps outsmarted her.

She caught a smell of burning mahogany wood. The main wall was close. The breeze grew stronger, feeding the unseen fire. Then all at once, the wind whipped from a different direction and her skin flushed with a new heat. The fire, the real fire, was close enough to be sucking at the air, feeding itself. Suddenly the air cleared — there was a break in the smoke from the lesser leading fire, and behind it they could see flames pushing up billowing black fumes. One solitary pine was utterly engulfed, and pitched its burning head before toppling to the ground.

"If a tree falls in the forest, and everyone there is burned to death, do they make a sound?" Mallory asked, but even he was affected by the horrible grandeur of the forest fire.

Lucy didn't need to give any orders. Without a word she turned away from the fire. They would have to circle more than she wanted to avoid the advancing conflagration, which would add to their time, but it was the only possible way of beating the advancing flames. If they could get to the car, the way to the road would probably be clear. Probably. If not, they might be trapped.

She kept them at a ground-eating trot. She would have liked to run, but her charges weren't up to that. The air cleared somewhat as they fled the fire, and though the smell was still heavy it wasn't dangerous to breathe. But the sky was beginning to darken, and gusts still sent red embers swirling hundreds of feet into the air, to rain down and spread new blazes.

A half-mile later she tightened their course. They would have to turn toward the fire again or they'd never make it to the car. A grueling, silent, interminable time later she knew, by instinct more than concrete navigation, that they were near her Volvo. She stopped, turned in one direction, than another. Mallory jumped on her indecision immediately.

"Don't tell me you're lost?"

At any other time she would have ignored him, but she was growing too frazzled to think about everything. "I'm not lost. The car's right around here, somewhere."

"You can't find the fucking car!" Mallory yelled, throwing up his hands.

"Shut up!" she growled. "Let me think!" She could feel the main fire growing closer, and all around them pockets of flame began to catch from the flying embers. The wind kept most of the smoke steered away from them, but soon, she knew, they would have to flee outright or die.

Then she saw the car. It sat, undamaged, much as she had left it, in a tangle of vines. But between them and the car was a stretch of leaping flames. The ground smoldered, the fuel almost consumed, but the fire seemed to magically die and revivify, sending up explosive ignitions whenever it found a patch of new tinder. Lucy had to close her eyes and fight back tears. The car was untouched, but the only way to reach it was through the fire.

She swayed against Edgar's strong chest, trying to draw strength from him. She was so tired, so tired... The smaller fires had almost surrounded them now, and she could hear the unearthly roar of the main conflagration close by. They either had to run away now, or...

Without thinking any further, without heeding Edgar's startled, then frantic cries, she shrugged off her pack and dashed toward the flames that separated them from the car. Ignoring the stitch in her side, her lungs that burned with smoke, and her rapidly heating feet, she sprinted through the flaming grass. Embers singed her arm hair and choked her, but she ran on, and a moment later, though it seemed an eternity, she reached her darling black Volvo. Nearby was the hollow tree filled with a season's supply of nuts and a king's ransom of uncut gems. She could come back for them anytime.

Laughing, she waved briefly across the smoke and hopped in. It took two tries to get the engine going after being idle so long, but she gunned it, made sure it would hold, and took off, as Mallory later said, like a bat into hell straight for the Battle brothers.

"Jeez," Mallory said, impressed, as she stopped just long enough for him to roll into the back seat. "You must have been doing, what, fifty, crashing through bushes on fire, sparks flying up behind your tires. I've never met anyone crazy like you are."

"Oh," she said lightly, "it wasn't as bad as it looked." But she smelled burning rubber, and knew she'd been lucky. Edgar saw that she was trembling, and she kept up an improbable speed, running down everything smaller than a sapling, until they couldn't see any hint of fire behind them.

But it was another four hours before they reached even the dirt road. She had escaped the fire by an unfamiliar route, and though the way was easy for a while, it wasn't long before she had to backtrack to avoid mud holes her car couldn't handle and foliage it couldn't pass. At one point she spent half an hour walking in front of the car with a machete, hacking through vines that blocked their path, only to come upon an unexpected deep ravine that forced them to back through the way she had so laboriously cleared. She came near to tears again, until Edgar told her some silly joke that revived her.

She found she only had to look at him to feel her courage rise, her strength return. Was this love? This heartening, this determined drive he seemed to inspire? Their hardship did this much — it gave what she felt a name. When she stood beside him up to her ankles in mud as they put their backs into freeing the car from yet another sucking rut, she looked over at him and realized, yes, I do love him. And she knew, then and there, that she would do anything to ensure his freedom and safety. Every gem, every ounce of influence she possessed, would be put to use for him. The debate that had played itself out in her mind since she met him ended. Edgar Battle had been thrown in her path; she'd be damned if she wasn't going to keep him!

Chapter 27

When they reached the dirt road, the first hint of civilization, they rested. Lucy scrubbed the ash from her face, and let Edgar tenderly clean the little burns from flying debris that dotted her arms and throat. Her face seemed hollow and her eyes were bloodshot, but he saw they were bright when she looked at him. He might have lost his sanctuary, he realized, but he hadn't lost her.

"Well," Mallory said, swishing his mouth with stale water, "Where to next?"

"I've been thinking about that," Lucy said. No place was as safe as her cabin, of that she was sure. The best alternative was to find a temporary shelter, and then, when the rains began and the danger of fire had passed, return to her land. Much of the area would be flooded soon, making any intrusion even less likely. They could stay through the summer, until she thought of a way to get them out of the country. Right now she needed a place for a few days at most.

She'd thought, for a time, she might bring them to the Seminole Big Cypress reservation. There were ceremonial sites that wouldn't be in use. No one would bother them there, and with her clout she could keep the tribes silent. But she decided it would be too much of a risk to let *anyone* see the Battle brothers. She was loved and respected by the Seminole and the Miccosukee, but she didn't think so highly of human nature to believe that there wasn't at least one man among them who wouldn't pass up the opportunity of collecting what surely must be a handsome reward. She didn't know what the figure was up to now, but two days ago it a quarter-million for the pair. It had risen steadily since their escape. Plenty of people would ignore an uncertain curse for the possibility of real, immediate fortune.

"I think our only choice is to go back into the woods again," she said. "There are hunting cabins all around the Everglades. Plenty of people know about them, but if we pick one of the most obscure ones we could probably stay there a few days without running into anyone."

"Aren't you getting sick of the woods yet?" Mallory asked his brother. But he replied, quite the contrary, he was just getting used to it.

"There won't be any way to hide you in a city. Not yet, anyway. I know a good spot to the south, but we'll have to get back on I-75. There are some jeep trails outside of Naples I think this car can handle. We'll be there in about an hour."

She wanted to be settled before midnight. She scanned the skies. Had the moon risen yet? Though the sky overhead was dark — it was between eight and nine — she couldn't even see any stars. The smoke, she thought.

She started the car, not so pretty as it had been, but in practical terms none the worse for wear, and drove slowly down the dirt road to meet the interstate.

Edgar didn't like driving at night. It made him loose his sense of direction entirely. He'd never learned to feel the rhythms of the moon and stars as he instinctively felt those of the sun, and barreling into the darkness, however well-lit the roads, made him feel like he was being herded into a labyrinth with no string, no trail of breadcrumbs left behind to give him any hope of escape. Every mile that passed beneath their tires, the farther he felt from safety, the closer to danger. The old ominous dread had returned, though he told himself it wasn't a premonition, only the ravings of a weary mind.

Their night ride brought back childhood nightmares, too, endless drives with his mother at the wheel, he in the back seat, curled alone and unseen with his face pressed against the window. He'd always felt abandoned, somehow, riding in the car at night, though his mother was only a foot or two in front of him. Everything was so still, so flat and dimensionless to a little boy who did not know the destination, who was tired but dared not sleep. They shouldn't have been traumatic rides. Usually they were only to or from his grandmother's house on the Jersey Shore late some Sunday night. But the way was always filled with imagined terrors as, pressed up against the window, he would fancy he saw things. What sorts of things, his mother would ask the few times he tried to tell her. But he couldn't describe them. When they drove through the city he would see people, in quick shadowed glimpses like ghosts, people on streets, in alleys, probably just bums and prostitutes and everyday people seeking diversion, but at night some trick of fancy would turn them into demon-possessed Heironymus Bosch beings, writhing in ecstatic torments.

The terrible part was that he could never slow down and actually *see* them. They came in flashes and peeks, half real, half capped by his imagination. They were all the more horrible for being only fleetingly seen; the unbelievable glimpsed is sometimes more real than when it is stared full in the face. He thought, in his young mind, that if he could only stop and have a good look at the things he thought he saw, even if they were true, even if they were more horrible than he had imagined, he would be less afraid of them after the confrontation. But his mother would never stop, and he faced the almost-seen creatures alone, without even her voice to ward them off, for she did not like to talk when she drove, it distracted her.

Between New York and his grandmother's house, they would pass through a long stretch of woods, and sometimes this was even worse than the city. People, he could understand, and even at six could see how some of them could turn into strange beasts and monsters at night. But his experience with trees was limited, and though he sometimes doubted the things he conjured up in the city, he was thoroughly convinced that under cover of darkness all trees turned into many-armed giants determined to snatch him out of the car. He was somewhat reassured when, after a little research, he discovered trees are firmly anchored by roots, even, he presumed, the evil night trees. In any case, none ever got him, but still he would press his little nose against the glass in fear, trying to watch every oak and birch and horse chestnut, knowing, as all children know, that nothing bad can get you if you stare unblinkingly at it.

He grew out of his childish fears eventually, but even as an adult he would sometimes see leering forms in his dreams that he recognized as vestiges of those night drives. And now, at forty, with Lucy Brightwing beside him and his brother in the back seat, he sometimes thought he saw a many-fingered hand snake out of the roadside and reach for him.

Lucy drove with her hand on his thigh, which he covered with his own big paw. Should I tell him about the jewels now, she wondered? No, there's still much to do before they can be sold, still more before the proceeds will be put to proper use. Until their course was more clearly laid out, she would not burden Edgar with hopes that, while they weren't false, were undefined and distant. Still, it was comforting to think of the millions hidden in the charred woods, enough, she hoped, for her own future and his.

Lost in her reverie, it was Edgar who spotted the potential trouble, and she had a heart-stopping moment of fear when her head snapped up to his word of warning. She thought it must be the dreaded roadblock. A moment later she saw that, like the last such scare, the excitement was all off to the side of the road, not blocking it. Relieved, she cruised toward the bright lights.

"It's nothing for us to worry about," she said.

"A road crew?" Edgar asked. "It's pretty late for that."

"Nope, not a road crew — a chain gang."

"What? You're shitting me." Mallory said. "I thought that was only in movies. Poor bastards. I wonder if any of them are thinking about escaping right now?"

"Thinking, but not acting. Look over there." The spotlights were intense, shining down on the dozen or so linked men from a high tower of collapsible scaffolding rigged to the transport bus. "That guard up there has a rifle, and there are probably a couple more inside the van, in the air conditioning, just waiting for anyone to make a break."

They were just approaching the gathering of men. The lights were so bright they could see the details of the scene a long way off. The men were all black, mostly middle-aged, with thin token chains around their wrists and ankles, enough to remind them what they were, not so much that they interfered with digging ditches, or picking up trash along the roadside. Each man was linked to his neighbor, so no individual had the power of choice, to run, and brave the rifle. Their eyes were listless and dispirited, everything from their slumped shoulders to their shuffling walks pointing to a lifetime of hopelessness. Lucy slowed to stare, then self-consciously turned away.

Edgar, looking at them, saw himself. Or rather, saw what he would have been. Lucy's hand on his thigh told him he had been reborn, plucked up from a dwindling life of incarceration, humiliation, and worse, to be swept along instead in the fierce, beautiful tide of Lucy's own life. He too turned away from the depressing sight, and brought Lucy's hand to his lips.

Then the car depressurized with the back window opening, and he heard Mallory shout "Souieeee! Pig, pig, pig!" Edgar only had time to wince in dreadful anticipation of the sound he knew would follow, the sound he almost believed he'd forgotten, Lucy to swerve madly to throw off his aim, before they heard the shots.

Mallory had half his body out the window, whooping like a madman. "You're free! You're free!" he shouted to the old men as they drove past. The tower guard was on the ground, shot cleanly through the chest as they pulled abreast of the chain gang. The guard who ran out of the bus at the sound of the commotion joined the first. Thanks to Mallory's expert, or lucky, shooting, no one was left to guard the prisoners. But they only stared dumbly at the fallen guards, at each other, and at the ground, kicking their feet nervously in the dust.

Lucy slowed, stunned. They'd been in the clear.

"Run, damn you!" Mallory screamed, but the prisoners, some of who had been prisoners for the last fifty years, began to file back into the transport van, to await the arrival of some new authority.

Edgar sat silent, the only motion of his body a steady rapid pulse flickering in the hollow at the base of his throat. It happened again, he thought grimly. Just as I knew it would. He should be beyond surprise by now. He should expect it of his brother, his crazy brother, his stupid brother... his insane brother. Just when he started to feel content, secure, even happy, in stepped Mallory to do the most senseless thing imaginable and ruin it all. He should have known it would happen again, he repeated to himself. But this would be the last time.

Around him, evil night trees reached out with swaying clawed arms.

"Stop the car," he said, quietly, evenly.

"Edgar, we have to go. We might still be able to..."

"Stop the car." And he reached over to shift to neutral and pluck the keys from the ignition, leaving her to coast to a stop along the roadside a quarter mile from the chain gang.

"But Edgar!"

"Mallory! Out of the car." Edgar's voice was stern, almost paternal, discipline commingled with love.

"Did you see that shit?" Mallory asked as he stepped out of the car. "Perfect chance for a getaway and those old guys just stand there! Do you think I should go talk some sense into them?"

"Stay right here, Mallory,"

" 'Sup, bro?" he asked, catching something new in Edgar's voice.

"This has to end now," Edgar said. "I've been taking care of you since you were a baby. But I'm not going to do it anymore." He drew his Glock and set it, very gently, against Mallory's forehead.

"Yeah, I catch wise, man," Mallory said, his own gun hanging indifferently at his side. "You didn't like my moves just now. It's cool, though, I got them all. We don't have shit to worry about."

But the gun never moved from his forehead. "I love you Mallory," he said, and his forefinger curled around the trigger.

Before he could pull it Mallory cried, "Get down!" as from out of the darkness new spotlights opened on them like glowing eyes, and a uniformed man stepped out with a shotgun. Mallory, reflexes ever sharp, raised his gun almost as soon as he was aware of the danger. The officer, part of the chain gang team, parked in darkness down the road, burst from the car, shotgun to shoulder, and immediately staggered from a shot to his bulletproof vest. He managed a single shot himself, wide scattered pellets that zinged past Mallory's arm, ripping the material and grazing his skin, before he was felled by a bullet to the knee and, when on the ground, another to the unprotected crown of his head. The brothers stood framed in the spotlight, their weapons now facing the same direction, though Lucy didn't know if Edgar had fired a shot. They could see no more motion from behind the headlight's unblinking glare.

"Whew!" Mallory said, laughing. "Close, huh? But we still got it, bro. You and me, together... the cops don't have a chance." He didn't see his brother's pained look as he turned away and circled to the car to Lucy's side. "Did you see that, girl?" he said through her rolled-down window. "Right out of the darkness, and we still got him! You stay here. I'm gonna go have a little talk with those poor chained-up bastards. You'd think one of 'em would have spirit enough to run. I'll be back in two shakes." And with his cocky, bouncy stride he strutted down the empty interstate toward the chain gang, whose members had settled themselves in the van to enjoy the air conditioning as they waited for order to be restored.

Edgar followed him with heavy steps, stopping, as Mallory had done, by Lucy's side of the car. She got out to stand beside him, and his eyes sought support for what he was about to do. She gave him nothing, lest he cast it back at her later. It had to be from him alone. But she looked at him with such fervent love and compassion that he had all the answer he needed. There would be no blame laid elsewhere. He wasn't doing this to save the world from future misery and pain at Mallory's hands; nor even for Lucy's sake. He was killing his brother, he knew, for completely selfish reasons, because he could not bear to ever see that look fade from Lucy's face. There was no chance of happiness to be found while his brother lived.

All around them, the world seemed to growl, a low rolling rumble that echoed in their bones. Edgar looked alarmed, but Lucy, her face radiant in the headlights, said, "Thunder! The rains have come. At last! The fire will be out soon. We can go back to my swamp." Edgar raised his gun to Mallory's retreating back. The skies opened fire with heavy cannonballs of rain.

Lucy was braced for the sound, and didn't flinch as three sharp reports rang out, louder than the thunder. She was so prepared, so calm and stanch that when the wrong man fell, when Edgar staggered and clutched at the car for support before crumpling to his knees, then pitching to his back, she was still looking expectantly at Mallory, waiting for him to die.

Then she was on her knees over her love, hands on his stricken face as his body writhed on black pavement still warm from the day's sun. For a moment, amid the pain, Edgar looked up at Lucy with wild regret. Then, with a quick shuddering sigh, his eyes flickered and closed.

Did Lucy speak? What could she say if she knew no charm to bring her love back from the dead. Did Lucy weep? Who could tell, for the deluge had come, steaming on the tarry interstate, washing soot and tears from her face. She had loved him, with a love she had fully acknowledged, for less than an hour, and now he was gone.

The realization that someone had shot him was an afterthought. She looked up, fairy opals of water on her hair and cheeks, and saw a dark uniformed shape emerge from the headlights.

The corrections officer, a woman with her hair pulled back in a high ponytail, stepped forward with her gun raised, pointed not at Lucy but at Edgar. She recognized Edgar, and the woman with him was a hostage if she'd ever seen one, battered, distraught.

"Step away from the suspect, ma'am," the officer said. "Are you hurt ma'am?"

Lucy didn't bother to think, knowing any pause might give her compassion. She stood obediently, but in her hand was Edgar's own Glock. When the snake has bitten you, she thought, when she has filled you with poison and stolen your life, does it do any good to kill her?

"It's okay, ma'am. It's over now."

Mallory spared her the damning decision. He shot the officer in the head, and Lucy turned away from her almost before she fell. She tried not to feel relief, tried not to wonder if she'd have done it herself, in the end. No witnesses, she thought numbly. I can still have my land, my tribe. Once Mallory is gone, it will be like I was never here.

The time between the first three shots, and the last one, was only a matter of a few seconds. Mallory came running up, now almost blinded by the rain. Lucy caught him before he could reach Edgar, holding him with her arms around his chest as he looked over her shoulder at his fallen brother. She felt the sobs shake him, but wouldn't let him go. She couldn't bear the thought of him touching Edgar. Her Edgar.

In a moment she pushed him away from her hard, looking at him sternly. "There's nothing else we can do."

"But what's going to happen now?" He was subdued. She though he'd be raving, kill the chain gang, her, himself, but he only looked confused and wiped ineffectually at his rain-spattered glasses. "Lucy? What's going to happen now?" For all his headstrong recklessness, he was used to having someone to follow. He might deviate from a course, but he still needed to have one set. He looked at her helplessly, a child waiting for guidance.

With Edgar gone, she thought, my obligation to Mallory ceases. I could bring him to the next town. Or I could just leave him here. Or, I could finish what Edgar set out to do. "Come," she said, taking his arm and leading him away from his brother's body to the thick woods that bordered the interstate. "We have to split up now. That officer called for backup, they'll be here any minute. I'll drive on, to lure them away. When they catch me, I'll give them some story that throws them off the tracks, say you stopped another car and crossed to the northbound lane. I'll think of something."

"But where will I be?" His voice sounded small in the rain.

"You'll be right here, where they won't think to look for you. Just walk straight into the woods. It's just like where I live. Go out about two or three miles and wait. When everything clears up here, say, by tomorrow night, I'll be able to come back for you."

She was sure he would refuse the plan. Who in their right mind wouldn't? But he only said, "How will you find me?"

She smiled at him. "I'm an Indian, remember? I'll track you. Don't worry. You just have to sit tight in the woods for a day, and

I'll come back and find you. Just stay in one place, and wait for me, ok? No matter how long it takes."

He nodded.

"Go in right here. The rain will stop in a little while, and you'll be dry and comfortable. Find a cozy place to take a nap, and I'll be back for you before you know it." Her voice was maternal and reassuring, and it pained her to see how he trusted her. She still had Edgar's Glock in her hand.

Obediently, Mallory started to walk through the palmettos that bordered the thicker woods, wading through them like waves, his hands trailing on their sharp points. He turned before he had gone three steps, and looked at her with a peculiar smile.

"Edgar wasn't really going to shoot me, was he?"

She answered automatically, "Of course not."

"Of course not," he echoed, and turned back to the woods. When he started walking, Lucy raised the gun. But almost at once she lowered it again.

She'd been active in the workings of fate too long. It was time, she decided with a sigh, to step back and let the world follow its own course. She would not shoot Mallory. Poor Mallory, brotherless and incomplete now. He must be left to make his own way. Her path, and that of the Battle brothers, had been side by side for a time. Now they diverged. She turned away from Mallory just before he disappeared, and walked past Edgar to the car. Already, the rain was washing the blood away.

As she drove off, she didn't let herself look in the rear-view mirror. She didn't want to see Edgar's premonition come true, that he was lying dead and alone on a roadside, wasted life ended in pointless, violent death.

For a time, Lucy drove in complete darkness, her headlights off to avoid unwanted attention, sticking to the pavement more by its feel beneath her tires than by sight. One siren passed her on the far side of the wooded median that separated north- and southbound lanes, then she had the road to herself again. When she'd passed enough bends she turned on her lights again, and drove, like any other traveler, homeward. She tried to cheer herself, contemplating her riches, her new nation. I'll work on the smokehouse, she thought, and get that composting toilet Nighteyes told me about. I'll plant a vegetable garden. I'll make a new boat, a new bow, a new house…

She sighed at her futile efforts, but refused to abandon them. She would have to think about Edgar again someday, have to mourn him. But she couldn't do it yet. The wound was too fresh, and if she yielded even a little now she would break down. She would be unhappy for a while, she told herself firmly, but after all, she had known him less a week, loved him less than an hour…

She swallowed hard and turned on the radio. She tuned in to the middle of a song from the sixties, a bouncy, desperate Simon and Garfunkel tune, assuring her it was going to be all right, that the worst was over now.

But it wasn't going to be all right, she thought through a forced smile. And as she drove to the Big Cypress reservation, it was a very long time indeed before the sun rose, a red and cheerless rubber ball, through the eastern thunderheads.

Chapter 28

The next day, Lucy took a dirt bike into the woods and gathered her fortune from its barely charred hiding place. The fire was gone, leaving bare black earth that would regenerate within a week or two now that the rains were here. Only a few hardwood trees, older, drier ones on their last legs anyway, had succumbed. Her house was intact. The fire never made it that far.

The morning after that, Lazarus Nighteyes got slightly more than he'd anticipated from Lucy's gems. He, Billie Bald Cypress and Lucy each got a tad more than four million, three of which Lucy immediately handed back to Nighteyes. He transferred the land deed to her, and passed the rest of the money on, grease for the legislative engine.

That afternoon Lucy Brightwing sat in the middle of a cluster of laughing, eager children.

Bald Cypress, pleased to receive his take, instantly forgave its tardiness and declared a feast and celebration for all who cared to attend. Lucy, the secret guest of honor, would have excused herself, but her position in life made it hard for her to avoid public festivities without a concrete excuse and she didn't have the energy to invent one. She was a ceremonial figure, and obligation was one of the prices of respect.

Though she grumbled a bit internally, she welcomed the distraction. She'd kept herself ceaselessly busy in the time since... but she didn't even like to put a name to the event. She still held back the waves of sadness that at times threatened to drown her, and she thought perhaps, if she kept them at bay long enough, the tide would turn and leave her calm.

Keeping occupied with plans for her reservation, and seeming to return to her normal life, helped stave off the questions that inevitably accompanied her homecoming. She answered Bald Cypress' first queries lightly, but discouraged him from asking more, saying, when he pressed her, that she got him what he wanted and how she did that was her own affair. Which, he acknowledged, was perfectly true, and though he still had his share of questions he was wise enough to know he'd get no answers from her.

"You were right," he said to Lazarus Nighteyes on the day of the feast.

"Is that quite like saying you were wrong?" Nighteyes asked archly, sipping at a dark, stimulating holly drink Lucy brewed for the occasion. Bald Cypress only *humphed* and fell silent.

The two men, each in a way a leader of his people, looked with satisfaction over the gathering in the field. It was by no means the entire population of Florida Seminole and Miccosukee, but it was a collection that could make a man almost feel his was not a dwindling people. Even an impromptu feast like this could gather nearly a thousand souls on a day's notice. Smells of cooking were carried on the breeze: deer and alligator, with the occasional intrusion of hamburgers and corn dogs; catfish, fry bread, and seasoned vegetable stews. At the far end of the field a group of drummers beat out rhythms generations old, to which wizened women moved their feet in shuffling dance. At night there would be more dancing and storytelling, with prizes given to the best entertainers. But already, Lucy Brightwing had attracted a group of children. Wherever she went, children always followed her like baby ducks, strung behind her when she walked, huddling close when she settled herself. Now they begged her for tales as if they were tidbits, and she teasingly threw them fragments of what she would tell at length later.

"Something happened to her while she was gone," Nighteyes

said, concern in his crinkled eyes.

"Yes," Bald Cypress returned. "She committed robbery, and she did it very well. That's all that happened to her."

"At least, all you care about," the other said under his breath. But he continued to watch her, sagely prying through her cheerful expression to some uncertain thing that lurked beneath. Once, across the distance, she caught him watching, and quickly looked away.

Nighteyes shrugged. "Whatever happened, it is only for her to know. As long as she is returned to us, I am content."

Bald Cypress looked at his Miccosukee counterpart narrowly. "She's my kin, Lazarus," he said, "but what is she to you, that you think so much about her secrets?"

Nighteyes laughed. "She is a very fine young woman," he said, "and a favorite of all our people. Not to mention the last of the Tequesta."

Bald Cypress rolled his eyes. "Must I constantly be reminded of that?"

"She must be, why not you?"

"An accident of birth set her higher in our people's eyes than you or I will ever be," Bald Cypress said, keeping his voice low enough so none of the passing crowd could catch his words. They would not be popular sentiments.

"An accident of birth, and accidents in the years that follow, put us all where we are, my friend. Don't be jealous of her because she makes herself loved. Her road has not been easy. Nor," he added, looking at her again with concerned, kind eyes, "do I think it will get any easier." With that he rose and abandoned the company he could only tolerate, for the sake of form, in small doses, to join the press of children around Lucy.

"May I listen too?" he asked.

"Of course," she replied in genuine welcome, though some of the young ones backed away in awe. "But wait, we can move to the tent so you can have a bench."

"Do I look too decrepit to sit on the earth with the rest of you?" he asked with amusement, and she spread her arms, inviting him to sit.

"I've been telling them the story of how fire came to the Tequesta," she said.

"Which story is that?"

"Why, the true one, of course! The rest are just pretty legends, but the Tequesta know the truth about, well, perhaps not everything, but nearly everything."

"And the Miccosukee," Nighteyes said, winking at the children, "are a very young people, and do not always know the truth. Therefore we must rely on Lucy Brightwing to set us straight."

She smiled at his gentle ribbing, but put the children aright. "There is no whole truth, only part truths. Some come very close to being complete, but they never really are. Therefore, it is sometimes best to choose the *prettiest* version of the truth, rather than the one you think is most correct. Now," she continued with her story. "Many years ago..." But she was instantly interrupted by a demand from a nut-colored six-year-old to know how much *many* is.

"Oh, ever so long before you were born, my sweet. Perhaps as much as nine or ten years." She cleared her throat and looked around to make sure there were no more questions before she resumed. "Many years ago, there was not a single drop of fire on the earth. All of the fire lived in the sky, in a very secret place. Fire was so proud it would never even pay a passing visit to earth, not even a quick how-do-you-do. But humans knew about fire, for the fire people would hold great balls, where they'd dance across the sky. That was lightning, but in those days lightning never deigned to set foot on the earth.

"Humans looked with envy on fire, wishing they could capture some of its brilliance for themselves. I am very sorry to have to tell you this, children, but it was greed more than need that made man desire fire. Fire is certainly nice in the winter, but even in north Florida it doesn't get very cold, and skins are enough protection. And I'm sure you all like cooked food better than raw, but raw food is just as healthy, especially fish, which is what they ate most of. Humans wanted fire because it was beautiful. It was like a glittering jewel." She flicked a glance at Nighteyes. "A jewel everyone longs to possess. Humans, who were beginning to think of themselves as the best things on earth, naturally wanted the best possessions. And so they schemed to get fire.

"For years they climbed trees and built ladders and jumped as high as they could in thunderstorms, trying any way they could think of to reach the fire that lived in the sky. But to no avail; the sky was just too high for them. They asked the birds, but none could fly high enough except the vulture. They promised him all the food he could eat, and riches for his entire family, so he made the attempt. But the fire people saw him coming and threw a bolt at him, so he only got his head feathers burned off for his trouble.

"Then, after many days of trying, the chief of the Tequesta felt a little tug on his trouser leg. At first he ignored it, thinking it only the pull of a thorn, but it came again, this time accompanied by a tiny little voice peeping, 'Please, sir, may I try to fetch fire for you?'

"The chief looked down and spied a young rat. The rat was really very young, hardly a teenager in rat years, but he stood high on his hind legs to seem taller. 'You!' the chief laughed. 'Fetch fire, where all others have failed? Ha!' But the rat was determined. He fluffed out his tail — in those days, you see, rats had tails like squirrels, only ever so much finer — no, you'll find out soon enough, no more questions!—and squeaked 'Let me try! I can do it!'

"Then the chief looked serious. 'But you will be killed, little friend. If the other animals couldn't succeed, how can you?' The rat, however, persevered. He had a great and worthy motivation for trying to prove himself. Rats have always had a difficult life, and their lot was even harder in those days. That year alone, four of his brothers died because they didn't have enough to eat. He saw what riches the humans were offering for fire, and he thought this might be the salvation of his people. He made the chief promise to provide food for his people, not just for his family, and not just for now, but for all rats, for all time. It was a considerable reward, worth far more than the temporary riches offered to other animals. But the chief was so certain the rat would fail that he didn't hesitate to make the promise. They clasped hands over it, and the rat departed.

"Now, how is a rat to get to the sky? And how is he to avoid being burned by the fire once he is there? And should he succeed in all this, how ever is he to get fire back down to earth? The answers are, in order, favors, cleverness, and sacrifice. These are the ways by which all things are achieved, oh my children.

"I won't tell you exactly how the young ratling managed to reach the sky, for I'm sure, if I told you his secret, you'd all try to go there yourselves and then your parents would come complaining to me." They groaned. "But I can tell you that he was always a very good and helpful rat, who throughout his young life had done favors for people whenever he could. He did them through good nature, not through forethought, but it turned out that a great many people owed him favors and were willing to help him. By calling in all the favors he had accumulated, he managed to get to the sky. The chief, if he had been a wise chief, should have known this, for it is a truth universally acknowledged that rats can get anywhere they set their minds on. It is their special talent.

"Before he left, he knew he had to take some precaution against being spied and burned straight away. The fire-people were very arrogant, so it would never occur to them that a little rat could get to the sky. What people do not believe, they do not see, and thus he knew that with just a little bit of caution on his part they would overlook him entirely. He disguised himself by rolling his whole body in orange and yellow pollen, until he was as bright and glowing as fire itself, then he traveled up to the sky while the fire-people were dancing.

"He found that in his disguise he could mingle among them unsuspected, and he had a good laugh dancing with all the little fire-children, with no one the wiser. But he still had the problem of how to get fire back to earth. Everything has to eat, he knew, and he'd stuffed his cheek pouches with dried grass, which is what rat-kind was forced to eat in those hard times. The fire licked at it readily enough, but it ate so quickly that the grass was gone before he could snatch at the fire and leap back down to earth. So he had to come up with another solution, and fast, for the heat was beginning to make him sweat, and soon the pollen would all slide off his body."

"I know what he did!" a little girl cried. "He..." She was shushed by the others, who wanted to hear the tale from its source.

"The rat looked all around for something else to burn, but as a rule the fire people eat nothing but air, and a rat can't carry that. He thought and thought, and he could only come up with one idea. The only thing that a fire might eat was... his tail." The children made little oohs and aahs, except for the little girl, who said, "I knew that," with a very self-satisfied air.

"It was terrible for him to think of. His tail was very beautiful, and he hated to ruin it. But worse than that, he knew it would be painful. But he'd come all this way — he couldn't give up now. He thought of his sweetheart back on earth, a shy, dear little rat girl. If he didn't get fire, the humans wouldn't provide for them. She might starve. That would be even worse than a burned tail. So he gritted his teeth and flicked his tail into the path of the next dancing flame that passed near him. Then, before anyone could stop him, he scampered back to earth at top speed.

"At first it was only frightening, and not too painful. But as the fire ate the fur on his tail he began to squeak in agony, and ran as fast as his little legs could go. He passed a stream, and he wanted more than you could possibly imagine to give up and plunge his tail in the cool water. But he could never live with himself if he failed after so much work. So he ran on and on, through the forests. As he ran, some of the fire fell off and started to eat the grass and trees. That fire decided that there was something to be said for the earth after all. Any place that had such delicious food couldn't be all bad. And that is why from that day on, lightning, the dancing fire, will at times visit earth of its own accord to eat some of the trees.

"But the rat didn't notice this. He just scampered on until at last he reached the human village and collapsed at the chief's feet, gasping, 'I have brought you fire!'

"Did the rat die?" asked a boy with braided hair.

"No, though he almost did. The chief's wife nursed him for three days, wrapping his poor burned tail in bandages and salve, and when he recovered all the other rats gathered around him, cheering. The humans cheered too, so happy with their fire. From then on, rats never had hair on their tails. But they consider it a small price to pay for the reward of always being fed by humans."

"But we *don't* feed rats," one child protested. Lucy couldn't tell if he felt bad that the deal was broken, or thought humans mighty clever, in getting fire for nothing. He was soon put straight.

"Oh, but you *do!*" she said. "The deal the chief made was that from then on, humans would store their grain all in one place. There, the rats could always help themselves whenever they were hungry. And whatever humans can't eat is always left out for the rats. We might call it our garbage, but the rats call it a banquet. No rat that lives near people has ever starved."

The children were delighted with the story, but naturally wanted more. "How do you know it wasn't a opossum that brought fire to people?" one asked. "Opossums have bare tails too," he further explained for the sake of the ignorant.

"The opossum lost his beautiful tail through vanity, not bravery," she said. "But that, my dears, is a tale my friend must tell you." She nodded to Nighteyes. "There's someone I have to see," she said, and stood, dusting off her legs.

Nighteyes agreeably started the story. "When the world began, the opossum had a long fluffy tail, silver with black stripes, and when he was not brushing it to a sheen, he was bragging about it..." But his eyes followed Lucy. He was more than a little surprised that she sought out Jimi Three Toes.

Chapter 29

Jimi had returned the same day as Lucy, with less fanfare. He'd found Lucy, but he hadn't brought her home. He'd gained two dependents and a bitter enemy.

He decided the best course of action was to pretend he'd never left in the first place, a feat rendered easy by the fact that no one had noticed his absence. There could be no advancement with Bald Cypress now, and he didn't think much of Lucy's nebulous hint that there might be a little something in it for him. It might mean a great deal for her to put in a good word with Bald Cypress, put him in the way of a more important position, but he wanted Bald Cypress to appreciate him for his merits, not just to humor Lucy Brightwing.

Still, there was some satisfaction in having, as it were, gone there and back again, even with nothing to show for it. He mostly occupied his leisure musing about exactly what Lucy was doing with Edgar Battle. It never struck him as particularly unusual that she should be in his company. In his view, Lucy was the sort of person those things happened to. She was exempt from the expectations one laid on ordinary people. It certainly never occurred to him to tell anyone about what he saw, least of all the law. Thoughts of the reward did nothing to sway him. He might have been imperfect in many ways, but as a Seminole he was loyal to Lucy, and as a man he was true to his oath. In these things, he was probably better than most men you'll meet.

When he spotted Lucy heading toward him at the festival he almost ran away. It was one thing for him to brood on the secret privately, quite another to be faced with her in the flesh (albeit with less of it exposed to view than last time) knowing he still held such potentially dangerous knowledge. But he stood his ground when she approached, and found that she didn't look particularly threatening. On the contrary, she looked friendly, if somewhat nervous.

"Hello Jimi," she said, and opened her mouth with a drawn breath to say more, but somehow it never managed to come out. Jimi politely took the burden of conversation on himself.

"How… umm… are you, Lucy?"

"Ok," she said, frowning at the ground. She wasn't sure why she wanted to see Jimi. It wasn't that she was worried about his confidentiality, for she understood his character. But he was the only living person who had seen her with Edgar, and it was a comfort, a very small comfort, to be with someone who was, simply by his existence, an affirmation of Edgar's life. She had sedulously avoided all forms of media, for she didn't want to hear the gloatings and mouthings of reporters and law enforcement as they analyzed Edgar Battle's life and death. She wanted to remember him in her own way, in her own time, not have his mug shots, and very likely his corpse, thrust at her on every newspaper cover, in every quarter-past-the-hour news break. But the gentle reminder she found in Jimi was pleasant.

"Hey Jimi, you want to grab a drink at the Skunk?" The Skunk, as in drunk as a, was a little tavern near the gathering grounds. That would make things easier, for the bar would be loud enough that they didn't have to talk. He agreed, and they walked away in silence until Lucy said, offhand, "Would ten thousand come in handy?"

"Dollars?" he asked, a catch in his voice.

"Yeah." She looked away from him.

"Uh, sure." Then, after scratching at the beard that was struggling to grow on his jaw, he added, "You don't have to, you know.

I wouldn't tell anyone."

Lucy laughed. "Aren't you worried I'll say ok? You're a good guy, Jimi. Good guys deserve something."

A few yards later she said, "You're working for Bald Cypress now, aren't you? You like it?"

"Of course. He's a fine man. I respect him a lot."

"This isn't getting back to him, Jimi. What does he have you doing? Washing his cars? Is that what you want to do for the next few years? You went to find me to impress him, didn't you?"

He admitted that was the case.

"I've got a tip for you, and you can take it or leave it, Jimi. What you're looking for, it isn't the best career. It's not as pretty as you think. But if you want in on one of the organizations, I'd suggest you think about Lazarus Nighteyes. Don't look so shocked!"

"But Bald Cypress is your uncle... great uncle... whatever."

"That doesn't mean I like him. Or trust him. And it certainly doesn't mean I have to look out for his best interests. He's a selfish old bastard without a sympathetic bone in his body. He won't do a thing for you unless he can get something out of it himself. Which describes a lot of us, I suppose, but he's in a position to make his character flaws particularly unpleasant for other people."

"*You* work for him."

"When it's convenient for me," she said with a shrug. "It has its advantages. But he doesn't give a shit for me, relative or not. This last thing I did for him, if I had screwed it up, like he thought I did, he would have tried to kill me. Well, maybe not, but he would have liked to. If I were anyone else, he would have, for sure. But Lazarus has a nice little set-up. Not quite as big as Billie's, but I have inside information that Lazarus just came into some extra cash, so he might not mind having a new guy on the payroll. If you're interested, I could talk to him."

Not sure whether this might be a test of his loyalties, he said, noncommittally, that he'd think about it, and they entered the bar.

"You still setting up your own reservation?" he asked just before they entered.

"Yeah, you interested in joining?"

"Nah, I'd lose my casino check. But there's a couple of girls I know who said they want to. Seminole girl named Sue Blue and her aunt Dolores Otter."

"Sue? I know her. She took a self defense class from me a year ago."

"You must be a hell of a teacher," Jimi said under his breath as they walked in, but she didn't hear him over the noise of the crowd.

"Smart little thing. What does she want to live in the boonies for?"

"She has a business proposition for you. Will you talk to her, whenever things get settled?"

She was in no mood for bother now, but said, "Sure." Lucy fanned herself with a menu and ordered a bottle of hard cider.

They sat at the bar. Lucy wasn't planning to stay long, and already almost regretted her invitation. She'd have to make small talk, all the while both of them skirting the one topic that engrossed her thoughts and must surely be on his. To forestall the questions she knew he longed to ask, which she resolved she would not answer, she said, "So you went on a quest, Jimi."

"A quest? You might say that."

"And what did you find?"

"Trouble. Then you. Not that it did me any good."

"Oh, don't worry, it will. But that's not what I mean. What did you find on the journey? What did you discover? You never went on a spirit-journey when you were young, did you? Not many people do these days. I was just wondering if this turned out to be yours."

Jimi played over his adventures. Somehow they didn't stack up to the mystical experience he always imagined a spirit-journey to be. "I don't think so," he laughed.

"Sometimes you don't realize you made a journey until it's over."

"Well, I haven't realized it yet," he said, downing half his beer and debating whether it would be acceptable to order a pitcher on her tab.

She smiled enigmatically. "Maybe it's not over yet." She noticed that he shivered at her words. It was a prerogative of the last Tequesta to say things in tones of profound meaning, and she sometimes had fun disturbing people with pseudo-prophetic words.

A bellow came from the door. Fagan Blue thundered in, shouting, "Jimi Three-toes, I'm gonna kill you!" Which, Lucy thought as she rose, holding her cider bottle loosely by the neck, made what she was probably about to do much easier to claim as self defense if it ever wound up in court. She didn't know what Jimi had done, but she had a soft spot for the bad-luck Indian, and Fagan was a notorious brute. So she calmly placed herself between them, while every other patron prepared, unobtrusively, to either jump to Lucy's aid or dive for cover.

"Stop," she said, and Fagan did. "One sentence. What did Jimi do?"

"Fucker stole my wife and tied me up for three days." He shoved forward, but didn't quite dare bump Lucy.

"And you, Jimi?"

"Sue tied him up 'cause he beats the tar out of her on a regular basis. She fed him, though, held a cup for him to piss in. I untied him this morning."

It was the bravest thing Jimi had ever done. Guilty, knowing it would have to end someday, he sliced Fagan's bonds and ran as fast as he could before the bull unstiffened and charged. To his surprise, there was no sign of immediate pursuit. Sue might have held a piss cup, but she was too squeamish to take care of the other business, and Fagan needed a long shower before feeling dignified enough to wreak revenge. Jimi went to the festival and almost forgot Fagan's wrath.

Fagan had spent the last three hours destroying Jimi's house and looking for Sue and Dolores, thinking that if he knocked his wife's teeth out he'd accomplish two things: revenge, and slicker blow-jobs. The ladies were in a sweat lodge with the tribe's champion stickball team, so Fagan decided to put that part off and focus on Jimi.

"She's leaving him," Jimi added, keeping Lucy between them. "She's terrified of him."

Lucy shrugged. "Sounds simple. Go home Fagan, and if you touch your wife again I'll castrate you."

He objected, there was a smashing tinkle of glass, and the cider bottle's jagged end pressed against Fagan's most prized posses-sion.

"Ok," she said over her shoulder to Jimi. "Sue and her aunt can come live on my reservation and work for me. Got that, Fagan?"

He grunted, and when she released him slunk out the door.

"Never ends, does it?" Lucy said, downing half of the new ci-der a grinning waitress brought her.

High in a corner over the bar, a small mounted television an-nounced that the news would be coming on after the next com-mercial, and she turned resolutely away, glad that the volume was low enough to make it easy to ignore. She didn't even know if Mallory had been caught yet. At times, when she let herself think of such things, she regretted not killing him. It would have been better to tie things up neatly. With Edgar gone, her interest in the Battle brothers over, she didn't fancy the idea of being dragged back in by any confession of Mallory's. But then, she reasoned, knowing him he wouldn't be taken alive.

She wondered how long he stayed out in the woods before he realized she wasn't coming back. More likely, though, investigators had dogs at the scene and tracked him to his place of concealment that very night. He was armed, there's be a shootout in which he'd be vastly outnumbered, and he'd be killed, putting an end to the legacy of the Battle brothers once and for all. Lucy allowed very little guilt to enter her feelings. If Mallory had been a different sort of man, she would have risked much to save him, for his brother's sake. But it would be madness to tie herself to Mallory alone.

And so she turned away from the television and talked to Jimi about the weather, always an engrossing topic in Florida. She was on the verge of excusing herself, to return to the outdoor festivi-ties for another hour or two before retiring to solitude and thought, when Jimi said, "I know I probably shouldn't ask..."

"Then don't!" she snapped. She'd been waiting for it, and al-most thought he would have the tact to let her escape without a reference to what he'd seen that day in the swamps.

Jimi frowned and looked down at his drink. He didn't want to offend or anger her — certainly not with that reference to ten-thousand which he scarcely believed — but he wanted to express his sympathy. He knew she could look for it nowhere else. "I just wanted to say I'm sorry for what happened to... him." Lucy half rose in her seat to flee from the unwanted conversation, but some kindness in Jimi's eyes held her. "I know it's none of my business, but when I saw the two of you together you both looked so happy. It doesn't matter what the particulars are, Lucy. It's just a shame when happiness has to end."

Lucy, touched, felt her eyes grow heavy. But she had not let herself weep since returning to the reservation, and she wouldn't start now. "Thank you, Jimi," she said, staring hard to keep the tears contained, and she lay one hand on his arm, turning to rise even as she did so.

"Lucy," he said, calling her back. "Are you going to try to see him?"

She only looked at him uncomprehendingly.

"If you want to, I was thinking about a way to do it. I know someone who works there..."

"See him? I don't know what you mean. At the morgue?"

"At the hospital," Jimi said. "I've thought of how you can do it."

Lucy looked at him, comprehension beginning to dawn even as she desperately fought back what surely must be false hope. If she let even a glimmer of hope in, it would crush her when it died. "Who are you talking about?" she asked, her voice so slow and distinct it seemed void of all feeling. "Do you mean Mallory? Has he been caught?" Her eyes looked almost angry, threatening him with dire consequences should he mislead her.

"Christ, you didn't know?"

"Know what, Jimi?" she said between clenched teeth, sitting back down and leaning close to him.

By way of an answer he pointed to the television, and Lucy lifted a chin held stoically set against any tremble. The news began, and the room fell suddenly silent, eager for the latest dose of Battle brothers saga. Lucy's eager attention was in no way remarkable in that room, and throughout the state others fell similarly hushed at the slightest mention of the topic.

The keenest observer would not have seen Lucy Brightwing move throughout that broadcast. She hardly heard the words. The picture was quite enough to immobilize her body even as her heart beat wildly against her chest. Bathed in the green fluorescent glow of an emergency room lay Edgar Battle. His face was slack, and what parts of him were not bandaged were bruised. But though his eyes were closed and she couldn't see his chest rise, wires and cords attached to his body connected to a machine whose face displayed the most welcome sight Lucy had ever seen: the blue trace line showing a slow, but regular, pulse.

Edgar Battle was alive.

They cut away from the hospital scene back to the anchor woman, who told the world that the eldest of the Battle brothers had been downgraded from critical to serious status after three surgeries to repair shattered lungs and blood vessels. Later that night, the anchor promised, they would speak with a noted ethicist on the merits of spending hundreds of thousands of dollars to save a criminal's life, only to have him condemned to death a short time later.

Lucy's lips parted, and she looked away from the screen, looked at nothing, not even thinking, only feeling a rush of sensations, of which the dominant was, of course, love, though it was followed closely by a desperate kind of fear. She looked back at Jimi for a moment, then without a word was racing out the door.

"Wait!" Jimi called. "What about..." But she was already gone, and wouldn't have stopped had she heard him. To himself, Jimi muttered the conclusion. "What about the ten thousand?"

With a sigh, he ordered a pitcher on Lucy's tab.

Lucy ran through crowds that stared, never noticing their looks. She sought one person among the hundreds, and when she spotted him standing alone near a cauldron set upon a tripod she came at him like a charging bear.

Lazarus Nighteyes held her at arm's length, his initial amusement turning to concern as she panted wordlessly, her breath like sobs. Never before had he seen such eloquence of features, never had a face spoken of so many conflicting emotions at once. "You look," he said softly, "as though you have been granted your fondest wish, at the most terrible price. Come. We will go to my tent. We will not be disturbed."

She sat cross-legged on a mat in his tent, a pavilion made of bright gaudy airy materials that would have been more at home on a medieval fairground than a Native American celebration. But it let the sporadic wind come through, and was waterproof, two advantages in a Florida summer.

Nighteyes examined her without seeming to do so as he puttered about to make himself comfortable, pouring a drink of water and filling his pipe. It was remarkable how much she looked like Two Moons, her mother, he thought. Neither looked very much like an Indian, and yet there was something in their bearing more than their features that pointed to a continuation of a long history.

Like her mother, she was beautiful, with a beauty of form as well as face: long supple limbs, an elegance of carriage, an instinctive pride that had nothing of haughtiness, a courage that scorned bluster. And like her mother, she was almost impossibly strong of will, not, again, in a way that was ostentatious, and yet Nighteyes knew that she could never be dissuaded from a course she had set.

She was going to ask him for his help now, he realized, and though he sensed it would cause him no end of trouble, he already knew there was no way he could refuse her. Even if she didn't invoke the old obligations that would practically force him to do her bidding, he would comply with whatever she asked.

She looked at him across the tent, with eyes so haunted he almost crossed to her side to comfort her. He could not imagine what could be troubling her, but his instincts were correct. Something had happened to her on her journey for the gems, some terrible course of events that had just now come to a head.

"Lazarus," she said, "I have something to ask you." Her voice did not waver because she kept it pitched so low, but he could see that she was trembling.

"Ask, then, my daughter." And indeed, he looked upon her with an almost paternal fondness and indulgence. She had never known a father's support, and her nearest relative, Bald Cypress, was hardly the sort she could love. Nighteyes was not surprised that whatever might be her dilemma, she should turn to him.

"I have a task before me," she said gravely, switching to formal Miccosukee. "An impossible task. And yet I must do it." She looked down at her hands. "I have done many things in my life.

Many difficult things. I have faced danger, and hardship, even death. But always I have believed I could succeed. I may have felt fear, but it was never fear of failure. This thing... I do not think I can do it. And yet I must. If I don't..." She shook her head. "No, it must be done. And you must tell me, Lazarus Nighteyes, who I have long respected and trusted; you must tell me, how am I to accomplish the impossible?"

"You gave me the answer yourself," he said gently. "Ask the rat who stole fire from the skies how all things, even impossible things, are achieved. Favors, and cleverness, and sacrifice."

She was silent a moment, then met his eye with a peculiar half-smile. "Lazarus, I have a favor to ask of you."

Chapter 30

A woman with two long black braids that curled at the tips passed her bag through the makeshift metal detector that had been set up at the entrance to the St. Michael wing of Salvista Hospital, near Ft. Myers on the banks of the Caloosahatchee River.

"That's ironic," she said to the guard on loan from the nearby prison at Yellow Fever Creek, as she filled out the requisite forms. "St. Michael is the patron saint of policemen. How many did he kill?" She shook her head. "My dad was with the Miccosukee PD."

She chatted easily with him as he escorted her down the long corridor. The astringent aroma of disinfectants assaulted her nose, a nose accustomed to smells of earth and trees. "He died a few years ago, a heart attack. But he had some close calls out there." She sighed. "Thinking about my dad, it will be hard talking to this guy. But the chief wanted me to be the one to try, for some reason."

"The Indian chief?" he asked, and she laughed. There was no mistaking her for anything other than an Indian, though he lacked the finesse to tell which kind. She wore an ankle-length traditional patchwork skirt, its intricate gaudy symmetry a radiant starburst amid the monotone of scrubs and uniforms. Her braids were tied with leather thongs, and a tight gorget of matched boar tusks circled her throat. Her ID tag told the world she was Molly Tsabanah, a lawyer for the Miccosukee Council.

"No, the chief of police for the reservation force. I just passed the bar a few months ago, and started working with the Miccosukee council. But yeah, the other chief wants me to do this too. I'm kind of scared. I don't know why they didn't pick someone with more experience."

He looked her up and down. "I got a pretty good idea. I don't care how bad this guy is, how hurt. After seeing nothing but cops and guards and doctors and FBI agents, he'll be happy to talk to a pretty girl. I don't know what he'll tell you, but he'll talk."

As they walked, the girl was trying to memorize the convoluted layout of the corridors.

"What are you going to be asking him?" the guard said.

"There was a murder on the reservation, and we think he and his brother may be responsible. What should I say to him? I've never done anything like this before."

"Oh, you'll do fine," the guard said. "You just be cool, and don't worry about him. He's in no shape to give you any trouble. Anyway, if he *does* give you trouble, I'll be there, along with about a dozen officers."

The woman smiled her gratitude, and congratulated herself that this guard, at least, accepted her for what she pretended to be. And why shouldn't he? She carried papers that confirmed her as Molly Tsabanah, along with a history that seemed to stretch back to her birth twenty-six years ago. It would take a lot of digging to uncover her real name, and she'd been sent with the right words from the right people. This time, at least, she would have no problem getting into Edgar Battle's heavily-guarded hospital room. She could, at least, see him, talk to him.

They reached the door, before which stood two uniformed, armed men, the black tape of mourning across their badges. They checked her credentials casually, cross-referencing her name with a brief list of approved visitors, and at last unlocked and opened the door.

She'd been steeling herself for this moment for days, while Nighteyes created her identity and pulled the strings necessary to arrange her visit. In that time Edgar had undergone two more surgeries, and survived an attempt on his life by the brother of one of the women Mallory had killed. The attacker, disguised as an orderly and carrying as his weapon a syringe of potassium chloride, was subdued before he could inject the lethal chemical, and security around the slowly recovering prisoner was increased. After so much work, it wouldn't do to have him killed before he could be sentenced to death. The policemen around the building guarded him like a prized possession.

Now she would see him, at last. But as the door swung open she only glanced briefly, almost indifferently at the white-shrouded bed, before turning to receive instructions from a policeman.

"You have ten minutes," he said mechanically, though he still spared a glance at her cleavage. "Sit in the chair provided for you, and do not lean toward, or have any contact with the prisoner. Do not hand him anything. Do not discuss the particulars of any case except the one you are investigating. Is that clear?"

She nodded, and one of the attendant doctors added, "If the patient becomes agitated you'll have to stop the interview. He's still very weak. We weren't sure he'd even live until a day or two ago."

She took her seat, a cushioned swivel stool a few feet from the bed, and at last allowed herself to lock on the face of her beloved.

Lucy Brightwing had labored hard for this moment, and she still wasn't sure what it would bring her. That day in Nighteyes' tent she promised him all the rest of her money, if only he'd assist her. "If you can help me with what I have to do, you can take as much as you want!"

"Check your ponies, girl!" Nighteyes said with a chuckle. "Why don't you try to bargain with me a little first! Let me hear what I have to do, and we'll see what it will cost you."

Lucy had hesitated. She was trying to think of some way to secure his help without giving her secret away, but found it was impossible. Though she balked at telling her story, she would have to confess the whole of her current mission, at least. He might ask, he might make assumptions, but she need not tell the reasons that lay behind it.

"You have heard, over the past few weeks, of the Battle brothers?" He confessed that he had. "And you know one of them, Edgar Battle, has been captured, badly injured."

She tried to school her voice, but when she spoke that adored name Nighteyes knew beyond the slightest doubt that she loved him. Poor girl! He could not imagine how it had come about, what peculiar events could have thrown them together. But somehow, she loved a killer. He didn't think to condemn her. Legends were full of the tales of women who loved gods, or animals, or bandits, or demons. Love is love, and cannot be denied. But he did feel sorry for her. Most of those legends, he recalled, ended badly.

"I need to rescue him," she said, straightforwardly, as though what she proposed was not the most foolhardy thing in the world. "And then get him somewhere safe. Will you help me do that?"

Later that night Lucy and Nighteyes had met again, in deeper privacy where they could speak freely, and after a great deal of discussion he agreed to help her in any way short of putting himself at risk. He would have to see just how many favors he himself could call in.

"You know this is a foolish wish, don't you, child?"

"No, Lazarus," she said with a beatific smile. "Not foolish. Not if it comes true."

"How far are you willing to pursue this folly? Will you give up your life for this man?" He expected a romantic, automatic affirmation. But then, knowing Lucy as he did, he realized he shouldn't be surprised when she returned a practical, "Not at all. *Give up* my life? No. But I will risk my life to save him. And if in the attempt I should die... well, I may think badly of the gods' decision, but I'll blame none but myself."

When they parted, Nighteyes lay awake for many hours. Shortly before dawn he came up with a plan. It was not much of a plan, but then, he knew, most things come about through luck and opportunity. He could get her inside, but after that, it was up to her. He could help her arrange sanctuary, but he couldn't transport Edgar there.

At nine, when etiquette determined it was late enough to make calls, he rang up the chief of police (whose luxurious boat had been purchased by a loan from Nighteyes,) the DA (whose pill-popping wife remained out of jail thanks to a word from Nighteyes) and the governor (whose checkered past remained hidden by Nighteyes' good graces) and had three brief, friendly conversations. In none of these conversations were any obligations mentioned. But all three men readily agreed to what seemed at the time to be a simple request.

By noon of that day, after one more call to a friend in Miami skilled at such matters, a new person was born. Molly Tsabanah sprang abruptly into the world, Athena from the skull of Zeus, complete with a history, a job, and her name on the short list of people approved to interrogate Edgar Battle.

Later that day, after a great deal of interference from secretaries, Lazarus met with a certain senator. He handed him a proposed rewriting of the section of the bill granting the Tequesta tribe its own reservation.

"I can't do this!" the senator said.

Lazarus put another stack of bills next to the three that already lay on the table.

"Come on, it's ridiculous. Sovereign borders?"

"It's a tiny parcel of land held by one girl. So she can set out no trespassing signs like anyone else."

"It's more than that, and you know it. You can't expect me to..."

Another stack. Another. The senator's eyes bugged. He had three kids at Harvard, a mother who needed in-home nursing. A mistress with his credit card. He skimmed the document again.

"It's a reservation with one girl, a tribe with one member. Who are you going to extradite? Who are you going to prosecute? It's nothing, no one will even notice, if you word it the right way. Legal matters to be handled internally. The Tequesta tribe to provide for its own law enforcement."

Another stack.

"Well..."

Chapter 31

Lucy was suitably impressed by the speed with which this was all conducted, but then, Nighteyes was one of those people who gets things done, a man who knew exactly how much of politics, of law, goes behind the scenes. He was skilled at those *sub rosa* machinations, knowing that, with the right incentive, the most important people can be convinced to do just about anything. He had spent his life subtly collecting these incentives from almost all of the people who mattered in the state, and many beyond. He'd held his own position so long, so successfully, not only because he collected such information and influence, but because he rarely made full use of it. A man who holds secrets of the powerful can be easily destroyed himself. But Nighteyes, as a rule, only knew, and smiled, and did nothing, thereby earning both the gratitude and tolerance of the people whose lives were effectively in his hands. When he did remind them, and called in a favor, they complied, almost universally without hesitation.

"I've gotten you in to see him," Nighteyes said, and when he had untangled her arms and recovered from the pleasant embarrassment her spontaneous warm embrace had stirred, he went on. "That is an important first step, but the rest will be largely up to you. You must get him out, and that might require one or two people be let in on part of your secret. Is there anyone you trust that much?"

"There is one who already knows something of this matter," she confessed, thinking how loath Jimi would be to find himself dragged into this mess again. But he would help her all the same.

"And is there another?"

"You?"

"I'm too old for this sort of thing, and I was never much good at violence, my early reputation to the contrary. No, this kind of action may be brought to the brink of success by cunning and luck, but there may come a time when blood is the only thing that will bring it to an end. I know what *you* can do, Lucy, but the simple act of moving a big man grown weak means you need at least one more person in the thick of it. Someone you can trust. Someone who would risk their own life for you... or for this man."

Lucy pressed her lips together, frowning. "I think I might know someone. If I can find him."

As dusk closed in around the reservation, Lucy had driven off in a borrowed car with stolen plates. She had some trouble finding the spot. To dissuade those hordes of macabre tourists who like to visit sites of tragedy, the road had been cleaned of blood, the grass, torn up by emergency vehicles, resodded, until that stretch of road seemed to the untrained eye like any other. But Lucy found it, almost feeling the ghosts of sadness rising up from the ground. She maneuvered her car into the foliage down the road, and set off to track a man she hoped she'd never see again, a man she was glad to be rid of. But Nighteyes was right. He was the only one, other than her, who would risk all for Edgar Battle.

He hadn't been caught yet, she knew, so he might actually still be out there, alone for all that time, waiting for her to return. That poor lost madman, alone and friendless, who trusted her so much that he would stay, waiting, three days in the wilderness. He'd been her responsibility too, she realized, not just Edgar. She'd taken them both, protected them both, interfered in the fates of not one but two Battle brothers, and she had been wrong to abandon Mallory in the end.

It is difficult to track a man in the darkness, and that night the moon was just a sliver past new. The trail was three days old, and

it had rained for much of the intervening time. It was an impossible task for anyone but a bloodhound — or Lucy. For an hour she
meandered within a few hundred yards of the interstate, trying to
pick up his trail, and at last found the first tracks, no more than
depressions in the earth and snapped twigs, things that to the
common eye would seem just than the random destruction of
weather and wild beasts. But to Lucy, these marks were a path,
and she followed the sporadic signs on her hands and knees for
another hour before the land turned marshy and she lost the trail
entirely.

She couldn't risk calling him. Though the woods were dense,
she couldn't know who else might be nearby. With a reward still
on his head, there would be plenty of people out looking for Mallory, and there could well be one like herself who, not knowing
where to start, decided to scout his last known location. So instead, she followed instinct. She retraced her steps to the last sign,
then allowed herself to wander as she thought he might. Thinking
like him, with his understanding of the wilderness, she tried to
recreate his steps. He would not climb that rise, she thought, for
even a slight elevation would be daunting to an inexperienced
woodsman. And that patch would have been too muddy, even
three days ago, so he would have skirted it for firmer ground. In
this way she wandered deeper into the woods, trying to move as a
lonely, frightened man might.

Three hours later, the stars sitting higher on their nightly arc,
she despaired of finding him. But she would not give up until
dawn at least. She needed Mallory now. As much as his unpredictable violence might be a liability, she needed his unswerving loyalty and physical strength in this endeavor. She hoped she wouldn't
need his psychosis and steady gun-hand, but it was good to know
they were there too. In all the world, there was only one other
person who loved Edgar. If she couldn't find Mallory she didn't
think much of her chances. But then, with him or without him,
she didn't think much of her chances.

It was luck alone that led her to Mallory shortly before sunrise.
Calling would have been no use, for when she found him, almost
stumbling over him in the burgeoning light, he was curled on his
side, unresponsive. For a moment she feared he was dead, then

thought, perhaps, asleep. But when she touched him and he opened his eyes, they were unfocused and delirious.

If she hadn't come when she did he wouldn't have lived out the day. She examined him as he raved, thrashing weakly as a newborn kitten, speaking, from parched lips, the same phrases that tore at her heart. *I waited,* he said piteously, *I waited forever, and nobody came. She promised she'd come, and she never, never did.* But he soon lapsed into unconsciousness, and for half a day he never knew her.

She could reconstruct his story well enough, and later, when he was well, he confirmed it. For a day or so he had waited, uncomfortable in the rain, anxious and grieving for his brother, but confident that eventually, he wouldn't be alone. Lucy would return. For a while, hunger hadn't mattered, and thirst was only a nuisance, not a great distress. But when the second day came, and he waited still, his thirst became so overwhelming that he drank from the clearest of the new-made rain ponds. It hadn't tasted offensive, and he didn't know what microorganisms can lurk in even the purest-looking water. Within hours he was stricken with gripping stomach pains, and by the end of that day he was too dehydrated to do more than crawl to the nearest puddle and again try to slake his thirst. He drank, was re-infected, and within minutes the water left his body violently. When she found him he was near death, dying of thirst while surrounded by water.

All that day she nursed him in the woods, cleaning the filth from his body as best she could while he was still unconscious, giving him water from her camelback sip by sip until he could keep some of it down. She let him lie with his head in her lap, and held him while his body purged itself of the last of the contaminants. Humans are well-equipped to handle most water-borne bacteria, flushing them out as soon as they are detected, and once he had untainted water Mallory began to rally. By the afternoon he could stand shakily, and at nightfall, with the support of her strong arm, he very slowly made his way out of the woods.

She took him to one of Nighteyes' safe houses, a rustic little one bedroom on the edge of dry rise in a spot known as Cow Bone Island north of the reservation. Though not hidden, it was isolated on a road everyone seemed to know to stay off of, and the few locals were all in the pay of the Miccosukee boss. An intruder would be instantly spotted, and as soon reported. The neighbors, none too near, knew they weren't expected to see what went on at that house.

Mallory was weak for several days, and even when his body was fed and hydrated looked wasted. But he didn't seem to blame her for his predicament, and she only said that she came as soon as she could, that the long investigation at the scene kept her away for so many days. He accepted this readily, especially when he heard the joyous news that Edgar was alive.

"And we're going to get him out," she promised him. "But this time, Mallory, you have to do exactly what I tell you."

He agreed, which she knew meant nothing, but at least he seemed pliant. Yet he was none too happy that she had no immediate plans to break his brother out of the hospital.

"This is the perfect time to do it," he said. "Once he gets to prison it will be impossible to get him out."

She told him there were almost as many guards at the hospital as there would be in prison. And more importantly, Edgar was still too badly injured to move, even if they could get past the guards.

"You'll have to wait," she told him, and after hinting at her connections with Indian organized crime, promised he'd be shot if he tried to leave the house. "I need your help," she said. "But if you do anything to screw it up, I'll kill you myself. If you want to save Edgar, you have to follow my orders. Clear?"

"You love him, don't you," he said more than asked.

She smiled, almost self-consciously. "Yeah."

"I am *so* glad I never killed you," he said, grinning. "Are you sure we can get him out?" he asked a moment later, as she was preparing to leave.

"No. But we'll try." She left him with food, cable, and violent video games, which she hoped might be enough to keep him occupied for a while. "I'll be back every few days," she promised. "But I can't make it any more often than that. Don't leave the house, don't even open the door. Remember, Edgar's depending on you."

That seemed to do the trick, but she drove away understandably nervous, wondering if, after all, it would have been better to leave him in the woods. Ah well, it was done now. And he would be useful, if he could be controlled.

Chapter 32

From his sickbed, Edgar opened bleary eyes to the usual crowd of blue uniforms and black suits that surrounded him. He wasn't in pain. The drugs they gave him kept him comfortable and sedate, as much, he fancied, for their own convenience as for his relief. But even without the drugs he wouldn't have been able to move. He knew, he had been told, how close he'd come to death. Those three bullets had shattered through bone and tissue so savagely that even the doctors had to admit it was more luck, and the strength of Edgar's own body, than their skill that preserved him. He was now missing a lobe of his left lung, several segments of blood vessels had been replaced by bits of his femoral artery, and a pig had unwillingly donated one of its heart valves for his use. But he was alive.

Fat lot of good it did him.

He'd been conscious, more or less, for a day, but his conscientious doctors were too pleased with their success to allow interrogations. The local PD, which had dibs on him until the other agencies could sort things out, tried to question him, but regardless of how they wheedled or threatened, he would only stare at them for a time, and close his eyes in supposed weariness until the doctors ordered them away. The FBI had no better luck. So far he'd said nothing, aside from mumbled answers to his surgeons' queries about his comfort, and he fully intended to maintain that stubborn silence.

His fate was sealed, he knew, and it would be a compromise of his dignity to try to bargain his way into a life sentence. To incriminate Mallory, to inform on Lucy, might have spared death, but it wasn't worth it. He died there on the roadside. So what if they resurrected him. His fantasy of freedom was gone. Lucy was gone. The only thing left to him was to preserve some measure of internal calm and self-possession. Soon, he decided, he would take a vow of silence. Let them threaten all they cared to, let them declare him insane and unfit to stand trial. He would speak to none of them.

Then that morning, amid the blues and blacks and the leaden shine of guns and handcuffs, he saw a swirling kaleidoscope of color. He focused his groggy gaze on a crazily patterned full skirt, the plunging lines of a white blouse, and looked, with moderate interest, at a face framed by long black braids, with wire-framed rectangular glasses over hazel eyes. Almost at once he turned away. There was only one woman he wanted to look at, and he never would again. He closed his eyes to resume his semi-lucid meditations.

Then something about that face struck him, and almost reluctantly he dragged himself out of that pleasant half-daze of pain medications, to look at it once again.

With a start, he almost said her name, then checked himself, both in prudence and embarrassment. The woman resembled Lucy Brightwing, certainly, but it could not be her. No one, he was sure, short of hospital staff or the law, could get near him. And though there was a resemblance, the differences struck him more strongly at first. The hair, the light eyes, a complexion fairer than Lucy's, freckles across her cheeks and the bridge of her nose. Even the contours of her face were different, the mouth held in a thinner line, a slightly different angle of cheek and jaw.

He only knew for certain it was Lucy when she spoke, for she made no effort to alter her voice. It was soft and low, lilting on certain syllables. "Edgar Battle," she said, with no trace of affection in her voice, only a veneer of public cordiality. "My name is

Molly Tsabanah. I'm an attorney with the Miccosukee Reservation, investigating a murder on Indian lands. I'd like to ask you a few questions."

There was nothing in her voice to indicate she'd ever known him, and he flinched at the coldness. Confused, he knew it was Lucy, his own Lucy. But what was she doing here?

A terrible idea dawned on him, one that was so disheartening his drug-addled mind caught hold of it with vicious glee and would not let go, so ripe was he for any form of lowness and tragedy. Maybe that staid, official-looking person before him was the real Lucy, a lawyer, one of that general *them* that included everyone who had been hunting him. Some force of thanatos and self-destruction forced him to think the worst, and though reason tried to dissuade him, he found himself almost believing that every moment she'd known him, every day he had loved her, had been no more than a ploy to secure evidence against him.

He didn't really believe this. His heart leapt and danced to see her, and somewhere deep inside he sighed, firmly convinced now that everything would be all right. Lucy is here! his soul sang, and he had absolute faith that she would take the situation firmly in hand and turn all danger aside, even as she turned away the raging sow that would have killed him.

And yet, hope is such a dangerous thing. After almost dying, after being stripped of everything that can possibly make a man's life worth living, he had very nearly resigned himself to the fact of his own failure and destruction. Resignation, acceptance of fate, if sincere, can make a man invincibly strong. So long as he knew he was doomed, nothing they could do to him would really touch him. Interrogation, indignities, trials, even execution would be no more to him than one long tedious dream between the end of his struggle and the end of his body.

But hope can crush the strongest heart, and he feared that should he let the smallest germ of hope enter him, it would unman him utterly. To know that he would die was almost soothing, and he could bear it with a composed mind. But seeing Lucy enter his room so calmly and easily among armed guards and officers, he began to lose that composure and think there might, after all, be the possibility of happiness.

Immediately he was tormented by the sister possibility of failure, the fear that anything he did wrong might rob him irrevocably of that hope. For that is the joy of hopelessness, that it allows, even encourages, inaction. In his first moments of consciousness he had indeed planned his escape, but before long the futility overwhelmed him, and he was happy to give up, reclining in despair's inviting arms.

Now, his mind was thrown into a tumult of activity as he tried to think, all in the course of a few seconds, what she was planning, and what he could do to help. Wisely, he said nothing until his mind was clearer.

"I don't think you'll get anything out of him, miss," said a burly officer who'd been on twelve-hour shift as one of Edgar's guards. "We've tried asking him questions, and he hasn't got a thing to say for himself." She heard one of the men in the corner murmur that if Edgar was left in a room alone with him, he'd certainly decide to talk before long. She glanced over, and filed that man's face away in her memory for future reference. There might be a day when she'd have the option of showing him mercy. She probably wouldn't.

Edgar disappointed their expectations. After an interminable pause he answered in a voice perfectly civil, though hoarse from disuse and the friction of tubes. "Pleased to meet you, Miss Molly." He held out a hand, bruised from IVs, to shake hers in introduction. At this weak gesture three guns were drawn and the burly guard sprang forward to intervene, ready to beat Edgar into submission at the slightest provocation.

Lucy—Molly — didn't react in the slightest to the rush. With a serene smile frozen on her face, she only said, with an apologetic shake of her head, "I'm not allowed to touch you, Mr. Battle." Edgar was the only one who read the longing beneath it.

Calm restored, she took out a small tape recorder, set it precariously on her knee, and started her queries.

"Where were you on the night of the ninth, Mr. Battle?"

He considered a moment, and then recalled. She had, advertently or no, chosen the night of the firefly expedition, and the memory provoked a smile on lips that had shown no such inclination for many days. "I was in the woods, somewhere," he said.

"In the Miccosukee reservation?" she asked.

"I don't know where it was, exactly," he replied truthfully. "I was hiding in the swamps."

She continued to question him, not pressing him on any particulars, calculating her inquiries to make no mention of Mallory, nor anything to connect her alter ego to the circumstances. He answered her with half-truths and lies that he took care to remember, in case he should want to stick to them later — or consciously amend them. Mostly he looked at her, keeping his face as neutral as possible, but drinking her in like cool water to a parched man.

His countenance might have betrayed some emotion (which the guards attributed to the interest a pretty girl can inspire) but Lucy's revealed nothing. She was reserved, with an edge of frost in her demeanor; efficient, superficially smiling when the situation called for it, a smile that seemed to quickly loose itself in insincerity before dying outright. No one who didn't know their connection would be suspicious. Even Edgar, who knew her friendship and strongly suspected her love, was plagued by pangs of doubt, still thinking, at times, can this really be Lucy? He was himself a practiced dissembler, but his skill was nothing to hers. But had he ever had so much at stake?

He listened to her speech for clues, for any hints she might be dropping about her plan. She must have one. Or had she only contrived to see him one last time, to give him the mixed comfort of her presence, adulterated, as it was, by the expectations it raised? If so, it was a feeble gesture, one he thought unlike her. She wouldn't go to such an effort merely to view him in his helpless misery. But he could detect nothing in either her words or her tone that seemed to point to a concrete plan. He filed away everything she said for later, hoping to dissect some secret code. He found none — as yet, she had none. She'd come to see him, to be sure, but more to see the layout of the building and gauge the strength of men guarding him. It was a reconnaissance mission, no more, and her course of action would develop depending on what she found there.

One of her chief goals was to discover how long she had until Edgar was well enough to be moved to prison, where security would be too high even for the devotion of love to breach. She might, for all she knew, have only a few days. Seeing Edgar now, awake and lucid, but still essentially immobile, she couldn't be sure how long it might be before his doctors relinquished their responsibility.

Though she could give no hint of her intentions, she trusted to Edgar's intelligence to further her cause, and his, by whatever means were in his power. To feign more weakness than he felt, to refuse to speak to any but her, would help her greatly in achieving her ends. Once he had time to mull things over, she was sure, he would come up with these things himself. He could prolong his stay in the hospital, and create the avenue by which she might be granted freer admittance to his company.

Her present visit was brief, if anything, somewhat under the allotted ten minutes. She gained no ground in her supposed investigation, and fully intended to return to press her case.

"Thank you for your time, Mr. Battle," she said with absent cordiality, and rose, turning to go.

Edgar looked hungrily after her, and then as she reached the door, the arms of policemen extending to usher her out, he called, "Miss Molly!" She turned back, just her head over her shoulder. He felt suddenly stronger, and with a measure of his old self he said rakishly, "Do you have a boyfriend, Miss Molly?"

The guards looked threatening, the doctors embarrassed, but Lucy swiveled her body to face him squarely and said, "Well, I don't know if he's boyfriend material, but there is someone I love." For the briefest moment her eyes softened, and Edgar felt his throat grow tight. But he only said, with forced cockiness, "Tell him to look out. When I feel a little better, I'll be giving him some competition." He winked, and Molly Tsabanah was shuttled out the door.

"You shouldn't tell him anything personal," said a man who identified himself as Detective Fallow, the officer in charge of the local investigation, as he walked her back down the corridor.

"I thought it might help," she said. "Make him feel easier next time I talk to him." She said it with the assurance that she would be back, and he didn't question it.

"You're not used to talking to criminals, are you?"

"It shows?" she asked with a nervous titter.

"Not much," he said. "I was actually pretty impressed. But you shouldn't ever give a criminal fodder for manipulation. Let them know you have a lover, kids, and they'll do anything they can to use it against you psychologically."

"They will?" she asked innocently. "I had no idea all criminals were so predictable."

"You been working with 'em as long as I have, you know what to expect," he said proudly, missing her edge of mockery entirely. Lucy chided herself, reminding herself to be careful. "It's even worse in this case, to give away anything about yourself. This guy has an accomplice still on the loose, you know. Of course, there's no way he can contact him, but he'll try to make you believe that his brother can track you down."

"Will he?"

"Oh, yes…"

"Track me down, you mean?"

"No, no. Impossible."

"Do you have any leads on the brother?" she asked.

"I shouldn't be talking about it, but yes. He's been spotted by a couple of people in the Panhandle. We think he might be heading to Texas, trying to get across the border."

"And once he's there he's safe?"

The detective laughed, a great guffaw that actually forced him to stop walking. "Ha! They can't keep anyone away from the old U.S. of A. They put up a little show, so we grease a few palms, then they hand over whoever we ask for. He'll be caught soon, anyway. Unless he's holed up somewhere, someone will spot him. There's a shitload… beg your pardon… a pile o' money sitting on his head. Hell, if he gets himself a good lawyer he can probably arrange to turn *himself* in and collect his own bounty!" This sent him into another spasm of laughter.

Evidently charmed by his wit, Molly asked him if he'd like a cup of coffee.

He accepted readily, saying, "Hospitals always have the best coffee. It's a shame they're such damned depressing places, or I'd spend all my breaks in a hospital cafeteria."

She let herself walk just a little closer to him, and they proceeded down the corridor, following the green line on the floor that promised every hundred feet to lead them to sustenance.

Once there, it took some effort to turn her thoughts away from Edgar's face and poor bandaged body, and focus her not inconsiderable charm on pleasing Fallow. She intended to bring the conversation around to those things she so vitally needed to know, but he obliged her, at least on one count, by making her a confession.

"I was really amazed that he talked to you... may I call you Molly?" She nodded, wondering if she'd remember to answer to that name. "He's been stubborn about talking to anyone in uniform, anyone at all, for that matter. We've been hogtied in how much pressure we can put on him to talk. Do you know, he got punched five or six times while he was still unconscious after surgery? No idea who did it, no one will rat out the culprit because they all want to take a swing at him. Wouldn't mind it myself, 'cept I'd rather wait until he's recovered. He'll feel it more, once he's off the pain medication. Not that you ever heard me say that, mind you. But he's killed quite a few deputies, and police, and troopers, and who knows who else, and in my opinion he deserves whatever he gets. But that will be up to judge and jury, won't it?"

Lucy nodded, but said nothing. She was trying to silence the retorts that sprang to her lips, trying to remember that she loved him, while the detective did not. He was only a man like any other, probably basically good at heart, who had a quite natural resentment of murderers. She tried not to blame him for his feelings, but never altered hers in the slightest.

"Anyway," he continued, "what it comes down to is I have a little problem." Lucy tilted her head to one side, interested. "Me and my boys are only going to have Edgar Battle until he's well enough to be moved. The doctors aren't quite sure when that'll be, maybe two more weeks. Maybe less. But that's all the time we have to get any kind of confession out of him. Then he goes to the feds, and we've lost our chance. He'll be convicted twenty times over before they ever get to his Florida crimes, and that means, unless he confesses freely, we might never know exactly what he's done in this state."

"But won't the FBI ask him about that too?"

"There's seven other states that have priority over us, chronologically speaking. If we don't get it now, well, I shouldn't say we'll never get it, but it'll be a long, long time. Plus, if you don't mind a little honesty, there's the glory factor. We caught him, when no one else could." At the cost of four more lives, Lucy thought. "That's a pretty big coup. Think how it'll look for my department if we get a full confession out of him before he even leaves the hospital. Commendations all around, not to mention more funding. And we've been mighty short of funding, lately. But he won't talk. You see the problem?"

"I'm beginning to. But what can I do?"

"Your interview today looked promising. Sure, you didn't get much, but at least he talked. That's better than any of us got. If we coach you a little bit, you might be able to coax a confession out of him."

"What makes you think that?"

"He liked you. Couldn't you tell?"

"I was just thinking about the questions I was asking him, and making sure the tape recorder was working. I don't much care about his personal opinions of me," she said coldly.

"Well, why should you? Be pretty sick if you did. But if he'll talk to you, if he likes you, you could be doing us a big favor."

"Just say I agreed to help you... and I haven't yet... I work for Miccosukee. If I get the confession, will you get the credit?" She smiled. "The Res police are short of funding, too, I think."

"Let me talk to your boys about that. I'm sure we can come to a mutually beneficial arrangement."

"No, let *me* talk to them. It might be tricky, but I bet I can convince them to let me take part in a joint operation."

"Good. Can you start tomorrow?"

"The day after. I have some business to finish up back at the Res."

"Thank you for helping us."

"Glad I can *be* of help." She reached her hand across the table to shake his, thinking of that other hand she longed to touch.

"This," he said, and knowing what he was going to say, Lucy flinched inwardly, "could be the beginning of a beautiful friendship." She smiled, a saccharine show of teeth, and excused herself with a bitter taste of bile rising in her throat.

Chapter 33

It was torment for them to see each other in the days that followed, all those words without a single breath of affection or fond memory. Lucy kept her disguise, and her act, up perfectly, palling around with the guards and officers behind the scenes, calmly questioning Edgar in the brief minutes his doctors allowed him to be disturbed.

Every day she could see signs of his recovery. The doctors reported progress, Edgar professed more weakness and pain than he felt, until he was almost ashamed at his apparent lack of stoicism. But the ploy worked, and though she soon thought he might be strong enough to walk, there was no talk of moving him. Fallow and his men were unwitting conspirators. Wanting to keep Edgar long enough for a full confession, they continually put off inquiries from the feds.

Not that Edgar showed any signs of making a confession. He talked, quite readily, but his stories were inconsistent, and focused mostly on his movements. He never made any reference to a crime. He told his story like a travelogue, and though his eloquence on the scenery of the eastern seaboard was really quite moving, he revealed nothing to incriminate himself or his brother.

Lucy was making progress of her own, gaining the confidence

of everyone in the hospital. She flirted unobtrusively with half of the men, and was unfailingly polite and respectful to the other half. She still had to go through the security checkpoint at the entrance to the St. Michael wing, walking through the metal detector, but her bags were never searched, and the guards had gotten in the habit of letting her possessions bypass the detector altogether. The first few times she pulled all her electronics out — a slim laptop, a tiny camera, and her recorder — and handed them safely around the scanner. Now only her person was subject to scans, mostly, she thought, so a stray belt-buckle or key chain could give a false reading, forcing them to examine her more intimately with the hand-held metal detector. She put up with these invasions cheerfully, and her good nature was acknowledged with a leniency that was far from standard policy. Everyone was convinced Molly was a conscientious, friendly, and rather sharp little investigator, and it wasn't long before they considered her part of the team.

Nearly every day, she pulled into a reserved spot in the hospital parking lot and after a briefing on the day's agenda went in to sit with Edgar. Maintaining her reserve except for rare moments — and even those moments were an act, for she couldn't let any sincerity enter her charade — she asked him questions about slayings, rapes and other mayhem, and still he did not confess.

By the afternoon she would head back to the reservation. It amused her to think that she would go from being the law's top assistant by day, to a scheming accomplice in crime at night. Every day she met with Nighteyes, but though they had added a few nuances to their plan it was still in its roughest outlines.

"There's no point in orchestrating every move," he advised her languidly. "Know what you're up against, know your escape route, have a quick getaway ready... and then don't let your courage and resolution fail you."

He was of the opinion that over-planning could be destructive in the end. "If you have it all laid out clearly before you, and something goes wrong, something unanticipated happens, it can spoil the whole thing. It'll fluster you, and you'll think the action is ruined just because the plan is ruined."

Think of it like a hunt, he said another time. You have your weapons, and you understand the nature of the beast. After that, you have to play it by ear. Maybe the bear runs away, maybe it charges you. Maybe you kill it on the first shot, and maybe you only wound it and have to track it for twelve miles.

"But if you're determined to succeed, you will," he concluded.

"Not if the bear eats you," she said with a sigh.

Some days, though not often, she went to see Mallory, taking secret routes and wearing yet another disguise to avoid detection. To her surprise and pleasure, he was proving extremely tractable. Apparently the thought of saving his brother put a check on his wilder impulses, and she began to think there could be hope of controlling him to the point where he might live a productive, or at least non-violent life. But she soon realized that though he obeyed her injunction against straying outside, nothing in his nature had changed. She had nothing to fear from him, any more than Edgar had, but he was by no means reformed.

For a day or two he was kept amused by the most violent video games and the Playboy channel. But before long he grew bored, and was forced to find what outlet he could in the confines of the small house. He searched it all over, destroying a thing or two just for the sake of diversion, until he finally stumbled on something designed to give him amusement.

Every home in Florida should be equipped with a live trap. Rodents are numerous, and it is convenient to have an easy, humane way of removing them from your crawl space or cabinet, to deposit in your neighbor's yard. This residence, stocked with everything necessary for a fortnight's stay, included the requisite trap, and when Mallory discovered it, and at length divined its purpose, he decided to have a natural history lesson.

It was perhaps fortunate, though not for his subjects, that he took up this new hobby. Having a project kept him contained. On the first day he set the trap in the house, but though he heard scuttlings all around him he failed to catch anything. The next night, braving the fictitious snipers Lucy had warned him about, he opened the back door just enough to deposit the live trap on the rear landing. Baited with peanut butter, this time it achieved the desired result, and in the morning when he reached out a hand to retrieve it, he found a citrus rat inside.

His game was delayed one more day. When he removed the

creature it promptly slipped through his fingers and escaped beneath the refrigerator, never to be seen again. The next morning there was another, or for all he knew, the same rat in the trap. Mallory held this one more firmly and was promptly bitten rather severely through the thumb. He instantly wrung the little creature's neck.

That provided him with some satisfaction, however fleeting, but he wanted to prolong his natural history study as much as possible. The next rat didn't have such an easy end.

Mallory showed the results of his experiments to Lucy, naturally assuming her native interest in animals extended to their mutilated corpses. She refrained from saying, or doing, anything, and told herself that as long as the rats held out (and in Florida they always would) Mallory could entertain himself. She needed him, so she left him to his shocking amusements, pitying the rats but glad he found something to distract himself from the interminable wait. He wouldn't have to wait much longer, and with only one trap at his disposal, she doubted the rodent population as a whole would suffer, whatever the sufferings of its individual citizens.

If she discussed her plans with anyone, it was Lazarus, never Mallory. Mostly, she pondered by herself in the little wooded cottage Nighteyes let her, or rather Molly, use. There was a rocking chair in the back, overlooking a stand of oaks, where she would sit by the hour with unfocused eyes, letting her mind run through different scenarios time and again, trying to play out each permutation. Sometimes, in her imagination, they were successful, getting off unharmed. But other times everything spiraled into tragedy. Whenever this happened she cut her musings short. She gladly envisioned victory, but even in her mind she refused to witness Edgar's death. Seeing it once had been enough.

It would soon be time to move Edgar, and Lucy thought she had a workable plan. It was simple, relying primarily on the trust she'd established among Edgar's guards. Confusion, quick threat, and quick escape just about summed it up. The plan was almost complete, only one component was missing. She needed an ally in the St. Michael wing, someone to provide distraction, to stir up chaos for just a few minutes. But that was impossible. No one else could get the necessary clearance, and she wouldn't even try to bribe those guards. They hated Edgar too much. If only there was a way to get someone else past the guards, just for a moment.

If only she lived in the antebellum south, she thought in one of her lighter moments. Then she could smuggle an accomplice in under her skirts, maybe even two. But even her full native skirt couldn't hide a man.

Despairing, for the thousandth time, she let her head fall back against the rocking chair's cushion and closed her eyes, listening to the heavy drone of yellow jackets as they foraged in the warming morning.

Then, she had an idea.

Chapter 34

The guards didn't see it, but Lucy was a predator that day. She glided with the easy stride of a hunting panther, her mind as cunning and quick as a thousand generals incarnate. She did not flinch when she looked into the cheerful faces of men she knew, within ten minutes, would be screaming at her with their weapons drawn. Yet she feared, in her very soul, not the bullets that would streak by her, nor the future that awaited her should she be captured, but the horrible dread of defeat. In her short, vital life, she had done much, but she'd never failed, not in anything. It never occurred to her before. Then, when it hadn't mattered, the world opened easily to her. Now that she finally settled her mind and her heart on the thing she craved most, the idea of losing it through her own inadequacy or ill-luck made her quake.

It was this last thought that steadied her as she got out of her rented white Corolla, and she clung to it. Luck would be the deciding factor, she knew, and she'd never been able to argue with luck. That was the responsibility of the spirits, in league with her ancestors. She would do all that skill and planning could accomplish, but in the end it was up to the gods, or the random gyrations of chance, to settle on one outcome.

For two days after her inspiration she was frantically busy,

shanghaiing Jimi to act as pack mule, carting mountains of supplies to her house in the swamp. This time she made sure he knew
the way, threatening him with the curses of the ages if he made a
single wrong turn. Then she collected her allies.

She didn't tell Mallory anything until the very morning of the
raid, when she ordered him into her car. She drove him down the
dirt path as close as she could get to her house.

"You wait here," she said. "No matter what."

"Will it be as long as last time?"

"No. Shouldn't be more than an hour or two." Or never. "And
be ready. When we come, we're coming fast. Shoot anyone who's
not us. Except this guy. Mallory, meet Jimi Golden."

On that day, Lucy carried more baggage than usual, and the
guards at the checkpoint remarked on it, but apparently didn't see
it as a threat.

"Can I leave this here, guys?" she asked the two men, who
were looking increasingly bored with their assignment as the days
progressed. Though there was some prestige in having anything to
do with the Battle brothers case, the long hours crawled by with
very few distractions, certainly none of the glamor or excitement
they might naively hope for.

"I'm going blading after I'm done here," she went on. "It's just
a change of clothes and my skates. Will you make sure no one
grabs it?"

They were happy to oblige the pretty Indian girl, even if her
usually ostentatious cleavage was concealed that day in a boxy traditional patchwork jacket that showed none of her curves.

With her shoulders held loosely she walked, as usual, to Edgar's room and cell, and after a brief discussion of the day's agenda took her accustomed perch on the swivel stool. She took a recorder out of her purse — a much larger bag than usual — and
tossed the open satchel nonchalantly near the cluster of officers
who had learned to stay unobtrusively out of her way when she
was interrogating the prisoner.

Then, with the adrenaline beginning its icy course through her
veins, she looked at Edgar.

She'd grown used to seeing him like this, degraded and diminished in body. He'd improved since her first visit, largely because

of her presence, but he'd grown thin, wasted from the many surgeries and prolonged inactivity. What a far cry for the robust man
she'd grown so fond of in the swamps! A ghost of the man he
was, his eyes were hollow and haunted even when he put on an
act of bluster. She could see, from the nervous jump of his muscles, that he guessed she'd act soon. He would be transferred to
federal custody any day. The men in suits who kept a presence in
the wing were growing restless for their turn, and would soon demand their prisoner, regardless of his health.

Today, for the first time, she let herself slip a little out of character, and for the space of a few seconds Lucy's loving eyes shone
through Molly's colored contacts and spectacles. She brought herself under control quickly enough, shaking her braids, but the effect lingered on Edgar through the first part of her questioning.
She gave him no overt signal, but as he mechanically answered
her, he knew this was the day.

"You won't have too long with him this time," an attendant
physician said as she composed herself. "We've reduced his pain
medication today, and I just noticed that his heart rate has increased significantly. You're back to ten minutes this morning.
Maybe a little longer this afternoon. But until he adjusts to the
decreased dose he needs to take it easy."

"He never seems the worse for talking to me," she said, but
made no objections. Ten minutes, she thought, should be enough
for what she had in mind. It would take just about that long for
her ally to be ready to assist her.

"Are you feeling better today, Mr. Battle?" Molly asked cordial-
ly.

"Fair-to-middling," he said.

"That's good," she replied. "You'll be getting a change of
scenery soon, then." Another brief spike on his pulse monitor.
Lucy emerged again, a fleeting twitch of brow, a movement of her
mouth attaching deeper meaning to her comment. Yes, it would
be today.

"I'd like to talk to you about your time in the woods," she began. Following her lead, he'd concocted a story that grazed along
the edges of the truth: that for some time he'd been hiding deep in
the Florida outback, though his version placed him in a northern

segment of the Osceola National Forest. It was a conceit that allowed them, in a tangential way, to speak of their time together.

"When you and your brother stayed there..." But he interrupted her, as he always did on this point.

"I wasn't traveling with my brother," he said. "I haven't seen my brother in almost three years."

"We'll let that slide, for now," Molly said coolly. "While you were living in the woods, what did you eat? Did you steal from cabins and farms?"

"I've never stolen a thing in my life," he insisted with wide-eyed innocence, and then laughed over her shoulder at the officers. "You'll have to find another crime to pin on me. No, I caught my own food when I lived out there." And at her request, he explained the fishing method she had taught him. "Best thing you ever tasted, fish you just caught yourself."

"You sound like quite a woodsman, Mr. Battle. Who taught you how to survive in the wild?"

"My ol' grandpappy," he said with a grin. "He was an Injun, and knew all there is to know about tracking and hunting and living off the land. Hey, I hear you're Injun, Miss Molly. That right?"

Fallow shot her a look that plainly warned *nothing personal*, but she ignored it and nodded, feeling her false persona slipping yet further away.

"Maybe you have a good Injun story to tell me, Miss Molly, huh? My ol' grandpappy used to tell me some humdingers. There was this one about snakes..."

Fallow cut him off. "We don't need any extra bullshit from you, mister. Just answer the questions, you got that? We're being real nice to you now, boy. But we don't have to be." His hand rested on his expandable baton.

Molly glared at him indignantly. "I thought you wanted him to talk," she said.

"Yeah, about his crimes. Not his ol' grandpappy."

"Why don't you let me do this my own way, detective. I've gotten more out of him so far than any of you have. Now I wouldn't be surprised if he clams up for the rest of the day."

Taking her hint, Edgar pressed his lips resolutely together, staring out at a nonexistent horizon.

"God *damnit*!" Fallow said. "We're only gonna have that bastard through tomorrow!" He crossed the room and grabbed Edgar by the fraying lapels of his hospital gown. "You talk, damnit, or I'm gonna rip your chest open again with my bare hands! We should have let you die on the street, you lousy cop-killing prick!"

At his outburst Molly stood abruptly, almost primly, and took a step back. Lucy longed to take Fallow by the throat and hurl him to the floor, but her ally, apparently, was not ready, and she couldn't risk any decisive action without his, or rather, their, help.

Fortunately, other men with cooler heads hauled Fallow off, with Edgar no worse for the assault. One of his subordinates whispered a word, and Fallow, looking more ashamed than angry now, said to no one in particular, "I've been standing all morning. I'm gonna go downstairs, get a cup of joe." The two men quit the room, significantly reducing Edgar's entourage. Now only two officers remained, along with a fed and the doctor. Much more manageable odds.

Chalk one up for luck, she thought.

The mild confusion sparked by the exodus might have been a good time to put her plan into action, and Edgar, thinking this, was ready. Any moment now, she would... do something. He couldn't imagine what. Subduing the guards in the room would be possible, but then what? How could they get down four floors and out of the hospital without being stopped? He had no idea of the layout beyond the confines of his room, but he assumed that like any hospital, it would be mostly narrow corridors and dead ends, a less than ideal place for a chase and a firefight.

The reduction in numbers only made the officers more edgy. As for the fed, she couldn't be sure. A cool, silent, perpetual presence, he worried her more than the others. He carried a gun, but wore it beneath a suit tailored specifically for that purpose, and it was far less ostentatious than the officers' bulky, obvious sidearms. He probably had another on his ankle, and who knows what other equipment secreted on his person. The officers were trained to kill, in theory, but in reality they rarely thought beyond controlling a suspect. They'd try non-lethal first, and they'd protect the civilian. She hoped. The fed, though... he might just shoot everyone at the first ruckus, and sort it all out later.

Edgar gave her a questioning look, which under the suit's stare she pointedly ignored. But she did say, coaxingly, "I'm sorry about that. I hope you can go on with our discussion. It should only be a few minutes more." Was there a special emphasis on those last words? Edgar stretched legs he found worryingly weak, and waited.

Lucy — it was certainly Lucy now — asked questions distractedly, for now she heard a sound, low and faint. For some time she was the only one to hear the noise, but after all, she'd been anticipating it. To the others, when it reached their notice, it was just another hospital sound, a subdued electrical drone and rustle from one of the many pieces of equipment that cluttered Edgar's sickroom.

Lucy slipped her left hand into her skirt pocket, her fingers brushing her bare thighs. The pocket had no bottom.

The first sharp cry of pain from behind her made her flinch, but she didn't turn. The electrical drone became more pronounced, and Lucy took off her non-prescription glasses, setting them carefully at her side. "Edgar, have you ever heard the story of the rat who brought fire to the earth?" she asked, as behind her all hell broke loose.

Brave men can handle such blatant attackers as human villains and charging rhinos and pouncing pards, but even the steadiest will go, at least temporarily, to pieces when attacked by an agile, tiny, inescapable enemy. Two days ago Lucy Brightwing found an underground swarm of yellow jackets just hitting their peak activity in the burgeoning summer. Insects, as every apiarist knows, can be subdued by either smoke or cold. She used the former to catch them, first rousing them to action by a few well-placed stomps, and then stunning them with a cloud from her smudge pot as they stormed out of their subterranean haunts. Stupefied, they were easy to collect in a paper bag, to rouse themselves some minutes later, understandably annoyed at being contained.

From there, she employed the second method. It took her a little experimentation before she determined exactly how long the yellow jackets could be chilled in the freezer without dying, and then, how long it took them to recover. It was, as it turned out, somewhat longer than from the effects of smoke: fifteen minutes or so before they regained their full faculties to emerge, mad as proverbial hornets, and seek revenge for the indignities they suffered.

Hornets are nothing. The wrath of a hornet is a mere baby's tantrum to the calculated strikes of their more smartly dressed brethren. Hornets try to sting. Yellow jackets try to kill.

They may not be brilliant strategists, but they are well-programmed ones. Like all insects, especially colonial species, they communicate with chemical signals, and they share their opinions freely. First they attack motion. Wave your arms in front of a yellow jacket and he, or far more likely she, will instantly dislike you, and advise all her compatriots to follow suit. Odor, shape, even color can annoy yellow jackets, and they seem to find the dark just as offensive as the bright. The agent's black suit and the surgeon's white coat provoked equal ire, while Lucy's cacophony of broken color splashes looked like a flower garden, not a threat. She wore no perfume, no hairspray, and was by yellow jacket standards relatively inoffensive.

That level of insect communication is like conversation, comparatively rational and polite. Beyond that is another level of pure instinctive rage, screaming chemical curses. When a yellow jacket is injured or killed, she releases a compound especially pungent and stimulating to her sisters. A yellow jacket of the same tribe who gets a whiff of that odor turns into a berserker, homing in on the site where its sister (or cousin) was killed and attacking with heedless fury. Unlike a bee, a yellow jacket is as agile as a fighter jet, and also unlike a bee, a yellow jacket can attack until it is exhausted, for it does not sting, but bites.

When the first guard was nipped he reacted instinctively, killing his diminutive attacker with a swift slap, smearing the signal for all-out assault across his uniform. There a brief delay, which one could not hope for in the wild, as the yellow jackets groggily bestirred themselves, and then three hundred of the little beasts rose in formation from Lucy's open purse and torpedoed toward their chosen target. Though the first deputy bore the brunt of the initial onslaught, the others weren't spared, their waving hands and unmanly cries making them enemies of the swarm. In the space of a second or two the men had their hands full, and Lucy, with hardly more than a surreptitious glance over her shoulder to gauge the degree of turmoil, stood as if in fear and curled her fingers around the knapped stone knife that had slipped easily through security. She turned, and when no one was looking took it out and dropped it on Edgar's bed, where he immediately snatched it up and hid it under the covers. Lucy looked in feigned alarm at the sight of man against nature, with nature clearly the odds-on favorite, and slid her hand into her other pocket, blocking Edgar with her body.

The guards and doctor never thought it was a plot. How could someone control yellow jackets? They dealt with it like an ordinary, if improbable occurrence, swatting and swearing, and never thought to radio for backup.

But the suit, as Lucy feared, had more composure, even through stinging bites that can make a grown man weep. He ignored the yellow jackets, ignored the undignified display of the other three men, and drew his gun. He pointed it at Lucy's chest.

For a moment she was dumbfounded, unable to move. The gun was just out of reach — he was better trained than Edgar had been.

"Step away from the prisoner," he said, and she couldn't tell if he was threatening her or Edgar. Time was running out. Only a few seconds had passed, but any moment now someone would think to open the door, call for help in a voice louder than the muffled shrieks each fresh bite elicited. Behind her Edgar fingered the knife. He was too weak to lunge, and could do nothing anyway with Lucy between them.

Lucy tuned out all sounds. Whatever the suit was saying had no effect on her. A yellow jacket crawled across the back of her neck, resting for a moment, and she could feel it cleaning its antennae with delicate, precise strokes of its forelegs before launching itself once again into the fray. Patience, her mother's voice whispered. Patience above all, in the hunt.

The suit suddenly lunged for her, pulling her roughly inside his guard, and raised the gun to Edgar. Lucy twitched loose the cord that held a wood and stone warclub against her thigh and drew it up through her pocket, catching the hollow above his jaw on the upstroke, knocking him cold.

"Take me hostage!" she said to her beloved, and Edgar felt his muscles thrill as the helplessness of weeks sloughed off him like a snake shedding its skin, and he stood, a man again, to pull the woman he loved against his chest and press a stone knife to her throat.

The yellow jackets had provided an effective smokescreen, and the guards didn't know what happened until the pair rose, coupled close as mating fireflies, and edged to the door, shedding wires and needles along the way.

No one knew what to do, so they ate precious seconds thinking while Edgar and Lucy shuffled down the corridor. Around the bend, through a heavy door, would be three guards at the metal detector.

They had their own worries. The bag of rollerblades held another few hundred angry yellow jackets. They hardly saw the pair, and they passed unchallenged.

She pressed the down button on either side of the hall, and waited, poised between, to see which would come first.

"The *elevator?*" Edgar asked incredulously, the first words he had spoken. "We're waiting for the *elevator?*"

If she wasn't so pleased with her success so far she might have been annoyed at him for questioning her plan. But this was no time for a spat, and she only laughed.

She had to admit, the wait was an anticlimax, almost an absurdity. She watched the light descend on one elevator, ascend on the other, both approaching the fourth floor. The one coming up stopped at the third, then after a breathless pause, descended. In the end, the one that had started on the ninth floor reached them first, mercifully empty.

"Jesus, Lu ... the *elevator?*" he said again as they got in.

"You can't do stairs in your condition. Now kiss me!" she insisted immediately, and thus kept him silent through the third floor.

"The car's parked right out front," she said. "A white Corolla. We just have to cross the lobby straight ahead, and through the automatic doors. I'm going to be your hostage, which should keep them off us until we get to the car. Just keep me between you and them. They won't shoot me."

The elevator, impossibly slow, pinged on the second floor. She got into position in front of him, pressing her buttocks provocatively against his groin. "Get ready," she whispered, as the elevator jerked a little bit, and resumed its descent. He snaked his left arm over her chest and rested the knife angled upward just below her jaw.

"You know that I love you?"

"Mmm-hmm," she replied, and the elevator doors opened.

Someone had thought to notify the troops. In the lobby, they assembled for battle.

They were lining up to storm the stairs (knowing no one uses the elevator in a crisis) when Edgar, Lucy snugly in tow, stepped out of the elevator. The men were almost to the stairwell, and Lucy and Edgar might have made it out the door without incident had Fallow not decided three cups of coffee was far too many before serious action, and left the group momentarily leaderless to visit the bathroom. He saw Lucy, and almost smiled and waved to her before he caught on.

To his credit, Fallow drew his gun with an admirable swiftness diminished only by the fact that he had forgotten to load it that morning. He had a kid at home, and always kept it safe.

The others noticed the escapees somewhat later, and the lobby erupted in commotion as doctors dove for safety, gurneys ricocheted off walls, CNAs quietly slipped out doors and RNs quite practically and cool-headedly dialed 911 and checked the blood supply for the transfusions they knew would be needed before long. Edgar and Lucy sidled to the door while Fallow and his boys clustered like a pack of defensive hens, clucking quietly amongst themselves and ardently wishing they had mounted the stairs a few seconds sooner, and avoided all this.

Fragments of their conversation caught Lucy's ear. "What do we do?" "Can you get a shot?" "Is that really him?" "Shoot the hostage. In the movies they shoot the hostage."

Oh, don't shoot the hostage, Lucy pleaded silently. It might have done some good if she'd actually said it out loud, but left to think for themselves they panicked.

The way ahead looked improbably clear, and Lucy began to hope their troubles were nearly over. Then came the explosive percussion of a gunshot. Maybe they were aiming for Edgar's head, but it would have been a tricky shot in the best of circumstances. In any event, they hit Lucy center-mass. Her chest caved in and she sank back against Edgar, gasping in agonized shock.

It was worse than she expected.

Chapter 35

Very likely, one of her ribs was cracked.

You think Lucy Brightwing would go into a firefight without a ballistic vest?

Chapter 36

"There's a police car at the entrance of the parking lot," Edgar said as he slid into the passenger seat. "And I hear sirens on the way. A lot of them."

"Then let's kiss this old dump goodbye," Lucy said, and drove slowly out of the lot.

"Can't you go any faster?" Edgar said, craning his stiff neck over his shoulder. "Come on! There's one after us!"

Lucy put on a little more speed as they left the lot.

"Is there something wrong with the car?"

"Nope."

"Let me drive."

"Don't be silly. Here, put your head down. Not like that. In my lap. Oh, that's nice."

"Lucy!"

"Hmm?" She was relaxed, blissful.

"They're going to catch up with us!"

"Yup."

"What? Is that what you want? Come on, we can at least try! Forget me, dump me here and get away. I don't care about myself, but you... don't do it!"

"Do what, Edgar?"

"Die with me! It's not worth it. I'm not worth it. Please!"

"Oh, Edgar," was all she could say. She didn't want to disillusion him. She loved her life far too much for such dramatic gestures of self-sacrifice.

Behind them, a linen service delivery truck pulled across the only exit from the hospital and stalled, smoke pouring from its hood. There was no way for those on scene to bypass the truck over the high surrounding curbs, and they had to wait helplessly for road deputies to get to the area. The driver, oddly enough, was not to be found.

Responding cruisers went to the hospital to pick up the trail, and were immediately surrounded by protesting masses of the Not Dead Yet society. This collection of invalids and amputees and sufferers with only fractions of their organs remaining would periodically and belligerently remind people they were still alive and needed the government to get moving on better health care. That particular day, the fittest of them were in wheelchairs, but the majority of them were on gurneys, or even on the ground atop stretchers, some carrying signs, those lacking appendages with short slogans scrawled across their naked bellies. A most distressing sight, even for trained professionals, and it quite upset the morale of the pursuing police who found it impossible to drive around them and their scattered prostheses.

Thrilled they'd finally gotten so much attention, the Not Dead Yets pounded on cruisers and screamed about their rights and generally created as much nuisance as possible, hoping the media would show up in time. The law tried to shoo them, but the protesters, thinking they were being denied their right to free speech, fought, bit, and hurled catheter bags before allowing themselves to be removed.

When after a hubbub of radio chatter units managed to head more or less in the direction Edgar and his hostage had fled, they ran across another stumbling block. Witnesses had been very clear in their description of the getaway car as a white Corolla, though there was some discrepancy about the plates. The BOLO went out, and as local forces mobilized they found to their dismay that practically every third car was a white Toyota Corolla. Each one was stopped, and all proved to be full of innocent tourists or businessmen or families. The police never knew they were duped; at least, there was no mention of it in the reports they filed that day. Had they investigated the matter further, they would have found an unusual number of car rentals over the past two days, and of those, many had specifically requested a vehicle of one particular make and hue. Had they probed a bit more, they might have found a disproportionate number of those renters to be of indigenous origin.

But eventually, Lucy saw blue lights in her rear view mirror. She pointed them out to Edgar but held to a steady pace.

"Faster!"

"Nope."

"They're going to catch us."

"We want them to. Well, not really catch us, but not lose us. I just had to cut their numbers back. We can deal with one or two following."

"I don't get it."

"You will. Oh, that idiot, what's he doing? Doesn't he know there's an innocent hostage with a knife to her throat? Must be a rookie."

Edgar looked back and saw the lone cruiser gun it until he was almost on their bumper.

"Do you have a gun?" Edgar asked.

"No, we don't need one. No killing on this, if we can help it. Get your head down. He's trying to pit us."

She saw the deputy accelerate, wild-eyed, and move to the side of her car to spin her. "I know they train you not to pit past forty miles an hour," Lucy said softly as she tapped the brake, slithered behind the cruiser and showed the rookie what a real pit looks like. He spun in front of her and stalled out on the shoulder, facing the wrong direction.

"There's another one, but that's okay, we're here."

They were on the dirt road that led, as near as any roads did, to her house.

"You're leading them here? Why?"

"You'll see. We still have to keep ahead of them. They'll get bogged down in the mud, but they'll be up with us in a minute or two. We don't have to get far." She flashed her headlights in the agreed-upon signal, and was answered by a triple flash from the woods.

"Oh, did I tell you?" Lucy said. "Mallory's here."

She skidded to a stop and ran around to the passenger side, half-hauling Edgar out.

Mallory stood grinning, a gun in each hand like a wild west outlaw. Lucy had to hand it to him. He might be a sick bastard, but he had cool down pat.

"What took you guys so long?" he asked, taking Edgar under the other armpit.

"We had to sign some insurance forms when we checked out," Lucy said as dragged Edgar along.

Edgar balked when he noticed someone, a weasel-faced Indian leaning against a tree.

"Easy there," she said. "He's on our side."

"Is that...?" Edgar started to ask.

"Yup," she replied. "Good thing I didn't kill him, isn't it?"

"Life is funny that way," Mallory agreed philosophically. "I've found, lately, that when I don't kill someone, they turn out handy down the road." Edgar and Lucy exchanged eyebrows. It wasn't quite progress, but might be built upon.

"That's it," Lucy said, sweeping a line with her forefinger. "That's the boundary. They can't come past here. Not," she added, "that we Indians aren't used to having our land rights violated. But this time if they do, it's war."

"What do you mean?" Edgar asked, but she didn't answer right away, and he didn't have the breath to ask again. He'd done well at the hospital, but now the inertia and transfusions and anesthesia and drugs and donated pig parts were catching up with him, and if it weren't for strong hands under each arm he would have collapsed. As it was, he managed to swing his legs in a semblance of a walk, and was proud enough to manage that.

When they came to the waterway, now considerably broader from the rains and runoff, Mallory lifted his brother like a damsel in distress and laid him gently in the prow. Lucy shoved off and poled homeward.

"We're safe now, bro," Mallory said.

"We're not safe," Edgar said. "We're surrounded, or will be

soon. We will never be safe as long as we're in this country."

Lucy laughed, the sound thrilling his blood and startling a family of coots. "We're not in this country anymore," she said gaily. "Well, not really. I got my land! I got my reservation! My borders are as secure as any nation's — legally, that is. They can't come in unless I give them permission, and they can't get you, Edgar. Not ever! You're safe here!"

His brain was still fuzzy as the last of the narcotics leeched out of him. "Why did you let them follow?"

"Because it's better if they know where they stand. That way the hunt ends. In just a few minutes they'll know there's nothing they can do. You're safe, Edgar."

It's just the drugs, she thought, the pain and the suddenness of it all. He's happy, right? He has to be.

"But... how..."

"Just a few lines in the bill no one noticed." Why mention the stacks of money now? "The Tequesta Res handles its own law enforcement, and there's no extradition. Border's sovereign. And it's official, as of yesterday. The government holds this land in trust for me, my people, and nothing can change that, not even the government itself. They can't get you, Edgar. They can't get us. We have everything we need here. We can stay forever!" She looked at him ecstatically, and Mallory lovingly pushed back the sweat-damp hair from his brother's forehead.

"Prison..." Edgar said weakly.

"Right, bro, you can forget all about prison now."

Lucy, sharper, said, "Edgar, what do you mean?"

But he was unconscious, his head against the dugout, hearing nothing but the plash of water on wood.

Chapter 37

Jimi smoked his Marlborough and leaned against the rented Corolla's trunk until its flashing red hazards met the whirling blue overheads of the two determined cops who made it that far into the wild. He managed to keep his cigarette in his mouth even when they slammed him to the ground, cuffed him, and subjected him to a search as humiliating as they could conveniently make it on such short notice.

"Who the hell are you?" they asked after they cleared the Corolla and asked for helicopter backup.

"Dude," he said, "this crazy lady picked me up while I was hitching and gave me fifty bucks to stand here."

"Why?"

"Had a message for you, and some papers."

The papers, a copy of the reservation grant and a map, had been in his pocket and so they, along with the rest of his cigarettes, an expired condom, a wallet with one crisp fifty inside and a nit comb with broken teeth, were now in the cops' possession. They scanned, using their flashlights in the shadowed boscage, while Jimi Three-Toes recited his memorized message.

"Edgar and Mallory Battle have been apprehended by the Tequesta Police Department and will undergo trial subject to the laws of the Tequesta Nation. Any attempt to cross the reservation border to retrieve them will be considered an act of war. She said the border is right over there."

"What did she look like?"

Oh, tall, dark, black eyes, curly topaz hair.

The consulted their radios, rechecked the BOLOs. "Did you see the two men? Was there another girl with them?"

"All I saw were the two guys and one girl."

"And this lady? The one who paid you. Who's she?"

"I think she's the chief here. Look, none of my business and you guys know what you're doing and all, but she didn't look like someone who takes any crap, if you know what I mean. Old school Indian, bows and arrows and shit. I'd be careful."

They thanked him for his concern by tossing him in the back of one of the cruisers.

More cops trickled in, then the FBI, then finally an officer with the Fish and Wildlife Conservation Commission. When he pulled up in his jeep the brass were trying to order the grunts into the woods. He looked them up and down and laughed. "You'll never make it out alive," he said.

"You go in then," a testy lieutenant snipped.

The FWC officer looked at the map attached to reservation grant. "This is Lucy Brightwing's place? I'll be damned, look what she got for herself. This for real? You've lost them, then. Do you know Lucy? Her people have lived out here for centuries. She's a legend. You can't go in, and she never has to come out."

"She'll have to come out for something. Food, medicine, hell, tampons."

He chuckled. "Not Lucy. That's home. She can stay there forever. If the Battle brothers are with her, out there, and you can't legally go in, you've lost them. They're gone, man. Might as well go home."

"But these guys killed dozens of people — cops, girls! They're animals! Are you telling me that even if we know where they are we can't get them? I mean, it might be hard, we might need to call out the Guard, or a tracker or something, but we can get them. We don't give criminals free passes in our borders! It's the USA, damnit!"

"No," he said. "This is the USA. That," he pointed through the trees, "is the Tequesta Nation."

Chapter 38

"Who the hell are you?" Lucy asked the two women sitting at her dining table.

"Didn't Jimi tell you?" the younger one asked.

"Wait, I know you. Sue Blue?"

"Yeah, and my aunt Dolores. We want to join."

"And we have an idea. A way to make money."

"Jimi said you'd take us in."

"Jimi said you'd protect us. We'll earn our keep. Tell her, Sue."

"Hold on," Lucy insisted, and settled Edgar into bed. He was ashen but conscious. "Are you feeling okay? I'm going to get this stuff out of my hair be Lucy again. Guess Molly's in a ditch somewhere, another Battle brothers' victim. Then I'll scout the border, make sure no one gets any ideas. Might even talk to them. But they can't come here. They can't set foot on the reservation, and if they do, I'll arrest them." She laughed. "Don't worry, Edgar. It's all good now."

She kissed him and turned to the women.

"Now what am I supposed to do with you?" The nerve of Jimi Three-Toes.

"We won't be any trouble," Sue said.

Lucy just looked Sue's provocative body up and down and

snorted. Mallory looked too, sans snort.

"Well? What's your big idea? What do you have to offer to the Tequesta Nation?"

The women exchanged looks. "You know how we can have casinos, because the laws don't apply to us?"

"The laws do apply," Lucy corrected. "Most of them anyway. This Res just has a few exceptions. Anyway, I'm not having a casino out here."

"Not a casino. No one would come out here when they can go to the Seminole casinos. But men will go a long way to get laid."

Lucy raised her eyebrows, immediately seeing possibilities.

"You mean... you want to have a whorehouse out here?"

"Legal, safe, tax-free. A swamp bordello."

"And you want to work in it, I suppose?"

"Me and Dolores. You'll find girls easy enough. Everyone trusts you, Chief Brightwing."

Chief? I guess I am.

"I'll think about it," was as far as she'd commit.

By nightfall the law enforcement helicopters had given up, though the news choppers still buzzed the treetops. Earlier in the afternoon Lucy, looking nothing at all like Molly, went to have a chat with the cops and feds still hanging out ineffectually where the dirt road died.

"What? Nothing higher than a lieutenant?" she asked, and melted back into the woods until they dragged a major out.

The next time she appeared she was dressed in full Tequesta rigout: a short skirt woven from moss fibers, deerskin leggings strapped over bare feet, and the proud naked bosom her ancestors had flaunted to the sun. She knew the power of panoply and distraction.

"The Battle brothers have committed infractions on Tequesta land," she told the major. "They will be held until such time as their guilt has been established, and they've served their punishment. Then, when the tribe has freed them, you will be at liberty to prosecute. Until then, it is a crime against my people to set foot on this land. Do so at your own peril."

"What if they come anyway?" Edgar asked later as they sat on the deck watching shadows of nightjars scoop up moths.

"Well, it would be like seizing drugs in an illegal search — not admissible. Of course, it's not like they'd give you back once they got you. So if they come, we fight. I have forty or fifty arrows. I have guns, a few rifles. Or we run again. Up to you. But I don't think you'll be running for a while."

Chapter 39

Lucy sat behind him with her legs looped around his waist, her chest comfortably against his back, her cheek on his shoulder. Three times she felt his breath catch, only to be exhaled in a sigh.

"What aren't you saying?" she asked him at last.

"I'm trying to thank you," he said, staring into the trees.

"There's no thanking between us," she said, rubbing him with her downy cheek. She'd have to put a stop to *that* right away. She didn't want a sense of obligation spoiling their affection. She knew as well as he did that if it came to debt, there was no way he could pay her back, other than with his love. "Don't think for a minute I saved you for anything other than selfish reasons. I was only thinking about my own happiness."

He tried to laugh, but gasped as the stitches in his chest pulled tight. "I... I don't know what I can do. I owe you my life, Lu." The words were inadequate, but he had to say them.

"You don't owe me a damn thing. When a Tequesta saves someone's life, the person doesn't owe his life in exchange. Quite the other way around. The person who did the saving takes on responsibility for the other, forever. Once you save someone, you're obligated to take care of them."

"But that's even worse," he protested. "If you've tied yourself to me for the rest of your life… if you still feel like you have to be responsible for me…"

"Edgar dear, when you feel better I promise I'll let you slave to support me. I'll stay at home and knit, and you can do all the hunting and gathering."

"Can we really live that way out here? For a long time, I mean? At least we have a little money. What I left in your trunk, I mean. The fifty thousand?"

"That's gone, Edgar. I'm sorry." She'd given it to Jimi for all his trouble, and as payment against future favors.

"You mean we're broke?"

"Umm…" It would just make him feel worse.

"Lu, this is the time to plan. How much of the fifty do we have left?"

"Ummm…"

Let's see. She started out with a little over four million. Two went to Lazarus Nighteyes for the land. One went toward the original reservation deal. Five hundred thousand went to the senator for the non-extradition rider. Another three hundred thousand to the hospital linen service, the Not Dead Yets, and the thirty Seminole and Miccosukee who all rented white Corollas on one particular day. About two hundred grand left. Not bad.

Then Lazarus asked her for a favor, and she couldn't say no. In return, he put that two-million she'd given him into a newly-created Fund for the Preservation of Paleoindian Heritage, from which, he told Lucy, she could draw whenever she wanted. In exchange she would provide occasional sanctuary to such members of his organization as needed it.

Total funds available: two million, two hundred thousand.

Current residents of the Tequesta Nation: One chief, one thief, one sociopath, two whores. Slated to slip in once things calmed down: one hit-man, one eagle-feather smuggler.

"How much do we have left?" he asked again. He was prepared for disappointment. It doesn't matter if she spent all the money, he told himself. She got you out, and that had to cost a lot. Still, she should have thought ahead and saved something.

"Edgar," she began, but faltered.

"I won't be mad," he said gently. "I promise."

It came out in a rush. "We have a little more than two million. Oh, and these." She pulled up her shirt to reveal a pouch lying flush against her stomach. She pulled it open, and a handful of small uncut rubies tumbled into Edgar's palm. "They're worth a little under a million real money, but we'd probably only realize half of that, the way we'd have to sell them." Always hold something back for emergency, her mother had told her, and she'd picked through the gems and taken a few she didn't think anyone would miss.

"Where did you…"

"Just before I met you I, um, pulled a heist. I took quite a few rocks like these. They were in the side panels of the car most of the time, then I put them in a tree when we came out here. That's what I went back to the car for. There were a lot more, but Lazarus sold them. Lazarus Nighteyes is the head of the main Miccosukee crime organization. I was doing a job for him and my uncle, the one I called that night. The total take was about twelve million, my cut was four, and this little bonus I skimmed." She trickled the rubies through her fingers.

"Why didn't you tell me before?" he asked, very softly.

"It was never the right time," she said, and he filled in the rest. You always thought we'd part, and until now you didn't trust me. There was too much to lose. After all, that's not the kind of information you give a thief, even one you like. But now it's safe to tell me. Like the firefly mound. You know there's nothing I can do to you now. What would I do with the treasure? Who am I going to tell?

This is what it comes to, he thought bitterly. I was a thief, and I thought I was a pretty damn good one, with my little wad in a duffel bag. Now it turns out I was even second rate at that. A random girl I picked up on the side of the road is a better criminal than I could ever dream of being. Millions! She got those millions on her own, and spent them on me, and here I am, a weak, stupid, two-bit thief after all.

"All the time, then, you were like me," he said. And yet so unlike! She found success at every turn, had luck and skill enough to share with him. He felt inadequate beside her. His life was safe, his future secure, but his triumph tasted bitter as defeat.

"What's wrong, darling?" she asked, caressing him, looking at him with loving, worried eyes.

"Nothing," he said, which always means everything.

He submitted to her caresses, and by and by the bitterness leeched away in her touch and the now-familiar drone and chirrup of night insects. Ah well, he thought. He loved her, a thing he never expected to happen, and that more than made up for any lingering feelings of emasculation. He didn't have to be the knight, as long he got to ride off with the maiden in the end. It just might take a while to get used to the fact that this maiden carried the sword and slew the dragons.

She lulled him with stories of her people, of gods who walk the earth in human guise, of mortals whose deeds are so heroic they aspire to godhead. Edgar began to think that in Lucy, last of her people, there must be the preserved and distilled magic of a thousand generations of Tequesta. When he remembered the things she had done, he was almost afraid of her.

But no, he decided as she curled her warm and very human body so comfortingly around his. She is no god incarnate, only a girl brave and clever as any old god, sweet and loving and sacrificing. Beneath the strength of her devotion, the passion that had saved him, he felt a very womanly softness in her love.

They didn't make love that night. He was still far too weak, and they half-expected an attack. They waited until Lucy made two outbuildings, one for Mallory, the other for Sue Blue and Dolores. Only then, two weeks later, did they finally have the leisure, inclination, privacy and ability to make love.

Lucy chalked her disappointment up to Edgar's incomplete recovery. Who can expect prowess from a man whose chest had been pried open a few weeks ago? It was enough, she told herself, to be wrapped in his embrace, and that first act of consummation was for her more symbolic than pleasurable. Anyway, the first one's always a freebie.

But when, as his strength increased, she was still disappointed, she began to get frustrated. It seemed that catty former girlfriend who said such embarrassing things in her radio interview hadn't been far off the mark. Now, she couldn't very well say, *geez, could you take a little longer please!* to a man whose ego was already fragile after being rescued and then put to shame in his chosen career. How could a man whose body promised so much supply so little when put to the test? There was no biological fault, no physical shortcomings. She guided him, tormented him, finally avoided him, all without saying that one thing that might help. Finally she loosed the pros on him.

When Sue and Dolores were done with Edgar, he was a new man. Expert, professional, unemotional fellatio is the best way to teach a man self-control. After an hour or two he was everything Lucy required. He debated whether to tell Lucy. To her relief, he never did.

Chapter 40

When it was clear no one was going to molest them, Lucy had a ceremony to make the Battle brothers, Sue, and Dolores official members of the Tequesta Nation.

They sipped the black drink until they vomited, which was the whole point, then ate the ceremonial three meats, fish, flesh and fowl. She sang them an abbreviated version of the history of their people, did a silly dance, then said, "Those wishing to join the great Tequesta tribe must prove themselves worthy by bravery or service. In times past I would have sent you off to kill an alligator with your bare hands, or harpoon a shark, or fight a band of Calusa, but your worth has already been proven. Edgar Battle, you stood your ground against a charging sow. You died and were re-born. You have shown you can carry a burden too heavy for any other man." She glanced at Mallory, then gestured for Edgar to dip his hands in a bowl of viscous mud she held out to him.

"Edgar, you are now Tequesta."

She turned to Mallory. "The swamps have tested you, and found you worthy." It was a stretch. He would have died if she hadn't come back for him, but she couldn't very well praise his skills as a warrior when she wanted to suppress them. He dipped his hands in the mud and immediately smeared it on his glasses when he adjusted them.

"Sue Blue, Dolores Otter, you have provided a great service to the chief of the Tequesta, for which we are infinitely grateful." The women giggled, and Edgar flushed deep scarlet. He still wasn't sure if Lucy knew what went on that night, though he could tell she was pleased with the results. The women muddied their hands and nudged each other, whispering.

"I welcome you to my tribe. You are now my family. From this day forth I will…"

They were interrupted by a rustle in the woods. A man emerged, gold hair, white teeth.

"Jack, you damned poacher! I didn't know it was you Night-eyes was sending!" She ran to the interloper and threw her arms around him, kissing him full on the mouth. "Oops," she whispered, and discreetly wiped her lips.

"Edgar, this is Jack. He's one of Lazarus' men. I didn't know you were coming today, Jack. You're just in time for the party." She leaned on his arm and walked him to her house, chatting blithely.

Edgar eyed Jack, who looked like a scruffy blond underwear model, a cocky Apollo poacher with that rakishness men hate and women can't resist. Suddenly, the wind dropped, which made the mosquitoes start feeding voraciously and the humidity settle under his collar like a noose.

Mallory punched him convivially in the chest, right at stitch-level. "That's it, bro. We're safe forever now." He ambled off after Dolores.

Safe.

Forever.

Forever.

His prison sentence had only been eighteen years.

Forever is a hell of a lot longer. Especially in the swamps.

The End

About the Author

Sullivan Lee is a former Florida deputy sheriff who would probably arrest every character in this book. She writes children's novels
under another name. Find her on Facebook or follow
her blogs, http://sullivanleewrites.blogspot.com and
http://lauralsullivan.blogspot.com